NEVERLANDERS

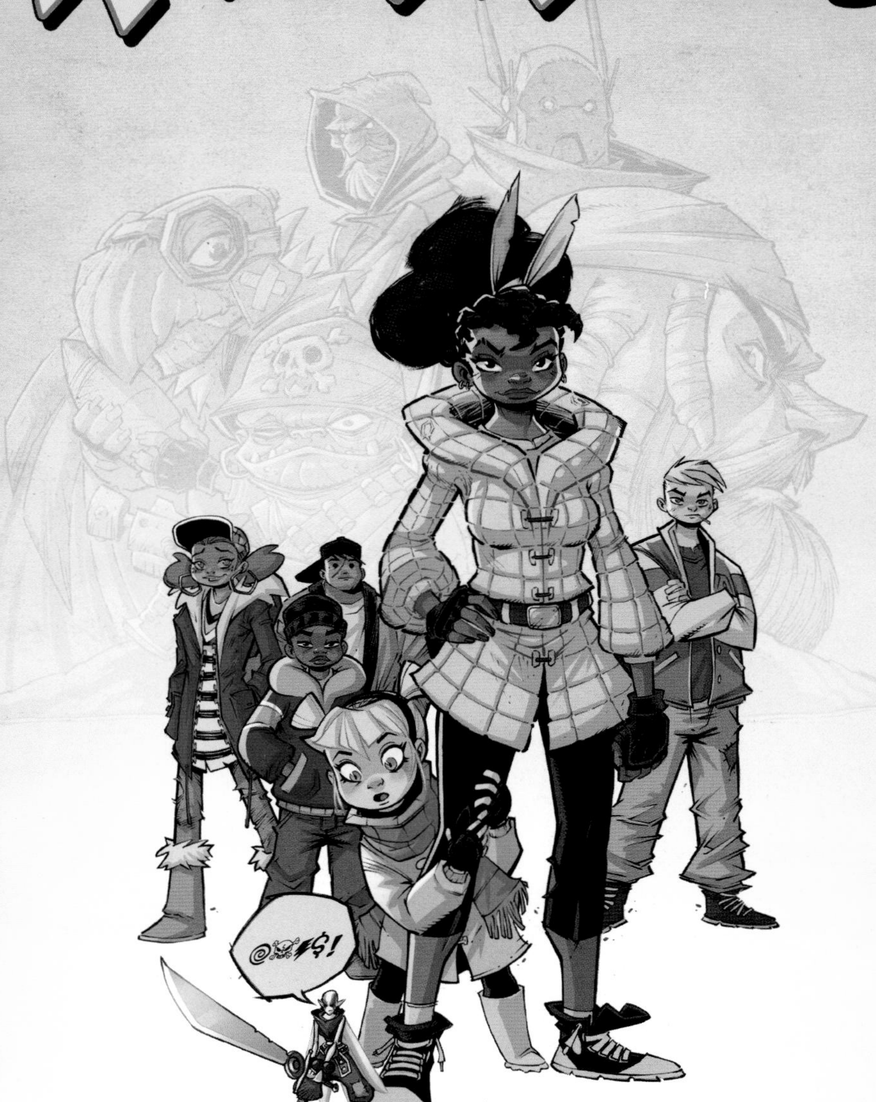

CREATED BY
TOM TAYLOR
AND
JON SOMMARIVA

RAZORBILL

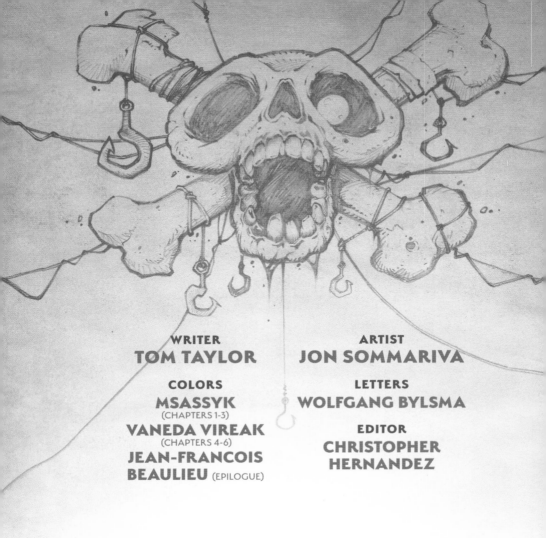

WRITER
TOM TAYLOR

ARTIST
JON SOMMARIVA

COLORS
MSASSYK
(CHAPTERS 1-3)
VANEDA VIREAK
(CHAPTERS 4-6)
JEAN-FRANCOIS
BEAULIEU (EPILOGUE)

LETTERS
WOLFGANG BYLSMA

EDITOR
CHRISTOPHER
HERNANDEZ

RAZORBILL

An imprint of Penguin Random House LLC, New York

First published in the United States of America by Razorbill,
an imprint of Penguin Random House LLC, 2022

Razorbill & colophon are registered trademarks of Penguin Random House LLC.

Visit us online at penguinrandomhouse.com.

Library of Congress Cataloging-in-Publication Data is available.

ISBN 9780593351710 (hardcover)
ISBN 9780593351758 (paperback)

Manufactured in Canada

10 9 8 7 6 5 4 3 2 1

TC

The publisher does not have any control over and does not assume
any responsibility for author or third-party websites or their content.

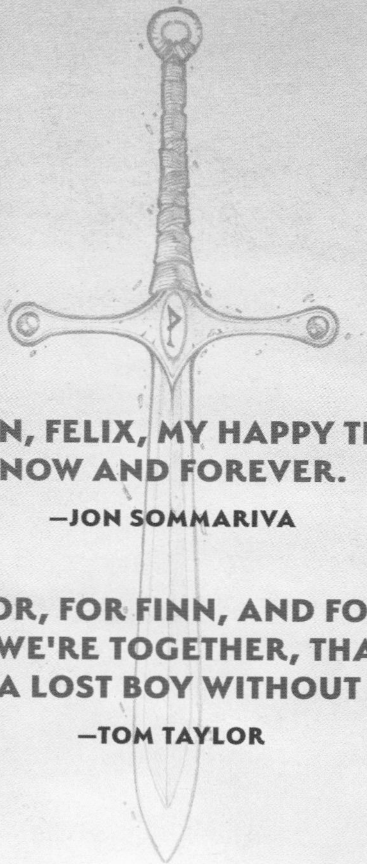

TO MY SON, FELIX, MY HAPPY THOUGHT
NOW AND FOREVER.
—JON SOMMARIVA

FOR CONNOR, FOR FINN, AND FOR MEGAN.
WHEREVER WE'RE TOGETHER, THAT'S HOME.
I'D BE A LOST BOY WITHOUT YOU.
—TOM TAYLOR

CHAPTER
ONE

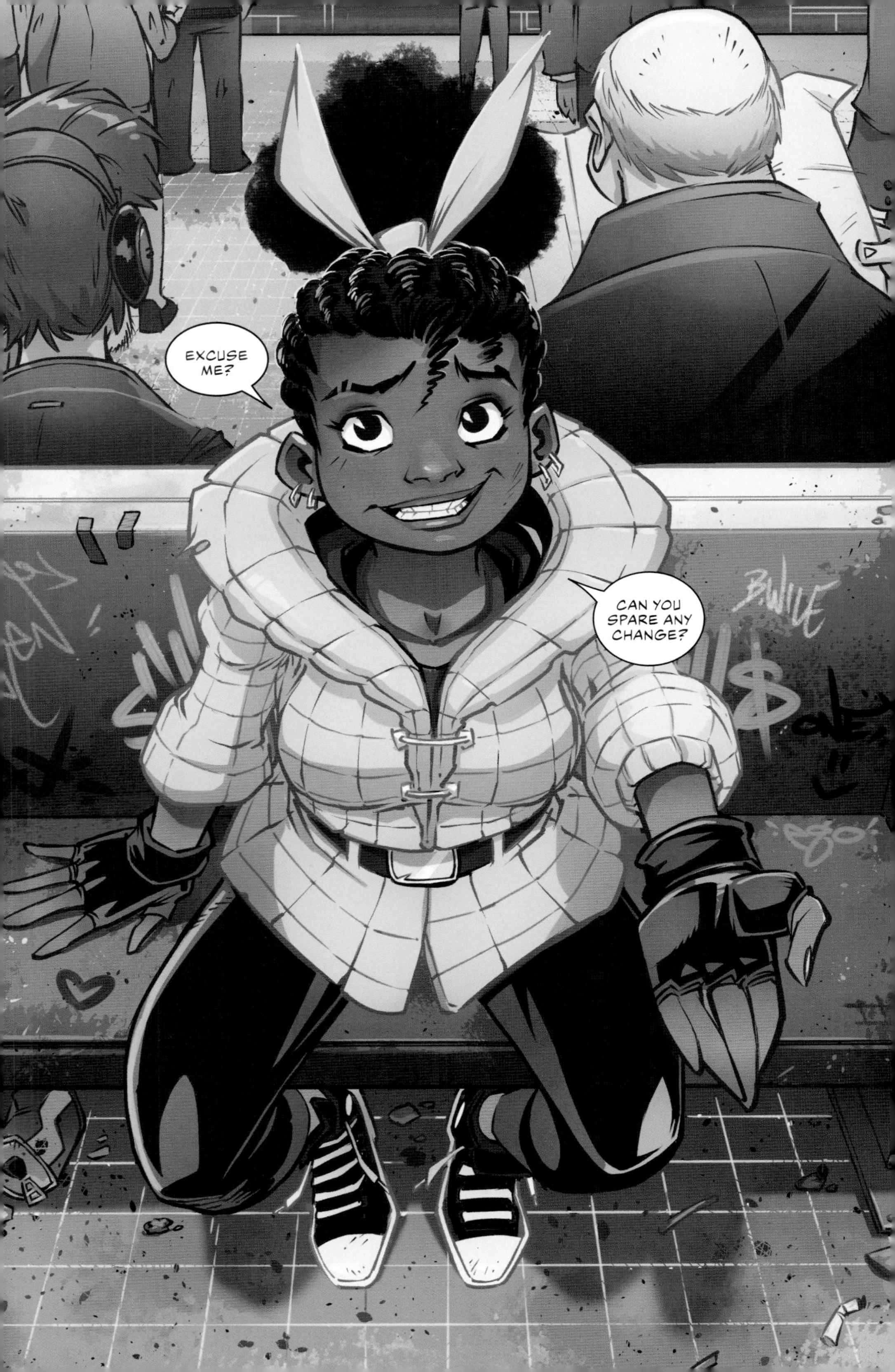
EXCUSE ME?
CAN YOU SPARE ANY CHANGE?

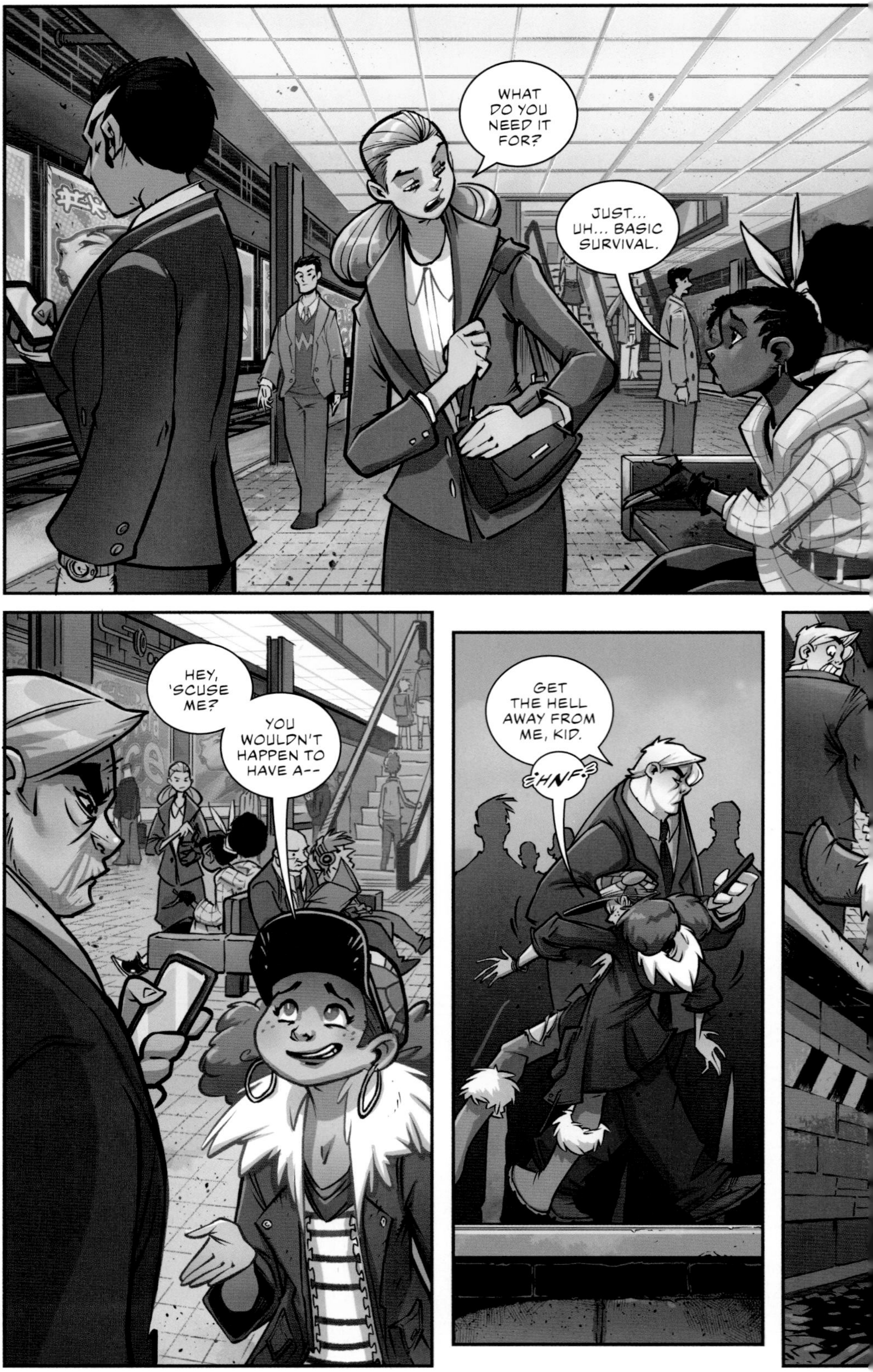
WHAT DO YOU NEED IT FOR?
JUST... UH... BASIC SURVIVAL.
HEY, 'SCUSE ME?
YOU WOULDN'T HAPPEN TO HAVE A--
GET THE HELL AWAY FROM ME, KID.
HNF

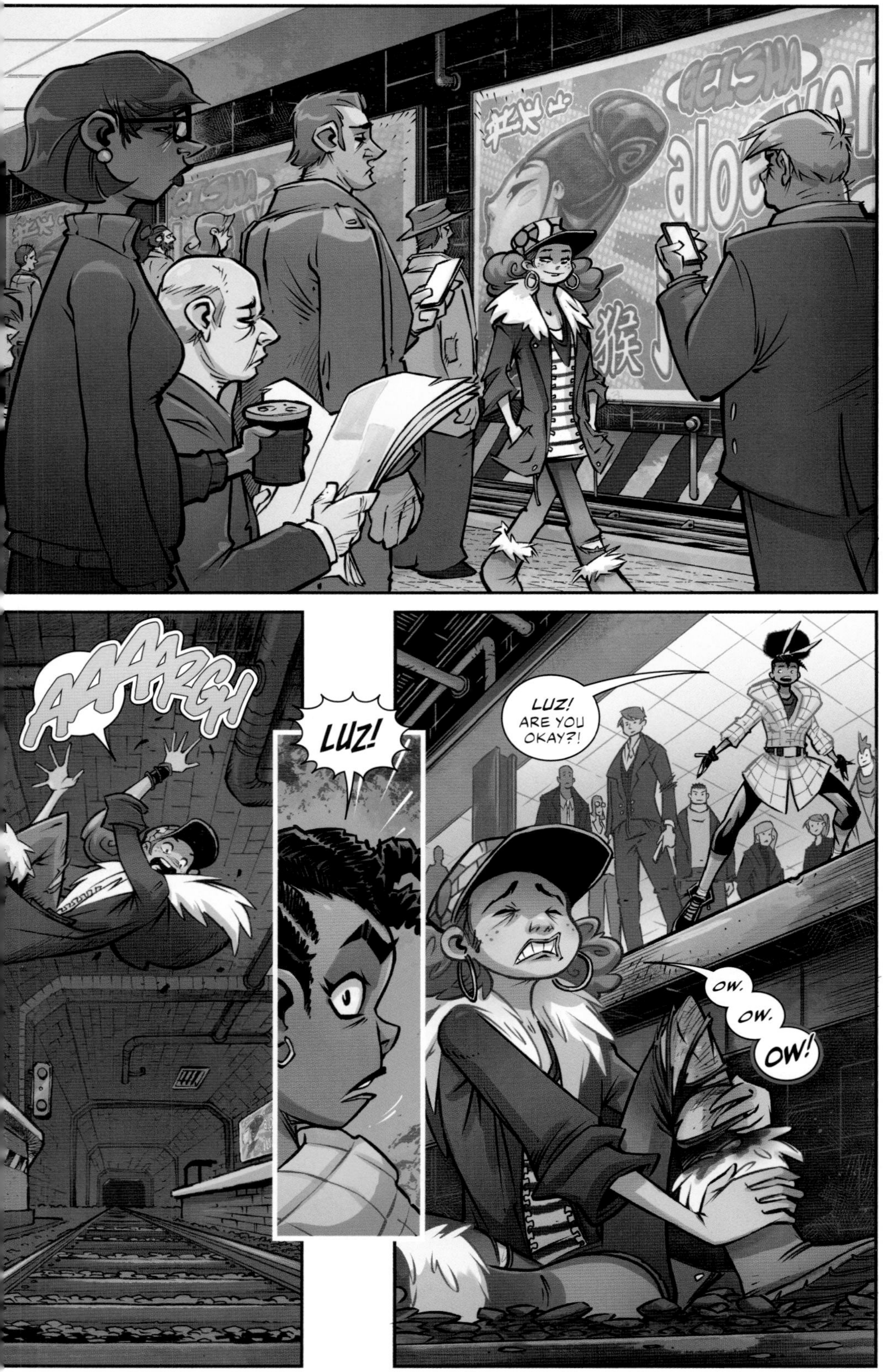
GEISHA
aloe
AAAARGH
LUZ!
LUZ! ARE YOU OKAY?!
OW.
OW.
OW!

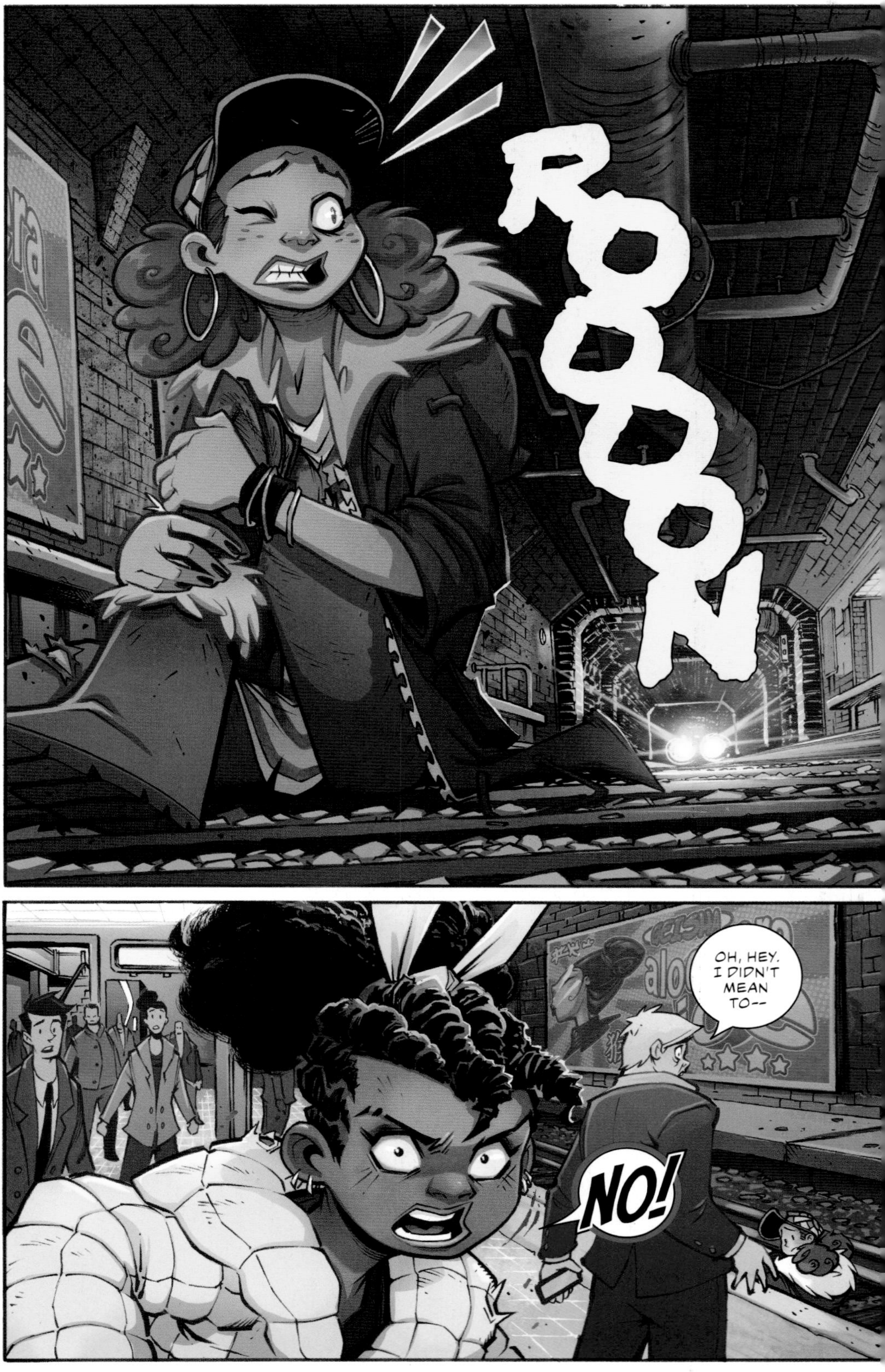
ROOOON
OH, HEY. I DIDN'T MEAN TO--
NO!

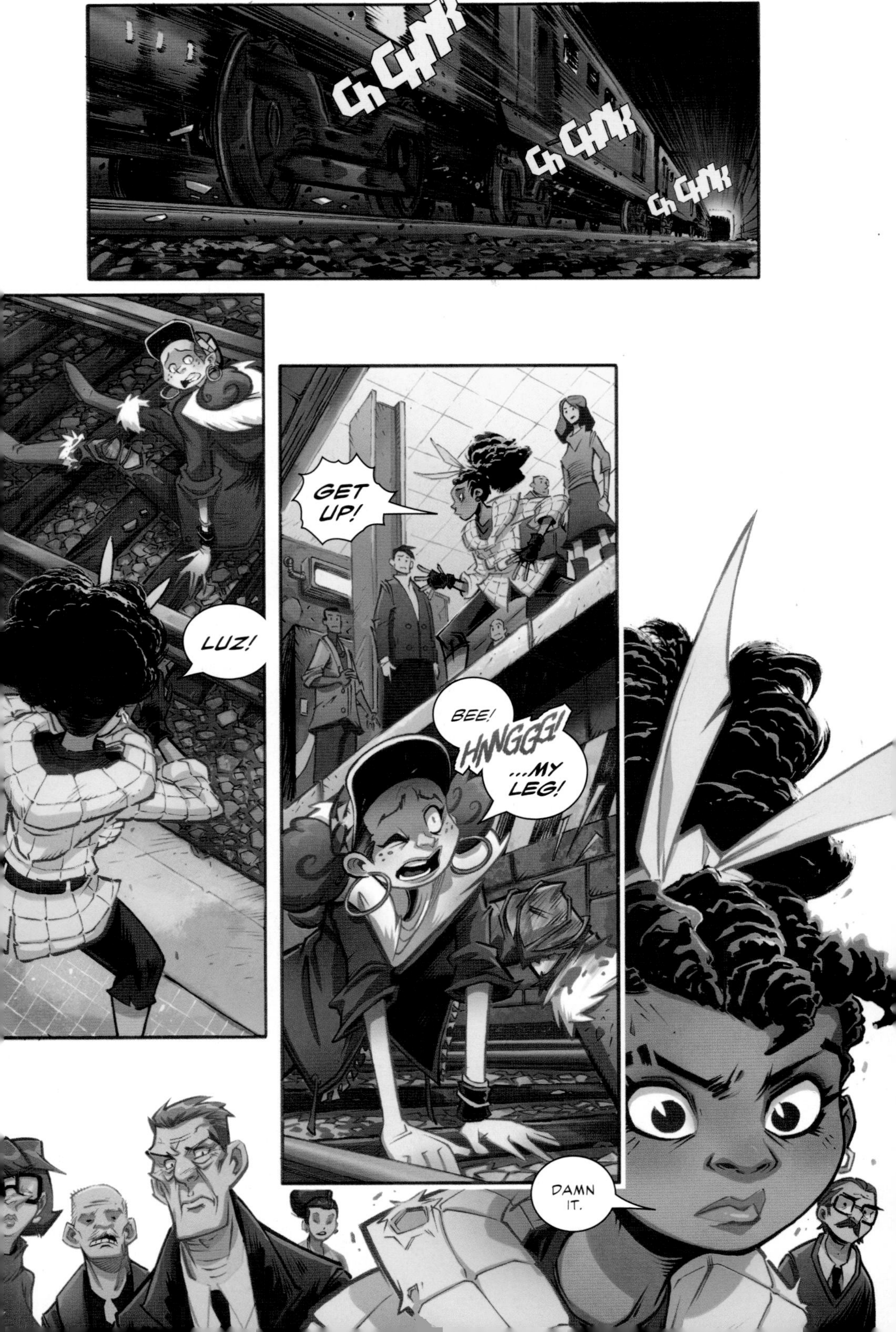
Ch CHNK
Ch CHNK
Ch CHNK
LUZ!
GET UP!
BEE!
HNNGGG!
...MY LEG!
DAMN IT.

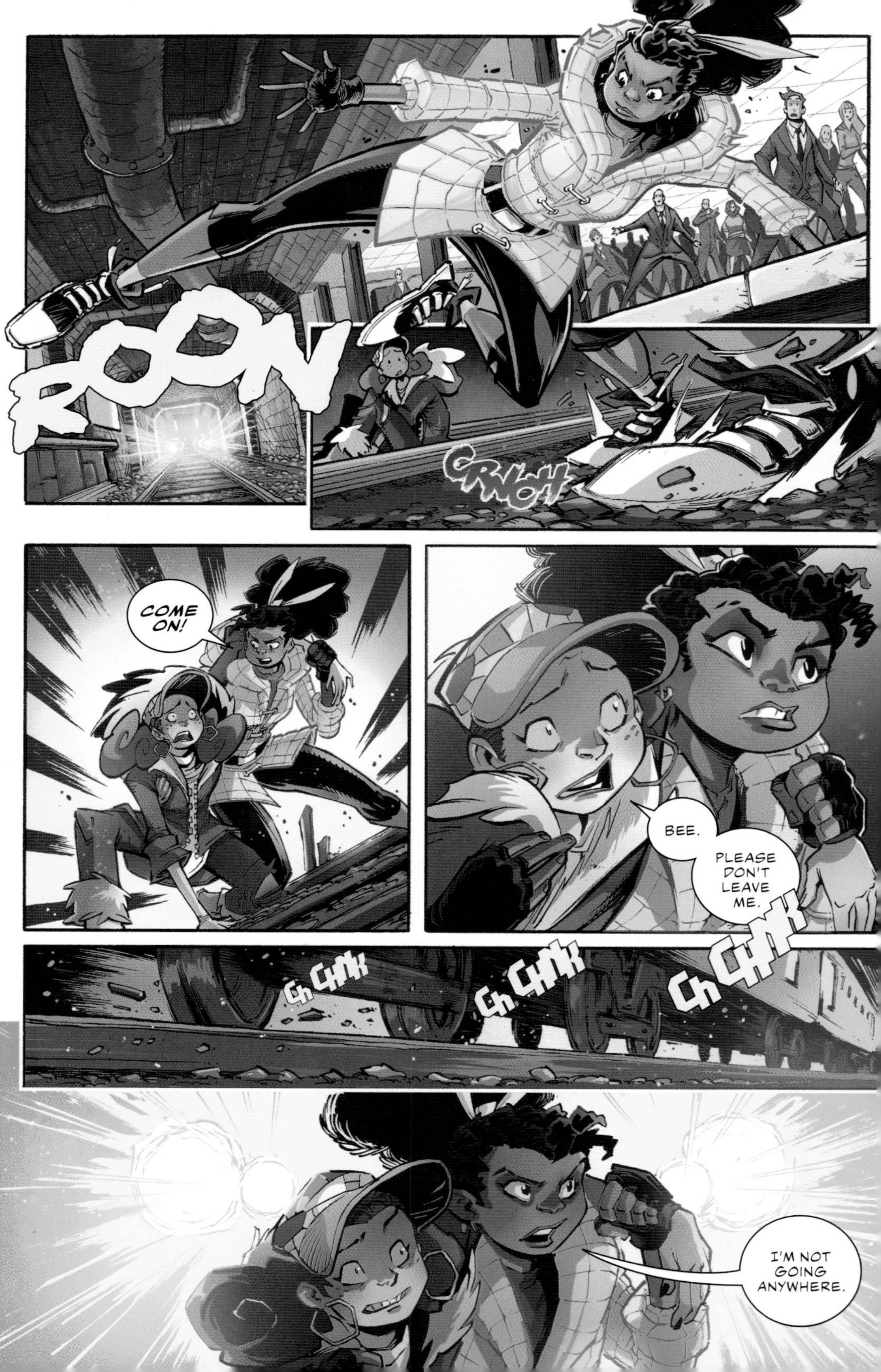
ROOON
CRUNCH
COME ON!
BEE.
PLEASE DON'T LEAVE ME.
CHUNK
Ch CHUNK
Ch CHUNK
Ch CHUNK
I'M NOT GOING ANYWHERE.

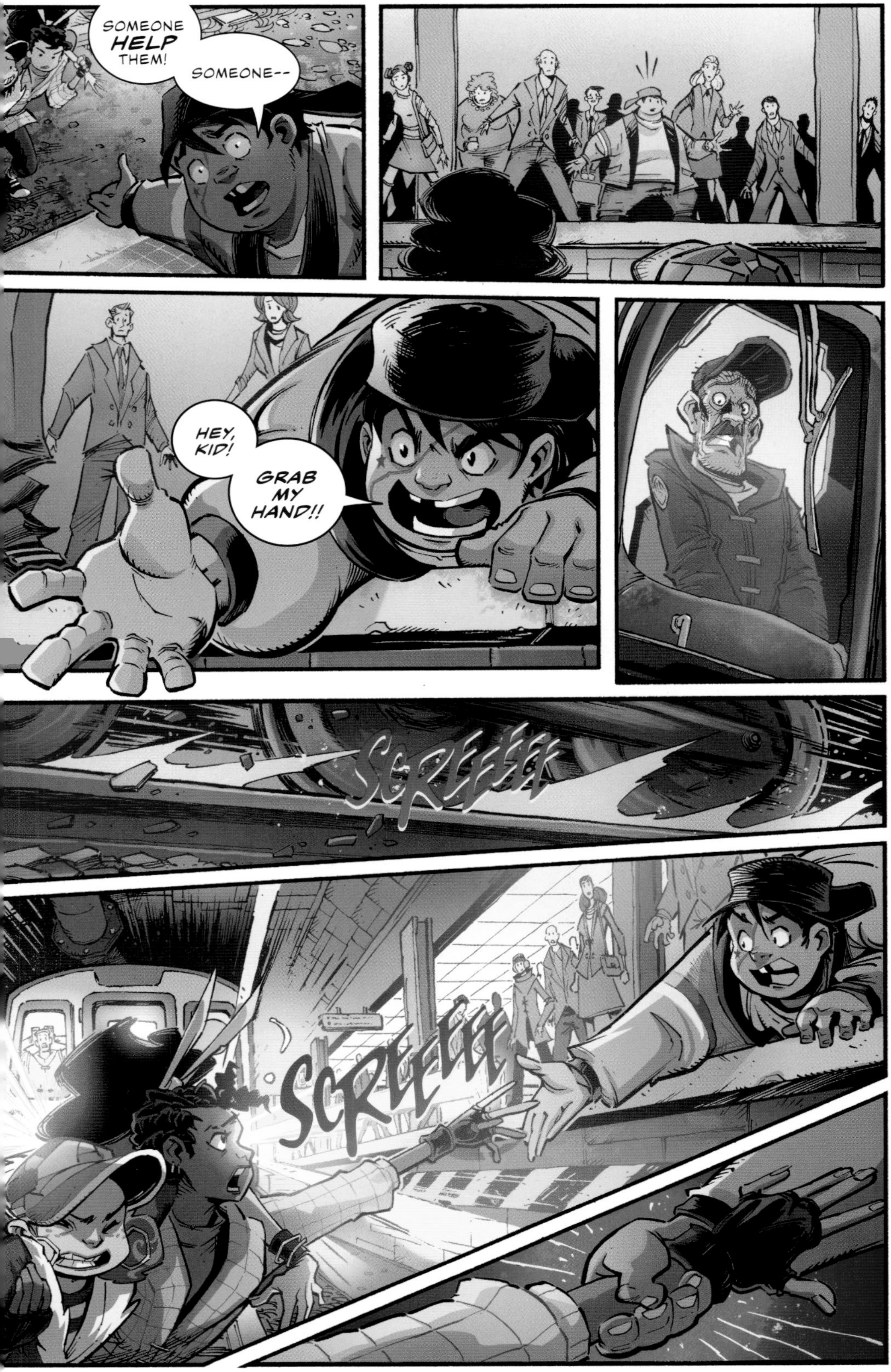
SOMEONE HELP THEM!
SOMEONE--
HEY, KID!
GRAB MY HAND!!
SCREEEEE
SCREEEEE

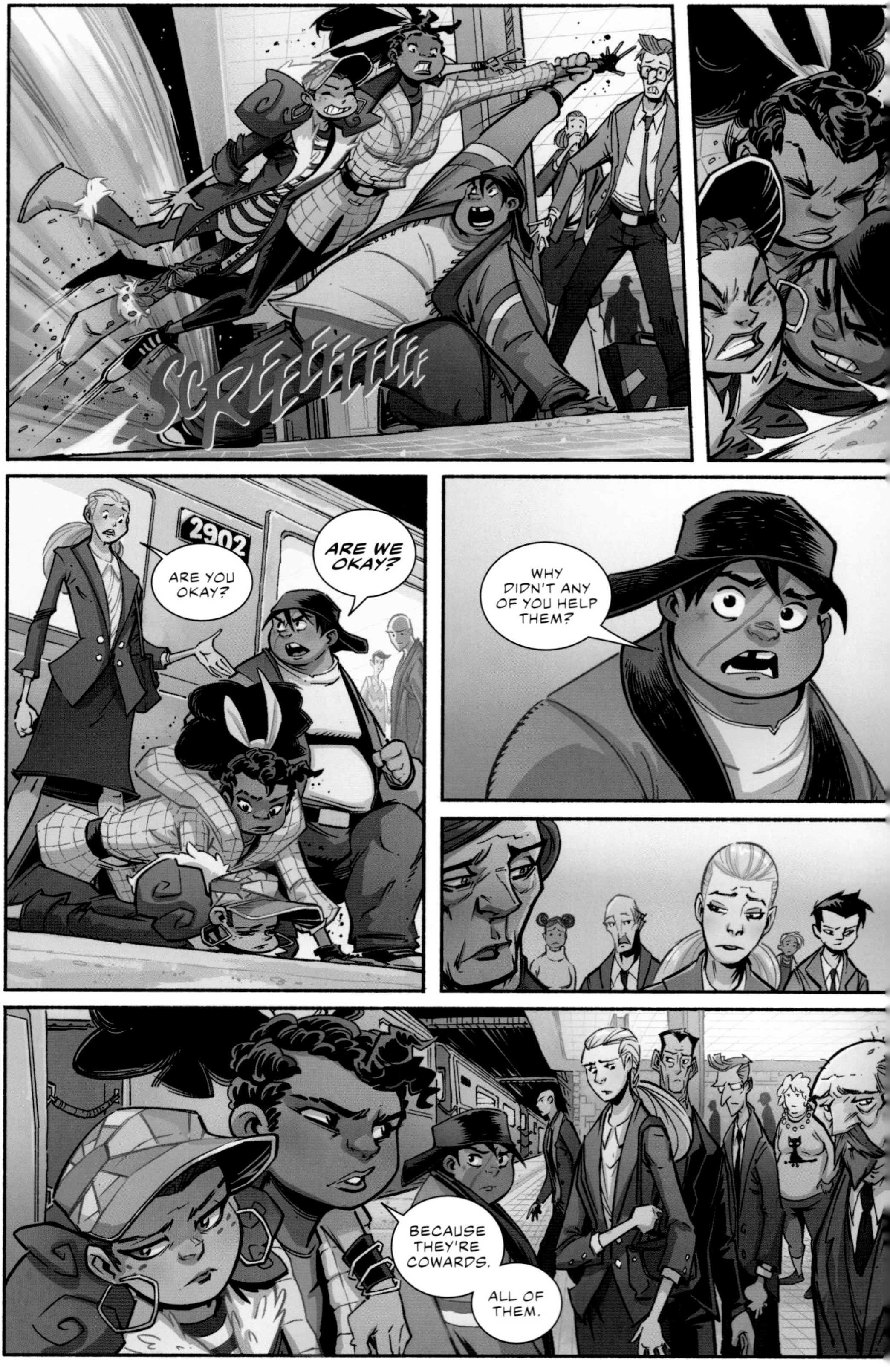
SCREEEEEEEE
ARE YOU OKAY?
ARE WE OKAY?
WHY DIDN'T ANY OF YOU HELP THEM?
BECAUSE THEY'RE COWARDS.
ALL OF THEM.

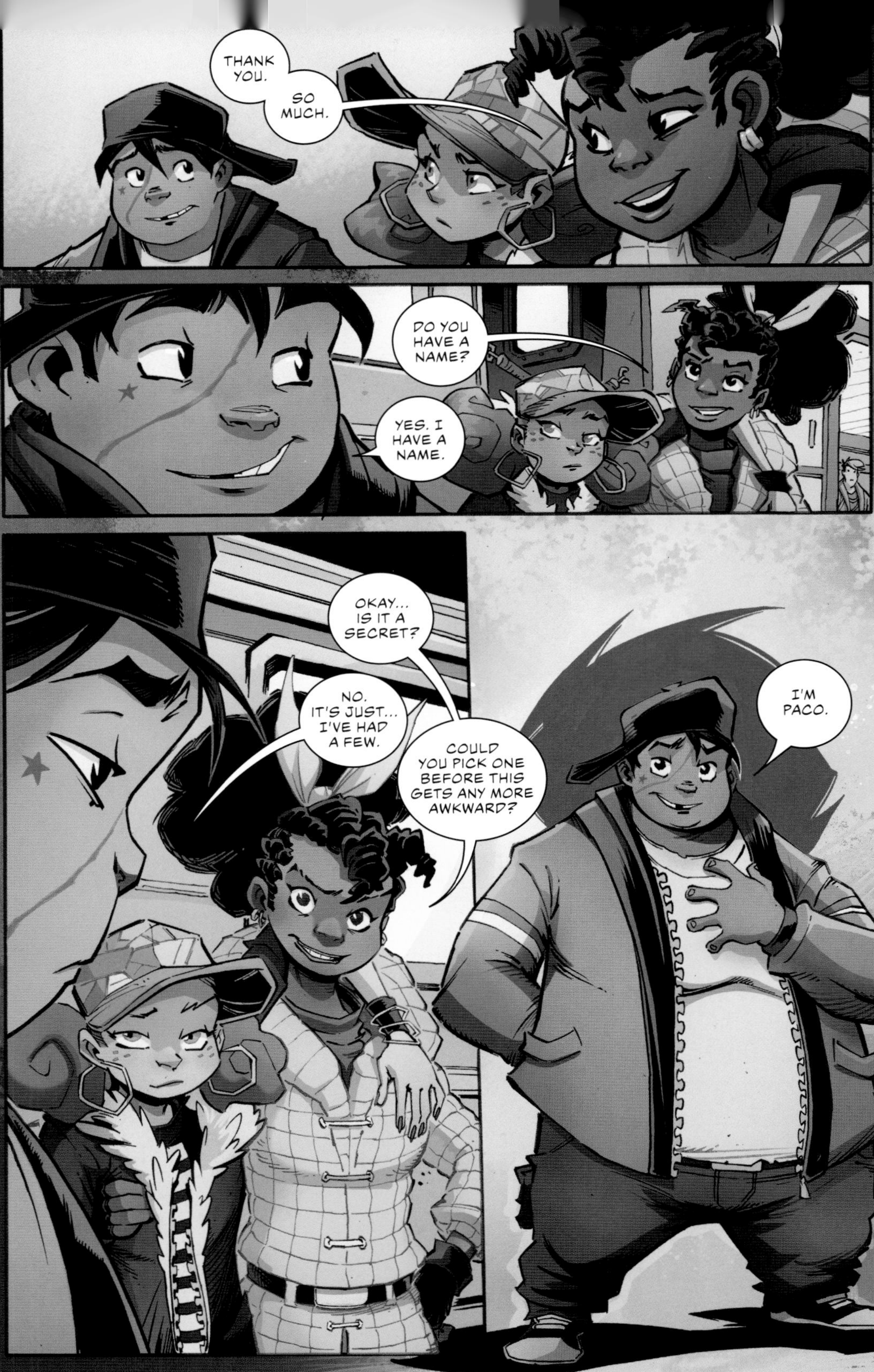
THANK YOU.
SO MUCH.
DO YOU HAVE A NAME?
YES. I HAVE A NAME.
OKAY... IS IT A SECRET?
NO. IT'S JUST... I'VE HAD A FEW.
COULD YOU PICK ONE BEFORE THIS GETS ANY MORE AWKWARD?
I'M PACO.

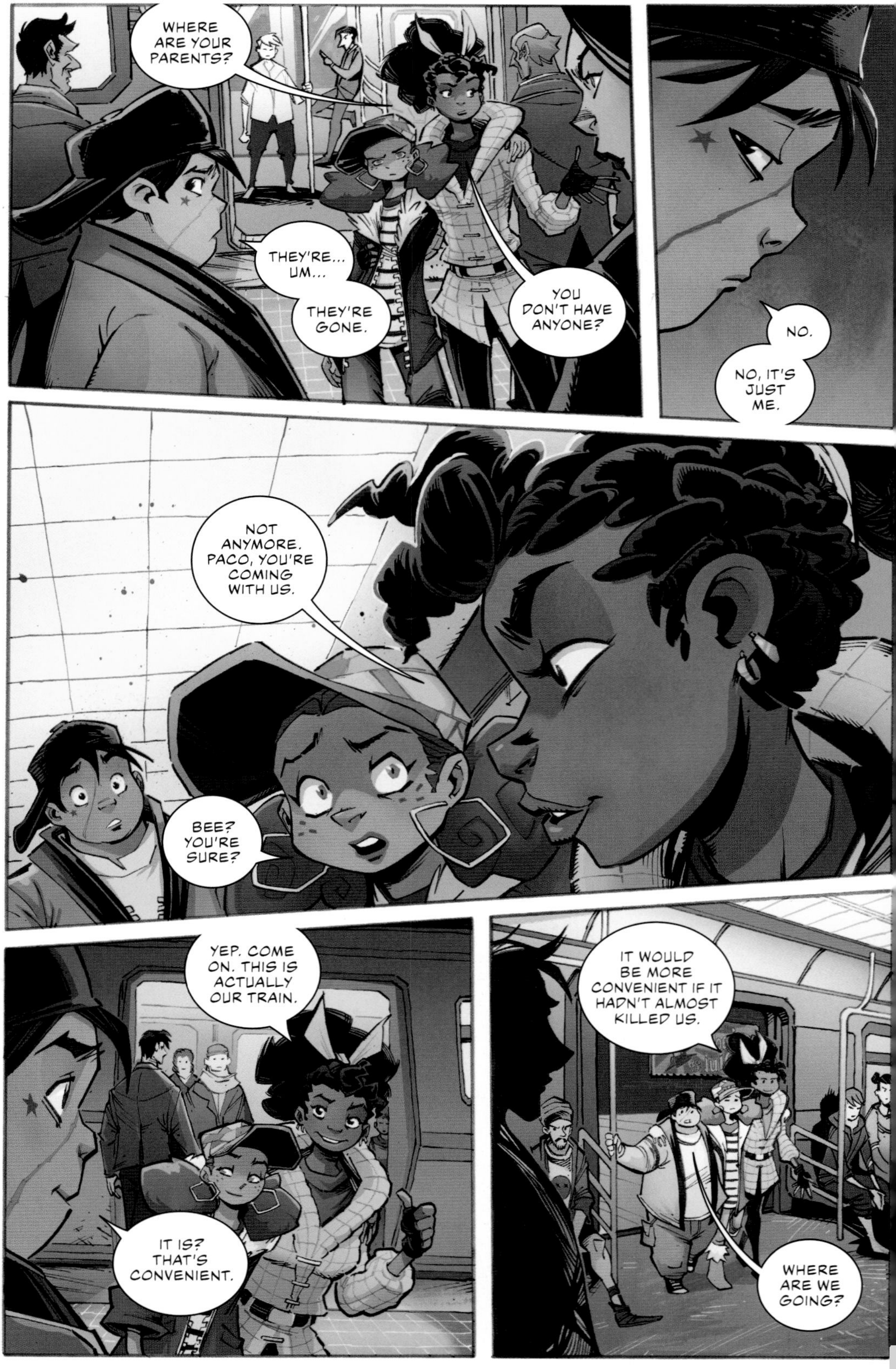
WHERE ARE YOUR PARENTS?
THEY'RE... UM...
THEY'RE GONE.
YOU DON'T HAVE ANYONE?
NO.
NO, IT'S JUST ME.
NOT ANYMORE. PACO, YOU'RE COMING WITH US.
BEE? YOU'RE SURE?
YEP. COME ON. THIS IS ACTUALLY OUR TRAIN.
IT IS? THAT'S CONVENIENT.
IT WOULD BE MORE CONVENIENT IF IT HADN'T ALMOST KILLED US.
WHERE ARE WE GOING?

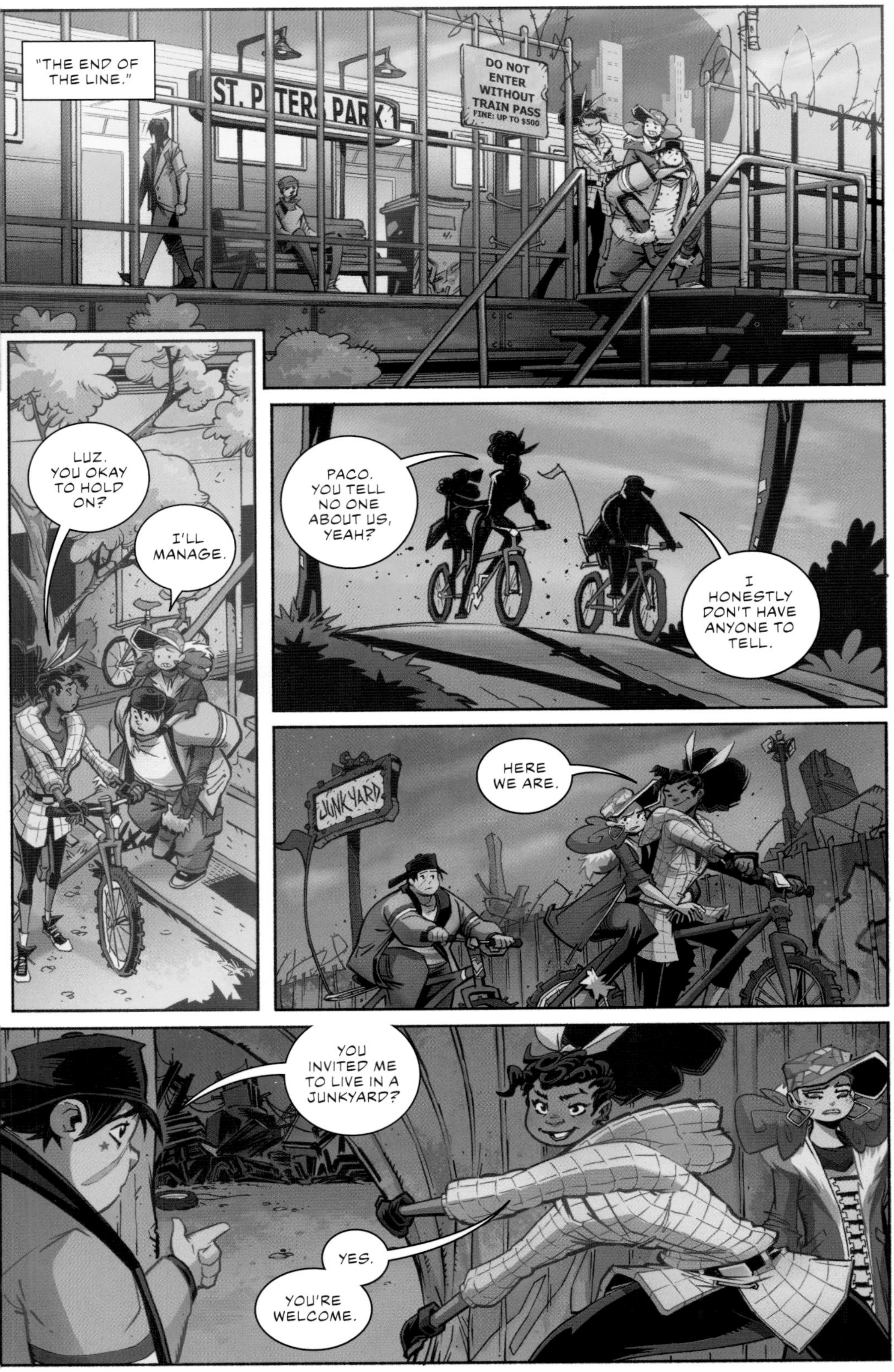
"THE END OF THE LINE."
ST. PETERS PARK
DO NOT ENTER WITHOUT TRAIN PASS
FINE: UP TO $500
LUZ. YOU OKAY TO HOLD ON?
I'LL MANAGE.
PACO. YOU TELL NO ONE ABOUT US, YEAH?
I HONESTLY DON'T HAVE ANYONE TO TELL.
JUNKYARD
HERE WE ARE.
YOU INVITED ME TO LIVE IN A JUNKYARD?
YES.
YOU'RE WELCOME.

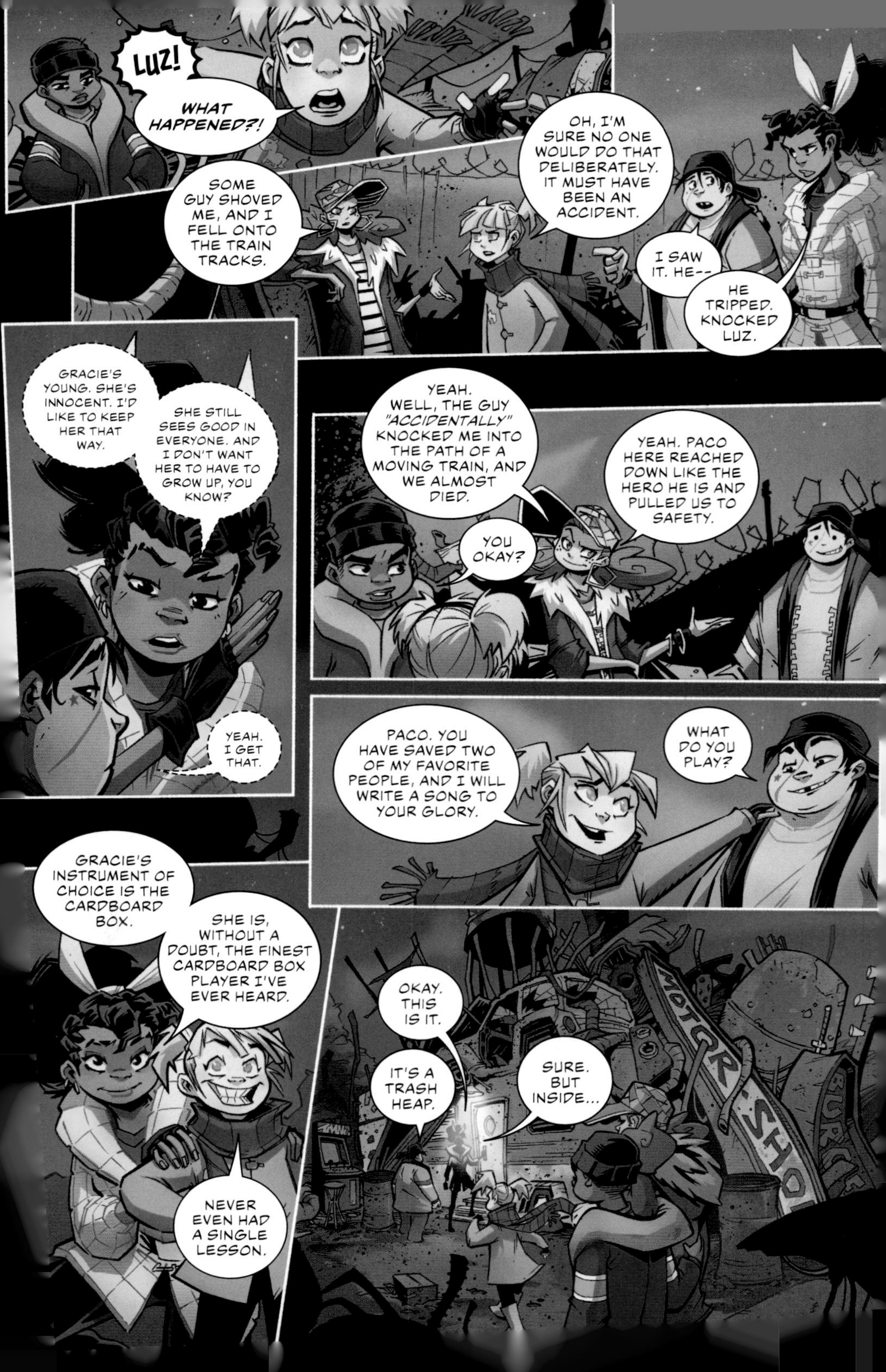
LUZ!
WHAT HAPPENED?!
SOME GUY SHOVED ME, AND I FELL ONTO THE TRAIN TRACKS.
OH, I'M SURE NO ONE WOULD DO THAT DELIBERATELY. IT MUST HAVE BEEN AN ACCIDENT.
I SAW IT. HE--
HE TRIPPED. KNOCKED LUZ.
GRACIE'S YOUNG. SHE'S INNOCENT. I'D LIKE TO KEEP HER THAT WAY.
SHE STILL SEES GOOD IN EVERYONE. AND I DON'T WANT HER TO HAVE TO GROW UP, YOU KNOW?
YEAH. I GET THAT.
YEAH. WELL, THE GUY "ACCIDENTALLY" KNOCKED ME INTO THE PATH OF A MOVING TRAIN, AND WE ALMOST DIED.
YOU OKAY?
YEAH. PACO HERE REACHED DOWN LIKE THE HERO HE IS AND PULLED US TO SAFETY.
PACO. YOU HAVE SAVED TWO OF MY FAVORITE PEOPLE, AND I WILL WRITE A SONG TO YOUR GLORY.
WHAT DO YOU PLAY?
GRACIE'S INSTRUMENT OF CHOICE IS THE CARDBOARD BOX.
SHE IS, WITHOUT A DOUBT, THE FINEST CARDBOARD BOX PLAYER I'VE EVER HEARD.
NEVER EVEN HAD A SINGLE LESSON.
OKAY. THIS IS IT.
IT'S A TRASH HEAP.
SURE. BUT INSIDE...
MOTOR SHOP

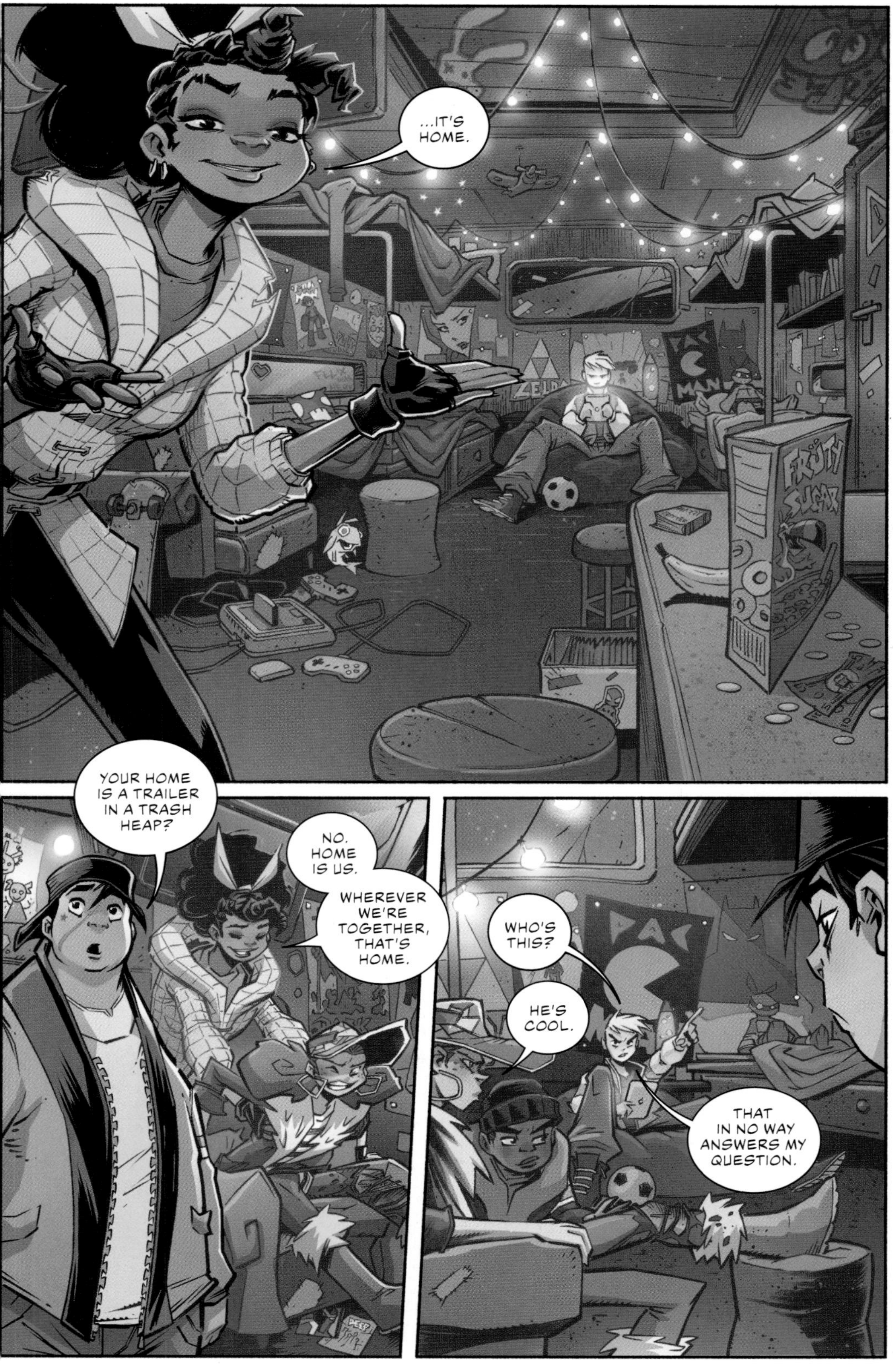
...IT'S HOME.
YOUR HOME IS A TRAILER IN A TRASH HEAP?
NO. HOME IS US.
WHEREVER WE'RE TOGETHER, THAT'S HOME.
WHO'S THIS?
HE'S COOL.
THAT IN NO WAY ANSWERS MY QUESTION.

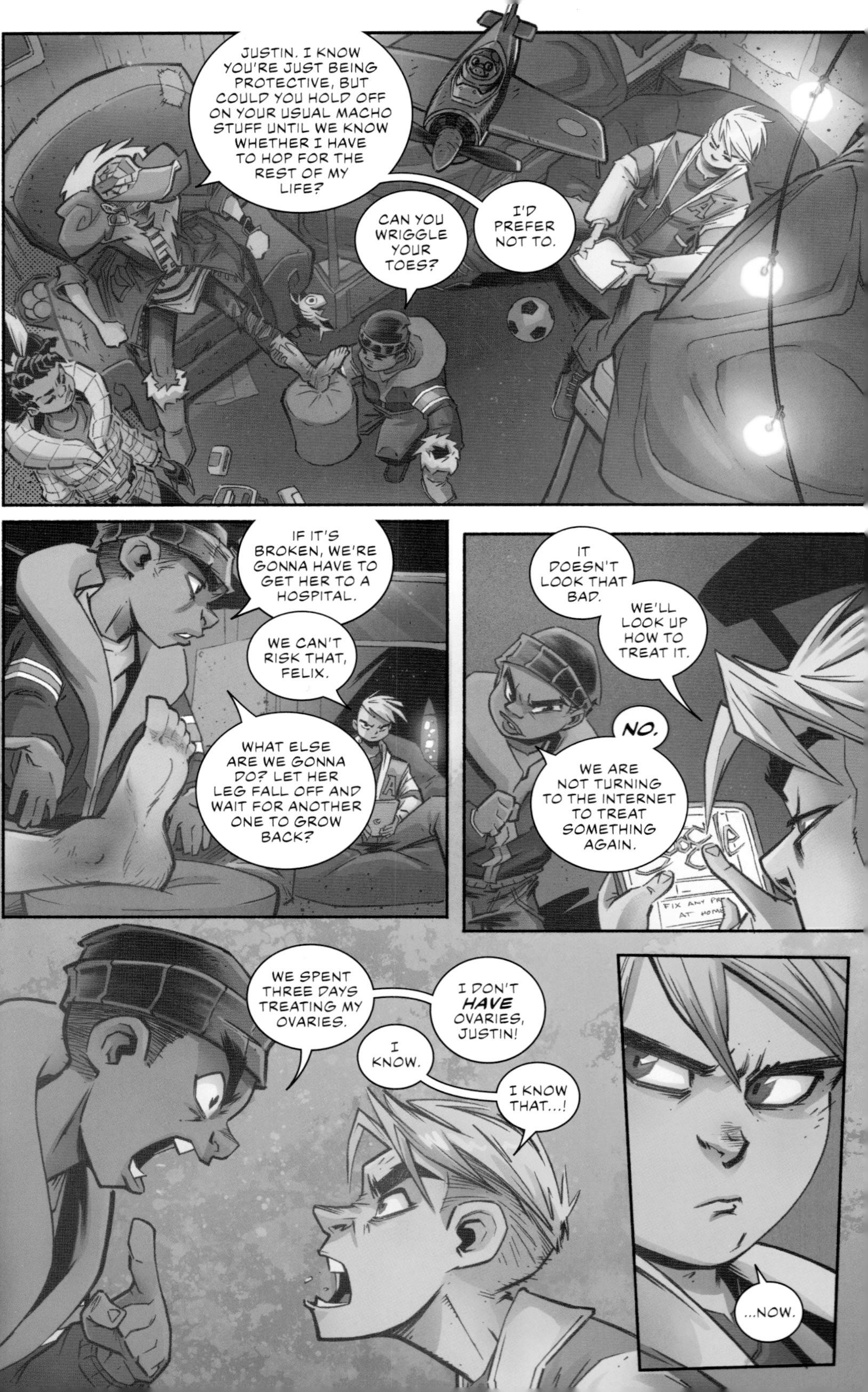
JUSTIN. I KNOW YOU'RE JUST BEING PROTECTIVE, BUT COULD YOU HOLD OFF ON YOUR USUAL MACHO STUFF UNTIL WE KNOW WHETHER I HAVE TO HOP FOR THE REST OF MY LIFE?
CAN YOU WRIGGLE YOUR TOES?
I'D PREFER NOT TO.
IF IT'S BROKEN, WE'RE GONNA HAVE TO GET HER TO A HOSPITAL.
WE CAN'T RISK THAT, FELIX.
WHAT ELSE ARE WE GONNA DO? LET HER LEG FALL OFF AND WAIT FOR ANOTHER ONE TO GROW BACK?
IT DOESN'T LOOK THAT BAD.
WE'LL LOOK UP HOW TO TREAT IT.
NO.
WE ARE NOT TURNING TO THE INTERNET TO TREAT SOMETHING AGAIN.
WE SPENT THREE DAYS TREATING MY OVARIES.
I DON'T HAVE OVARIES, JUSTIN!
I KNOW.
I KNOW THAT...!
...NOW.

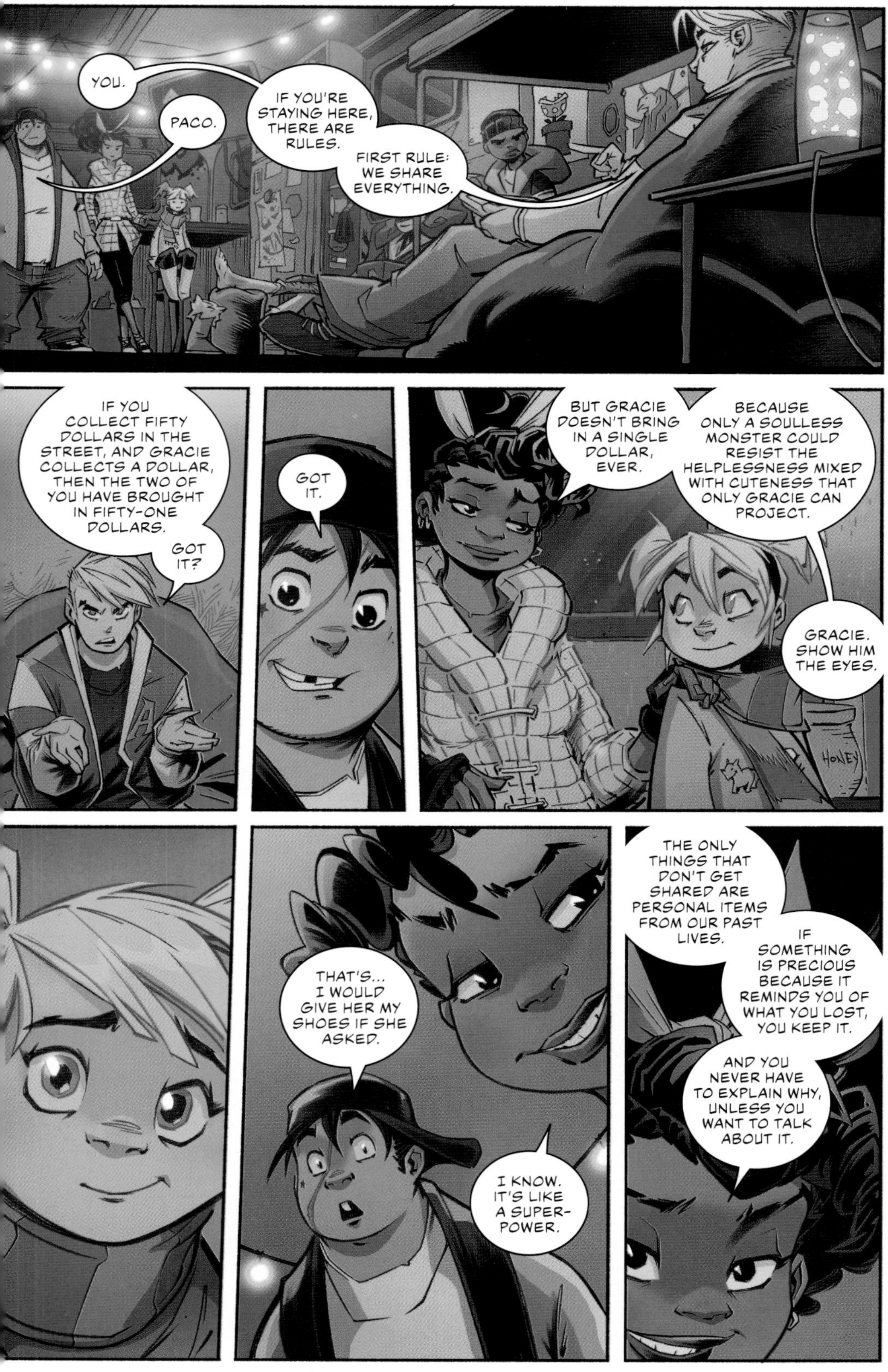
YOU.
PACO.
IF YOU'RE STAYING HERE, THERE ARE RULES.
FIRST RULE: WE SHARE EVERYTHING.
IF YOU COLLECT FIFTY DOLLARS IN THE STREET, AND GRACIE COLLECTS A DOLLAR, THEN THE TWO OF YOU HAVE BROUGHT IN FIFTY-ONE DOLLARS.
GOT IT?
GOT IT.
BUT GRACIE DOESN'T BRING IN A SINGLE DOLLAR, EVER.
BECAUSE ONLY A SOULLESS MONSTER COULD RESIST THE HELPLESSNESS MIXED WITH CUTENESS THAT ONLY GRACIE CAN PROJECT.
GRACIE. SHOW HIM THE EYES.
HONEY
THAT'S... I WOULD GIVE HER MY SHOES IF SHE ASKED.
I KNOW. IT'S LIKE A SUPER-POWER.
THE ONLY THINGS THAT DON'T GET SHARED ARE PERSONAL ITEMS FROM OUR PAST LIVES.
IF SOMETHING IS PRECIOUS BECAUSE IT REMINDS YOU OF WHAT YOU LOST, YOU KEEP IT.
AND YOU NEVER HAVE TO EXPLAIN WHY, UNLESS YOU WANT TO TALK ABOUT IT.

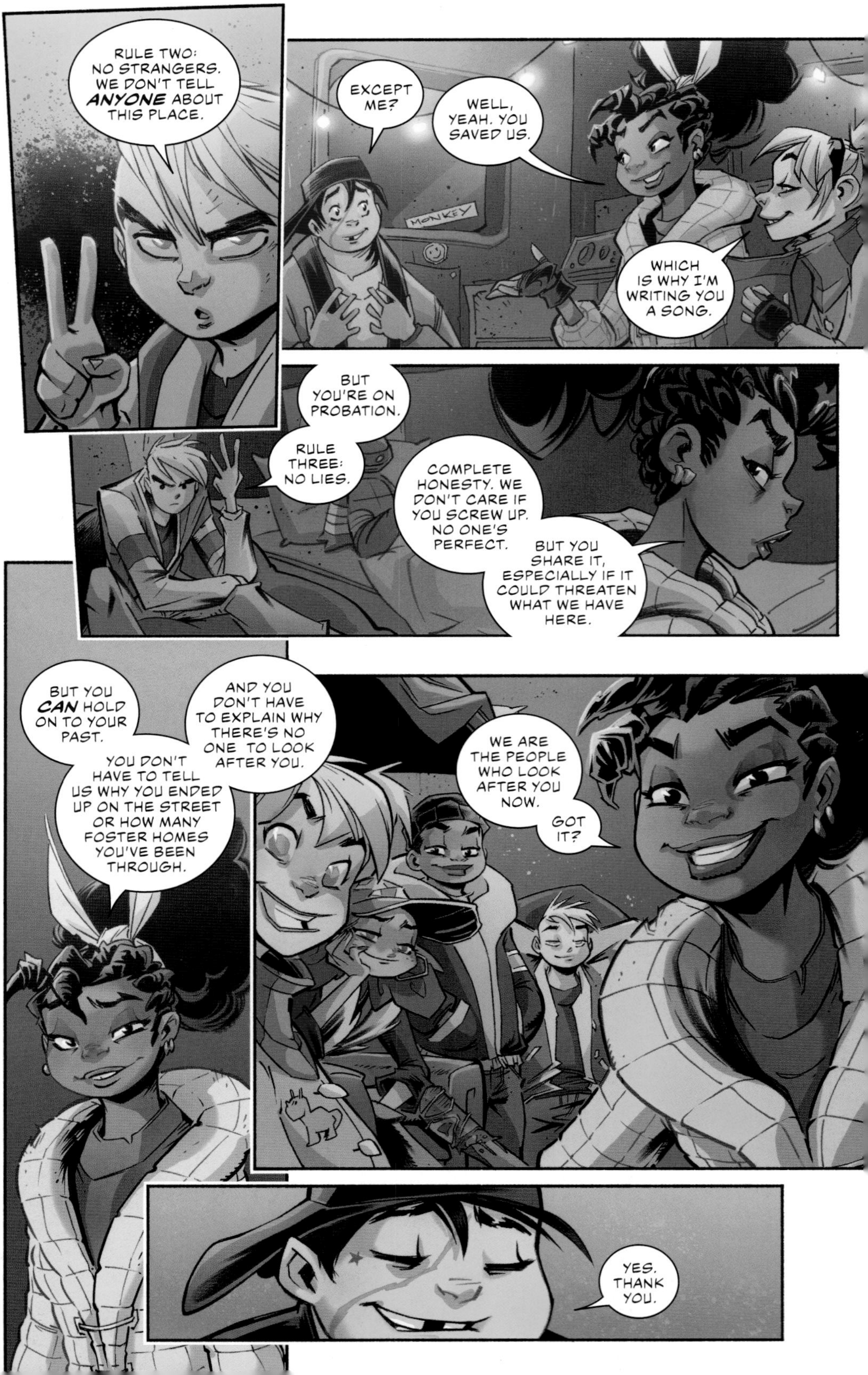
RULE TWO: NO STRANGERS. WE DON'T TELL ANYONE ABOUT THIS PLACE.
EXCEPT ME?
WELL, YEAH. YOU SAVED US.
MONKEY
WHICH IS WHY I'M WRITING YOU A SONG.
BUT YOU'RE ON PROBATION.
RULE THREE: NO LIES.
COMPLETE HONESTY. WE DON'T CARE IF YOU SCREW UP. NO ONE'S PERFECT.
BUT YOU SHARE IT, ESPECIALLY IF IT COULD THREATEN WHAT WE HAVE HERE.
BUT YOU CAN HOLD ON TO YOUR PAST.
YOU DON'T HAVE TO TELL US WHY YOU ENDED UP ON THE STREET OR HOW MANY FOSTER HOMES YOU'VE BEEN THROUGH.
AND YOU DON'T HAVE TO EXPLAIN WHY THERE'S NO ONE TO LOOK AFTER YOU.
WE ARE THE PEOPLE WHO LOOK AFTER YOU NOW.
GOT IT?
YES. THANK YOU.

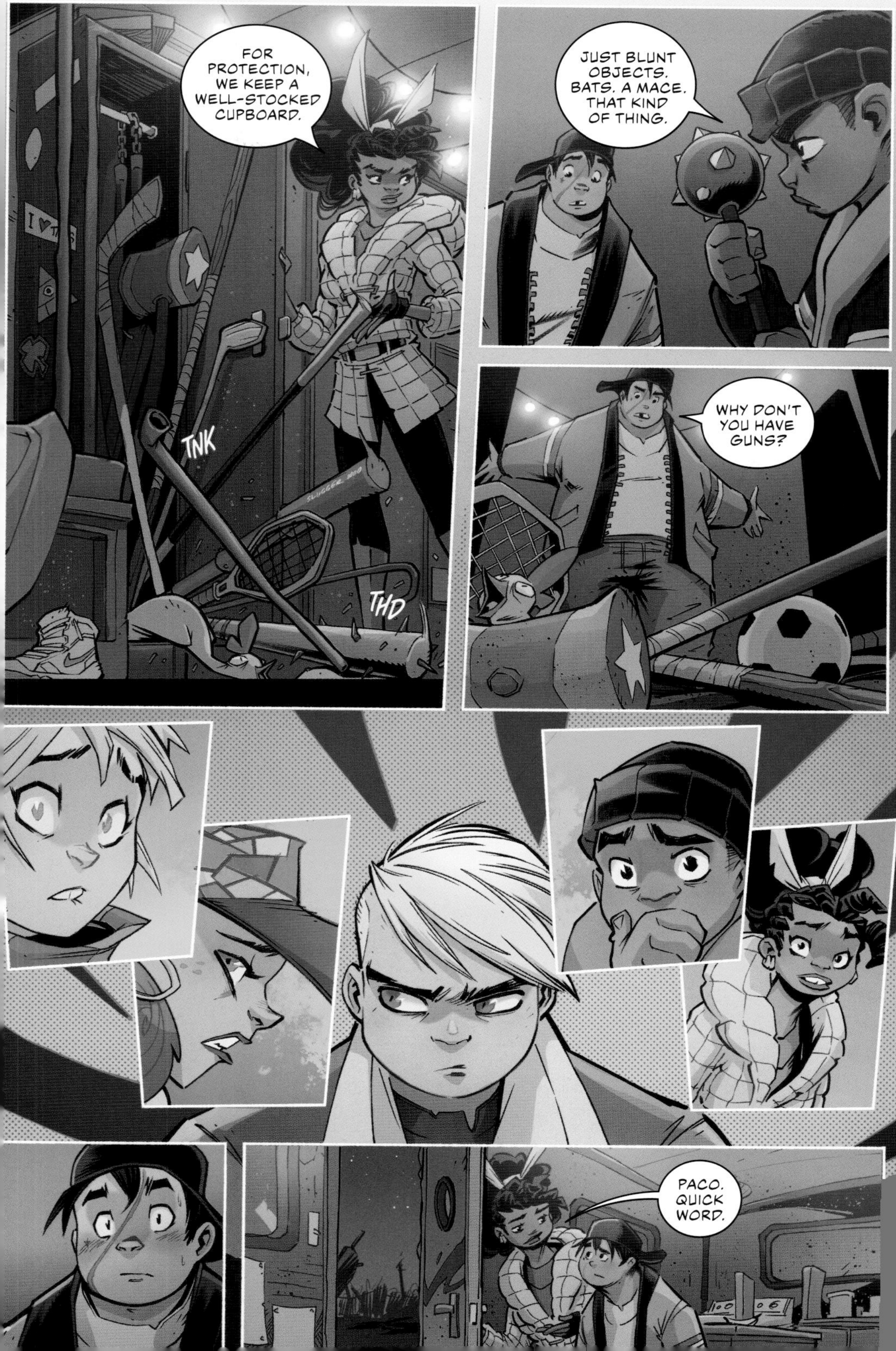
FOR PROTECTION, WE KEEP A WELL-STOCKED CUPBOARD.
TNK
SLUGGER 1000
THD
JUST BLUNT OBJECTS. BATS. A MACE. THAT KIND OF THING.
WHY DON'T YOU HAVE GUNS?
PACO. QUICK WORD.

THE BIG GUY IN THERE, JUSTIN... THERE WAS A SHOOTING AT HIS SCHOOL.

HE RAN. HE NEVER WENT BACK.

OH.

YOU *NEVER* BRING A GUN ANYWHERE NEAR HERE. GOT IT?

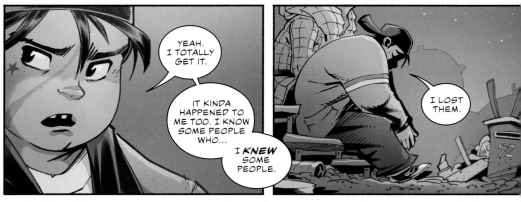

YEAH. I TOTALLY GET IT.

IT KINDA HAPPENED TO ME TOO. I KNOW SOME PEOPLE WHO... I *KNEW* SOME PEOPLE.

I LOST THEM.

I'M SORRY.

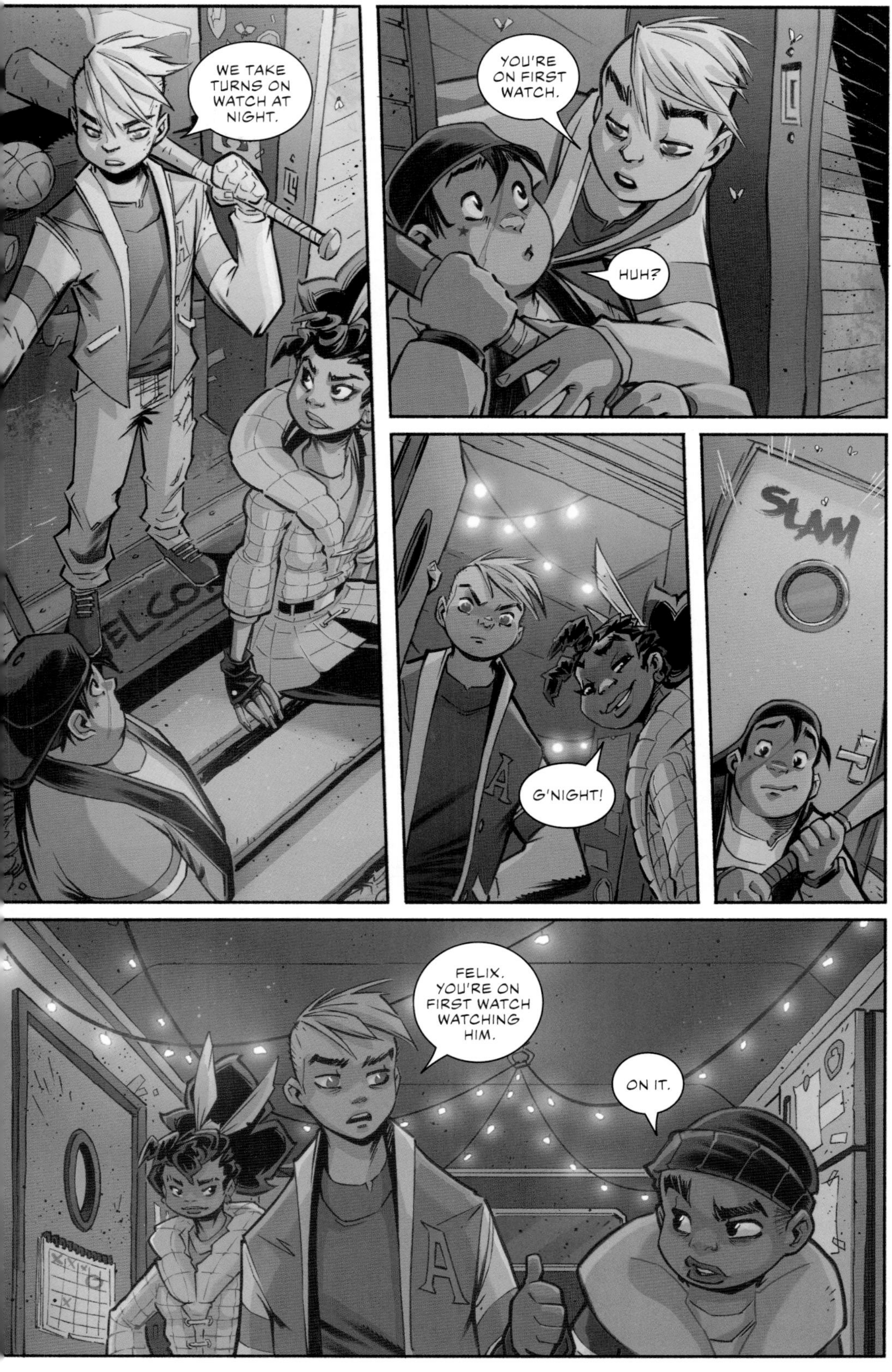
WE TAKE TURNS ON WATCH AT NIGHT.
YOU'RE ON FIRST WATCH.
HUH?
G'NIGHT!
SLAM
FELIX. YOU'RE ON FIRST WATCH WATCHING HIM.
ON IT.

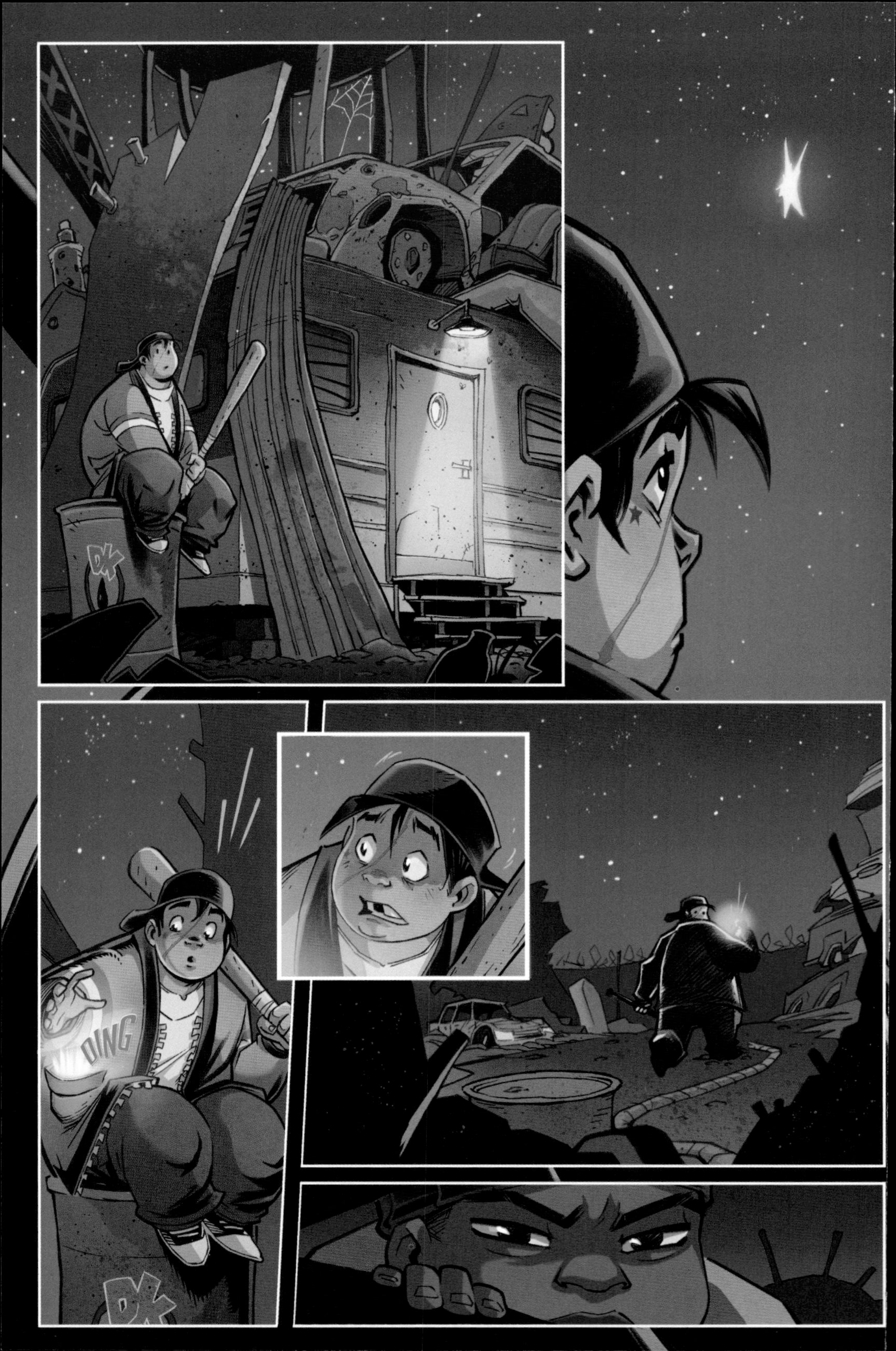
DING

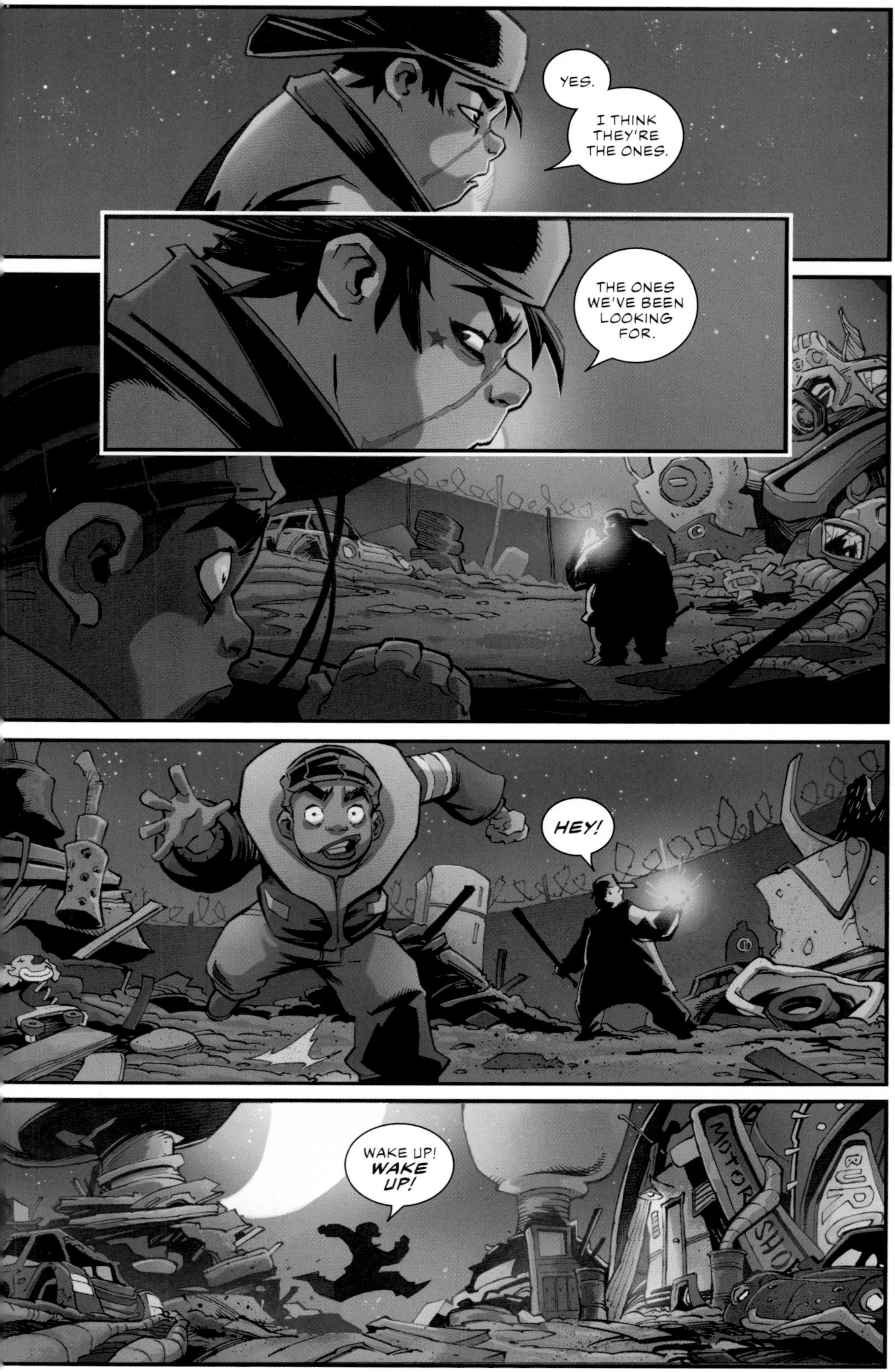
YES.
I THINK THEY'RE THE ONES.
THE ONES WE'VE BEEN LOOKING FOR.
HEY!
WAKE UP! WAKE UP!
MOTOR

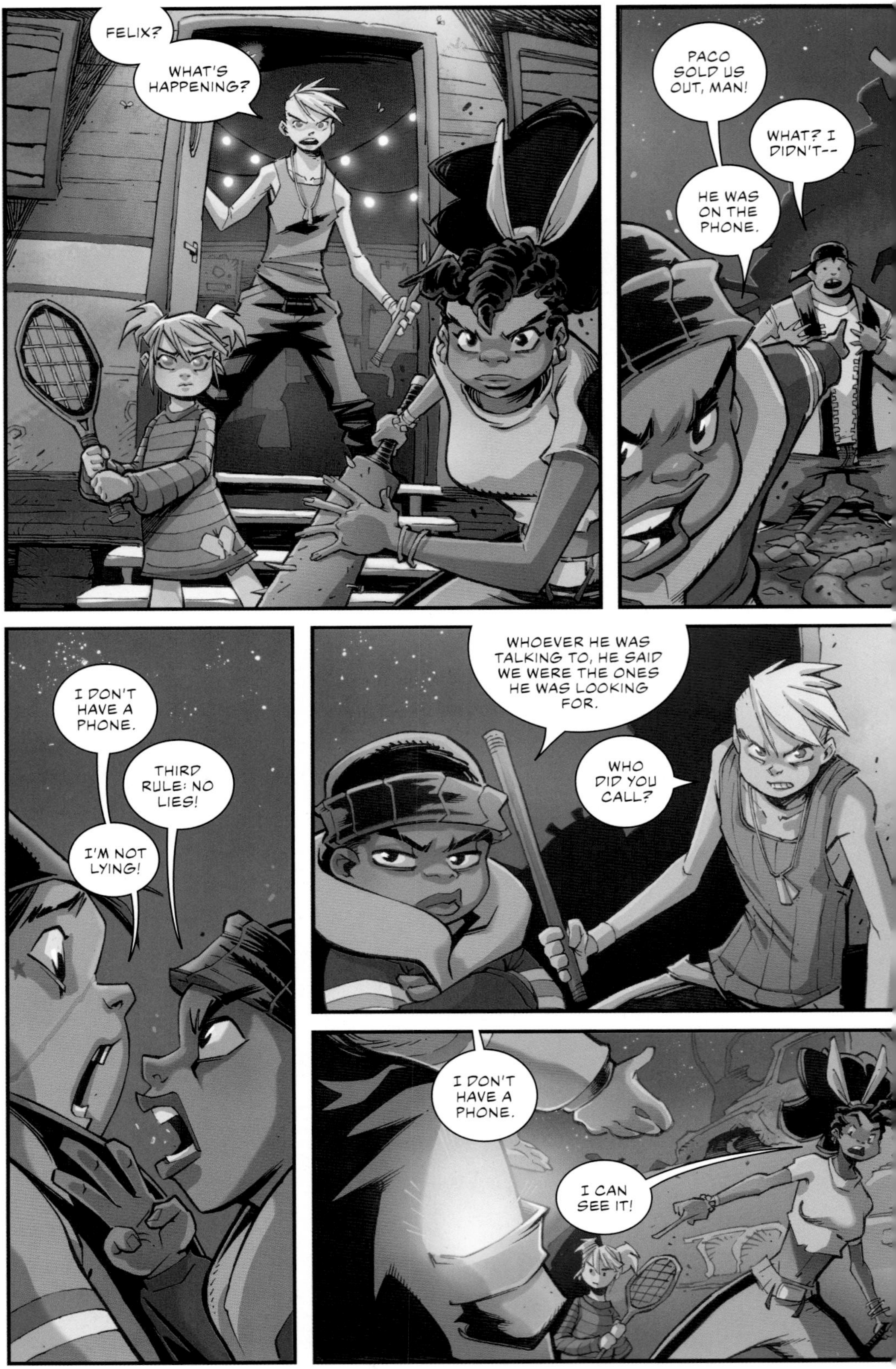
FELIX?
WHAT'S HAPPENING?
PACO SOLD US OUT, MAN!
WHAT? I DIDN'T--
HE WAS ON THE PHONE.
I DON'T HAVE A PHONE.
THIRD RULE: NO LIES!
I'M NOT LYING!
WHOEVER HE WAS TALKING TO, HE SAID WE WERE THE ONES HE WAS LOOKING FOR.
WHO DID YOU CALL?
I DON'T HAVE A PHONE.
I CAN SEE IT!

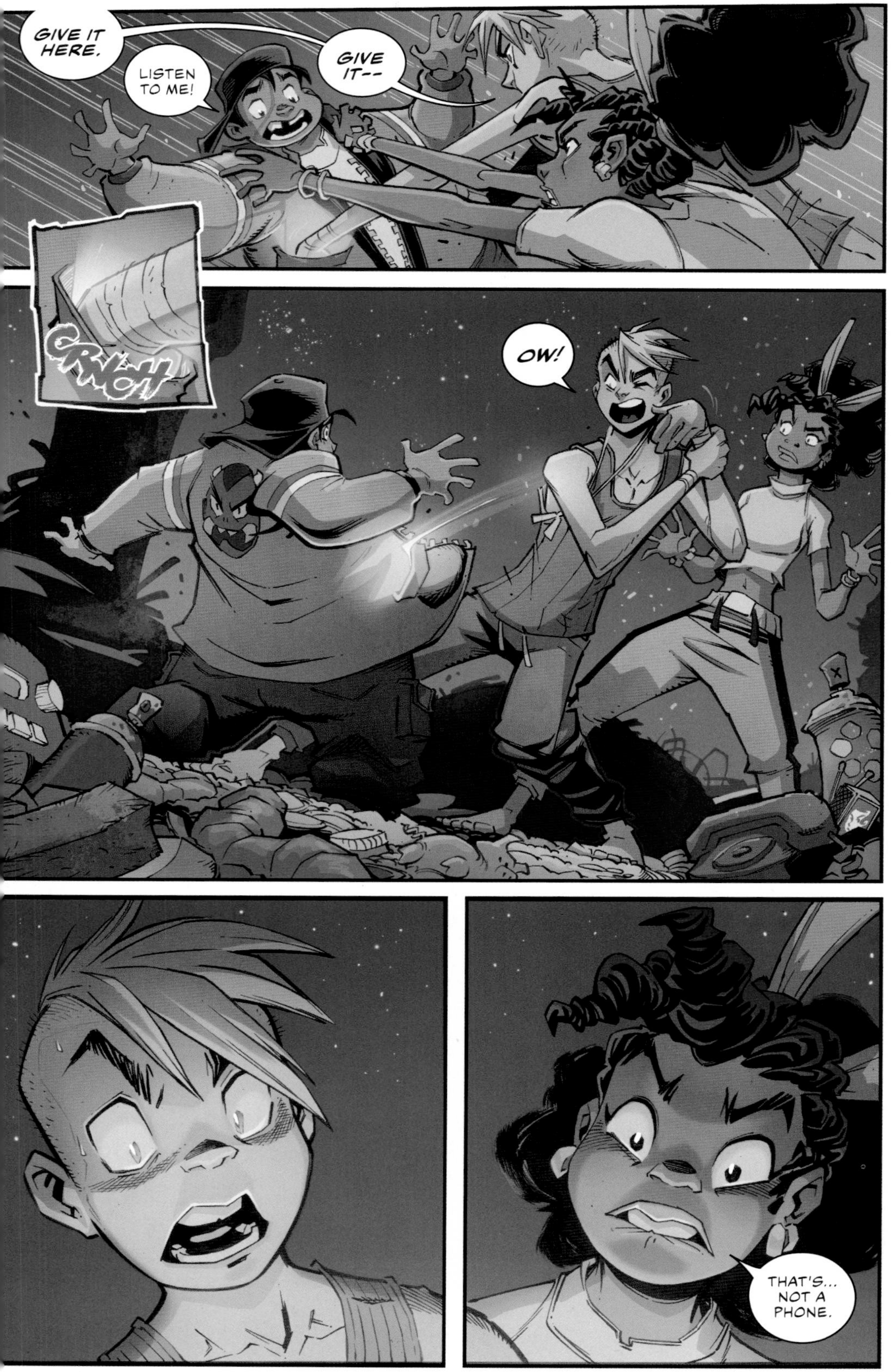
GIVE IT HERE.
LISTEN TO ME!
GIVE IT--
CRUNCH
OW!
THAT'S... NOT A PHONE.

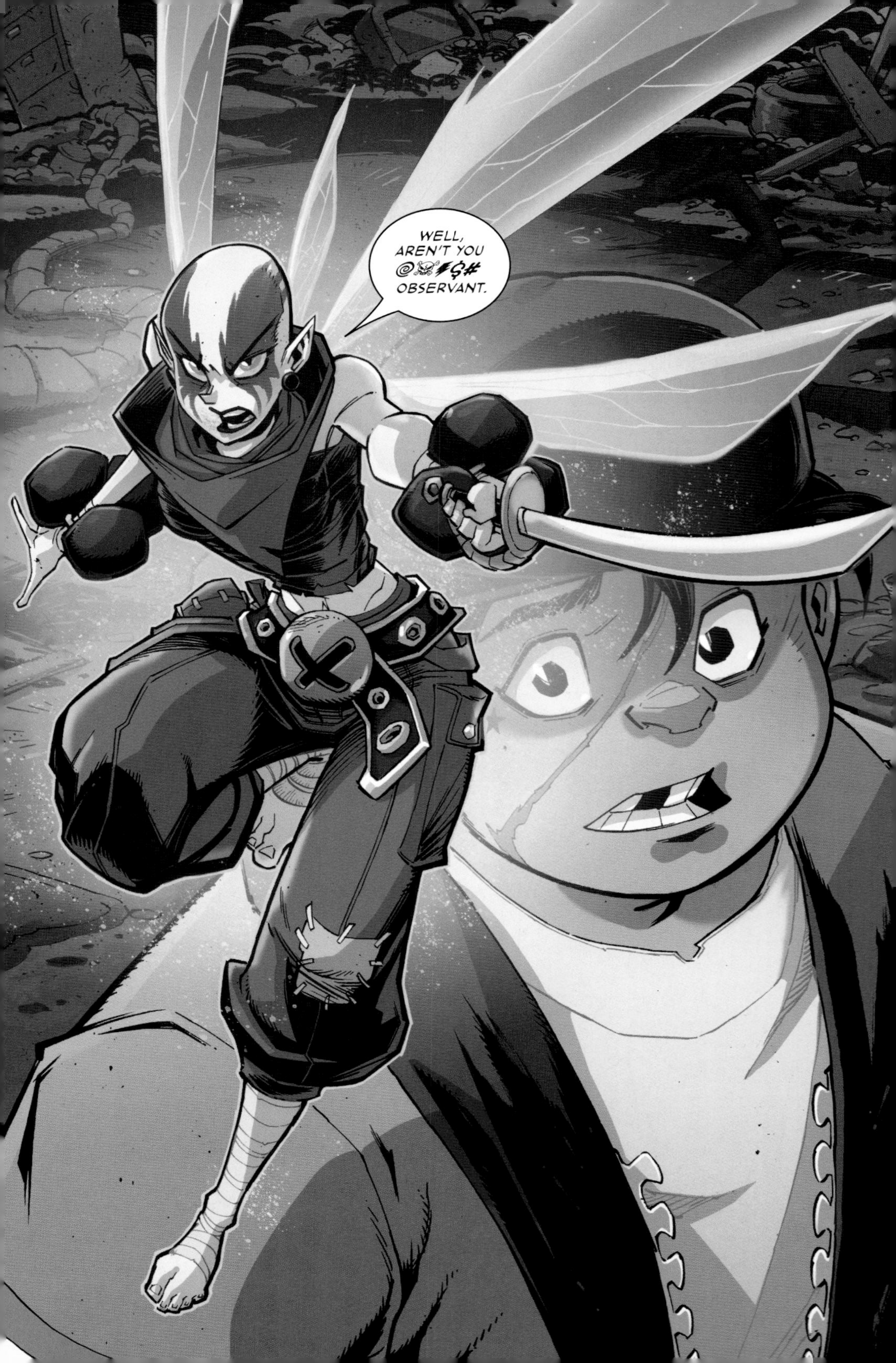
WELL, AREN'T YOU @☠⚡$# OBSERVANT.

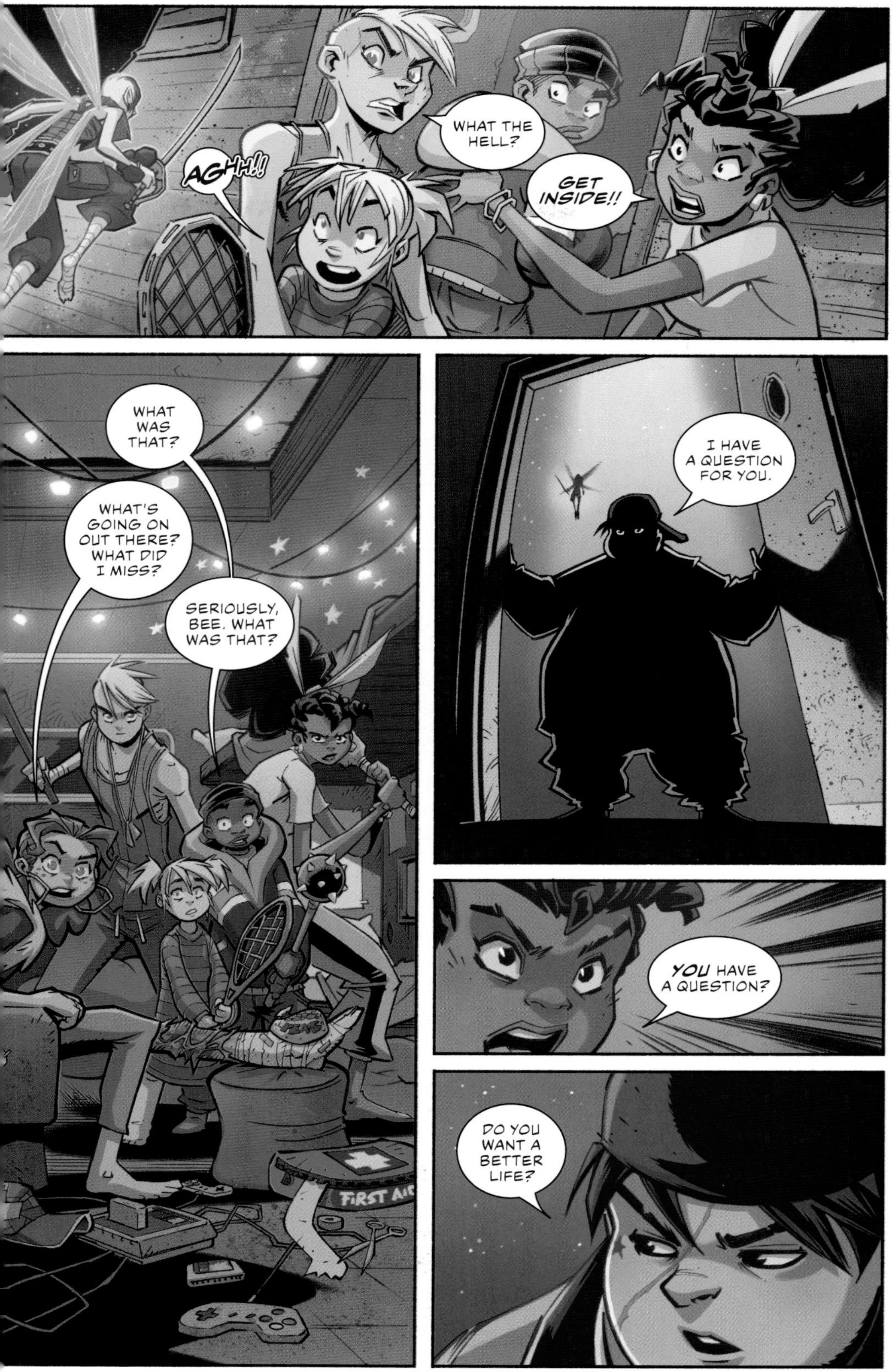
AGHH!!
WHAT THE HELL?
GET INSIDE!!
WHAT WAS THAT?
WHAT'S GOING ON OUT THERE? WHAT DID I MISS?
SERIOUSLY, BEE. WHAT WAS THAT?
I HAVE A QUESTION FOR YOU.
YOU HAVE A QUESTION?
DO YOU WANT A BETTER LIFE?
FIRST AID

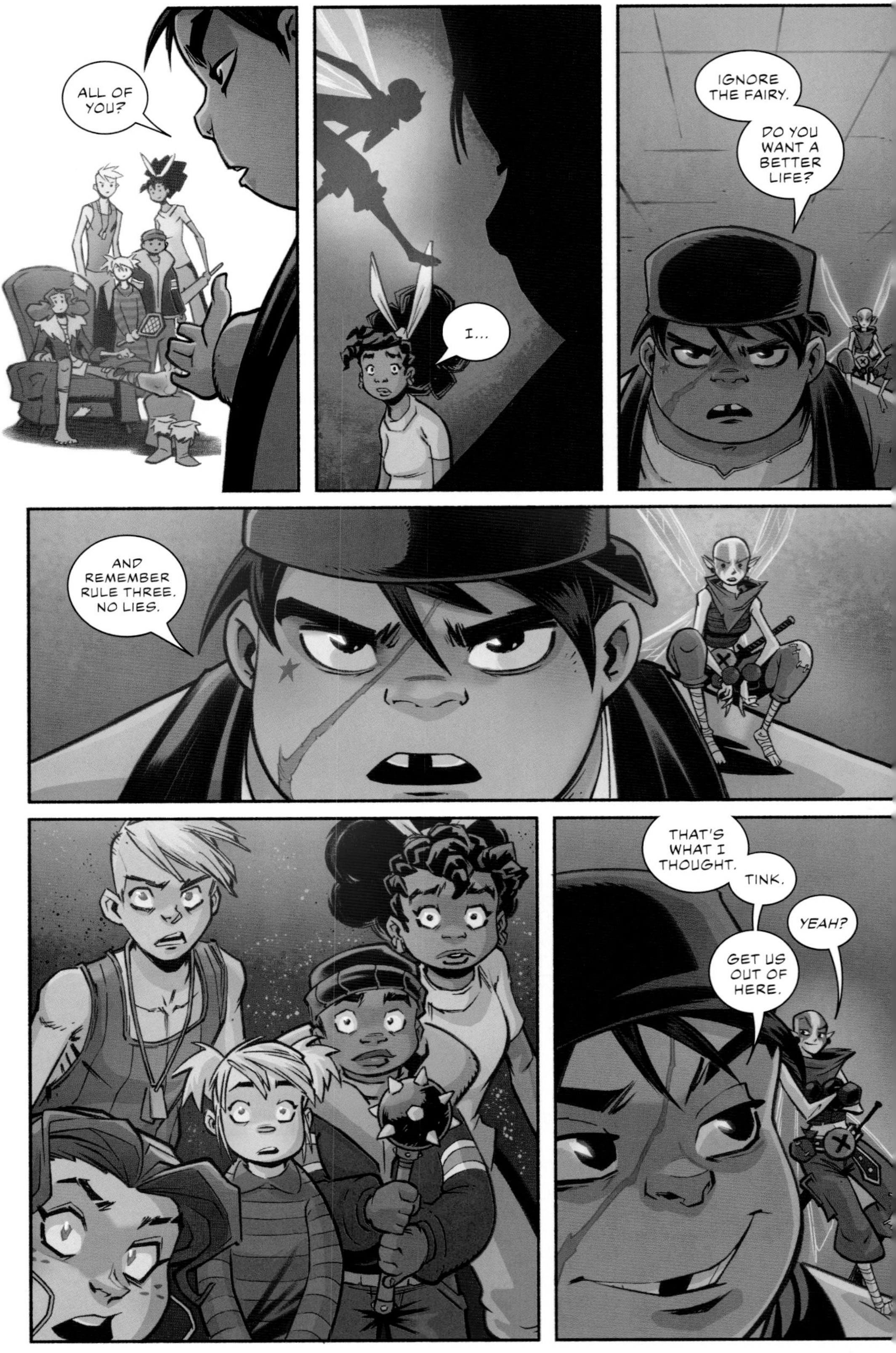
ALL OF YOU?
I...
IGNORE THE FAIRY.
DO YOU WANT A BETTER LIFE?
AND REMEMBER RULE THREE. NO LIES.
THAT'S WHAT I THOUGHT.
TINK.
YEAH?
GET US OUT OF HERE.

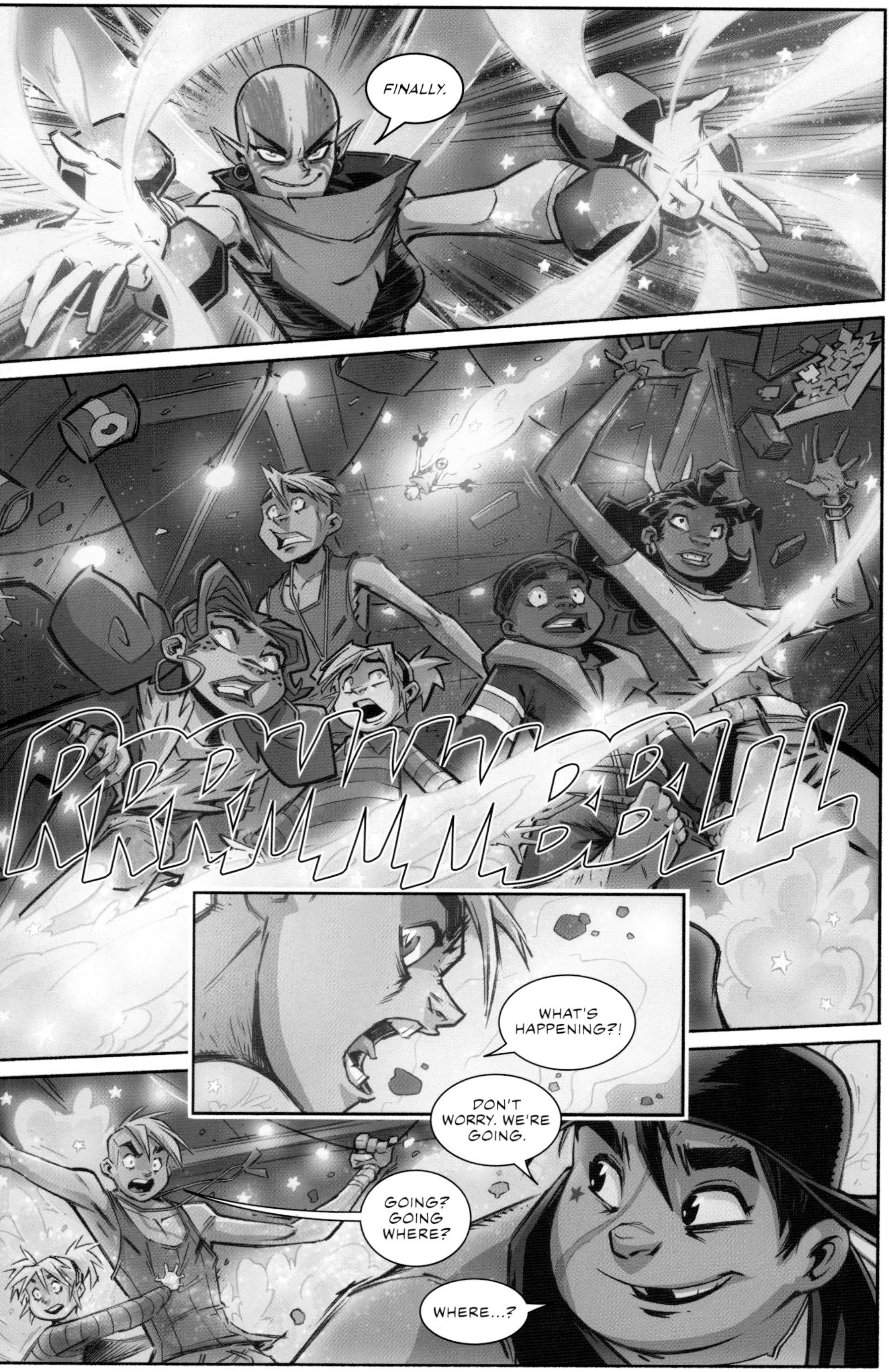
FINALLY.
WHAT'S HAPPENING?!
DON'T WORRY. WE'RE GOING.
GOING? GOING WHERE?
WHERE...?

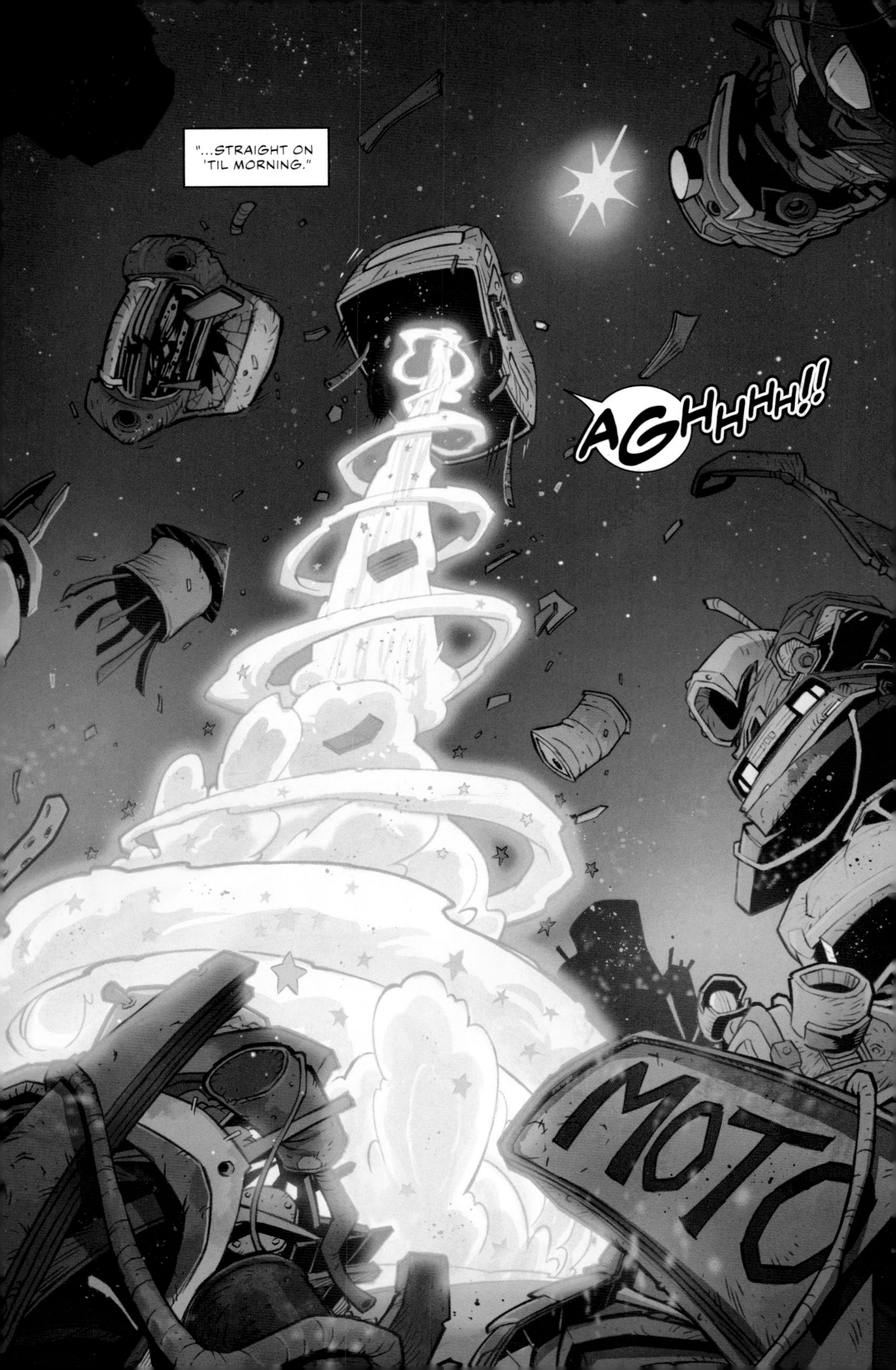
"...STRAIGHT ON 'TIL MORNING."
AGHHHH!!
MOTO

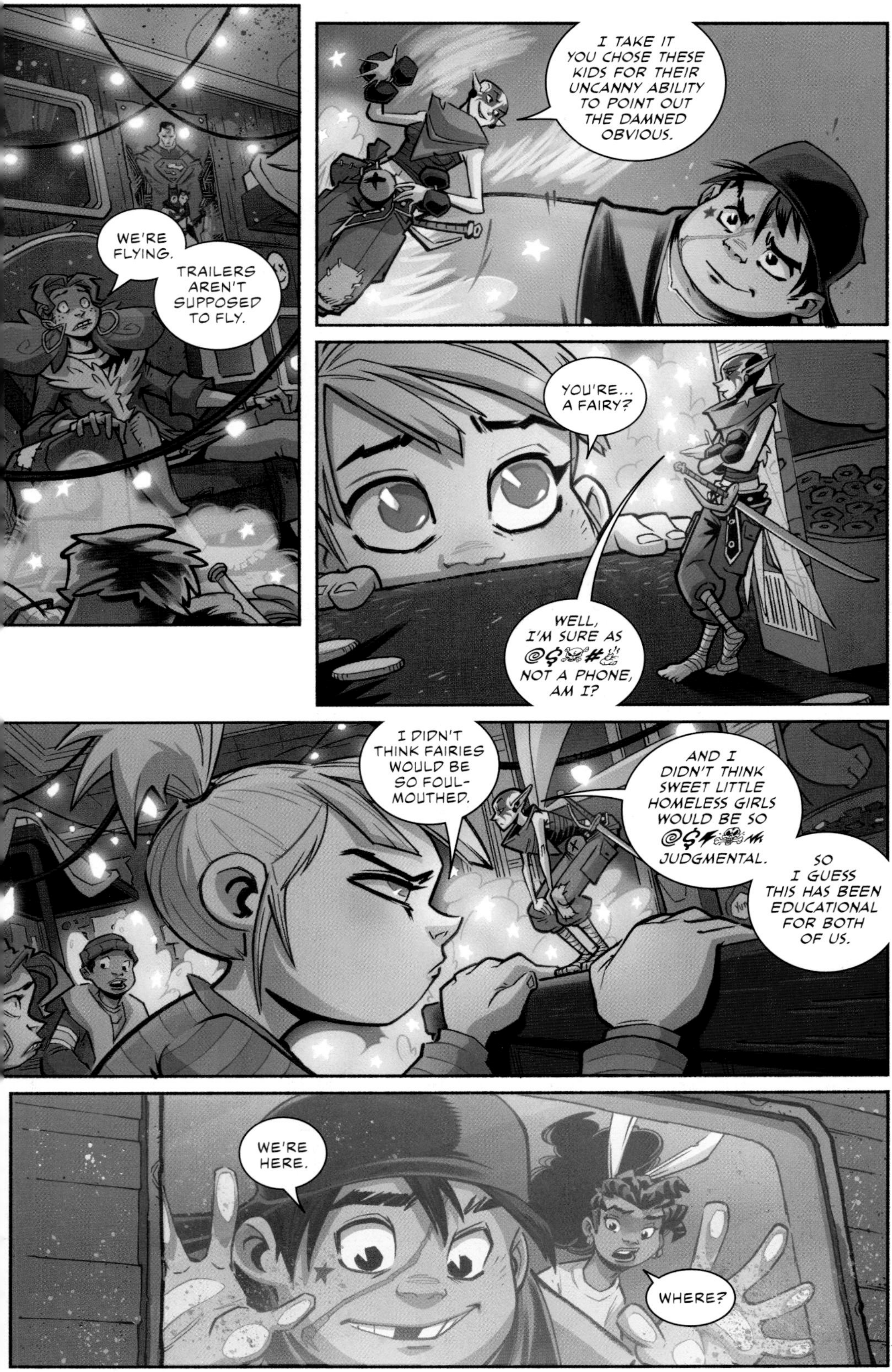

WE'RE FLYING.
TRAILERS AREN'T SUPPOSED TO FLY.
I TAKE IT YOU CHOSE THESE KIDS FOR THEIR UNCANNY ABILITY TO POINT OUT THE DAMNED OBVIOUS.
YOU'RE... A FAIRY?
WELL, I'M SURE AS @$☠#☝ NOT A PHONE, AM I?
I DIDN'T THINK FAIRIES WOULD BE SO FOUL-MOUTHED.
AND I DIDN'T THINK SWEET LITTLE HOMELESS GIRLS WOULD BE SO @$⚡☠✗ JUDGMENTAL.
SO I GUESS THIS HAS BEEN EDUCATIONAL FOR BOTH OF US.
WE'RE HERE.
WHERE?

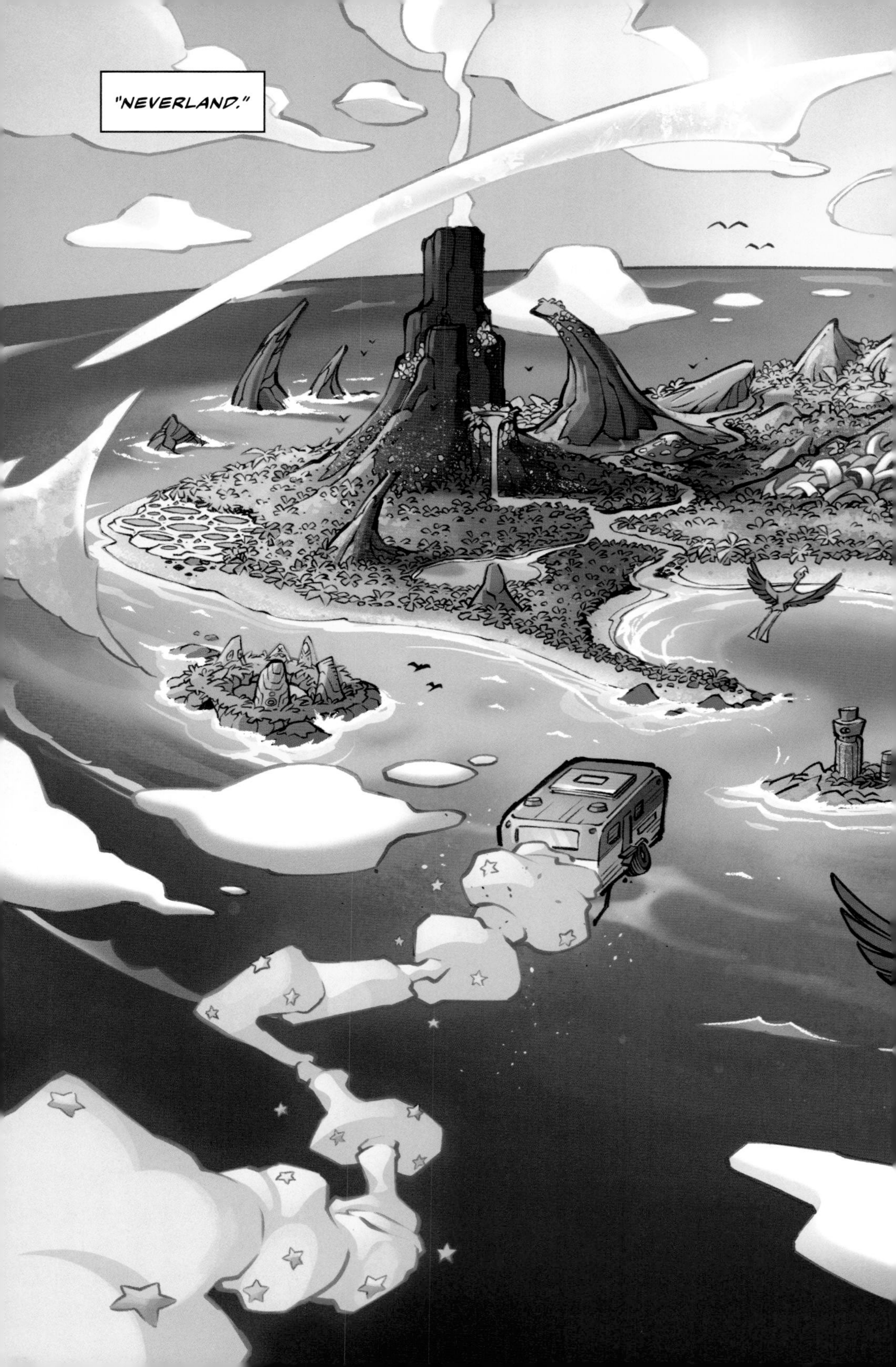
"NEVERLAND."

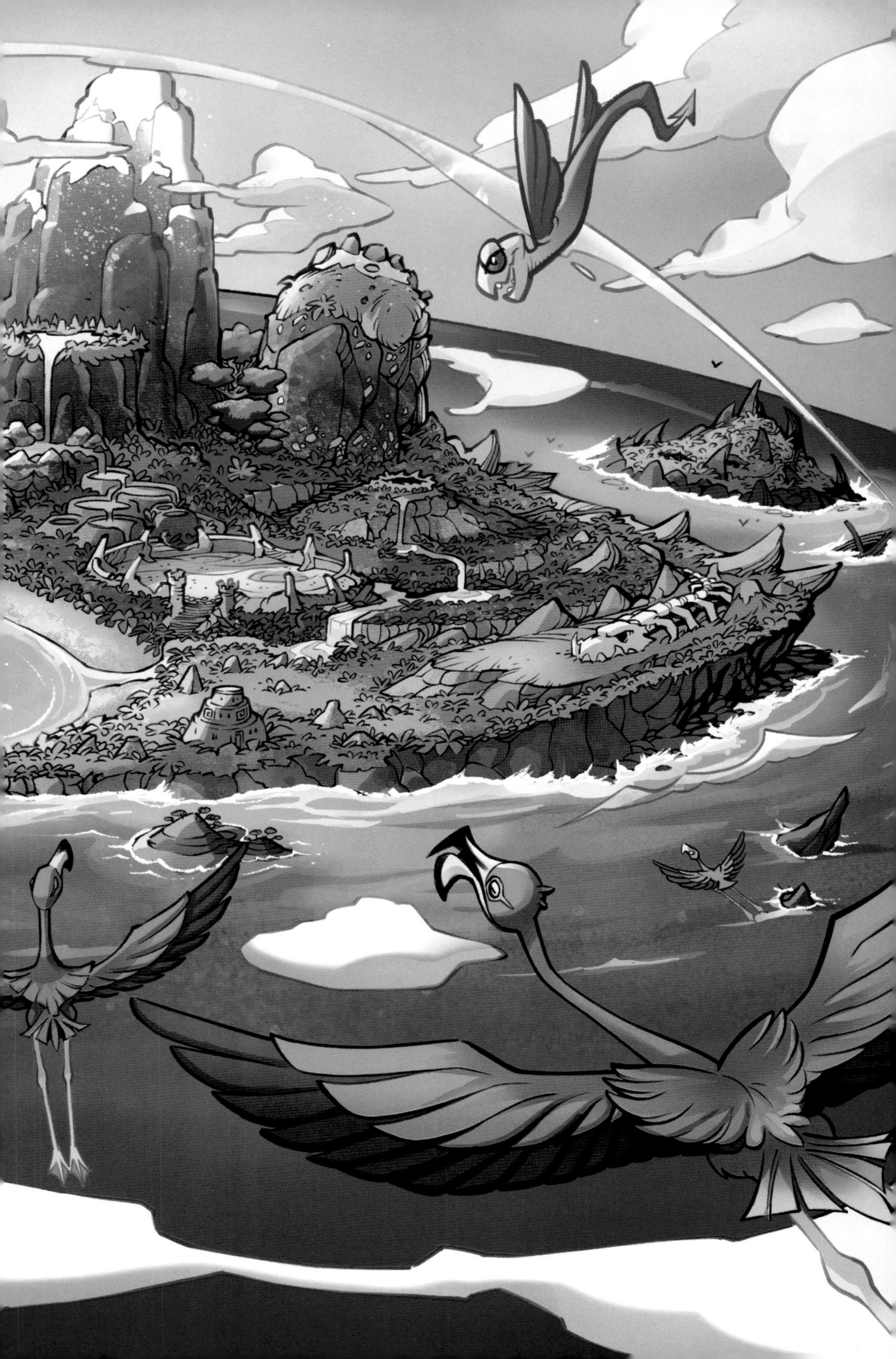

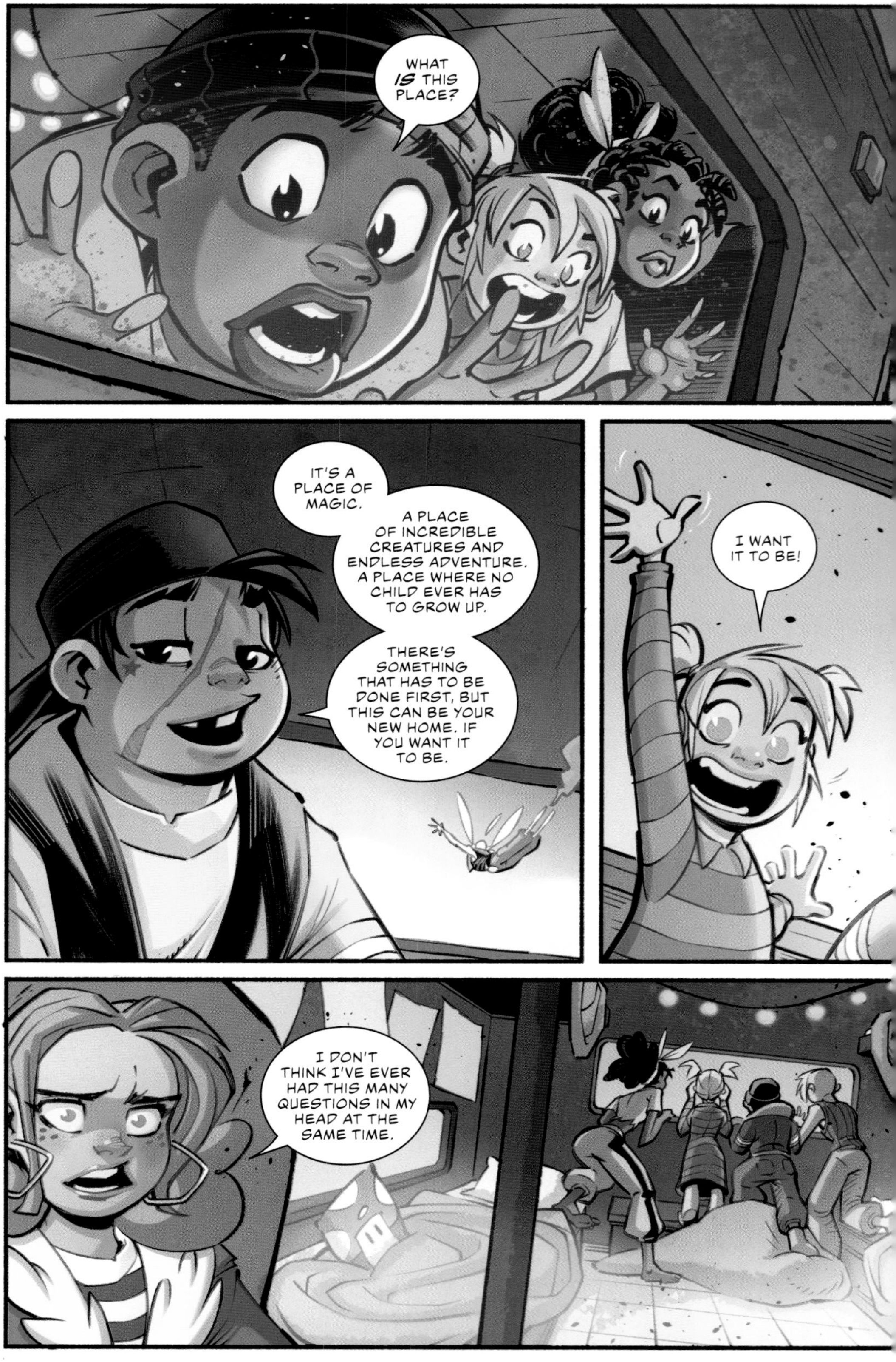
WHAT *IS* THIS PLACE?
IT'S A PLACE OF MAGIC.
A PLACE OF INCREDIBLE CREATURES AND ENDLESS ADVENTURE. A PLACE WHERE NO CHILD EVER HAS TO GROW UP.
THERE'S SOMETHING THAT HAS TO BE DONE FIRST, BUT THIS CAN BE YOUR NEW HOME. IF YOU WANT IT TO BE.
I WANT IT TO BE!
I DON'T THINK I'VE EVER HAD THIS MANY QUESTIONS IN MY HEAD AT THE SAME TIME.

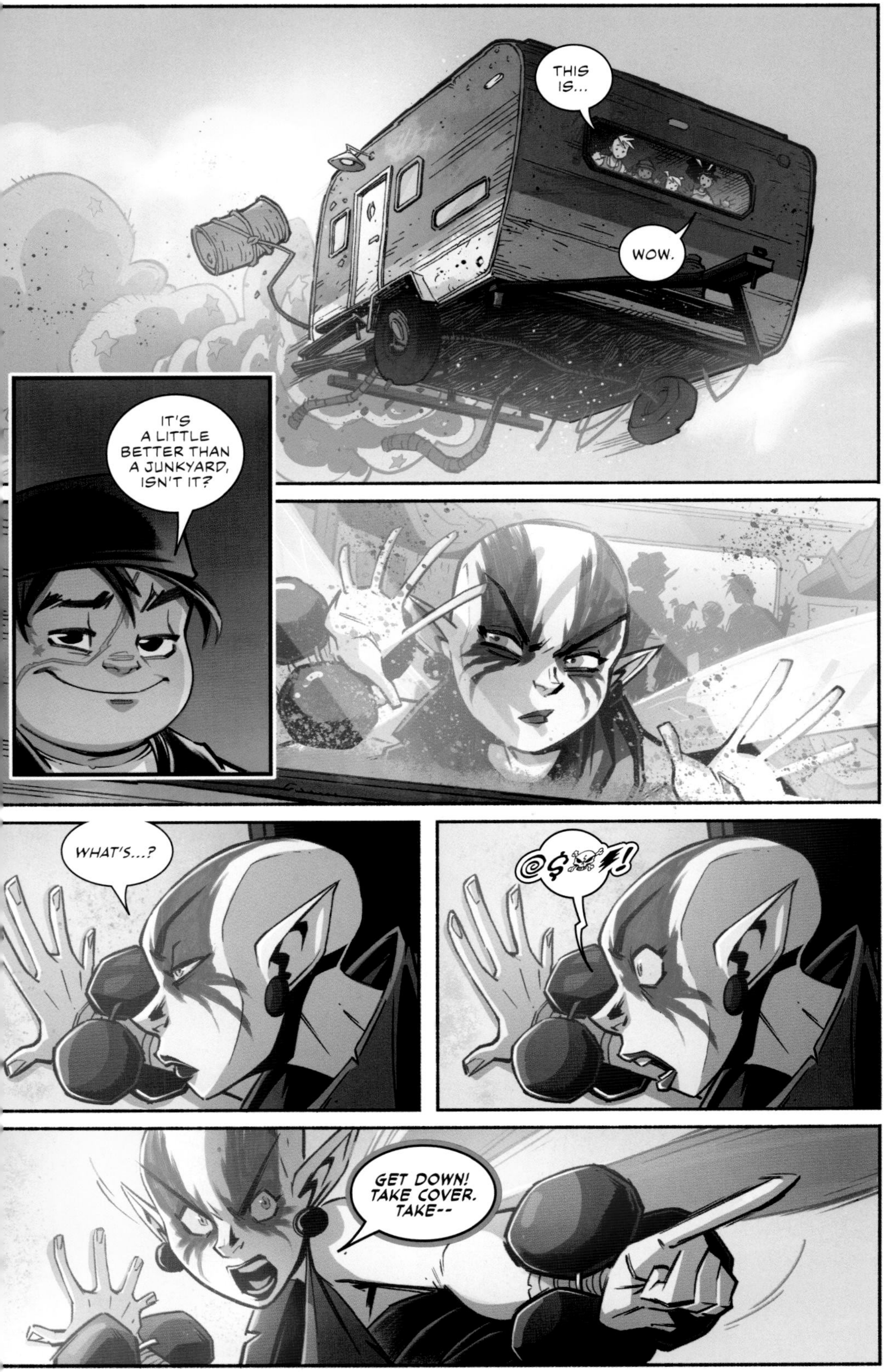
THIS IS...
WOW.
IT'S A LITTLE BETTER THAN A JUNKYARD, ISN'T IT?
WHAT'S...?
GET DOWN! TAKE COVER. TAKE--

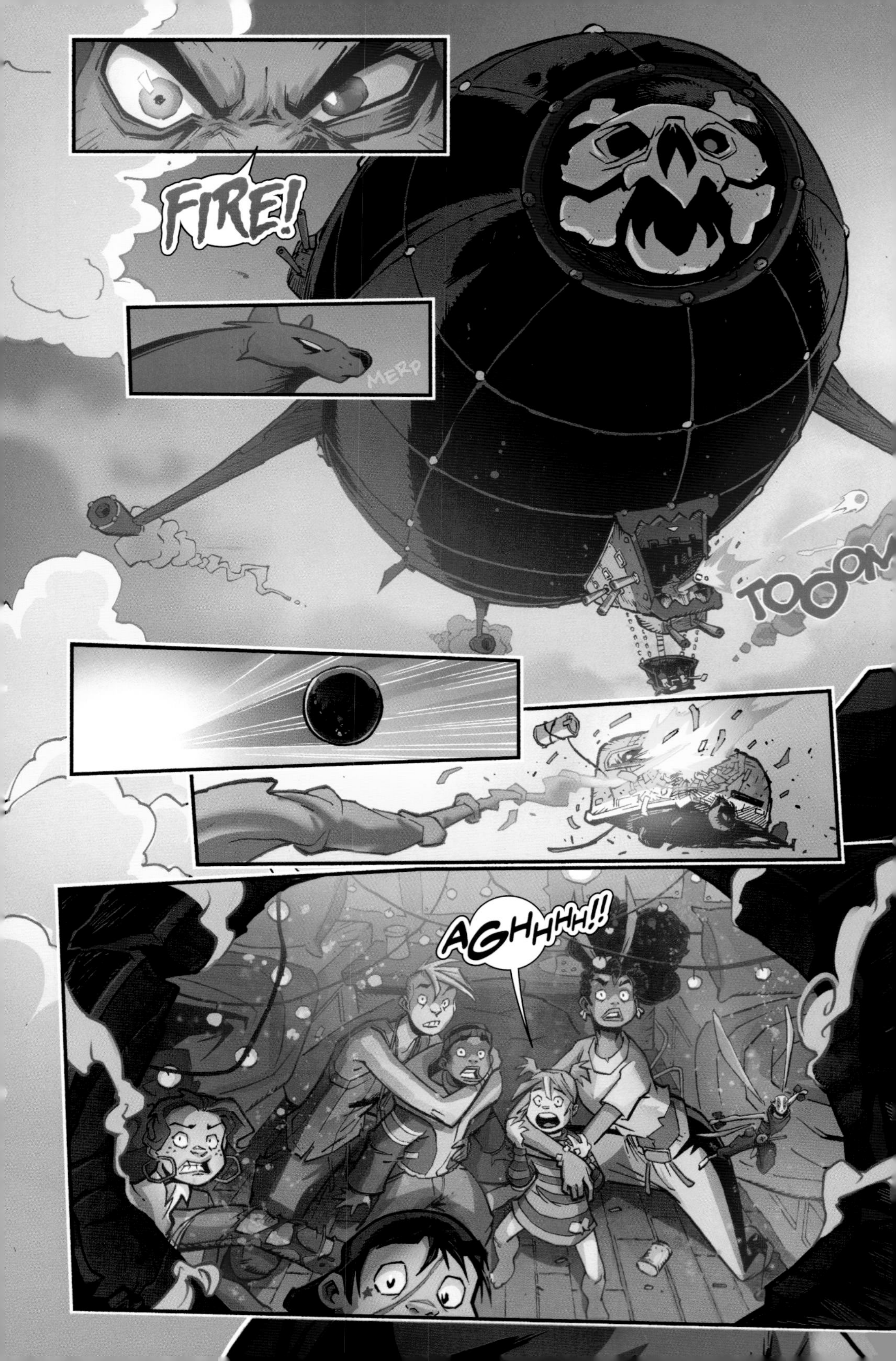
FIRE!
MERP
TOOOOM
AGHHHH!!

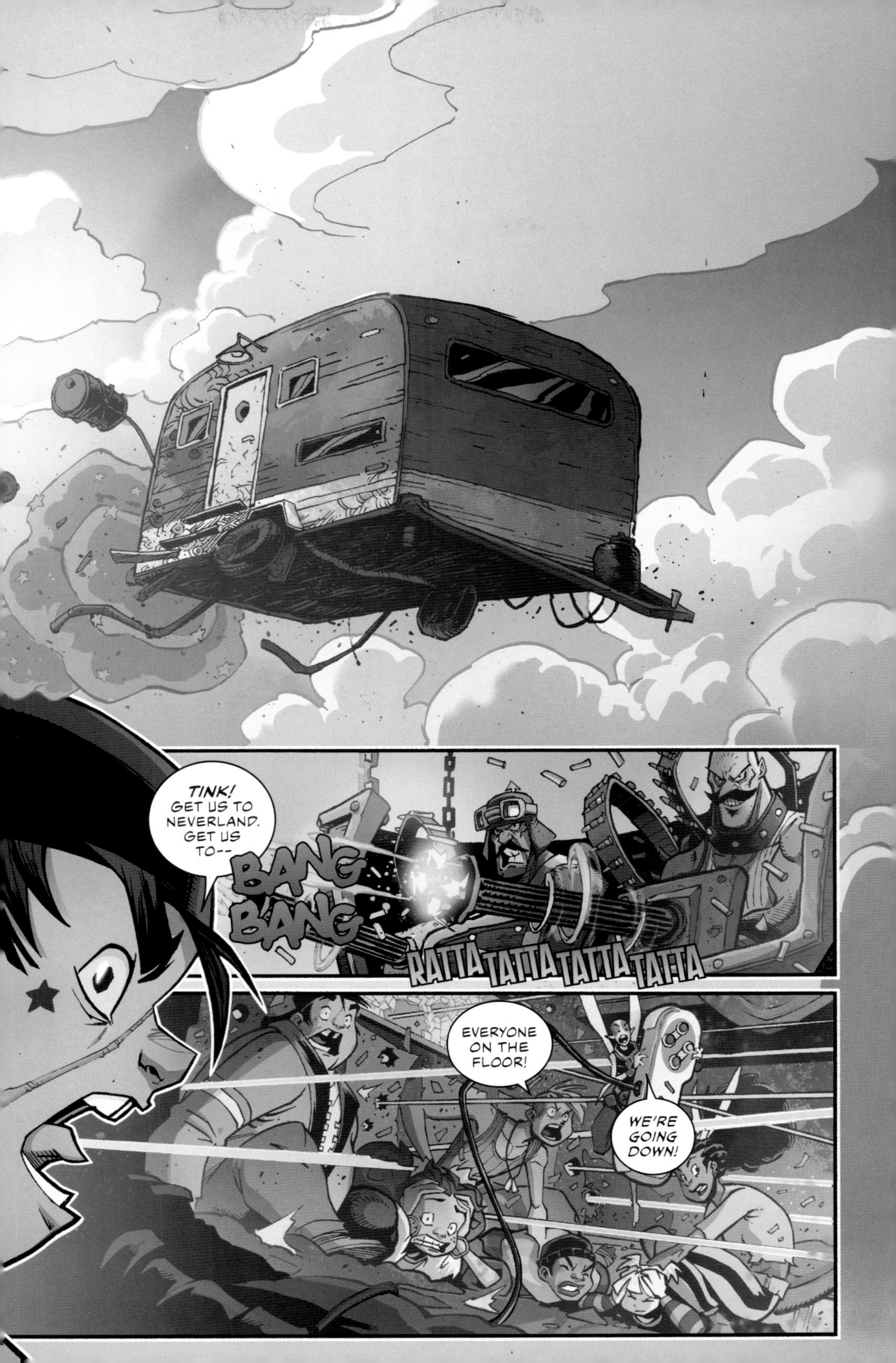

TINK! GET US TO NEVERLAND. GET US TO--
BANG BANG
RATTATATTATATTATATTA
EVERYONE ON THE FLOOR!
WE'RE GOING DOWN!

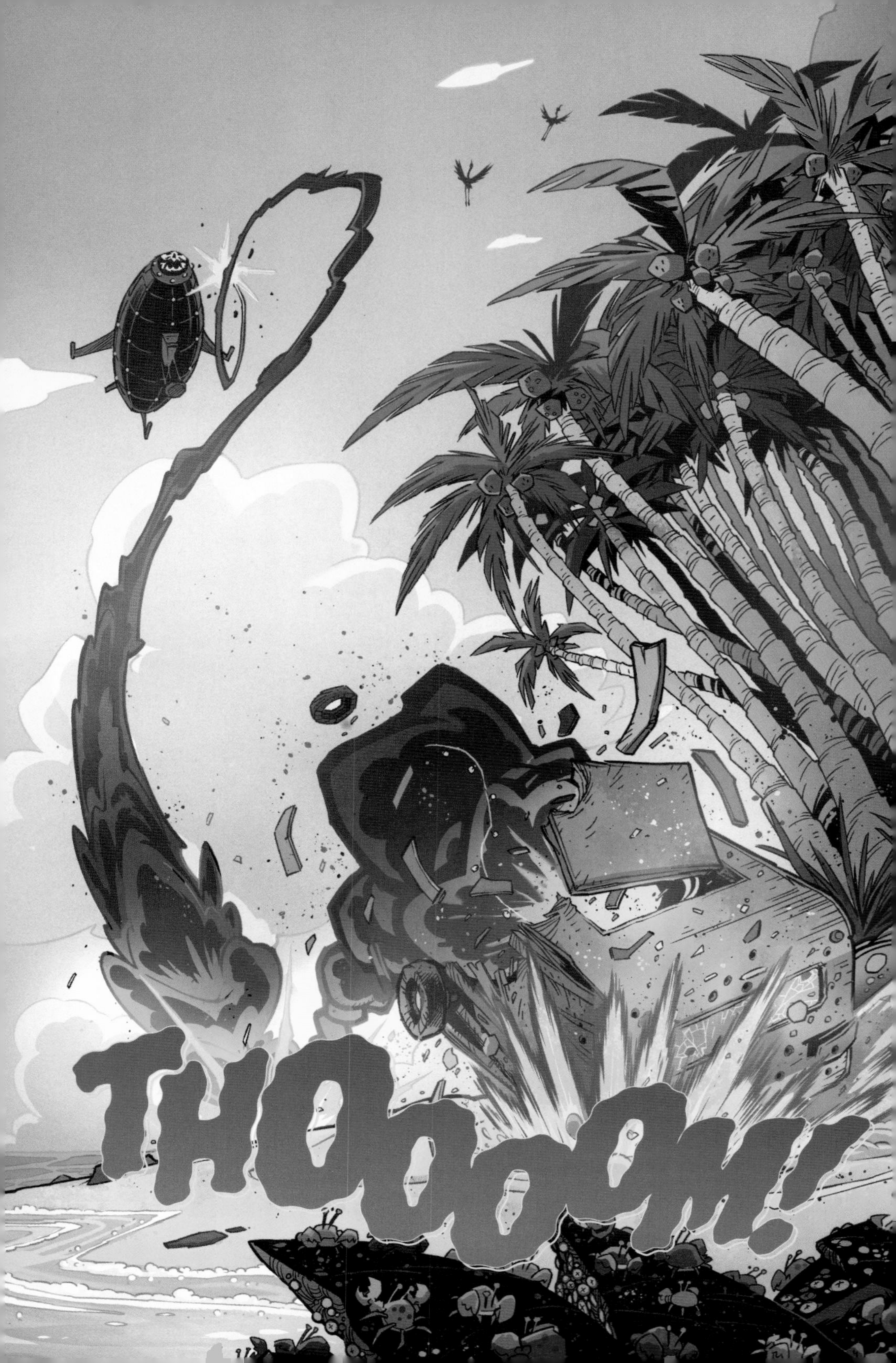
THOOOOM!

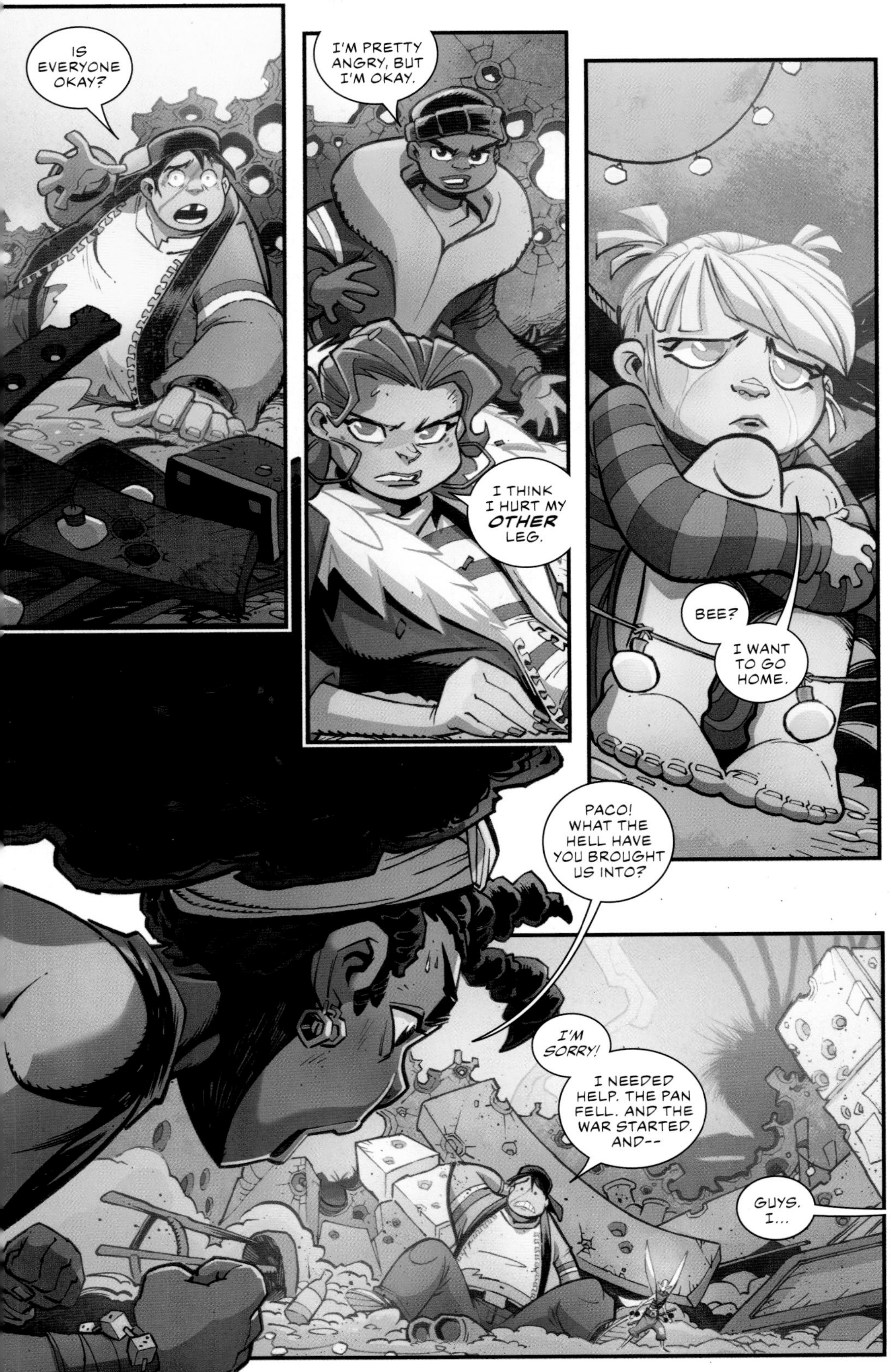
IS EVERYONE OKAY?
I'M PRETTY ANGRY, BUT I'M OKAY.
I THINK I HURT MY *OTHER* LEG.
BEE?
I WANT TO GO HOME.
PACO! WHAT THE HELL HAVE YOU BROUGHT US INTO?
I'M SORRY!
I NEEDED HELP. THE PAN FELL. AND THE WAR STARTED. AND--
GUYS. I...

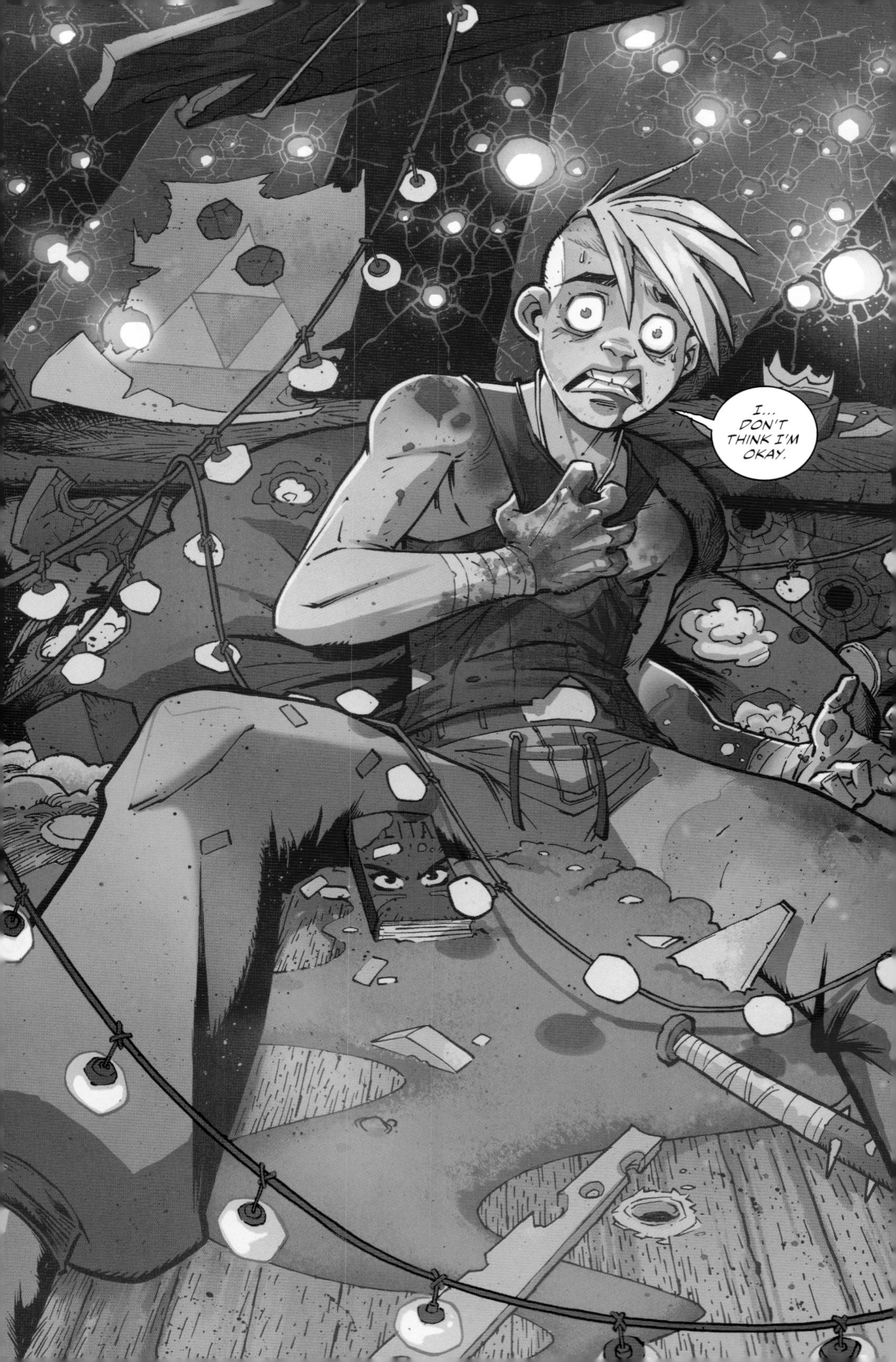
I... DON'T THINK I'M OKAY.

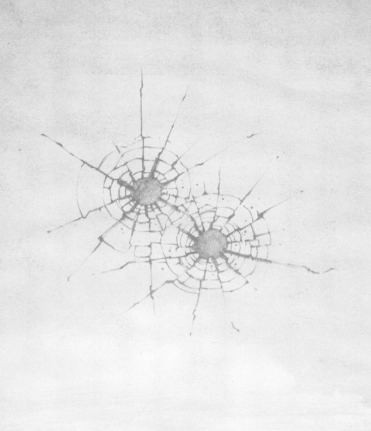

CHAPTER
TWO

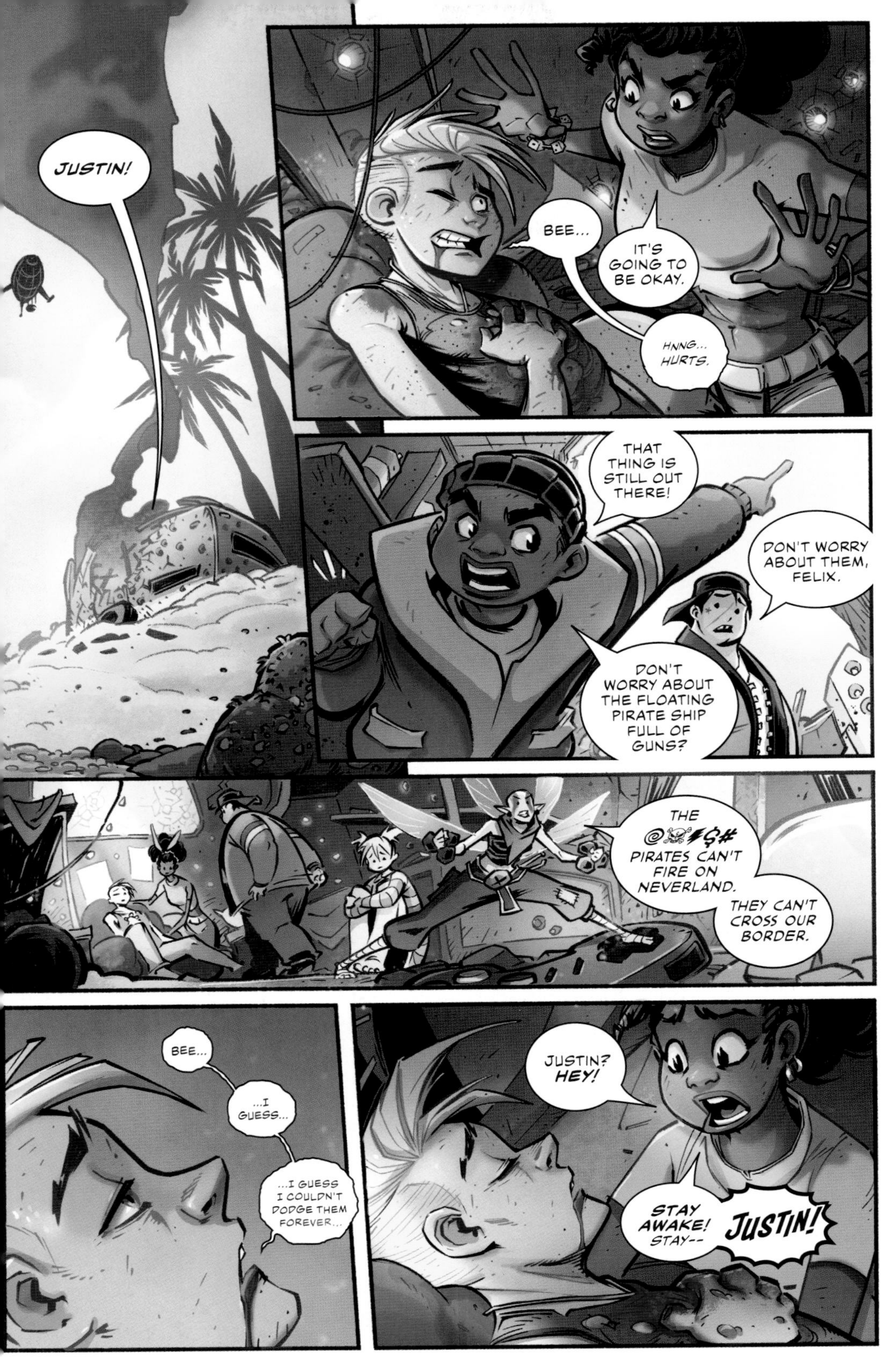
JUSTIN!
BEE...
IT'S GOING TO BE OKAY.
HNNG... HURTS.
THAT THING IS STILL OUT THERE!
DON'T WORRY ABOUT THEM, FELIX.
DON'T WORRY ABOUT THE FLOATING PIRATE SHIP FULL OF GUNS?
THE @☠#$# PIRATES CAN'T FIRE ON NEVERLAND.
THEY CAN'T CROSS OUR BORDER.
BEE...
...I GUESS...
...I GUESS I COULDN'T DODGE THEM FOREVER...
JUSTIN? HEY!
STAY AWAKE! STAY--
JUSTIN!

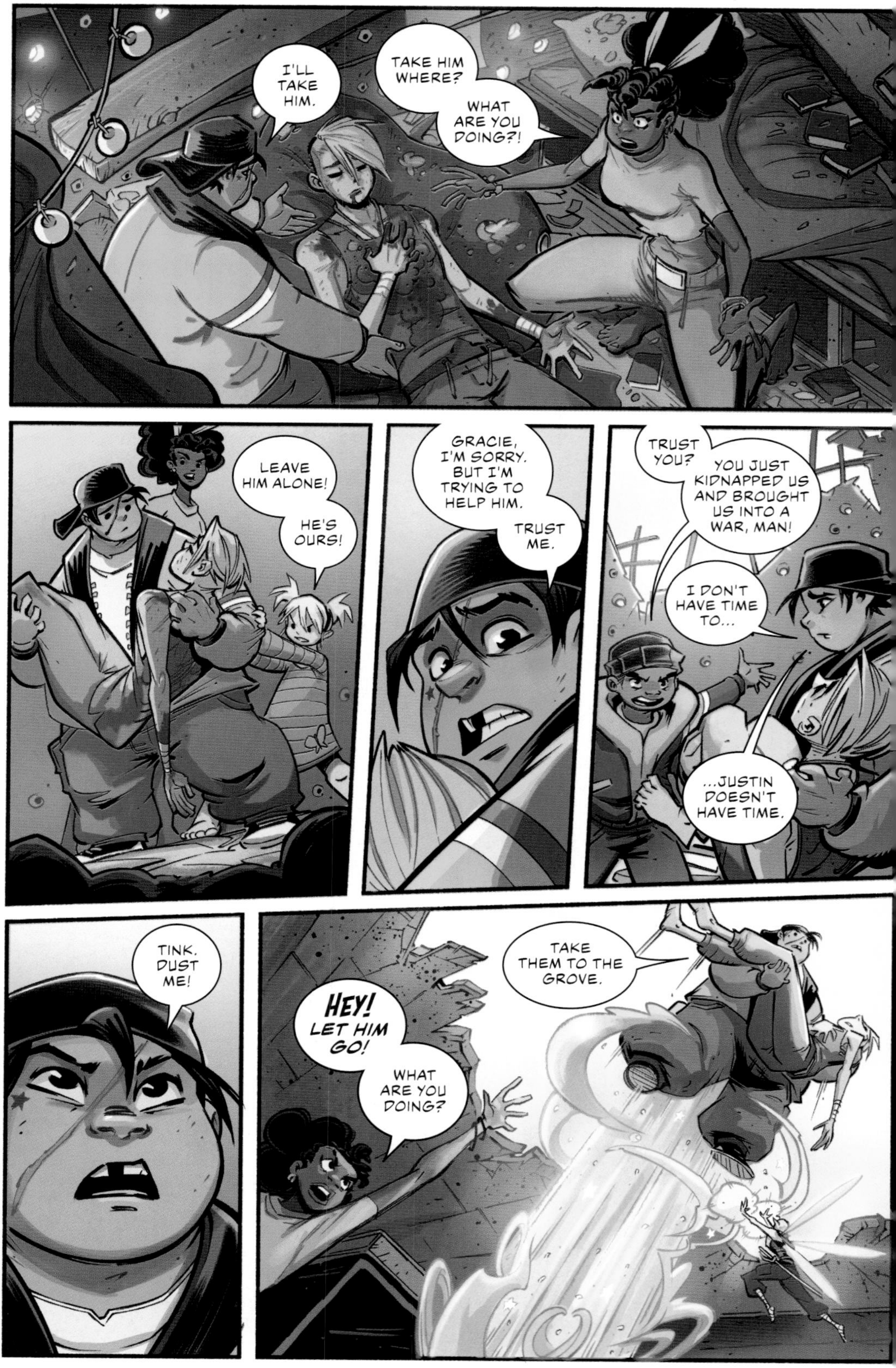

I'LL TAKE HIM.
TAKE HIM WHERE?
WHAT ARE YOU DOING?!
LEAVE HIM ALONE!
HE'S OURS!
GRACIE, I'M SORRY. BUT I'M TRYING TO HELP HIM.
TRUST ME.
TRUST YOU?
YOU JUST KIDNAPPED US AND BROUGHT US INTO A WAR, MAN!
I DON'T HAVE TIME TO...
...JUSTIN DOESN'T HAVE TIME.
TINK. DUST ME!
TAKE THEM TO THE GROVE.
HEY! LET HIM GO!
WHAT ARE YOU DOING?

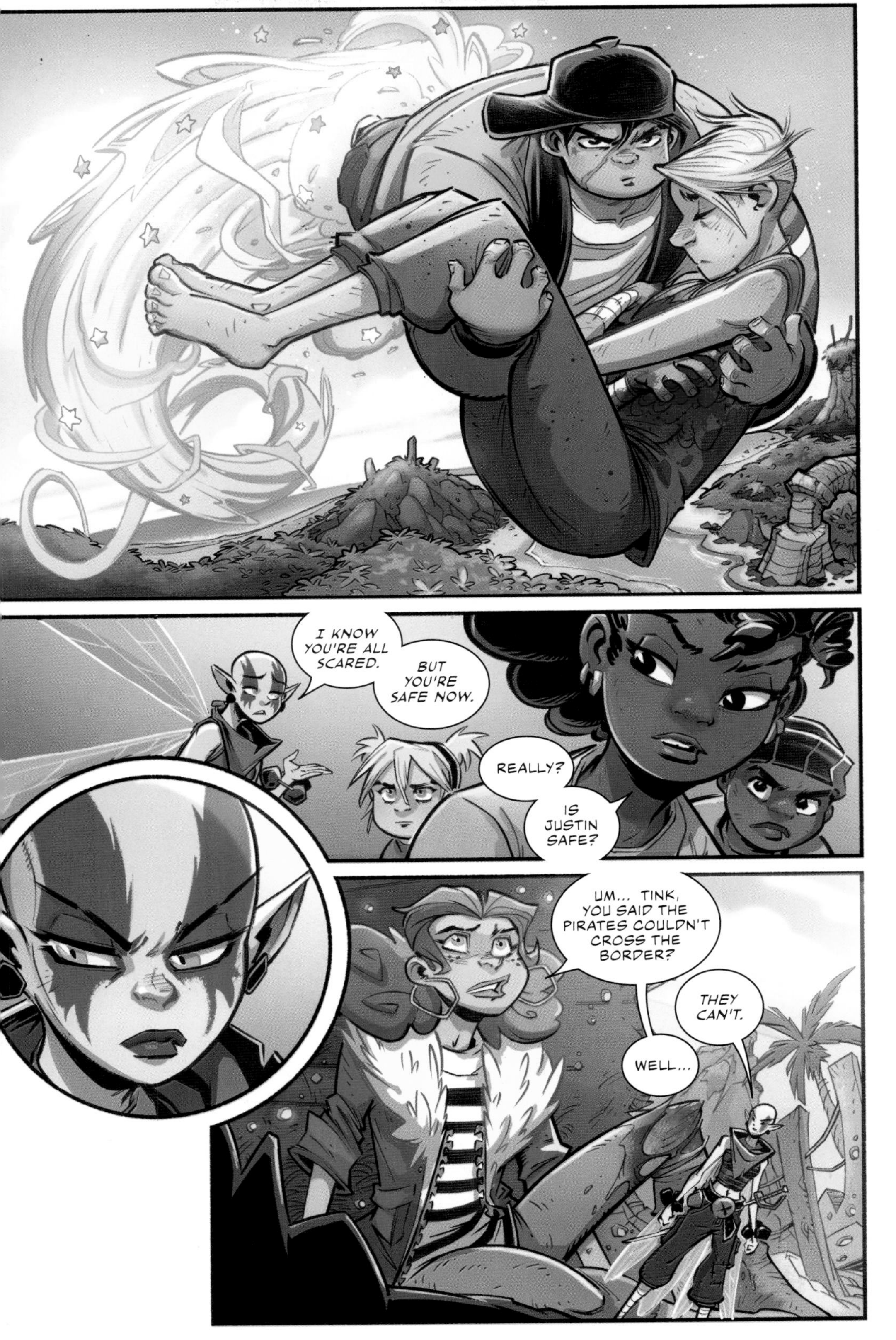
I KNOW YOU'RE ALL SCARED.
BUT YOU'RE SAFE NOW.
REALLY?
IS JUSTIN SAFE?
UM... TINK, YOU SAID THE PIRATES COULDN'T CROSS THE BORDER?
THEY CAN'T.
WELL...

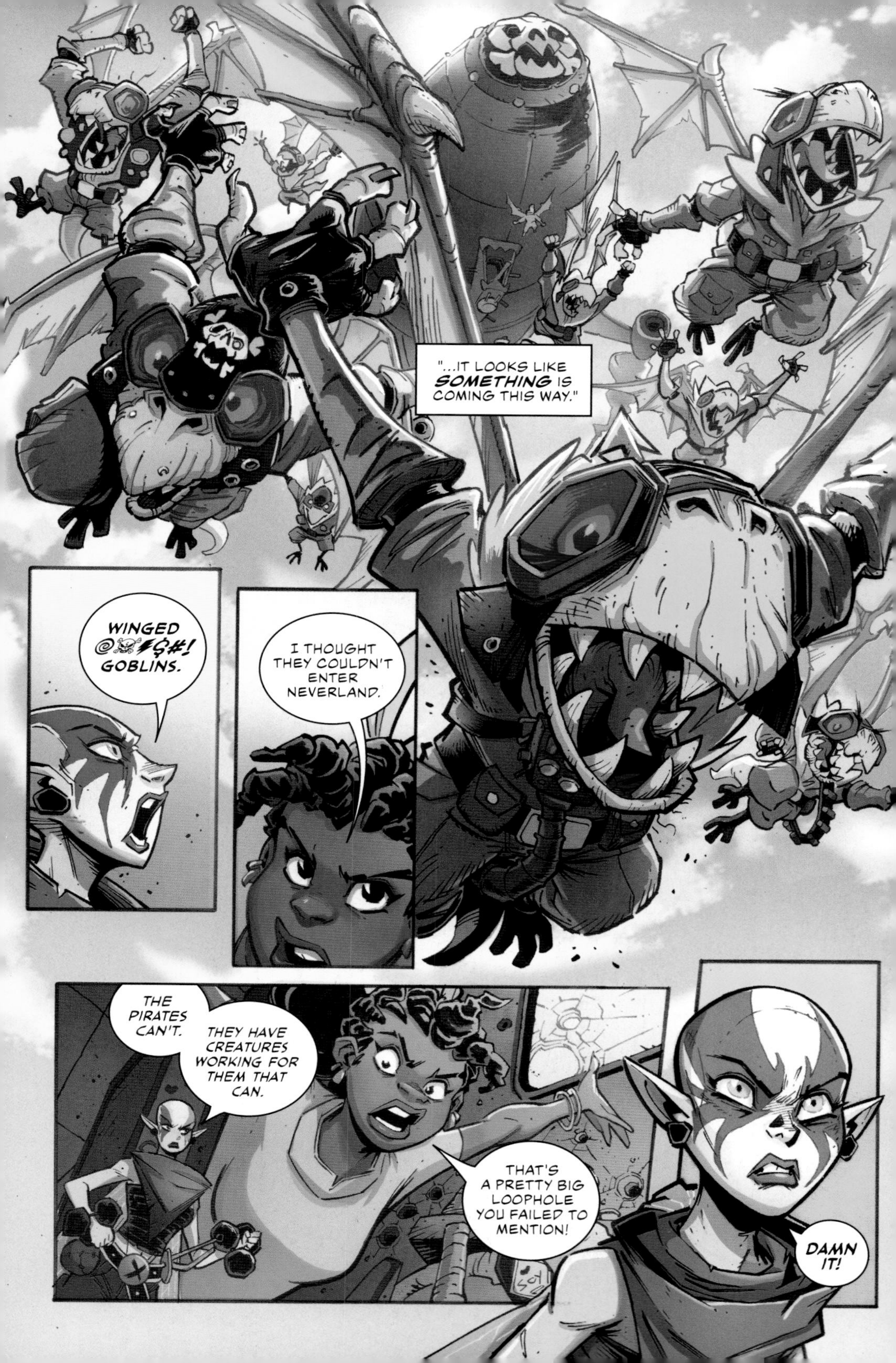
"...IT LOOKS LIKE SOMETHING IS COMING THIS WAY."
WINGED @☠⚡$#! GOBLINS.
I THOUGHT THEY COULDN'T ENTER NEVERLAND.
THE PIRATES CAN'T.
THEY HAVE CREATURES WORKING FOR THEM THAT CAN.
THAT'S A PRETTY BIG LOOPHOLE YOU FAILED TO MENTION!
DAMN IT!

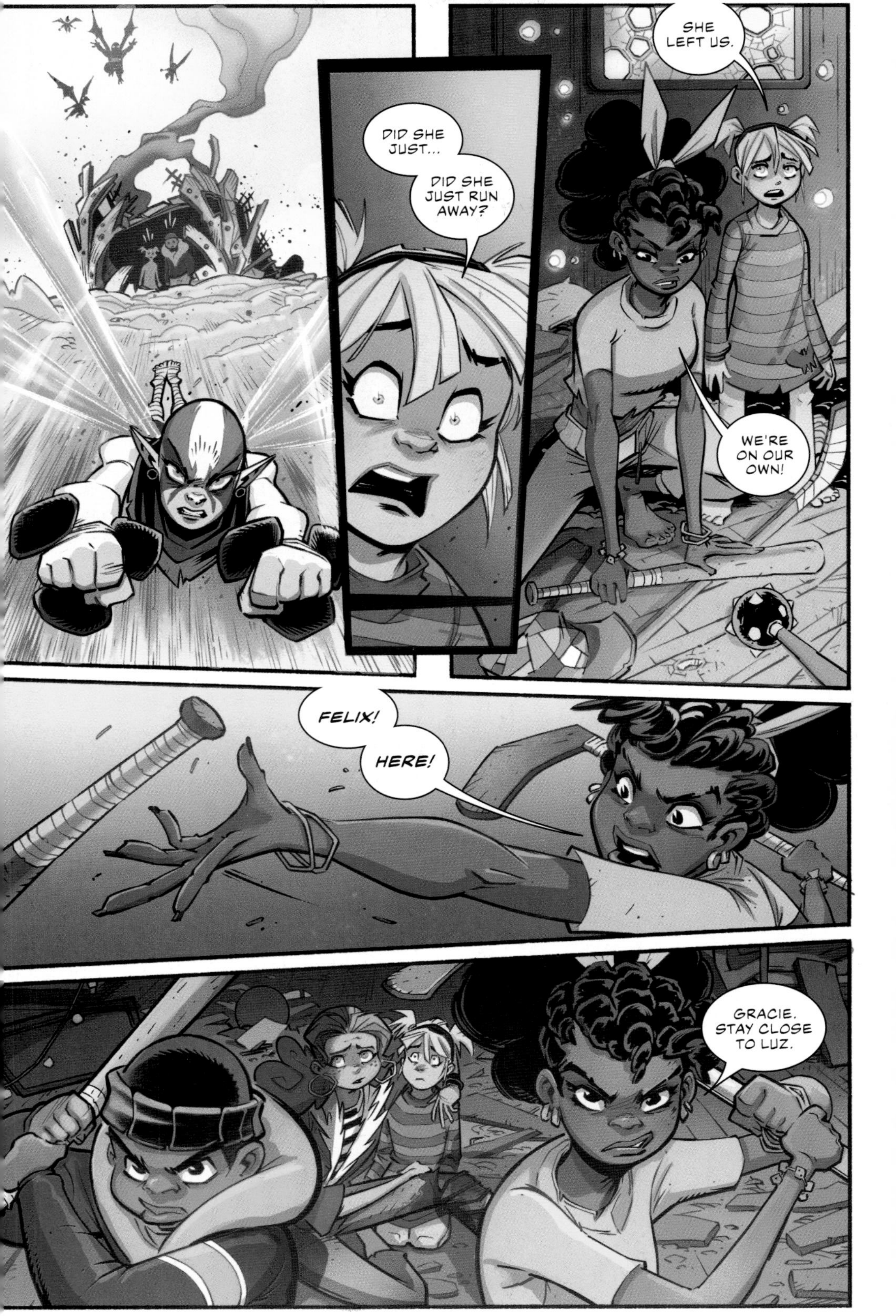
DID SHE JUST...
DID SHE JUST RUN AWAY?
SHE LEFT US.
WE'RE ON OUR OWN!
FELIX!
HERE!
GRACIE. STAY CLOSE TO LUZ.

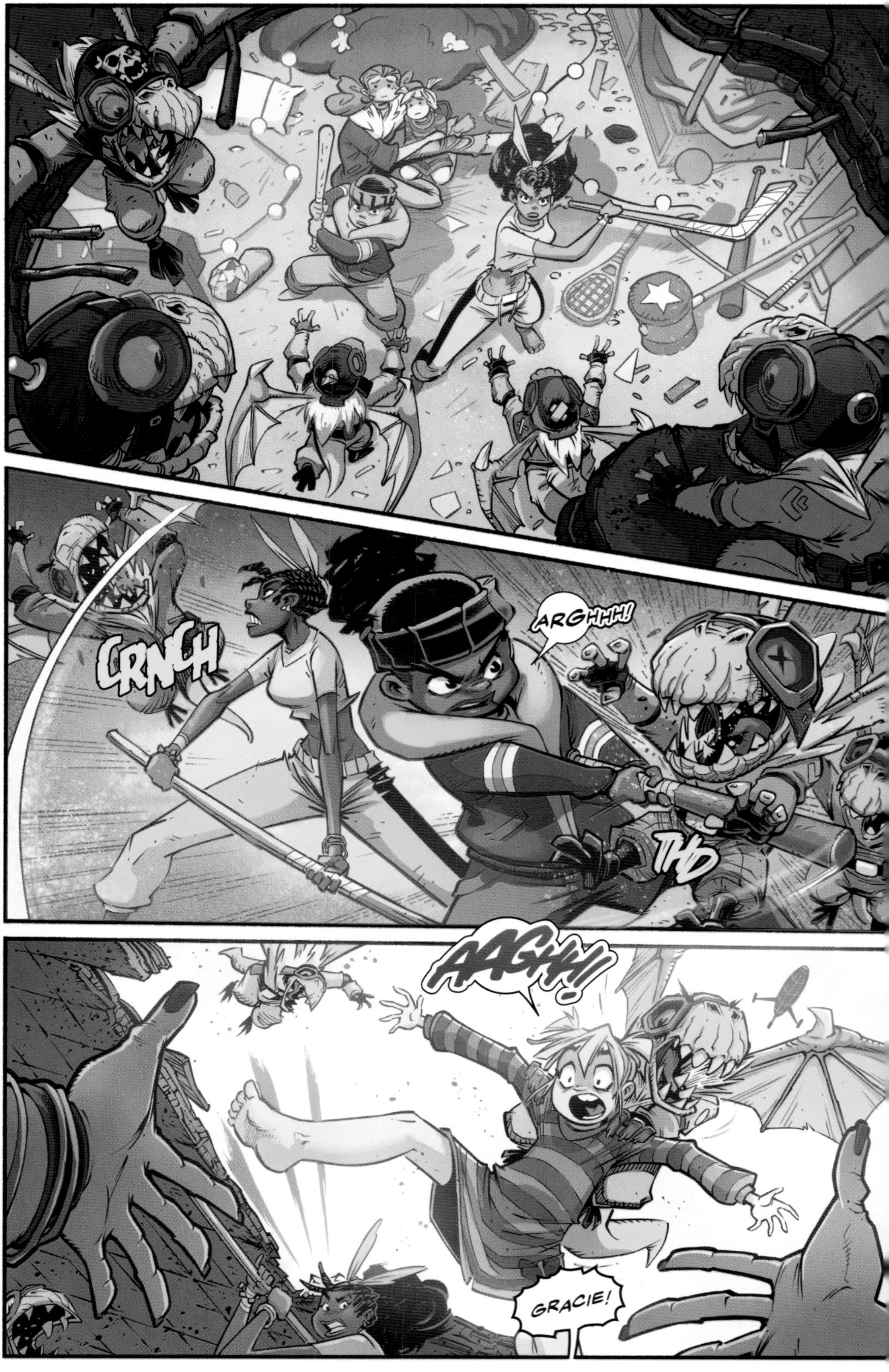
CRNCH
ARGHHHH!
THD
AAGHH!
GRACIE!

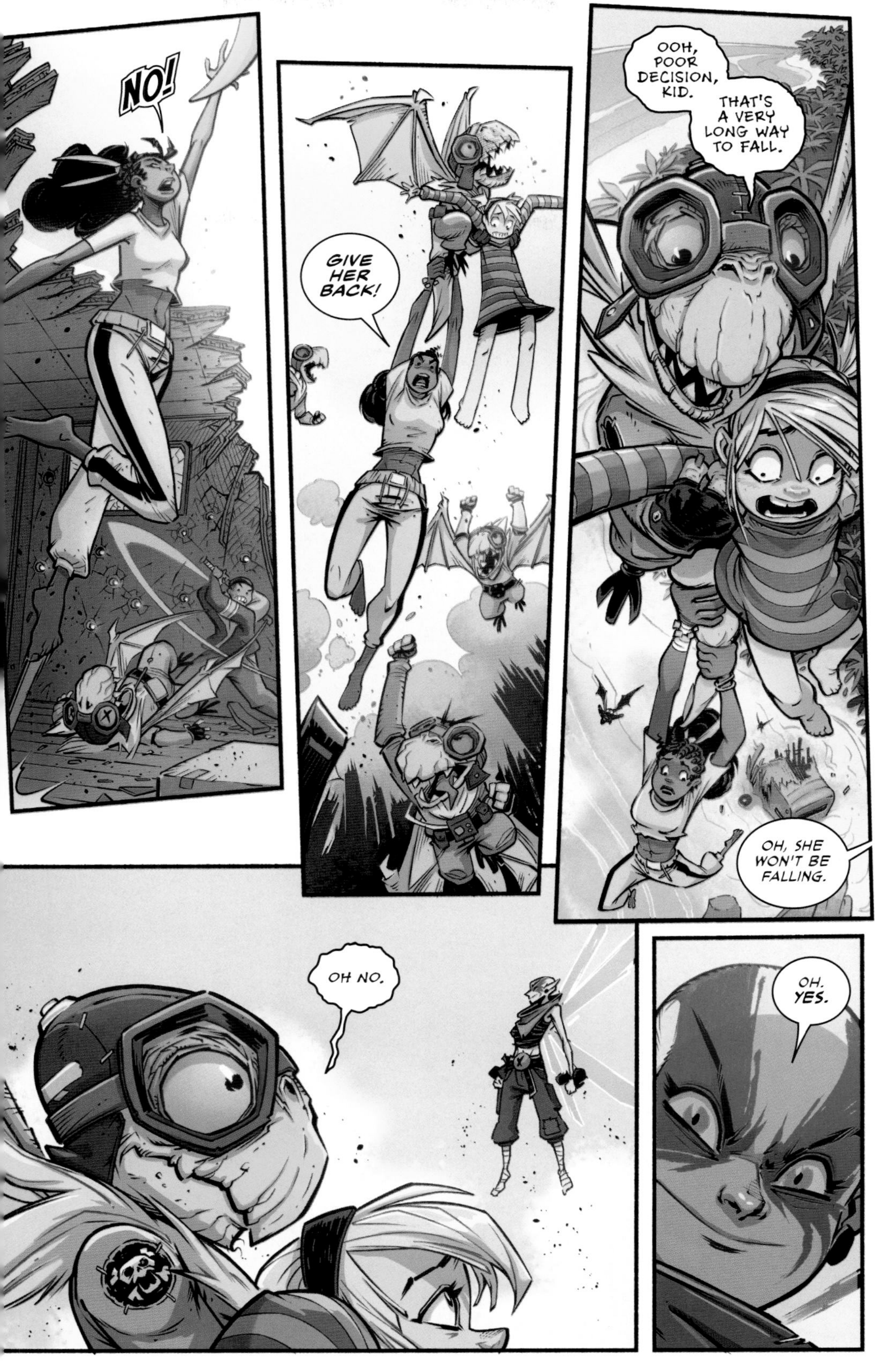
NO!
GIVE HER BACK!
OOH, POOR DECISION, KID.
THAT'S A VERY LONG WAY TO FALL.
OH, SHE WON'T BE FALLING.
OH NO.
OH. YES.

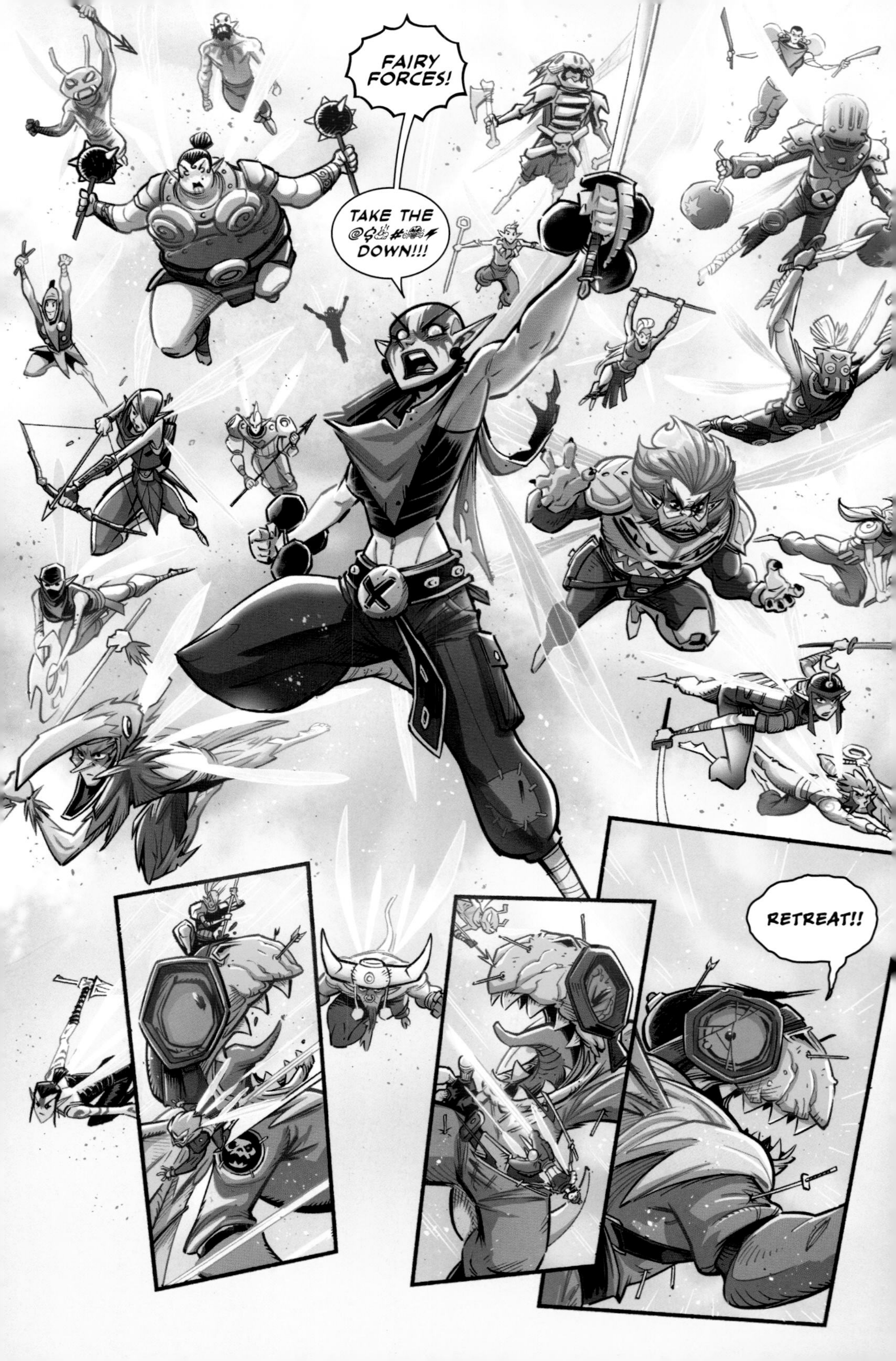
FAIRY FORCES!
TAKE THE @$#* DOWN!!!
RETREAT!!

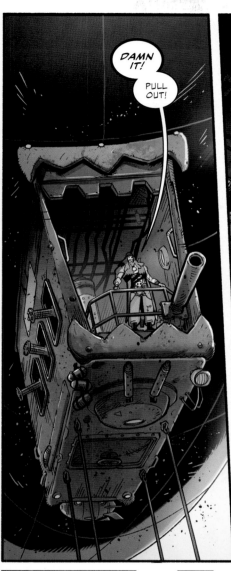

DAMN IT!

PULL OUT!

OH, PACO! YOU RESOURCEFUL YOUNG MAN.

WHAT HAS HE DONE NOW?

HE'S FOUND HELP.

BUT WE'RE SO CLOSE.

WE NEED TO HIT THEM HARD AND QUICKLY...

I KNOW.

...BEFORE THEY REALIZE WHAT THEY CAN BE.

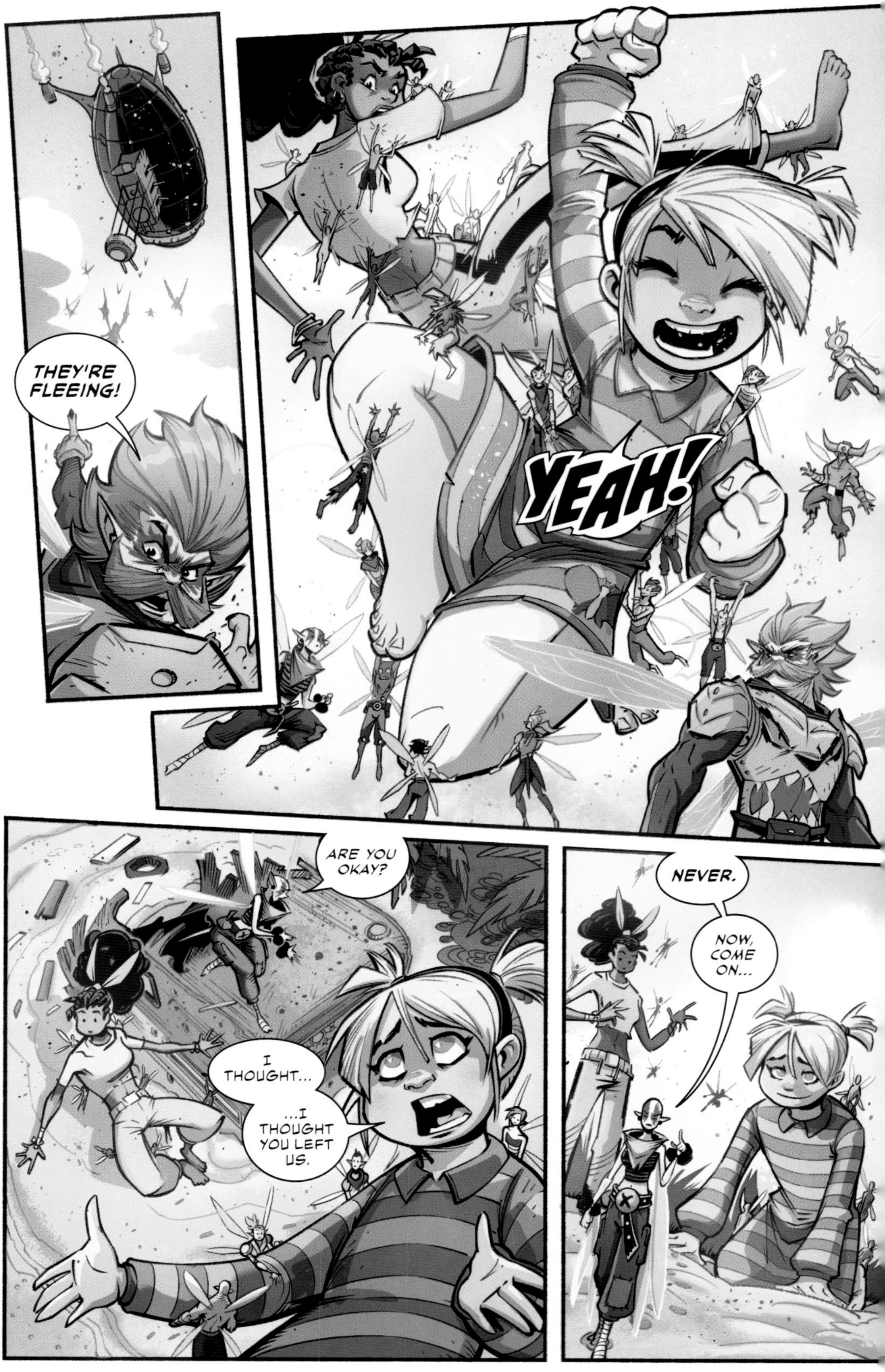
THEY'RE FLEEING!
YEAH!
ARE YOU OKAY?
I THOUGHT...
...I THOUGHT YOU LEFT US.
NEVER.
NOW, COME ON...

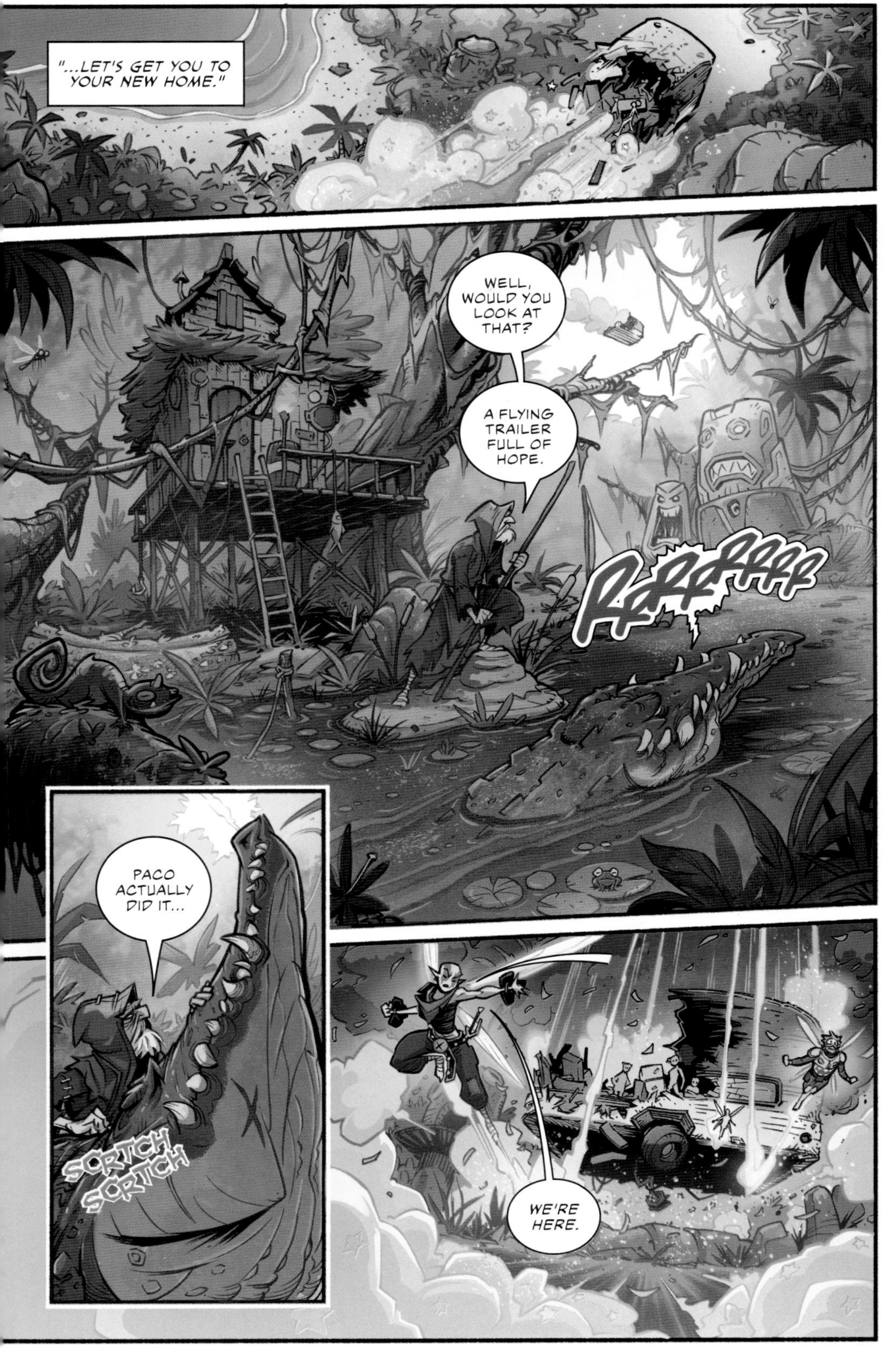

"...LET'S GET YOU TO YOUR NEW HOME."
WELL, WOULD YOU LOOK AT THAT?
A FLYING TRAILER FULL OF HOPE.
PACO ACTUALLY DID IT...
SCRTCH SCRTCH
WE'RE HERE.

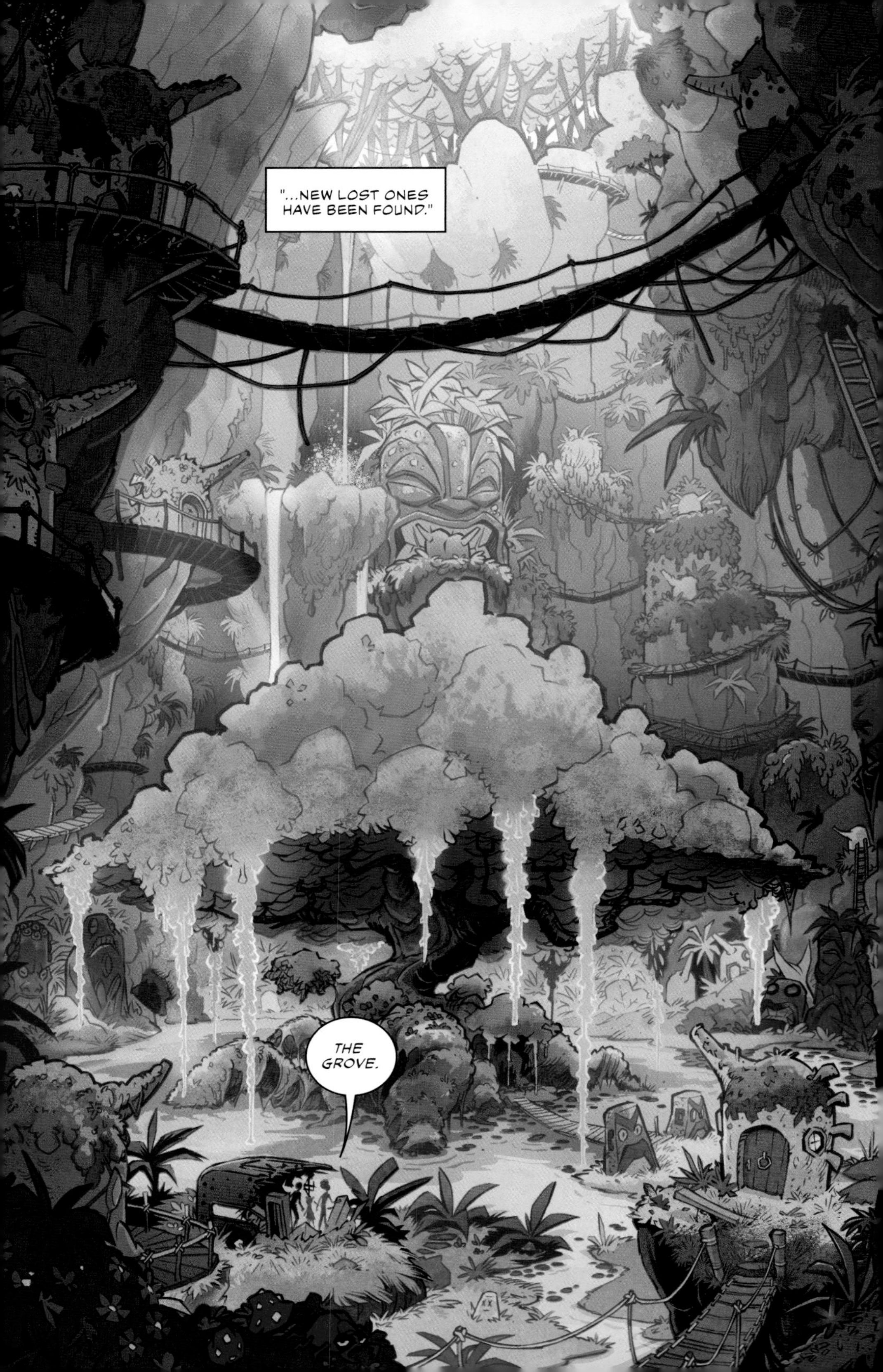
"...NEW LOST ONES HAVE BEEN FOUND."
THE GROVE.

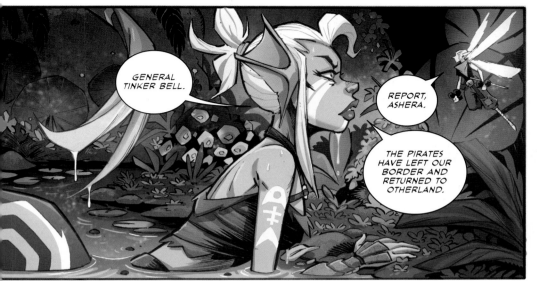

GENERAL TINKER BELL.

REPORT, ASHERA.

THE PIRATES HAVE LEFT OUR BORDER AND RETURNED TO OTHERLAND.

WAIT... YOU DID IT?

YOU ACTUALLY *DID* IT?

NEW LOST ONES!

WHAT'S WRONG WITH THAT ONE?

IS SHE BROKEN?

I NEVER THOUGHT I'D SEE A *MERMAID.*

I ONCE CUT THE LEGS OFF MY DOLL AND STUCK ON A REAL FISH TAIL.

IT SMELLED LIKE THE MARKET, BUT IT WAS BEAUTIFUL.

YOU! PACO! WHERE'S JUSTIN?

IS HE...?

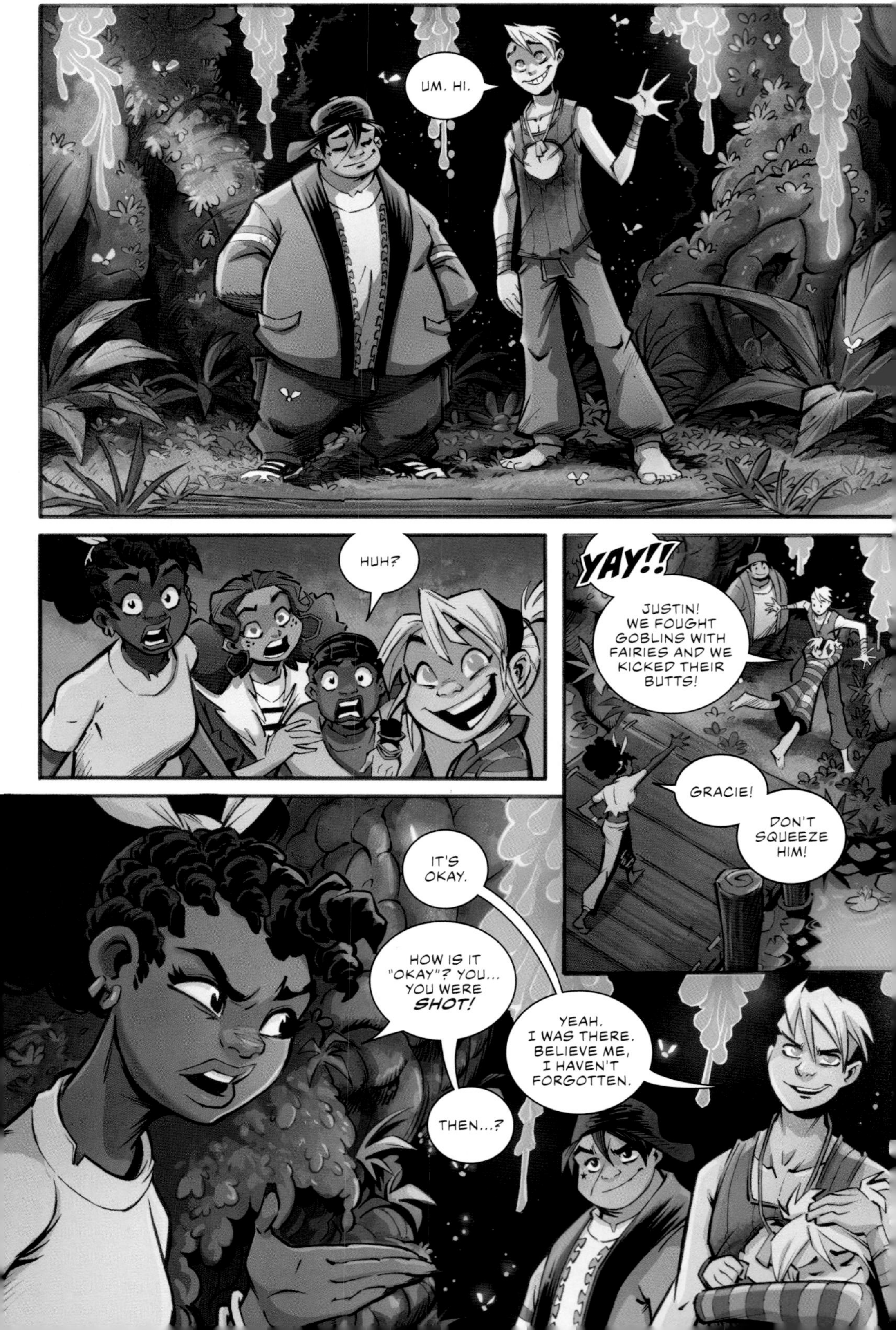
UM. HI.
HUH?
YAY!!
JUSTIN! WE FOUGHT GOBLINS WITH FAIRIES AND WE KICKED THEIR BUTTS!
GRACIE!
DON'T SQUEEZE HIM!
IT'S OKAY.
HOW IS IT "OKAY"? YOU... YOU WERE *SHOT!*
YEAH. I WAS THERE. BELIEVE ME, I HAVEN'T FORGOTTEN.
THEN...?

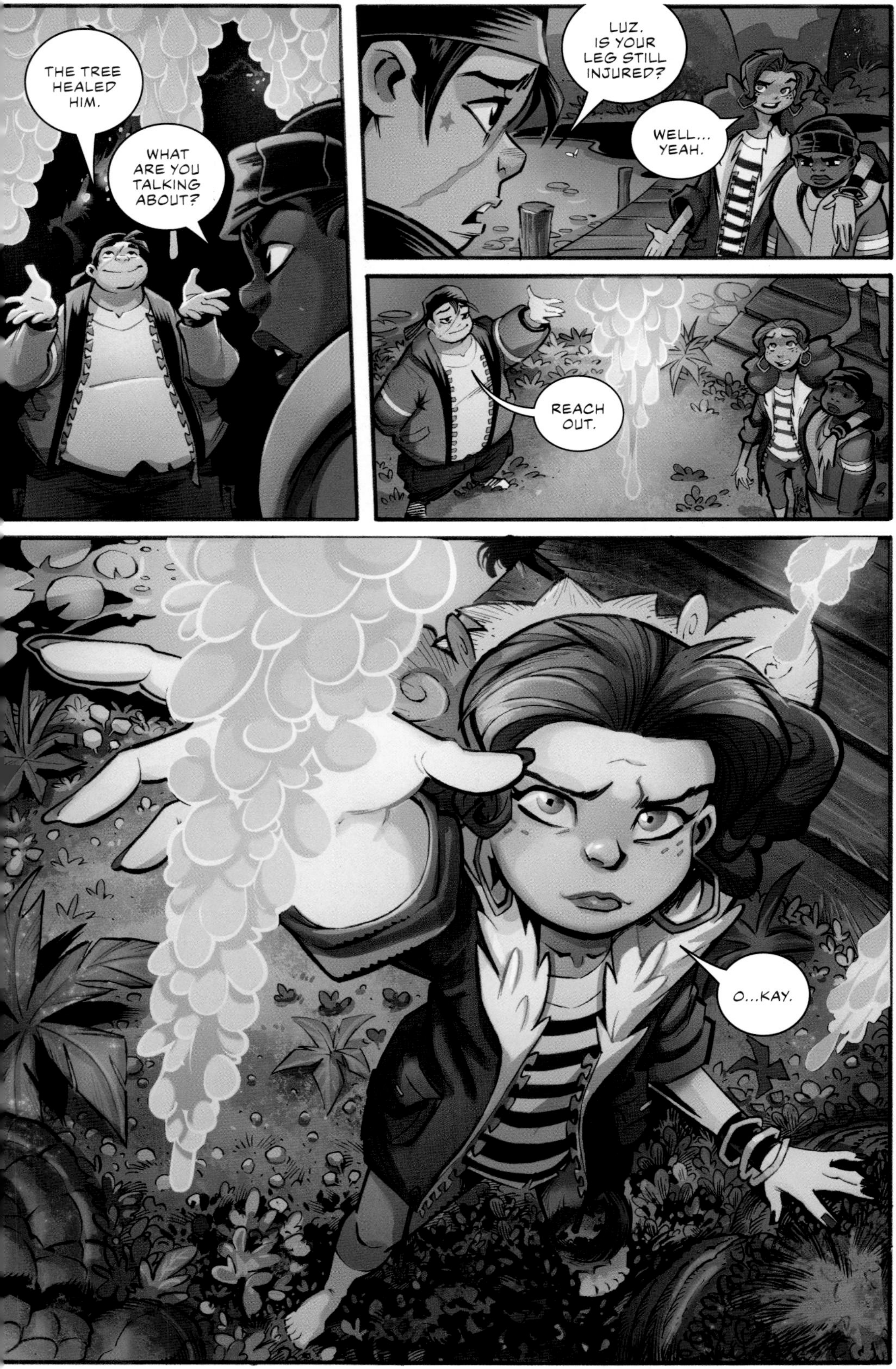
THE TREE HEALED HIM.
WHAT ARE YOU TALKING ABOUT?
LUZ. IS YOUR LEG STILL INJURED?
WELL... YEAH.
REACH OUT.
O...KAY.

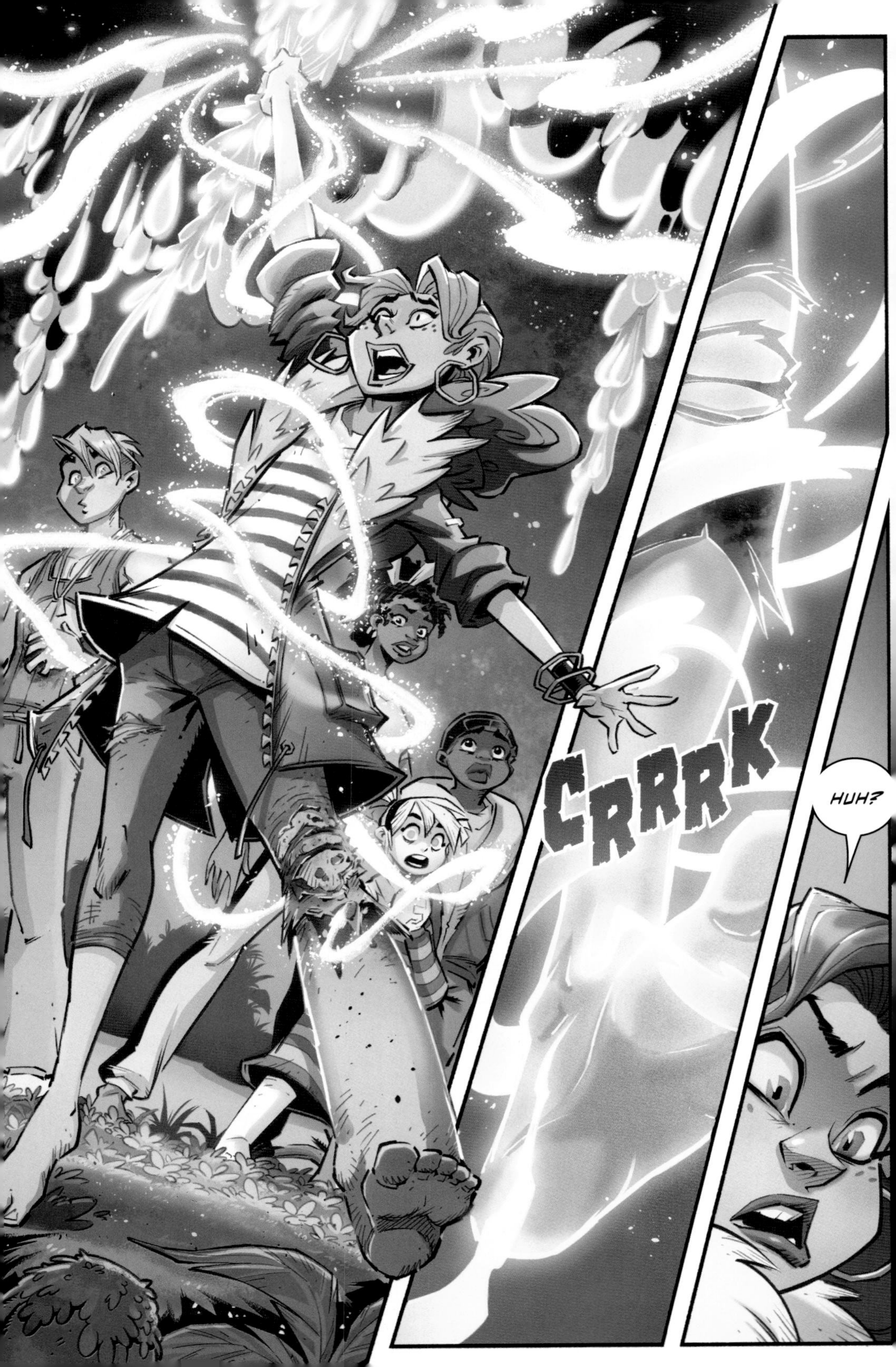
CRRRK
HUH?

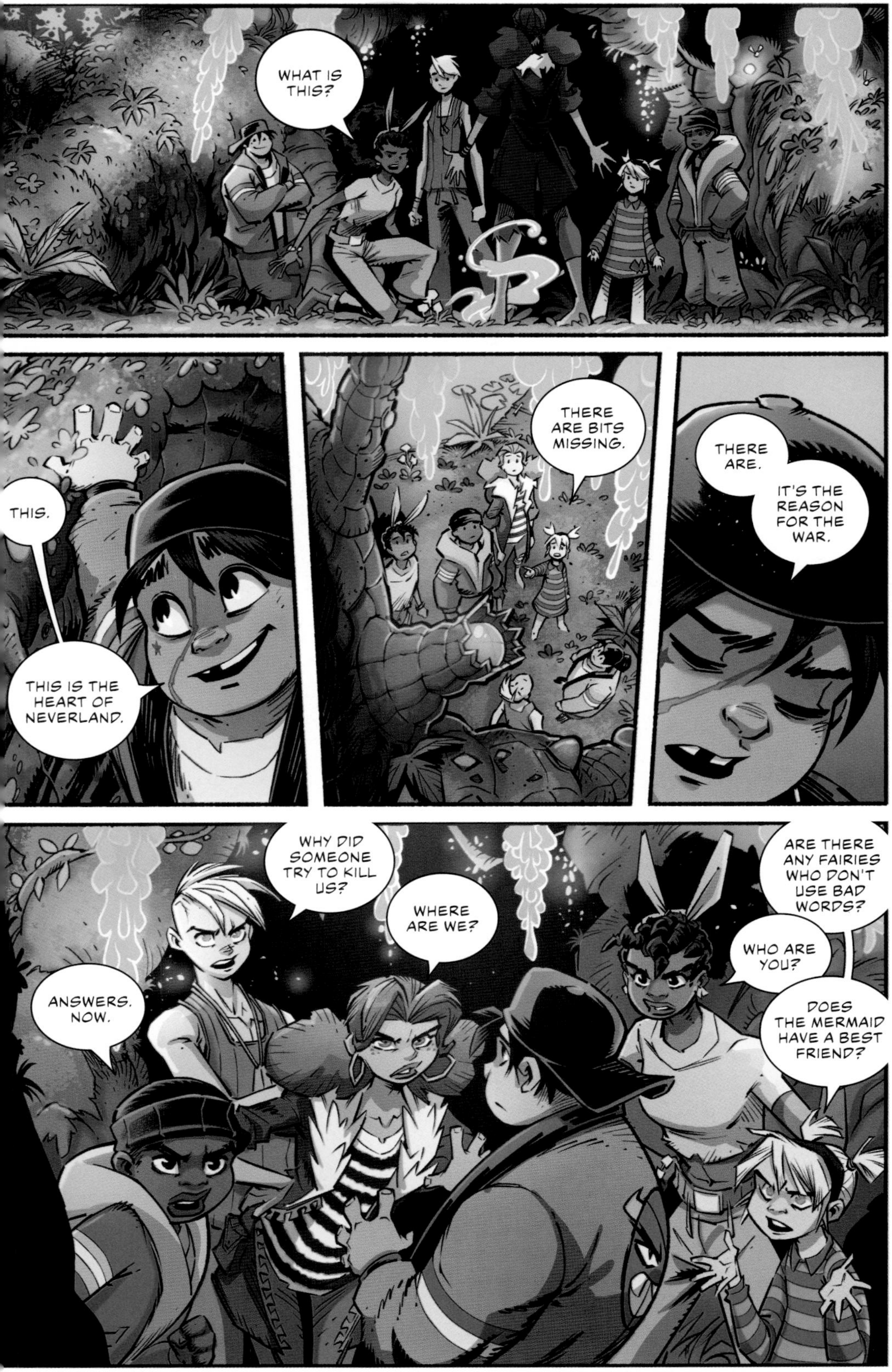
WHAT IS THIS?
THIS.
THIS IS THE HEART OF NEVERLAND.
THERE ARE BITS MISSING.
THERE ARE.
IT'S THE REASON FOR THE WAR.
ANSWERS. NOW.
WHY DID SOMEONE TRY TO KILL US?
WHERE ARE WE?
ARE THERE ANY FAIRIES WHO DON'T USE BAD WORDS?
WHO ARE YOU?
DOES THE MERMAID HAVE A BEST FRIEND?

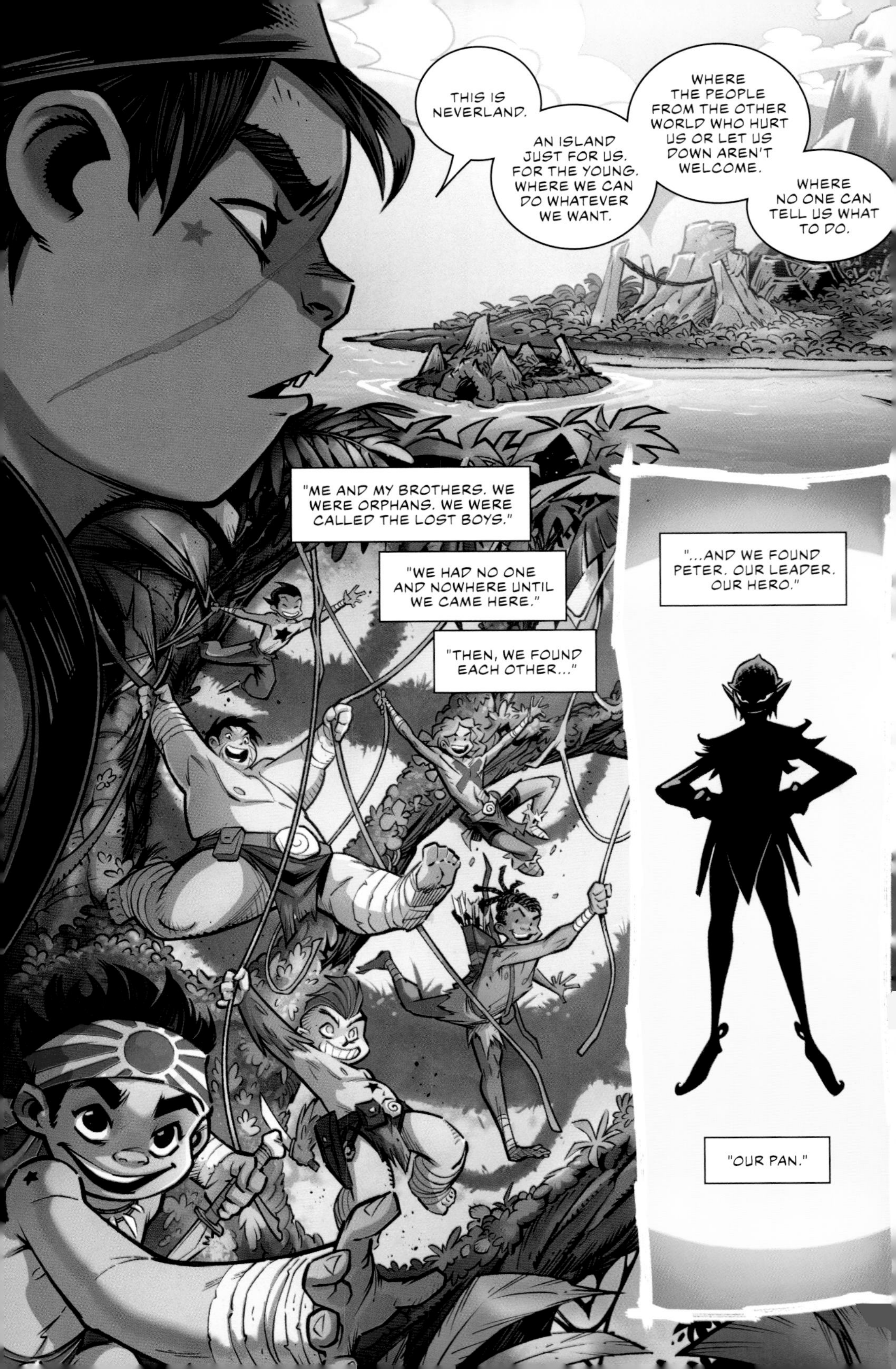
THIS IS NEVERLAND.
AN ISLAND JUST FOR US. FOR THE YOUNG. WHERE WE CAN DO WHATEVER WE WANT.
WHERE THE PEOPLE FROM THE OTHER WORLD WHO HURT US OR LET US DOWN AREN'T WELCOME.
WHERE NO ONE CAN TELL US WHAT TO DO.
"ME AND MY BROTHERS. WE WERE ORPHANS. WE WERE CALLED THE LOST BOYS."
"WE HAD NO ONE AND NOWHERE UNTIL WE CAME HERE."
"THEN, WE FOUND EACH OTHER..."
"...AND WE FOUND PETER. OUR LEADER. OUR HERO."
"OUR PAN."

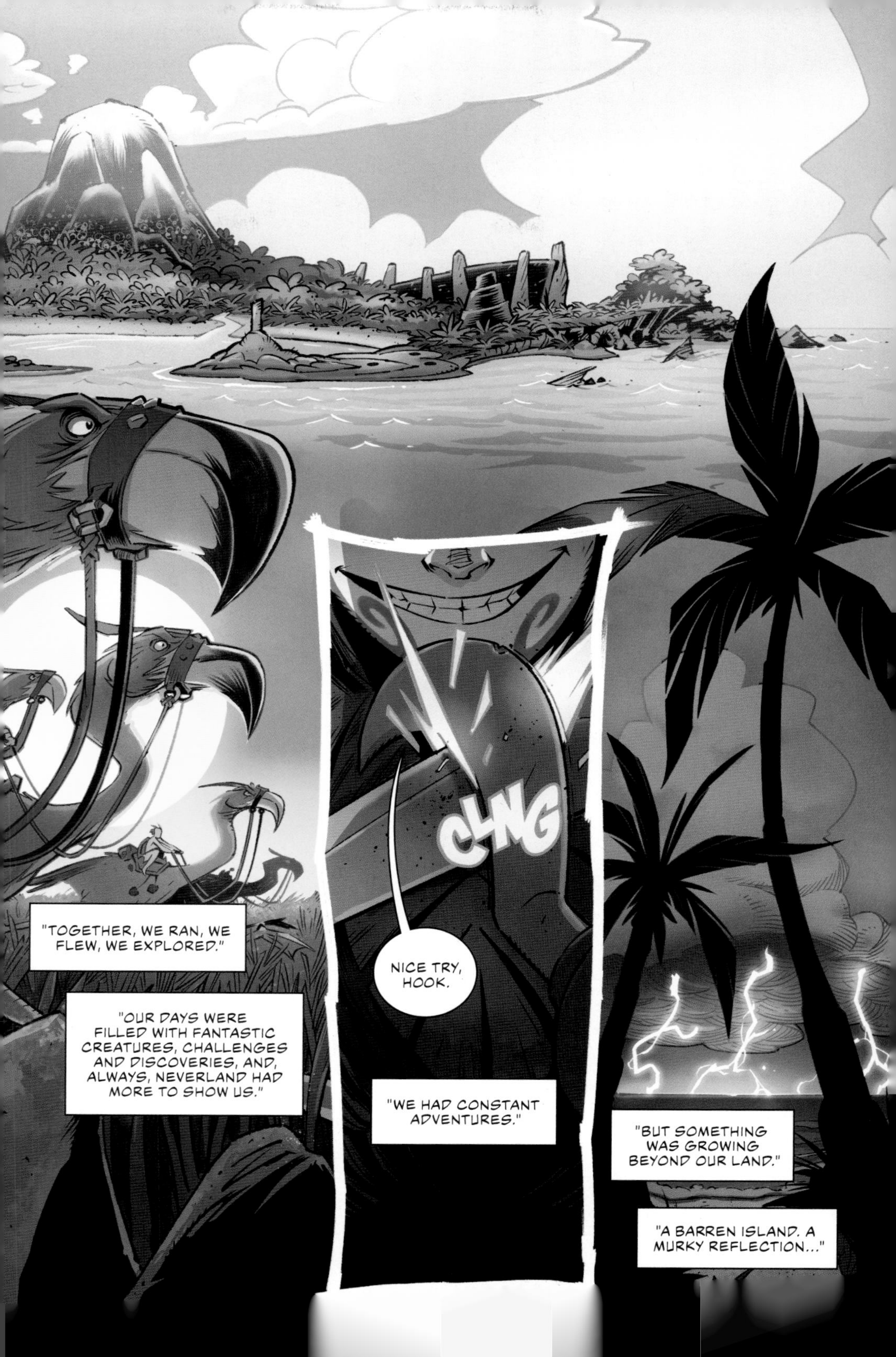

"TOGETHER, WE RAN, WE FLEW, WE EXPLORED."
"OUR DAYS WERE FILLED WITH FANTASTIC CREATURES, CHALLENGES AND DISCOVERIES, AND, ALWAYS, NEVERLAND HAD MORE TO SHOW US."
CLING
NICE TRY, HOOK.
"WE HAD CONSTANT ADVENTURES."
"BUT SOMETHING WAS GROWING BEYOND OUR LAND."
"A BARREN ISLAND. A MURKY REFLECTION..."

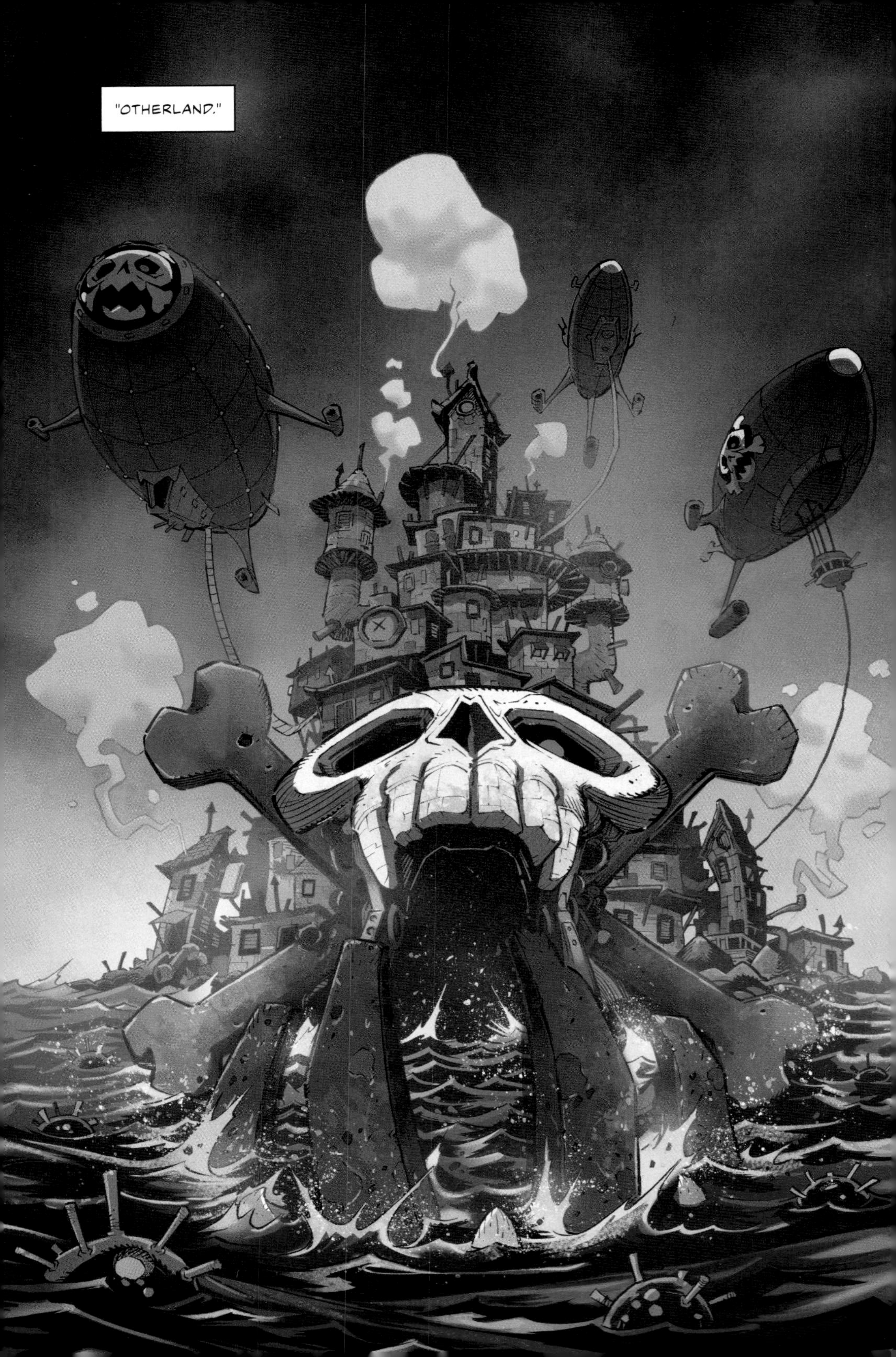
"OTHERLAND."

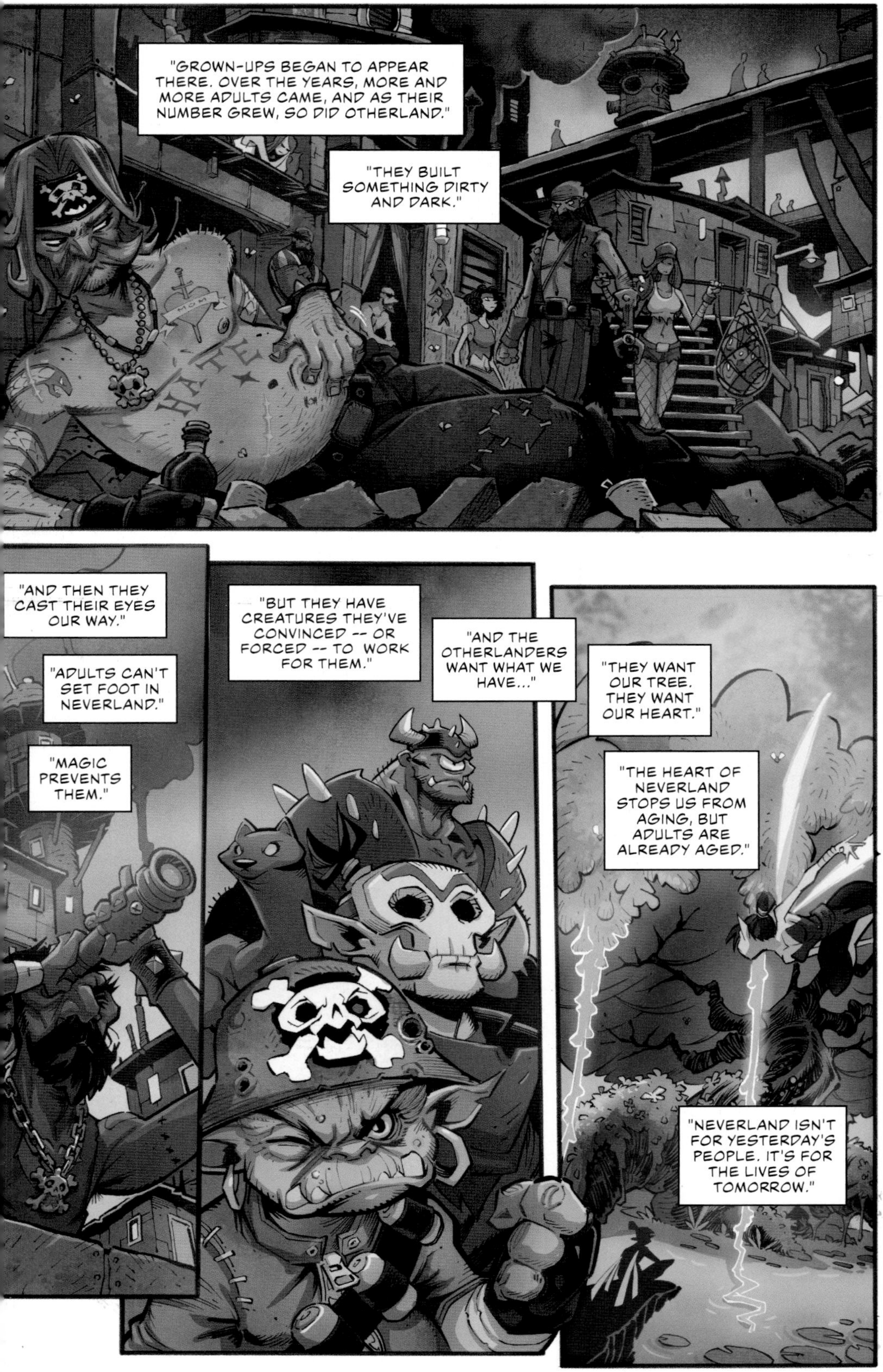
"GROWN-UPS BEGAN TO APPEAR THERE. OVER THE YEARS, MORE AND MORE ADULTS CAME, AND AS THEIR NUMBER GREW, SO DID OTHERLAND."
"THEY BUILT SOMETHING DIRTY AND DARK."
MOM
HATE
"AND THEN THEY CAST THEIR EYES OUR WAY."
"ADULTS CAN'T SET FOOT IN NEVERLAND."
"MAGIC PREVENTS THEM."
"BUT THEY HAVE CREATURES THEY'VE CONVINCED -- OR FORCED -- TO WORK FOR THEM."
"AND THE OTHERLANDERS WANT WHAT WE HAVE..."
"THEY WANT OUR TREE. THEY WANT OUR HEART."
"THE HEART OF NEVERLAND STOPS US FROM AGING, BUT ADULTS ARE ALREADY AGED."
"NEVERLAND ISN'T FOR YESTERDAY'S PEOPLE. IT'S FOR THE LIVES OF TOMORROW."

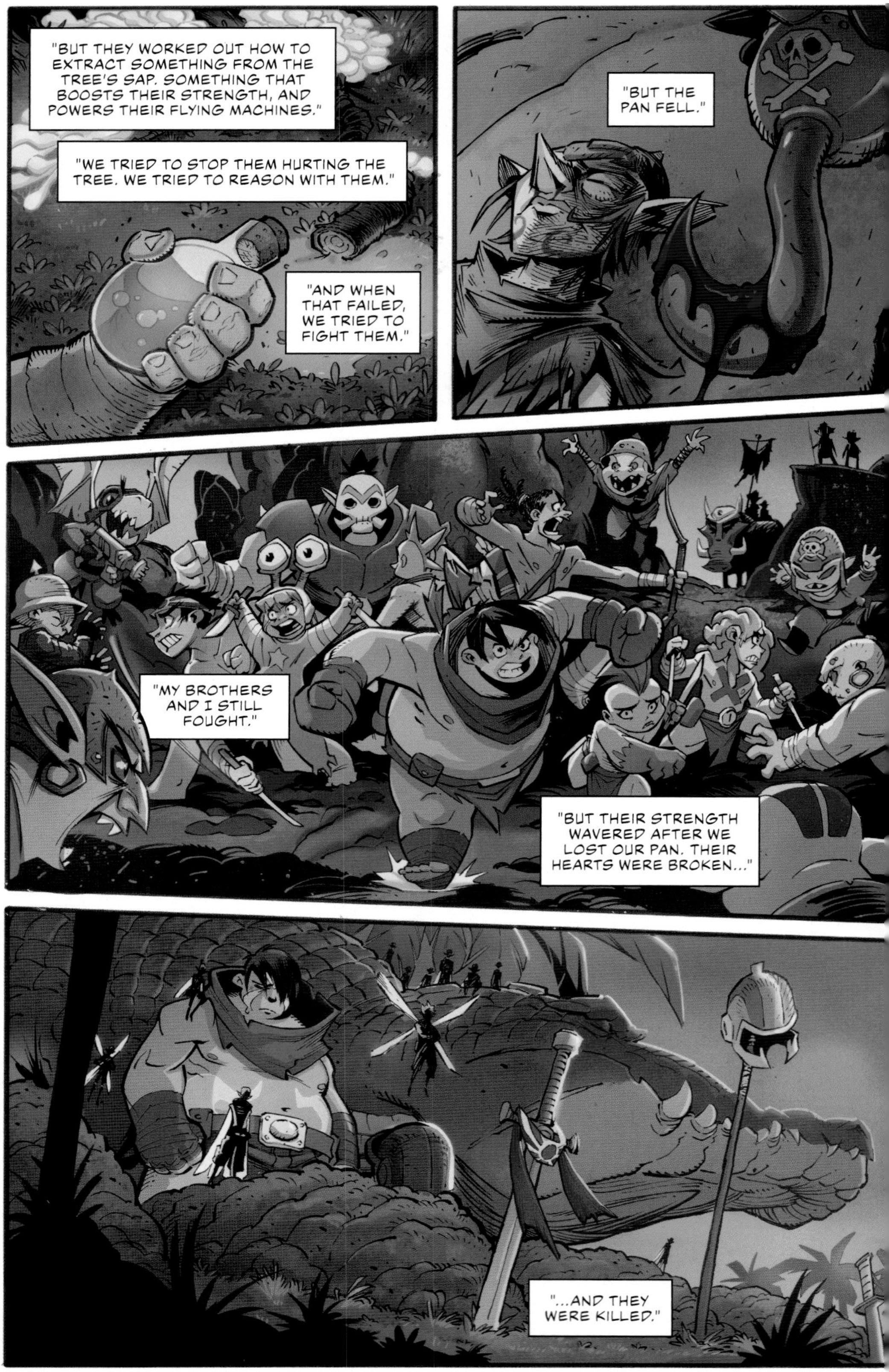
"BUT THEY WORKED OUT HOW TO EXTRACT SOMETHING FROM THE TREE'S SAP. SOMETHING THAT BOOSTS THEIR STRENGTH, AND POWERS THEIR FLYING MACHINES."
"WE TRIED TO STOP THEM HURTING THE TREE. WE TRIED TO REASON WITH THEM."
"AND WHEN THAT FAILED, WE TRIED TO FIGHT THEM."
"BUT THE PAN FELL."
"MY BROTHERS AND I STILL FOUGHT."
"BUT THEIR STRENGTH WAVERED AFTER WE LOST OUR PAN. THEIR HEARTS WERE BROKEN..."
"...AND THEY WERE KILLED."

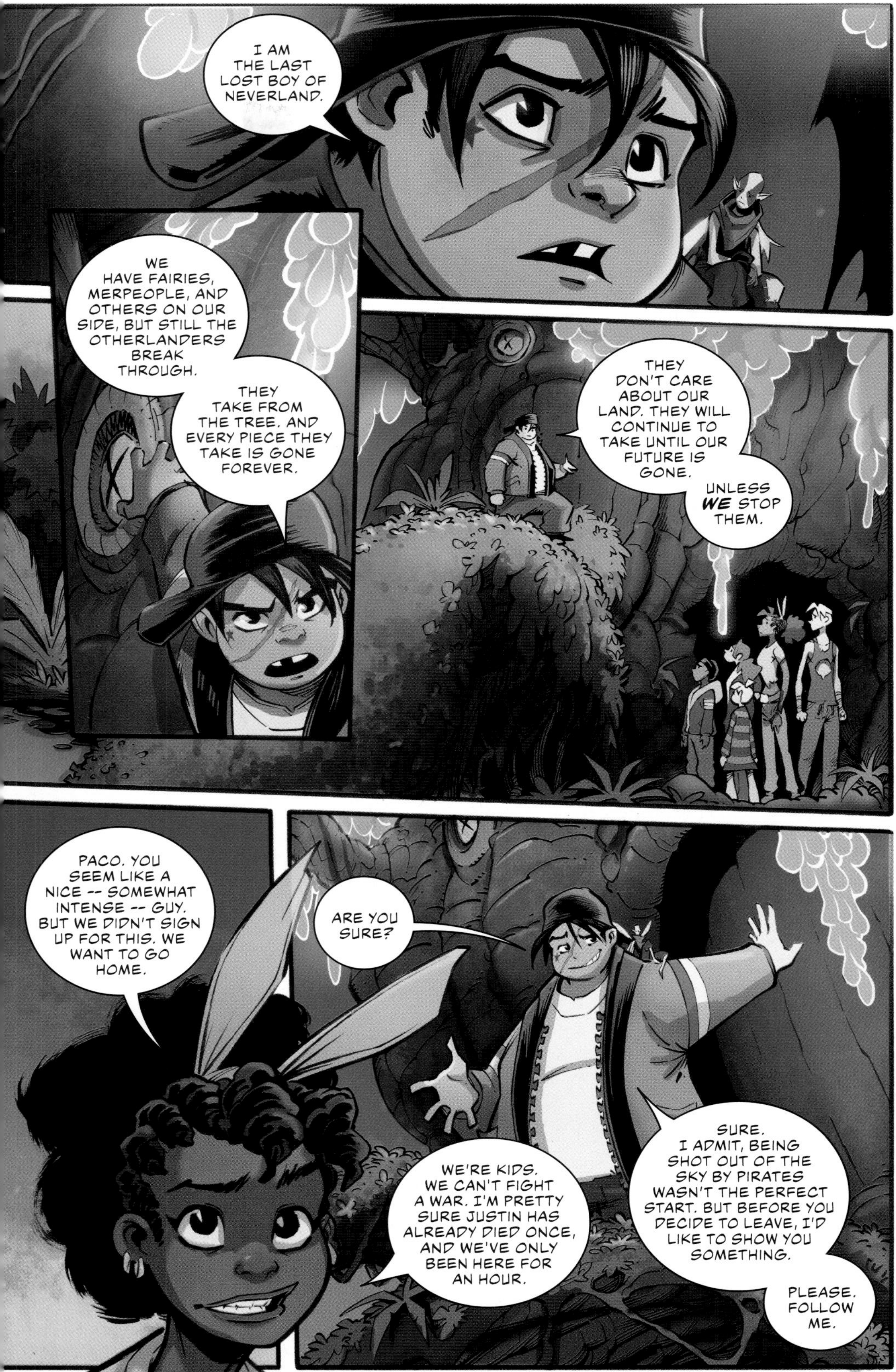
I AM THE LAST LOST BOY OF NEVERLAND.
WE HAVE FAIRIES, MERPEOPLE, AND OTHERS ON OUR SIDE, BUT STILL THE OTHERLANDERS BREAK THROUGH.
THEY TAKE FROM THE TREE. AND EVERY PIECE THEY TAKE IS GONE FOREVER.
THEY DON'T CARE ABOUT OUR LAND. THEY WILL CONTINUE TO TAKE UNTIL OUR FUTURE IS GONE.
UNLESS **WE** STOP THEM.
PACO. YOU SEEM LIKE A NICE -- SOMEWHAT INTENSE -- GUY. BUT WE DIDN'T SIGN UP FOR THIS. WE WANT TO GO HOME.
ARE YOU SURE?
WE'RE KIDS. WE CAN'T FIGHT A WAR. I'M PRETTY SURE JUSTIN HAS ALREADY DIED ONCE, AND WE'VE ONLY BEEN HERE FOR AN HOUR.
SURE. I ADMIT, BEING SHOT OUT OF THE SKY BY PIRATES WASN'T THE PERFECT START. BUT BEFORE YOU DECIDE TO LEAVE, I'D LIKE TO SHOW YOU SOMETHING.
PLEASE. FOLLOW ME.

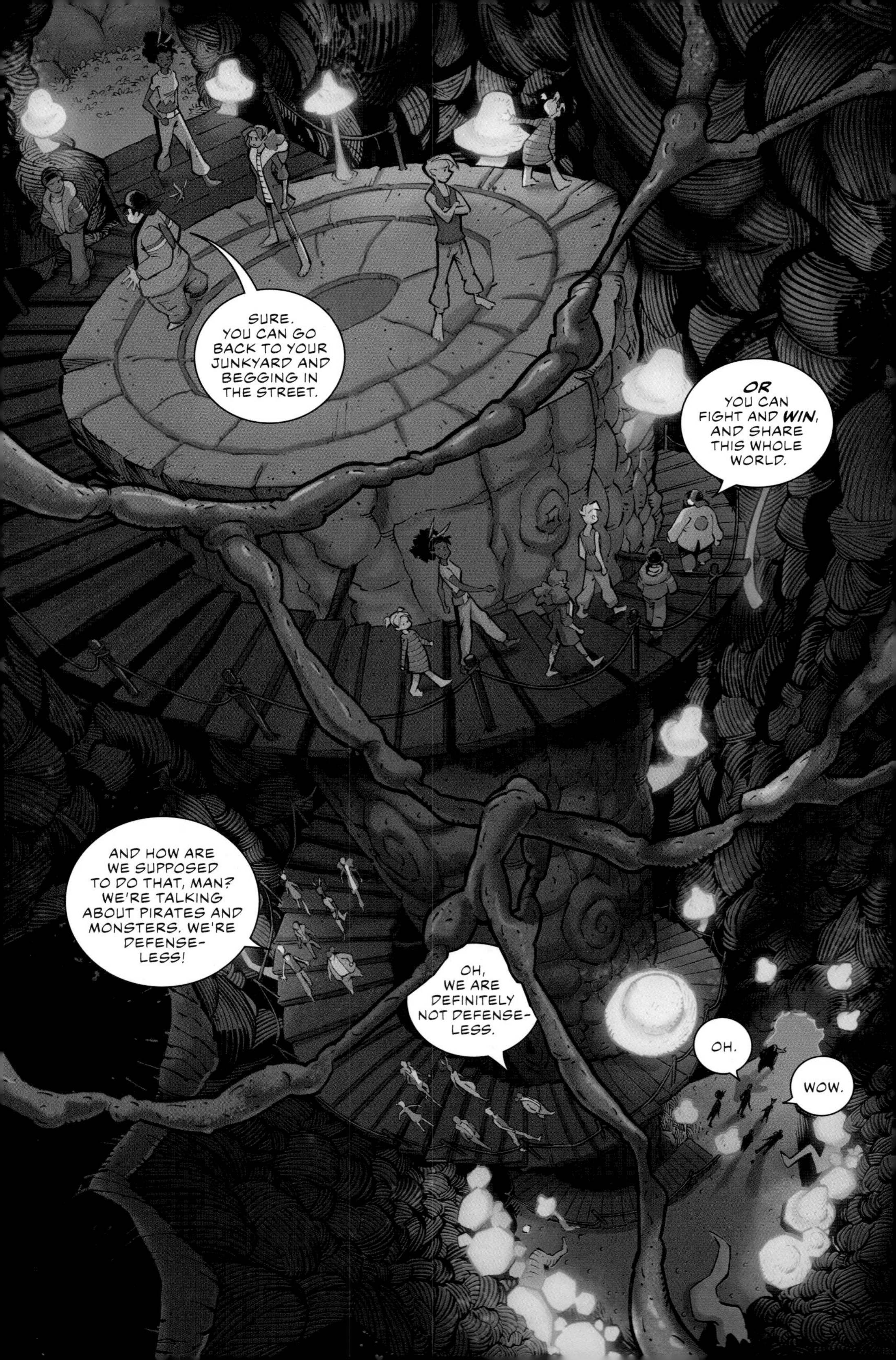
SURE. YOU CAN GO BACK TO YOUR JUNKYARD AND BEGGING IN THE STREET.
OR YOU CAN FIGHT AND WIN, AND SHARE THIS WHOLE WORLD.
AND HOW ARE WE SUPPOSED TO DO THAT, MAN? WE'RE TALKING ABOUT PIRATES AND MONSTERS. WE'RE DEFENSE-LESS!
OH, WE ARE DEFINITELY NOT DEFENSE-LESS.
OH.
WOW.

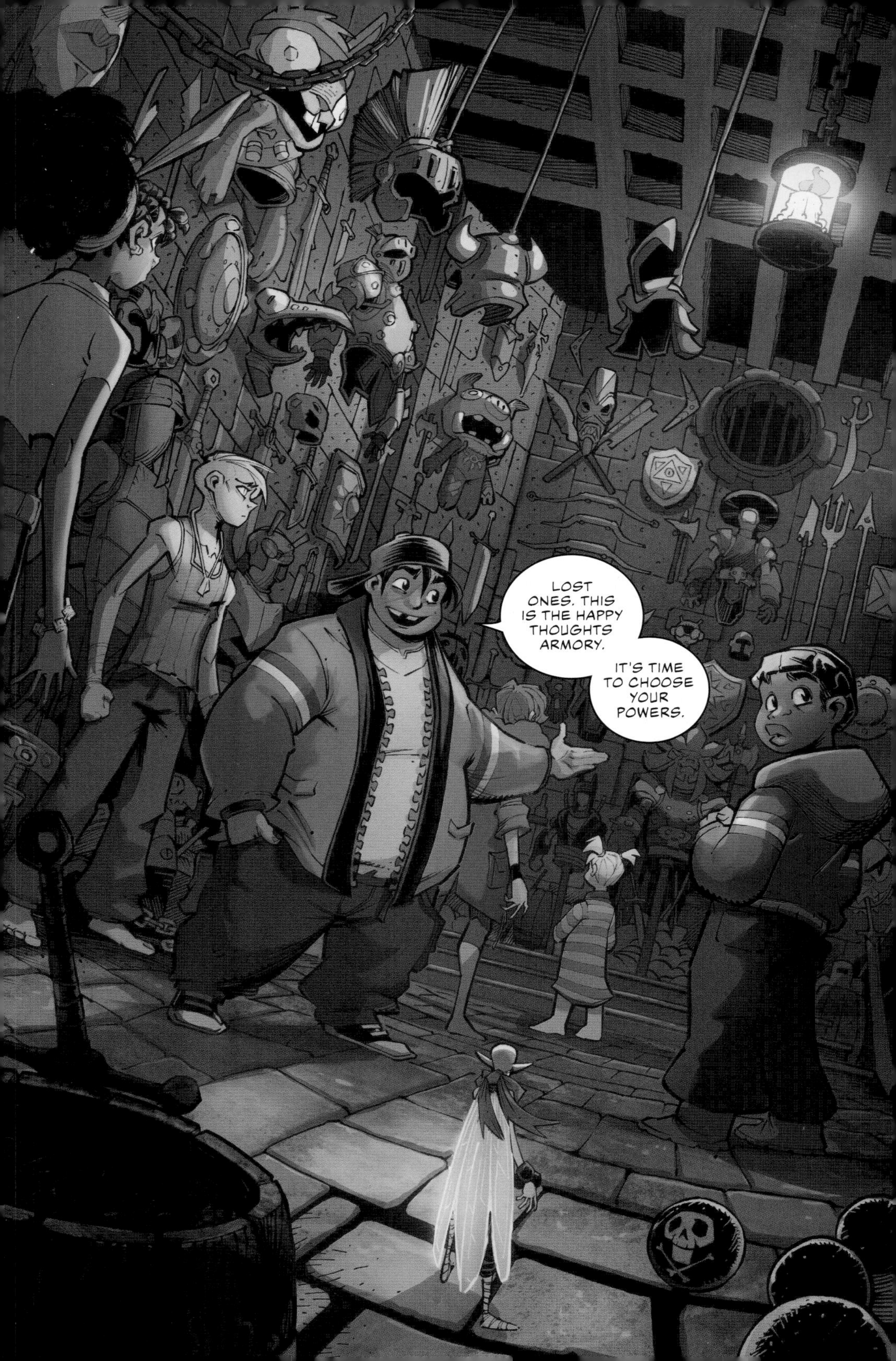
LOST ONES. THIS IS THE HAPPY THOUGHTS ARMORY.
IT'S TIME TO CHOOSE YOUR POWERS.

CHAPTER
THREE

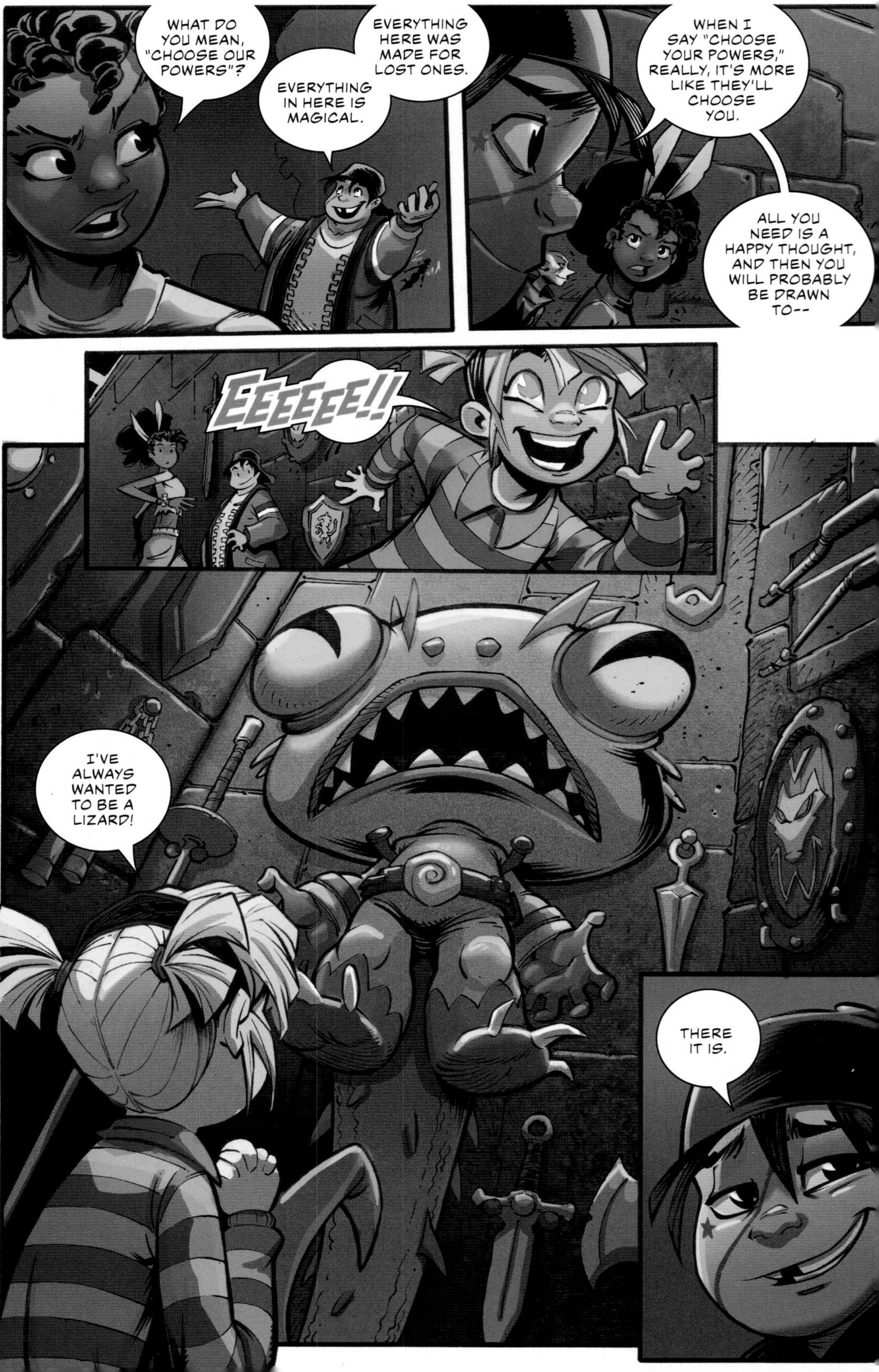
WHAT DO YOU MEAN, "CHOOSE OUR POWERS"?
EVERYTHING HERE WAS MADE FOR LOST ONES.
EVERYTHING IN HERE IS MAGICAL.
WHEN I SAY "CHOOSE YOUR POWERS," REALLY, IT'S MORE LIKE THEY'LL CHOOSE YOU.
ALL YOU NEED IS A HAPPY THOUGHT, AND THEN YOU WILL PROBABLY BE DRAWN TO--
EEEEEE!!
I'VE ALWAYS WANTED TO BE A LIZARD!
THERE IT IS.

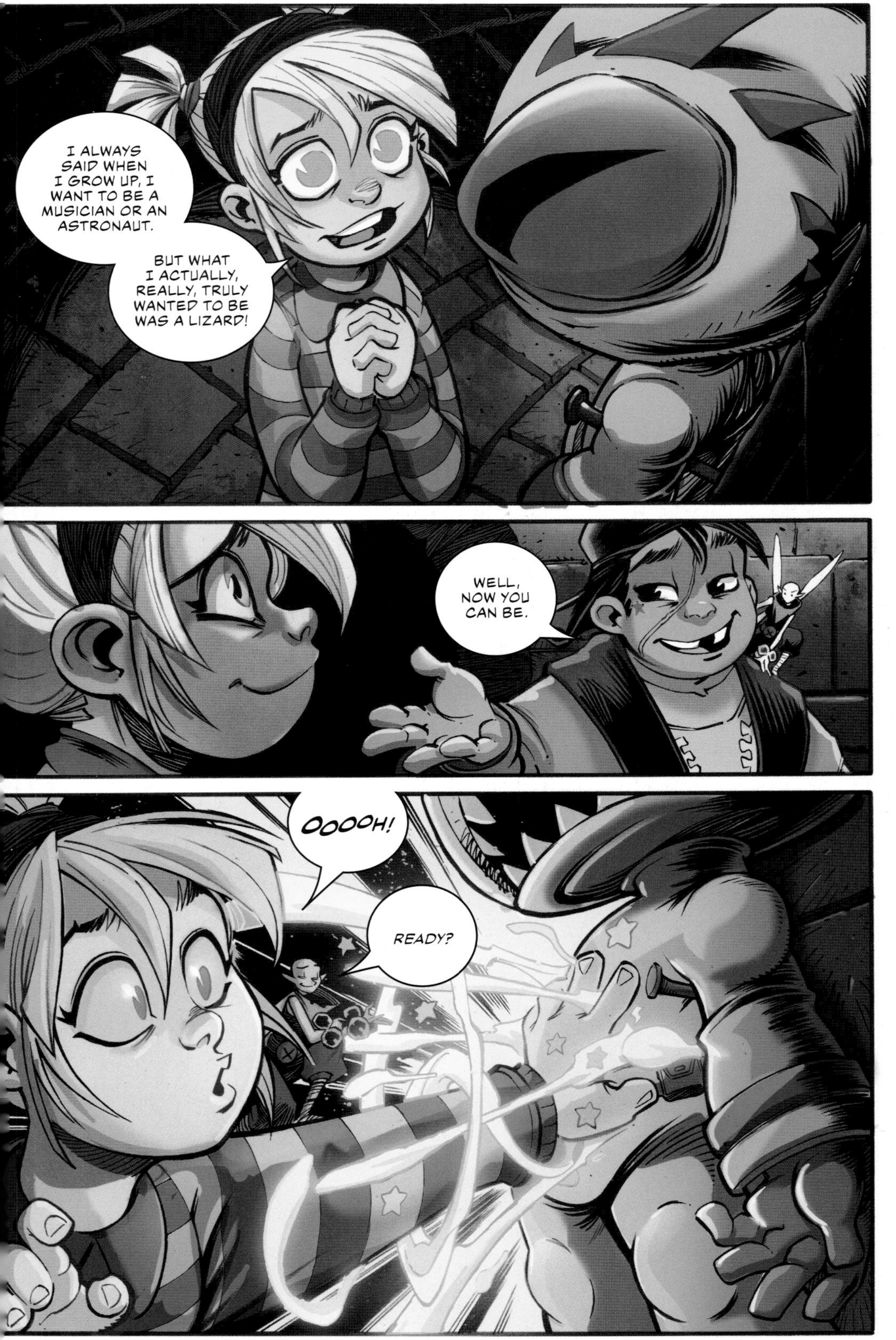
I ALWAYS SAID WHEN I GROW UP, I WANT TO BE A MUSICIAN OR AN ASTRONAUT.
BUT WHAT I ACTUALLY, REALLY, TRULY WANTED TO BE WAS A LIZARD!
WELL, NOW YOU CAN BE.
OOOOH!
READY?

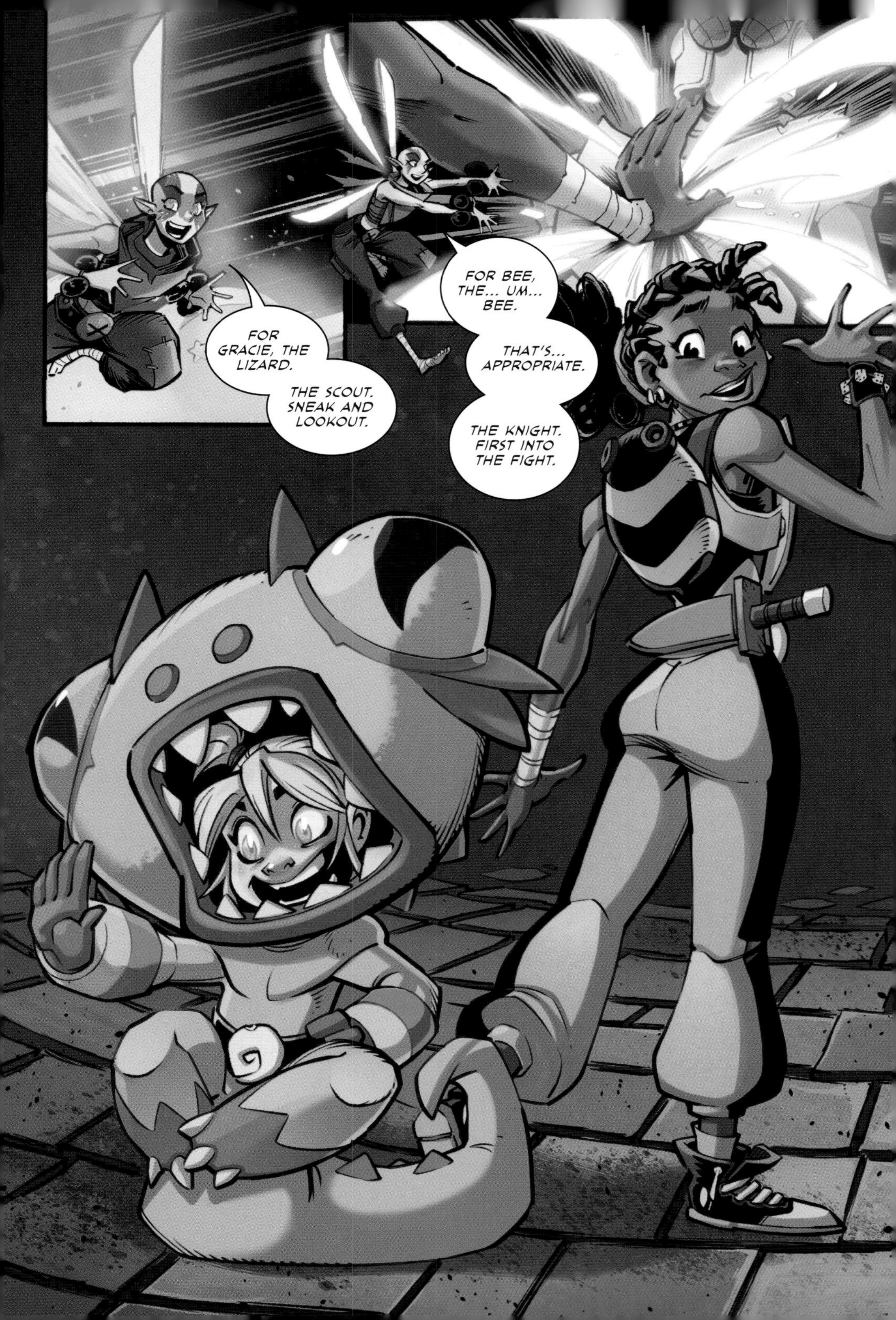
FOR GRACIE, THE LIZARD.
THE SCOUT. SNEAK AND LOOKOUT.
FOR BEE, THE... UM... BEE.
THAT'S... APPROPRIATE.
THE KNIGHT. FIRST INTO THE FIGHT.

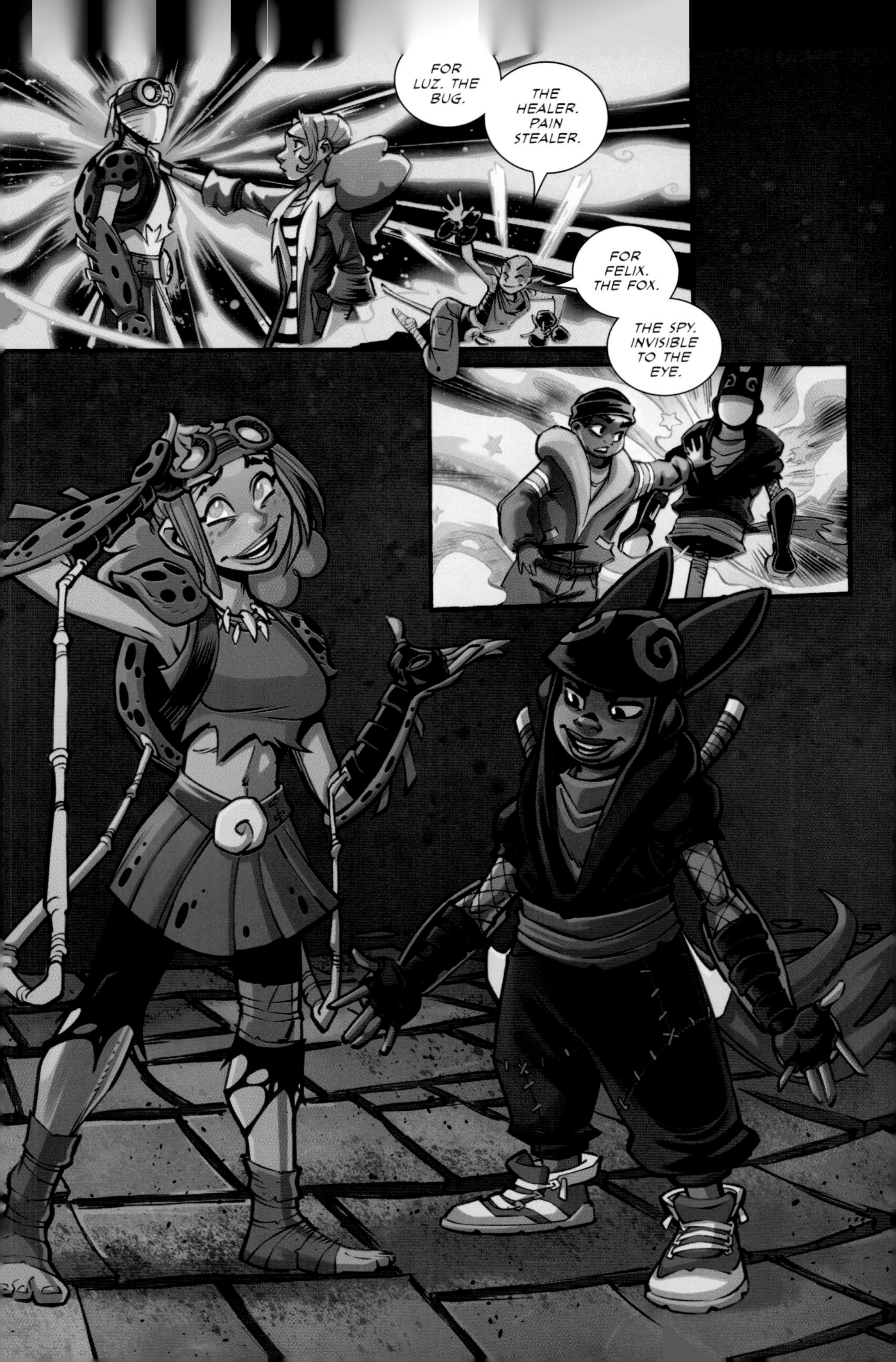
FOR LUZ. THE BUG.
THE HEALER. PAIN STEALER.
FOR FELIX. THE FOX.
THE SPY. INVISIBLE TO THE EYE.

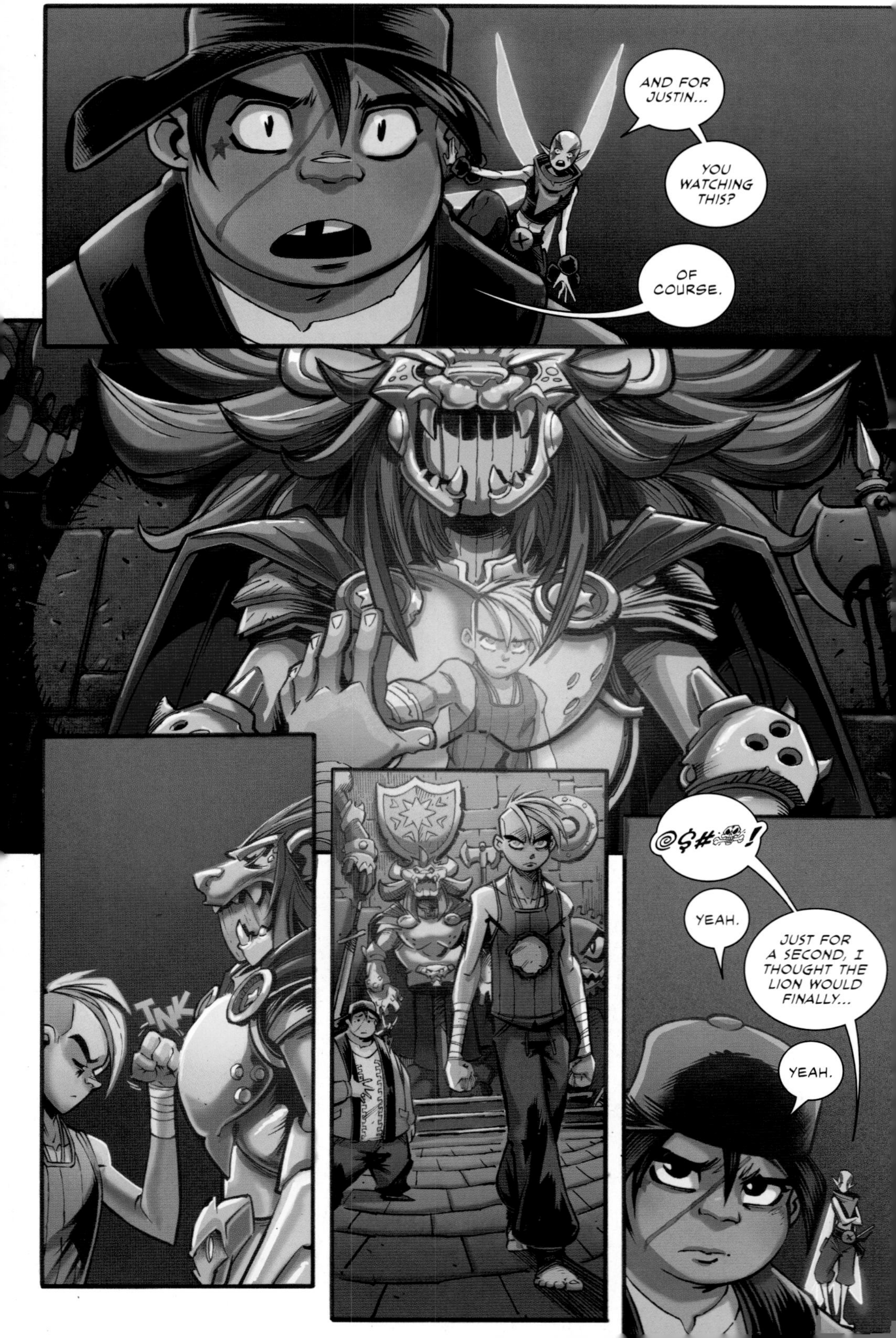
AND FOR JUSTIN...
YOU WATCHING THIS?
OF COURSE.
TNK
@$#☠!
YEAH.
JUST FOR A SECOND, I THOUGHT THE LION WOULD FINALLY...
YEAH.

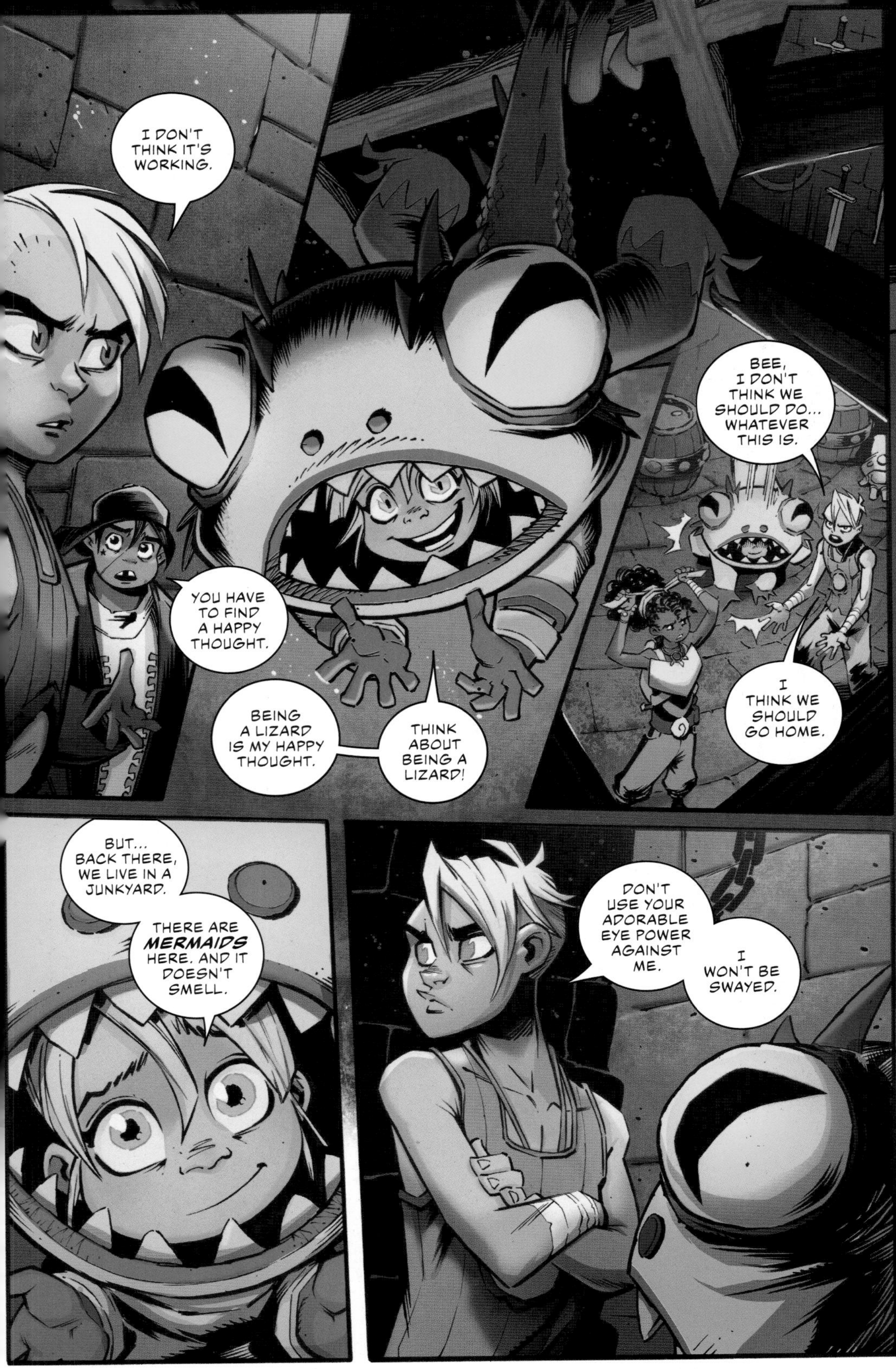
I DON'T THINK IT'S WORKING.
YOU HAVE TO FIND A HAPPY THOUGHT.
THINK ABOUT BEING A LIZARD!
BEING A LIZARD IS MY HAPPY THOUGHT.
BEE, I DON'T THINK WE SHOULD DO... WHATEVER THIS IS.
I THINK WE SHOULD GO HOME.
BUT... BACK THERE, WE LIVE IN A JUNKYARD.
THERE ARE MERMAIDS HERE. AND IT DOESN'T SMELL.
DON'T USE YOUR ADORABLE EYE POWER AGAINST ME.
I WON'T BE SWAYED.

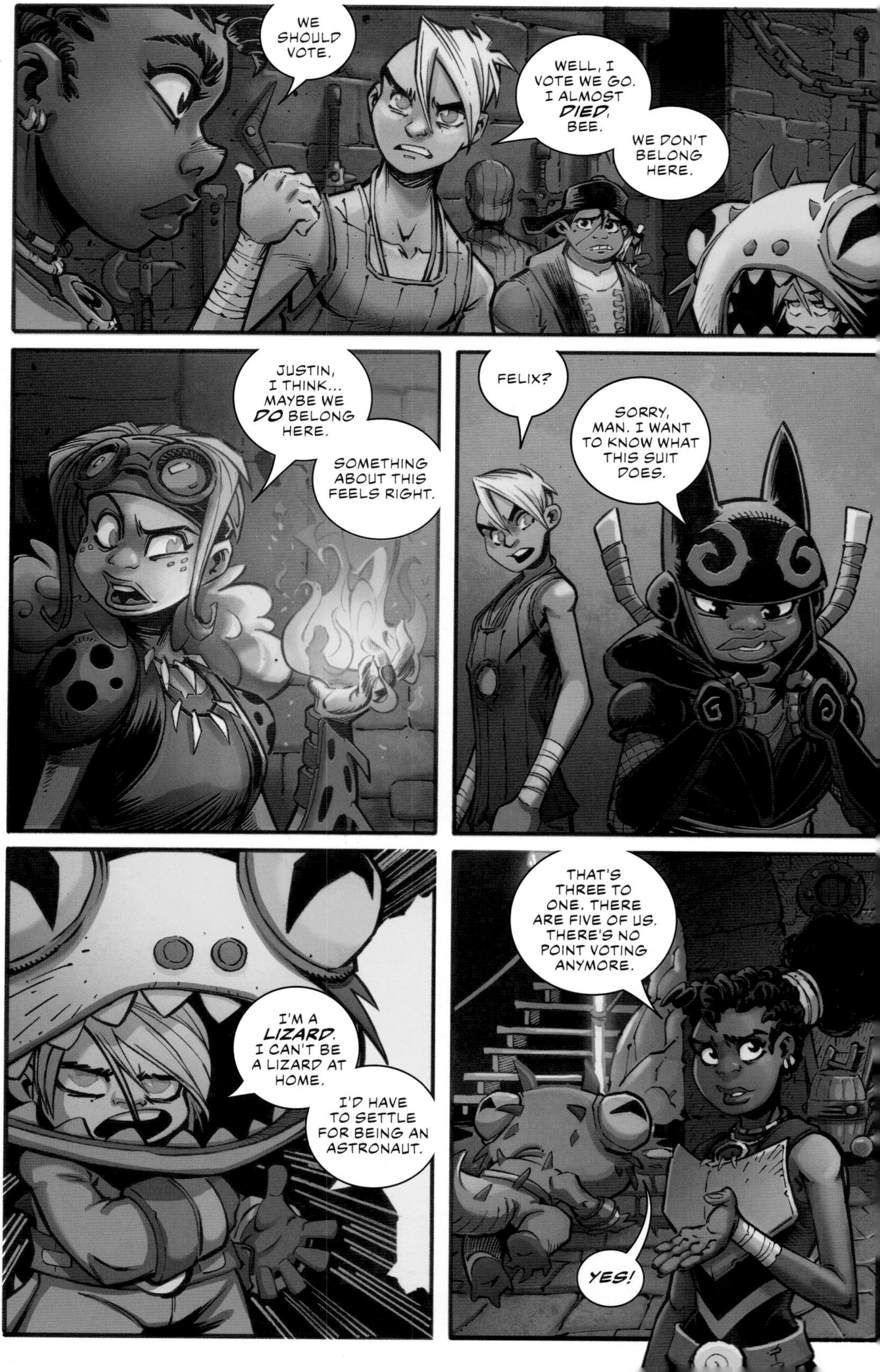
WE SHOULD VOTE.
WELL, I VOTE WE GO. I ALMOST DIED, BEE.
WE DON'T BELONG HERE.
JUSTIN, I THINK... MAYBE WE DO BELONG HERE.
SOMETHING ABOUT THIS FEELS RIGHT.
FELIX?
SORRY, MAN. I WANT TO KNOW WHAT THIS SUIT DOES.
I'M A LIZARD. I CAN'T BE A LIZARD AT HOME.
I'D HAVE TO SETTLE FOR BEING AN ASTRONAUT.
THAT'S THREE TO ONE. THERE ARE FIVE OF US. THERE'S NO POINT VOTING ANYMORE.
YES!

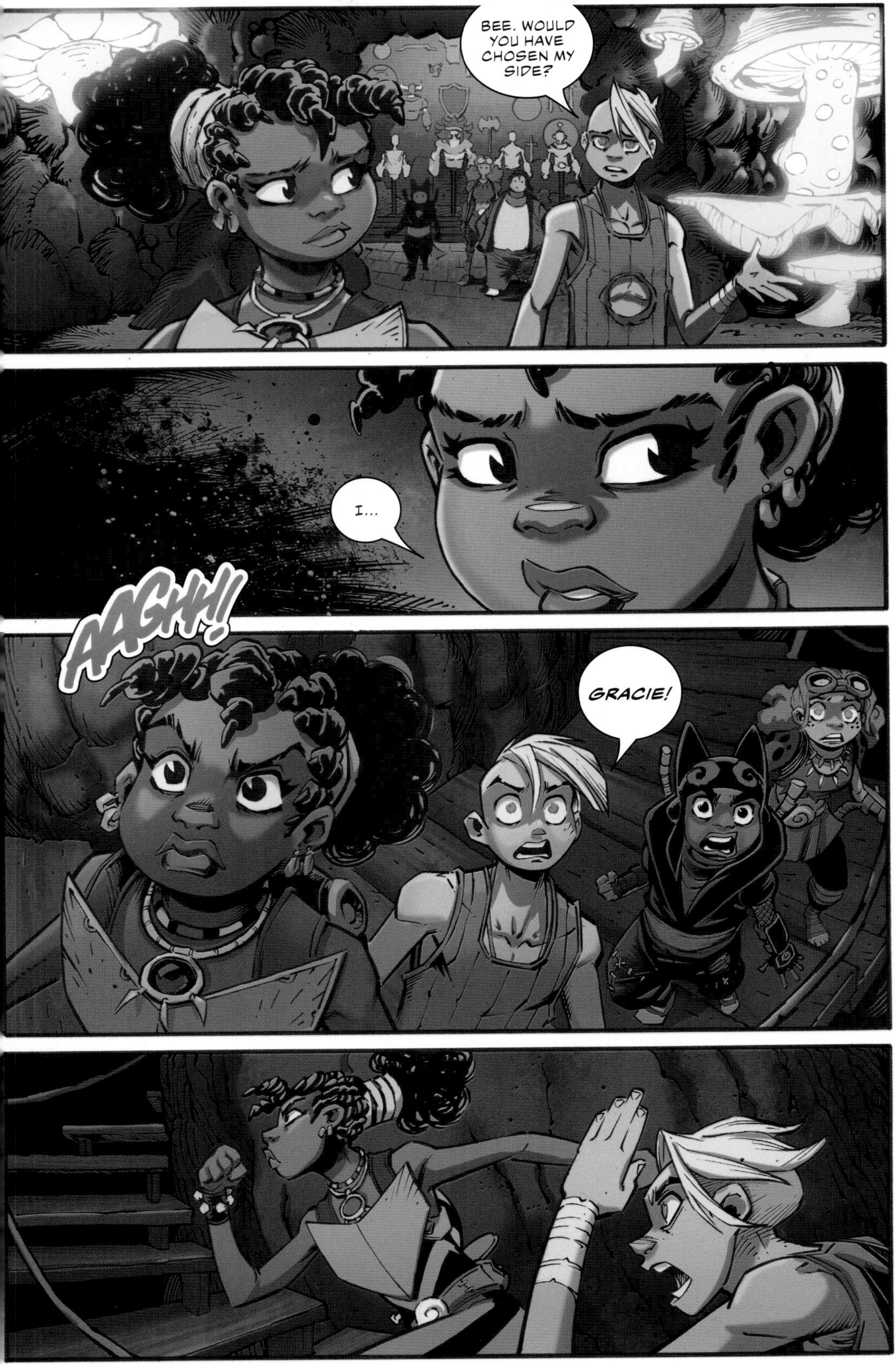
BEE. WOULD YOU HAVE CHOSEN MY SIDE?
I...
AAGHH!!
GRACIE!

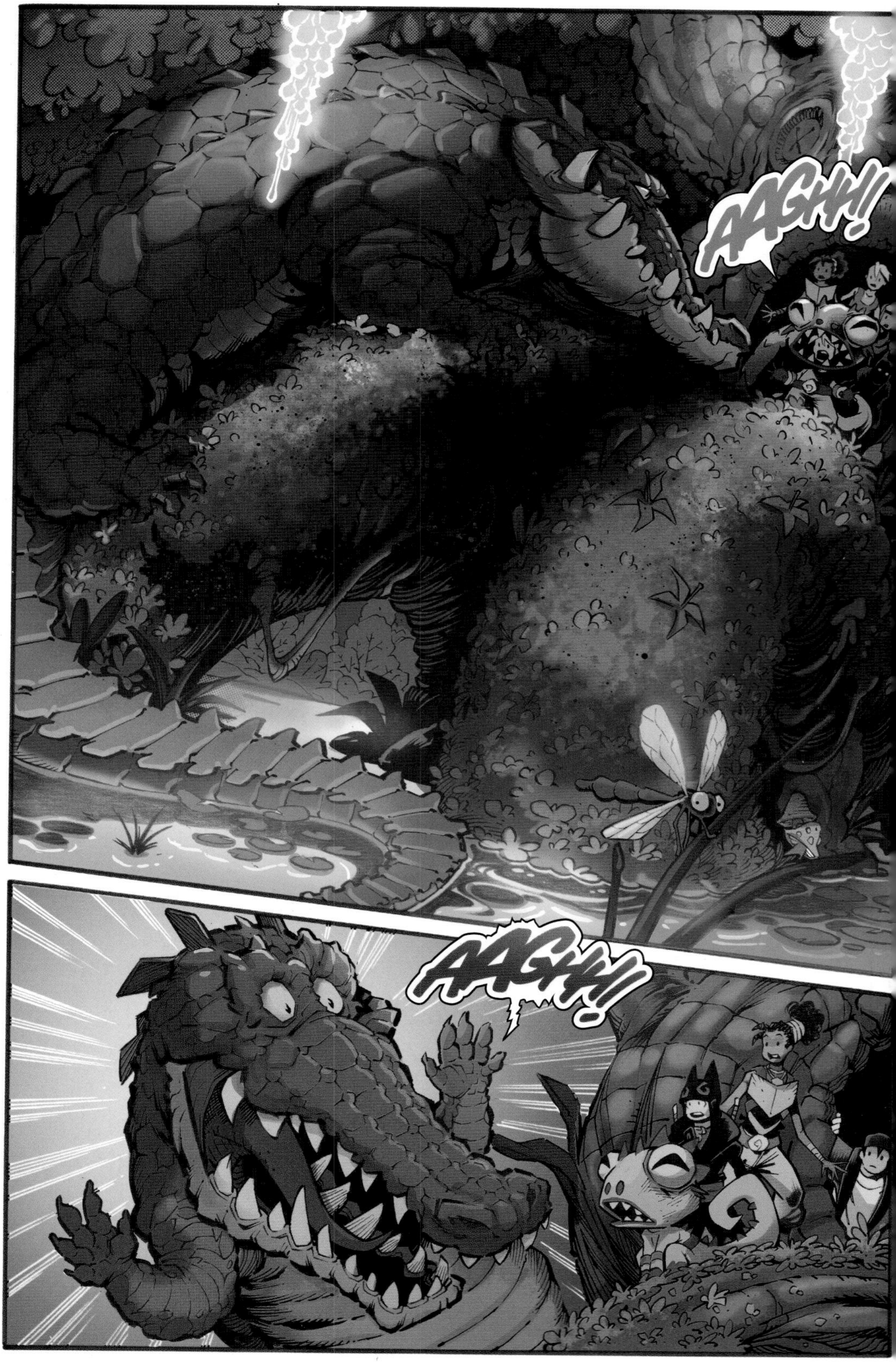
AAGHH!!
AAGHH!!

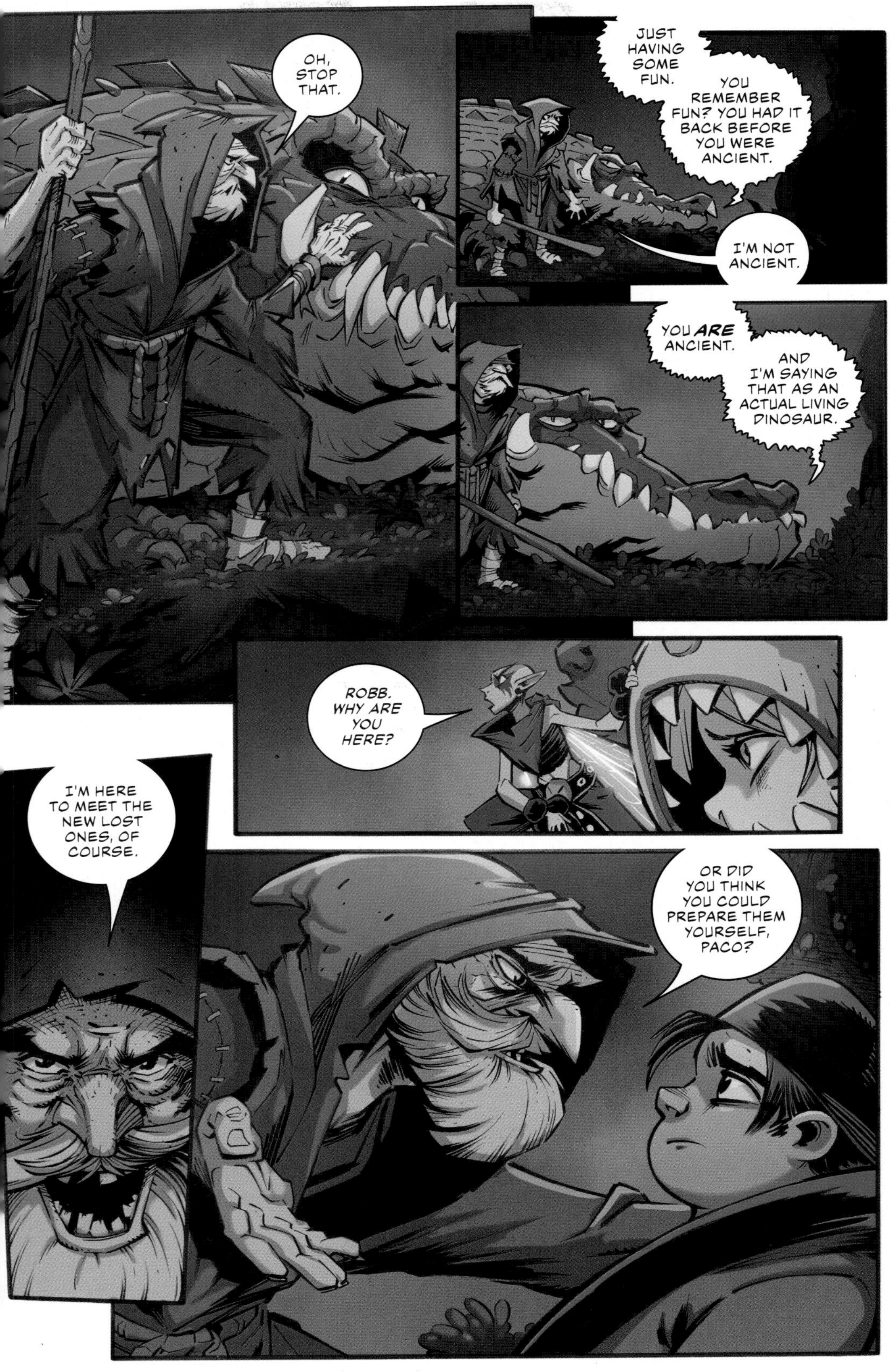
OH, STOP THAT.
JUST HAVING SOME FUN.
YOU REMEMBER FUN? YOU HAD IT BACK BEFORE YOU WERE ANCIENT.
I'M NOT ANCIENT.
YOU ARE ANCIENT.
AND I'M SAYING THAT AS AN ACTUAL LIVING DINOSAUR.
ROBB. WHY ARE YOU HERE?
I'M HERE TO MEET THE NEW LOST ONES, OF COURSE.
OR DID YOU THINK YOU COULD PREPARE THEM YOURSELF, PACO?

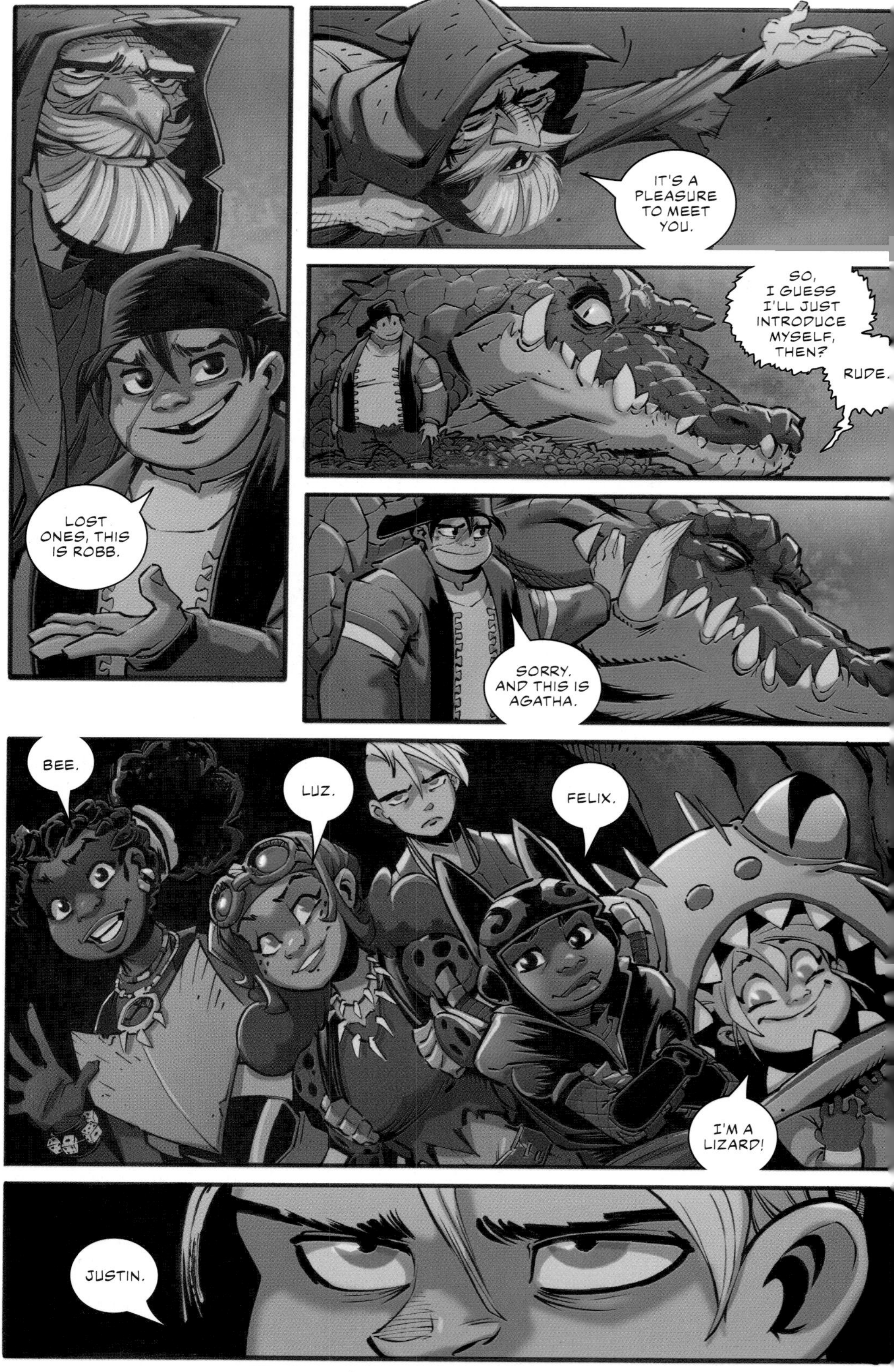

LOST ONES, THIS IS ROBB.
IT'S A PLEASURE TO MEET YOU.
SO, I GUESS I'LL JUST INTRODUCE MYSELF, THEN?
RUDE.
SORRY. AND THIS IS AGATHA.
BEE.
LUZ.
FELIX.
I'M A LIZARD!
JUSTIN.

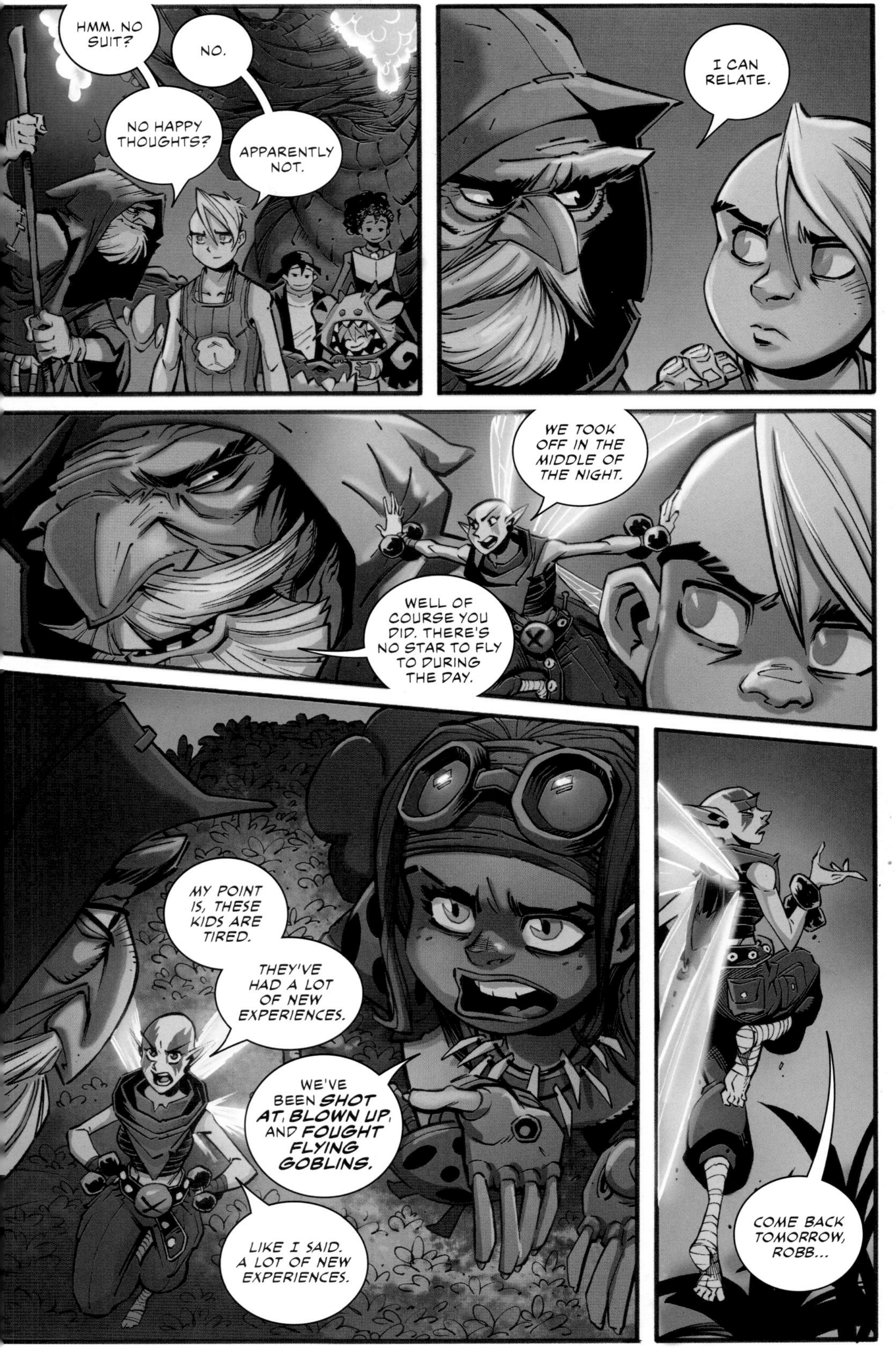
HMM. NO SUIT?
NO.
NO HAPPY THOUGHTS?
APPARENTLY NOT.
I CAN RELATE.
WE TOOK OFF IN THE MIDDLE OF THE NIGHT.
WELL OF COURSE YOU DID. THERE'S NO STAR TO FLY TO DURING THE DAY.
MY POINT IS, THESE KIDS ARE TIRED.
THEY'VE HAD A LOT OF NEW EXPERIENCES.
WE'VE BEEN SHOT AT, BLOWN UP, AND FOUGHT FLYING GOBLINS.
LIKE I SAID. A LOT OF NEW EXPERIENCES.
COME BACK TOMORROW, ROBB...

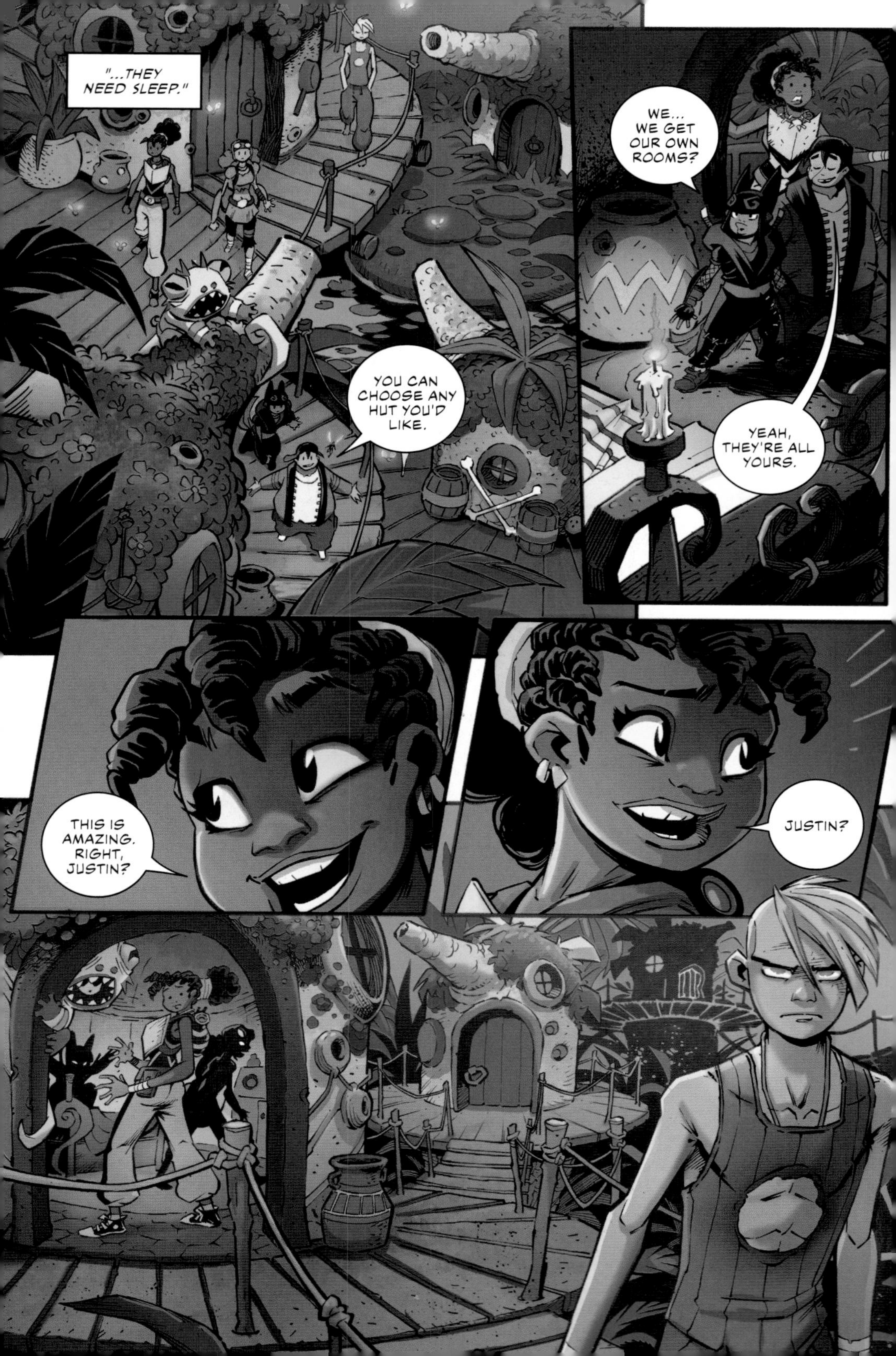
"...THEY NEED SLEEP."
YOU CAN CHOOSE ANY HUT YOU'D LIKE.
WE... WE GET OUR OWN ROOMS?
YEAH, THEY'RE ALL YOURS.
THIS IS AMAZING. RIGHT, JUSTIN?
JUSTIN?

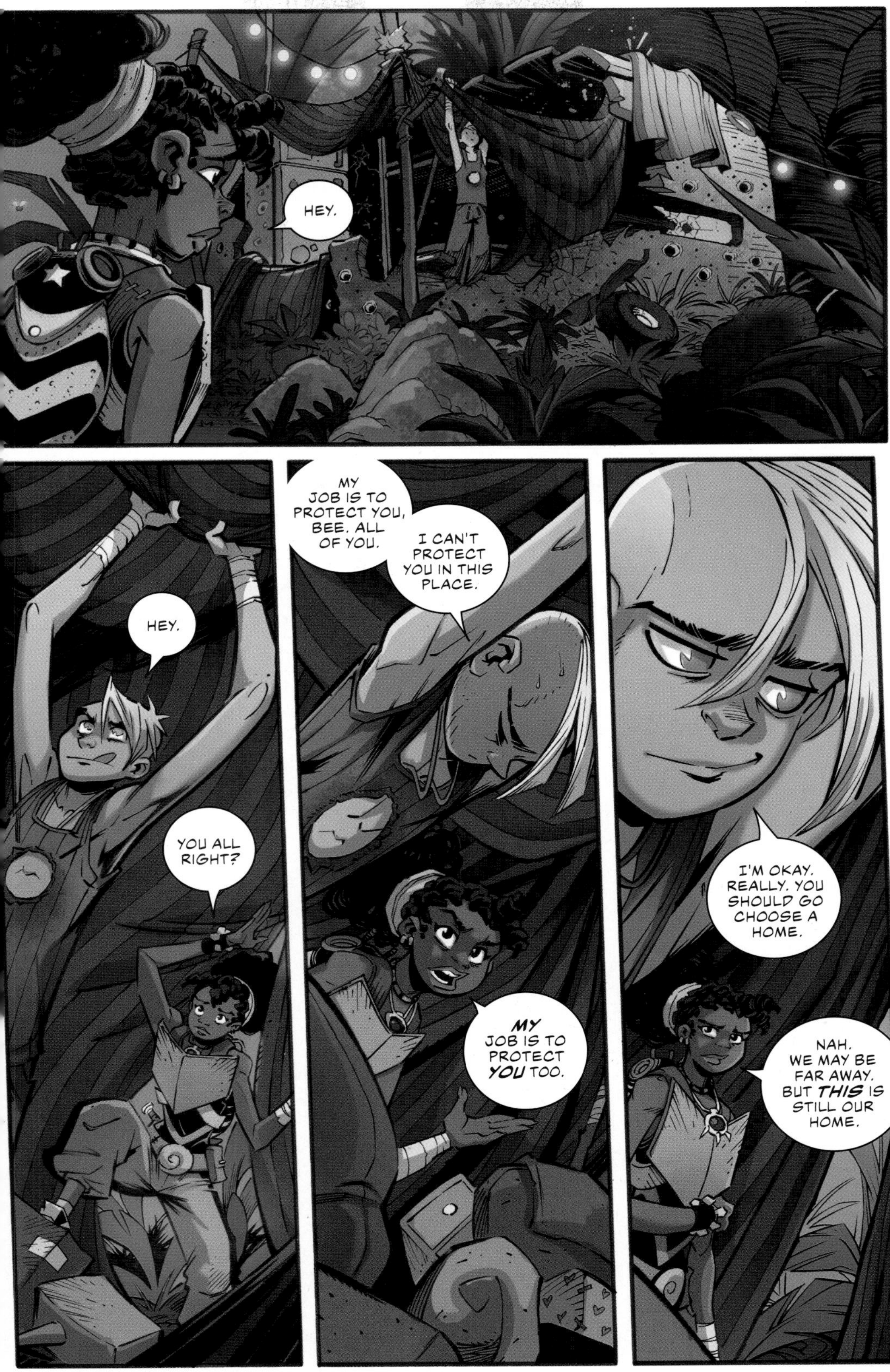
HEY.
HEY.
YOU ALL RIGHT?
MY JOB IS TO PROTECT YOU, BEE. ALL OF YOU.
I CAN'T PROTECT YOU IN THIS PLACE.
MY JOB IS TO PROTECT YOU TOO.
I'M OKAY. REALLY. YOU SHOULD GO CHOOSE A HOME.
NAH. WE MAY BE FAR AWAY. BUT THIS IS STILL OUR HOME.

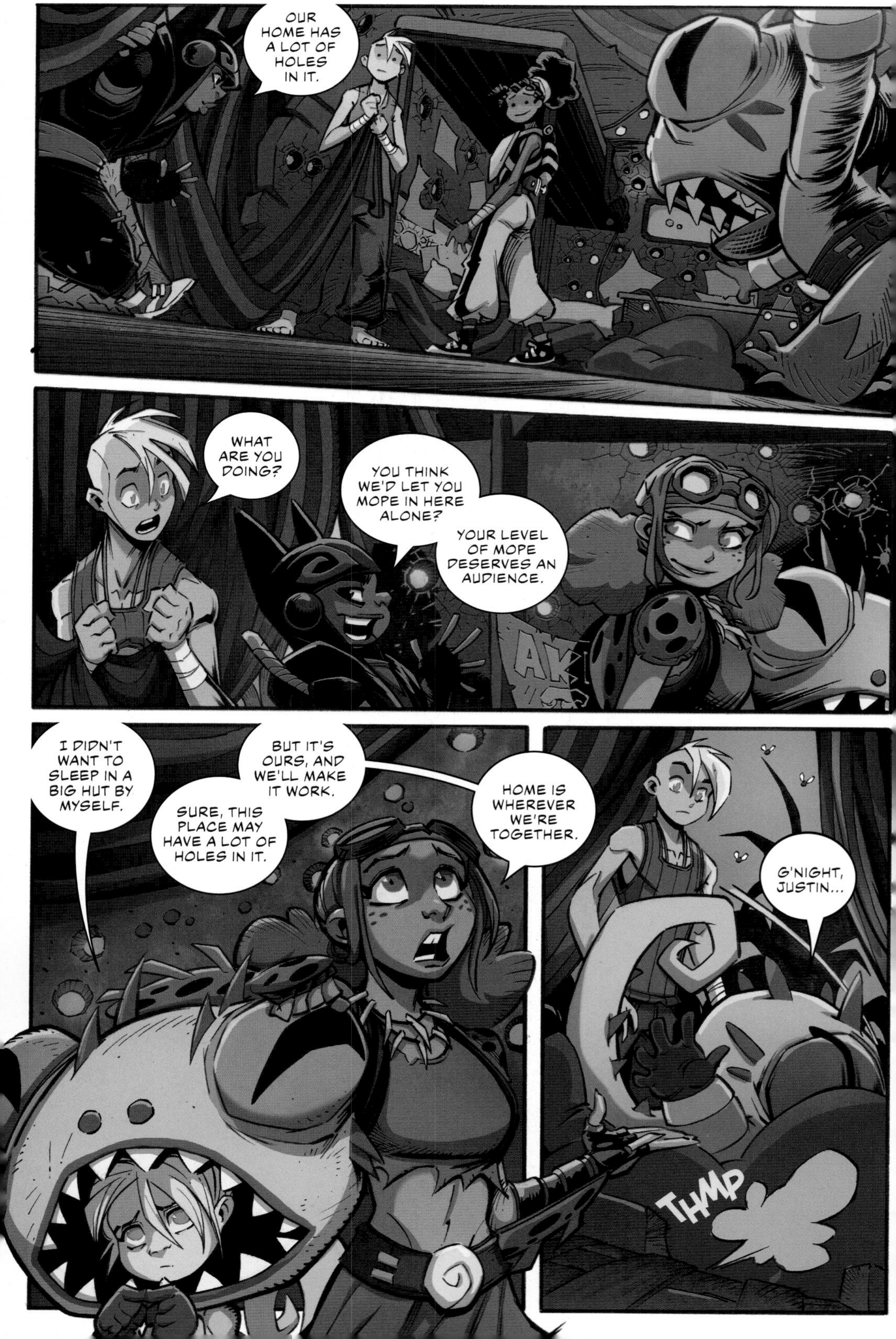
OUR HOME HAS A LOT OF HOLES IN IT.
WHAT ARE YOU DOING?
YOU THINK WE'D LET YOU MOPE IN HERE ALONE?
YOUR LEVEL OF MOPE DESERVES AN AUDIENCE.
I DIDN'T WANT TO SLEEP IN A BIG HUT BY MYSELF.
SURE, THIS PLACE MAY HAVE A LOT OF HOLES IN IT.
BUT IT'S OURS, AND WE'LL MAKE IT WORK.
HOME IS WHEREVER WE'RE TOGETHER.
G'NIGHT, JUSTIN...
THMP

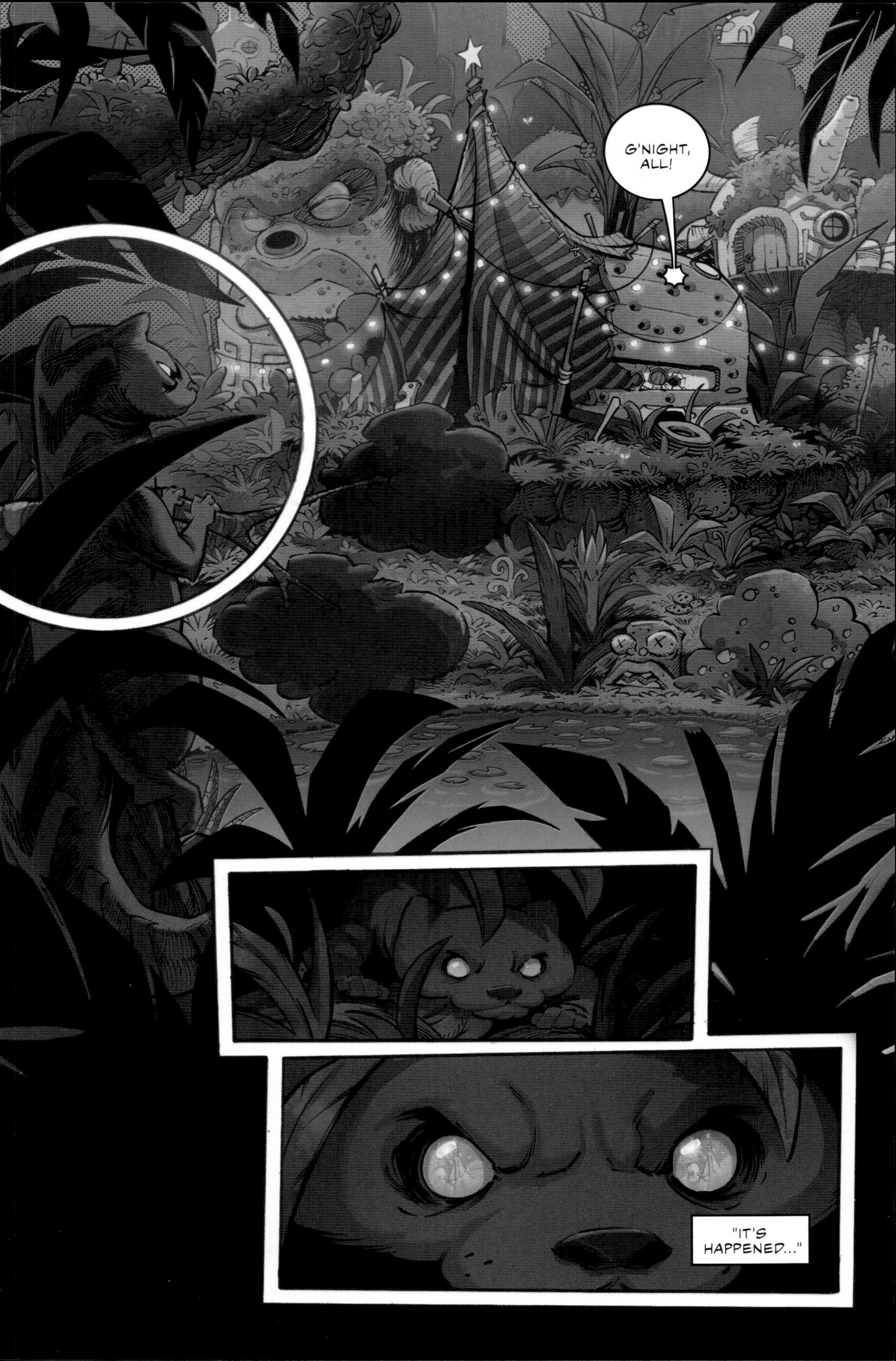
G'NIGHT, ALL!
"IT'S HAPPENED..."

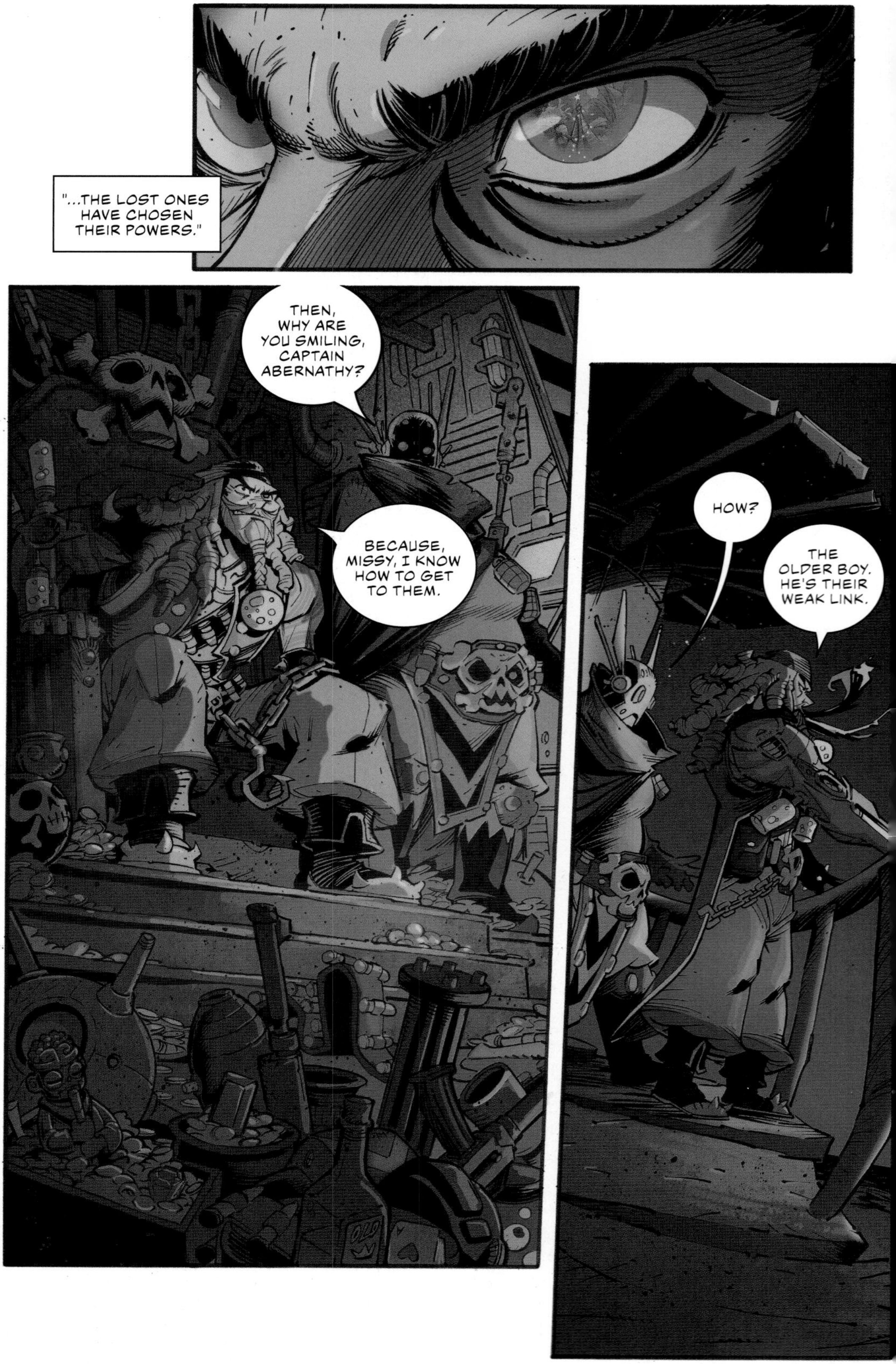
"...THE LOST ONES HAVE CHOSEN THEIR POWERS."
THEN, WHY ARE YOU SMILING, CAPTAIN ABERNATHY?
BECAUSE, MISSY, I KNOW HOW TO GET TO THEM.
HOW?
THE OLDER BOY. HE'S THEIR WEAK LINK.

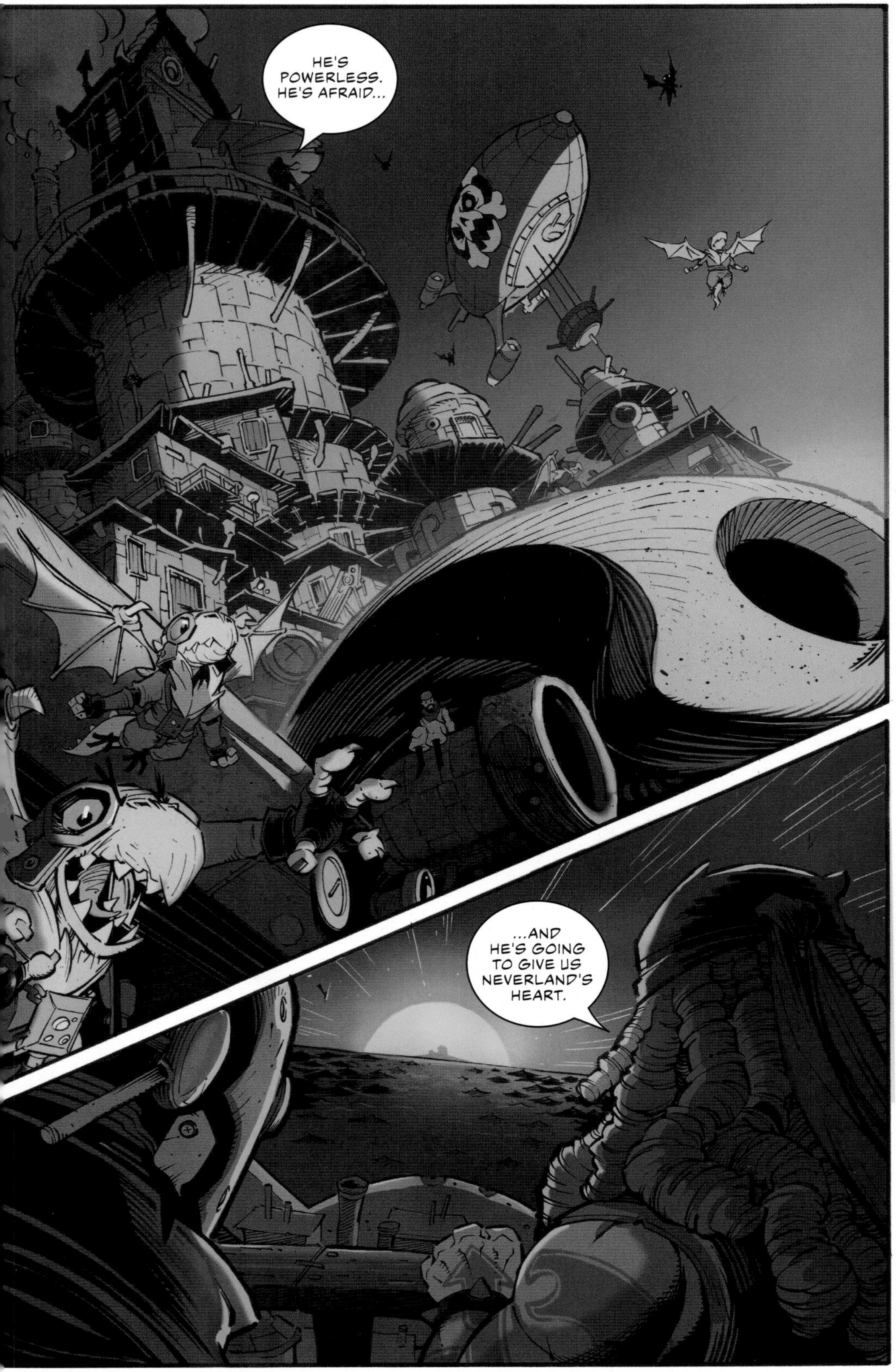
HE'S POWERLESS. HE'S AFRAID...
...AND HE'S GOING TO GIVE US NEVERLAND'S HEART.

CHAPTER
FOUR

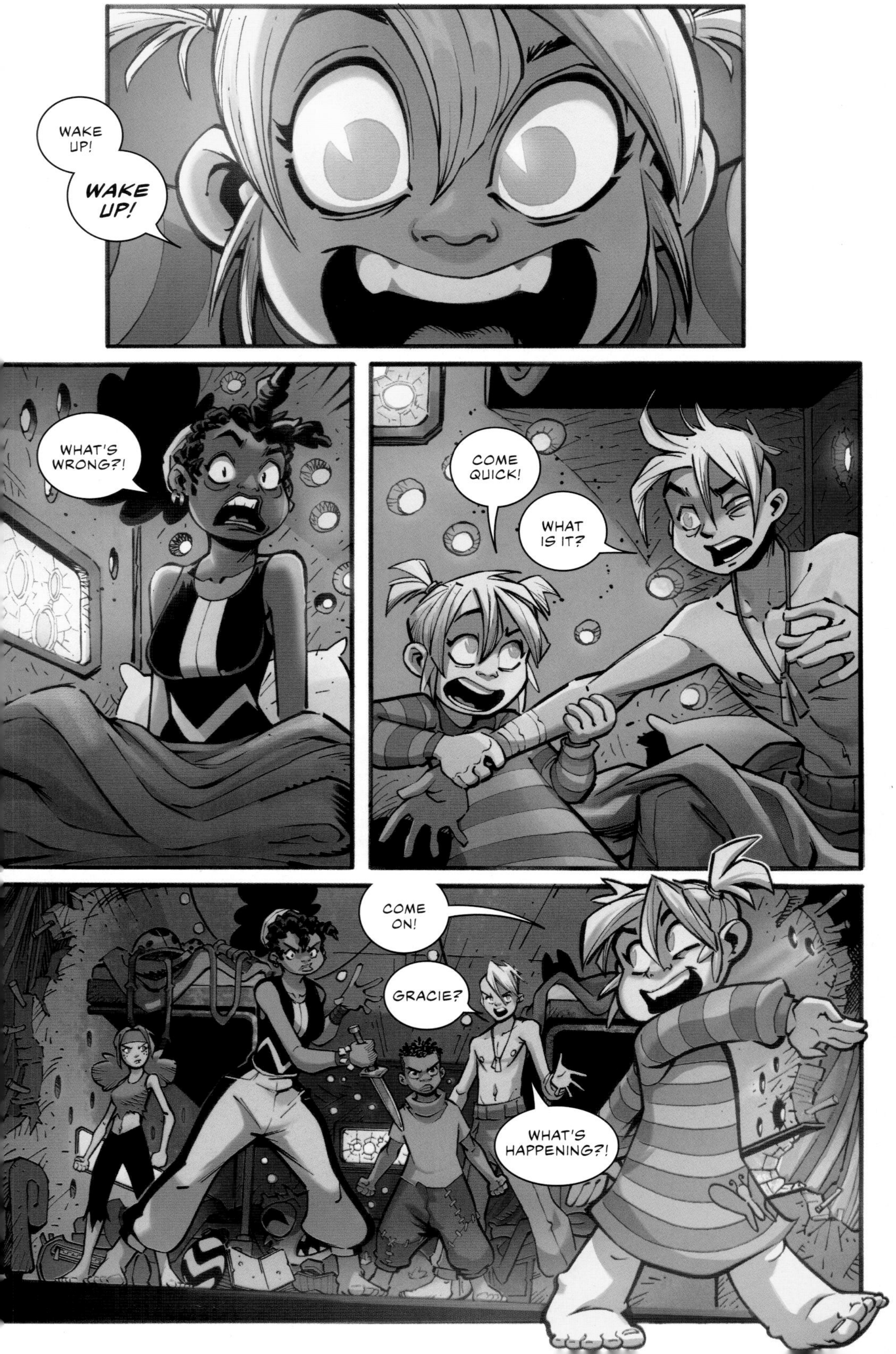
WAKE UP!
WAKE UP!
WHAT'S WRONG?!
COME QUICK!
WHAT IS IT?
COME ON!
GRACIE?
WHAT'S HAPPENING?!

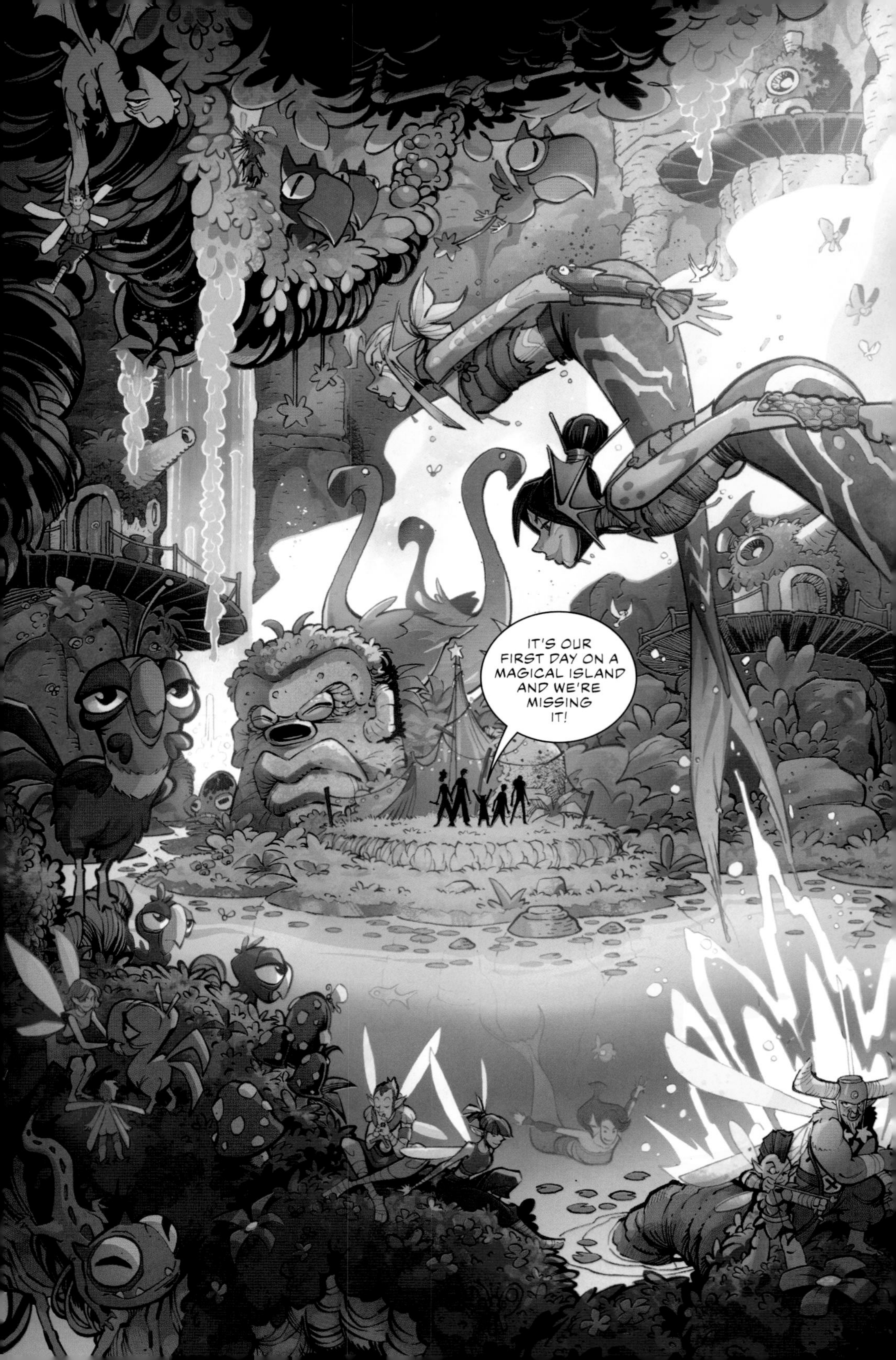
IT'S OUR FIRST DAY ON A MAGICAL ISLAND AND WE'RE MISSING IT!

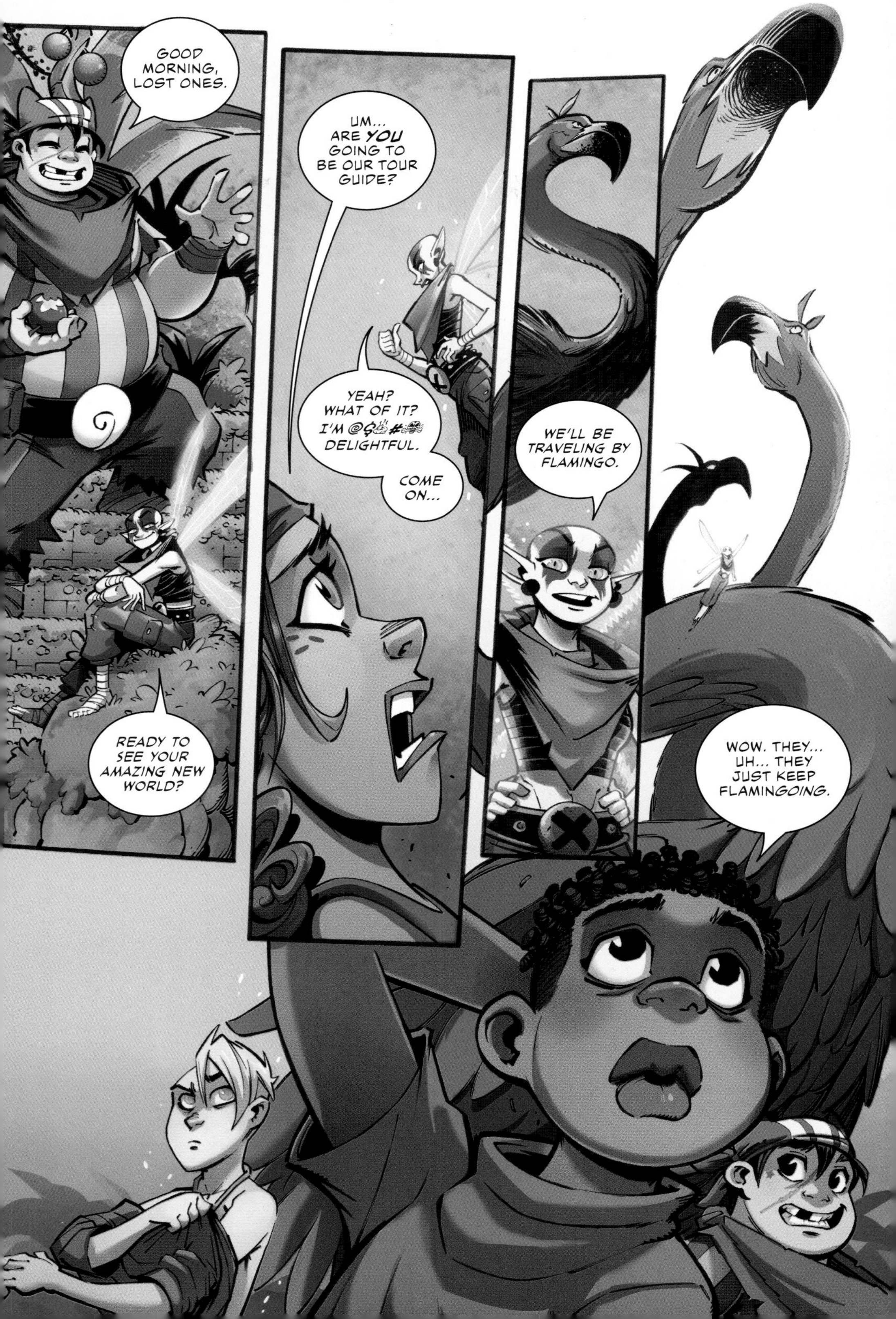
GOOD MORNING, LOST ONES.
READY TO SEE YOUR AMAZING NEW WORLD?
UM... ARE YOU GOING TO BE OUR TOUR GUIDE?
YEAH? WHAT OF IT? I'M @$#!* DELIGHTFUL.
COME ON...
WE'LL BE TRAVELING BY FLAMINGO.
WOW. THEY... UH... THEY JUST KEEP FLAMINGOING.

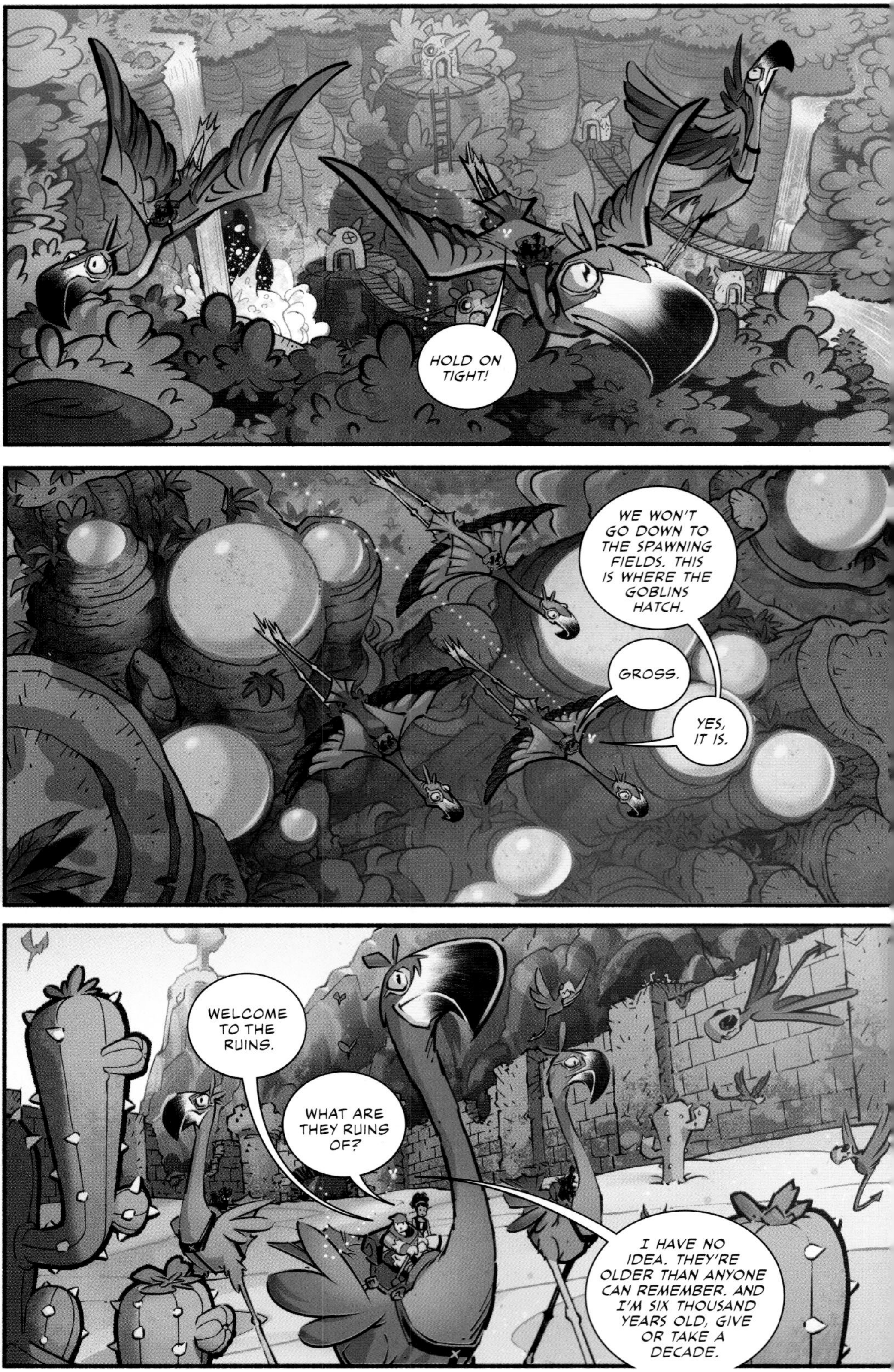
HOLD ON TIGHT!
WE WON'T GO DOWN TO THE SPAWNING FIELDS. THIS IS WHERE THE GOBLINS HATCH.
GROSS.
YES, IT IS.
WELCOME TO THE RUINS.
WHAT ARE THEY RUINS OF?
I HAVE NO IDEA. THEY'RE OLDER THAN ANYONE CAN REMEMBER. AND I'M SIX THOUSAND YEARS OLD, GIVE OR TAKE A DECADE.

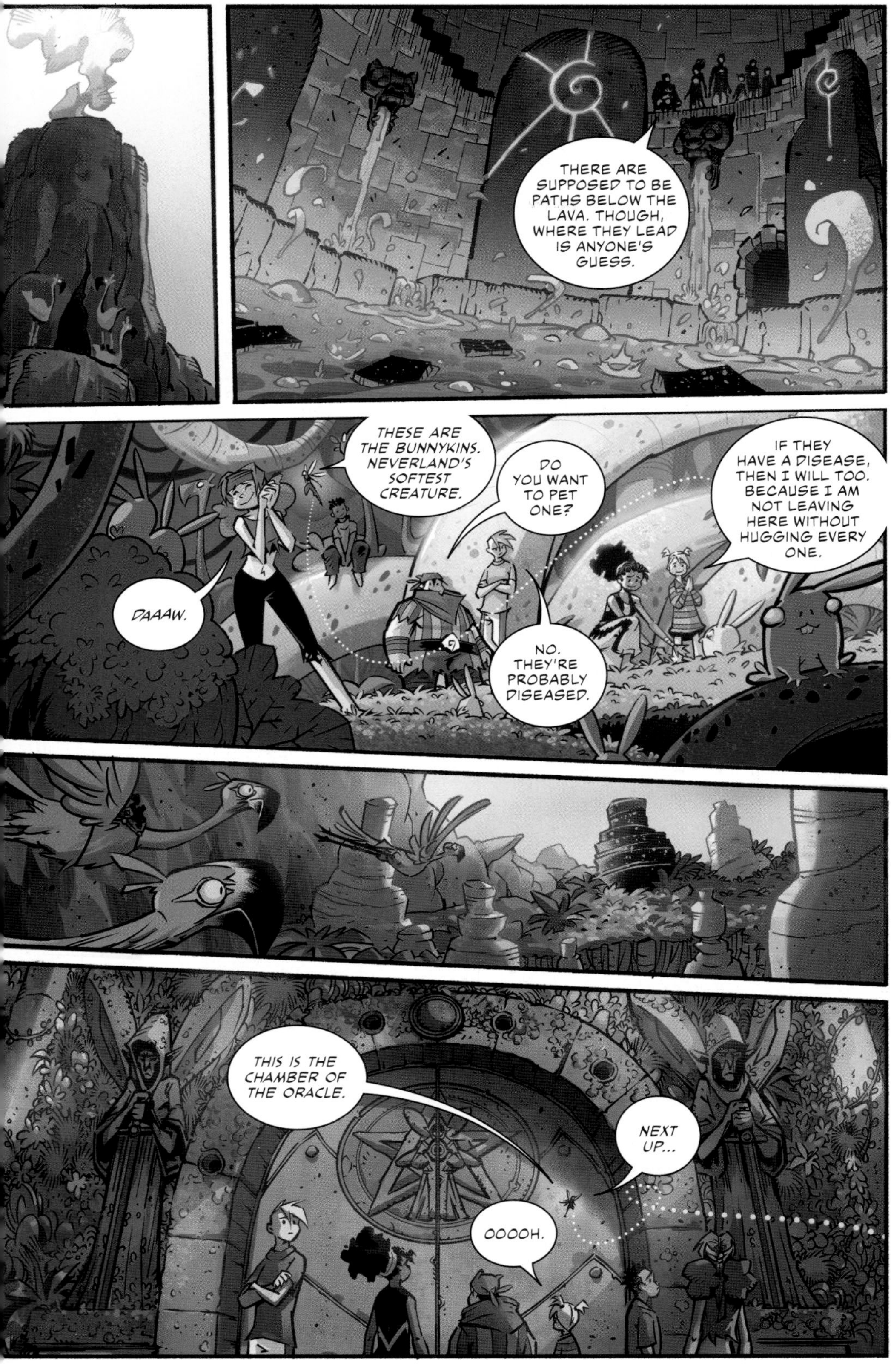
THERE ARE SUPPOSED TO BE PATHS BELOW THE LAVA. THOUGH, WHERE THEY LEAD IS ANYONE'S GUESS.
THESE ARE THE BUNNYKINS. NEVERLAND'S SOFTEST CREATURE.
DAAAW.
DO YOU WANT TO PET ONE?
NO. THEY'RE PROBABLY DISEASED.
IF THEY HAVE A DISEASE, THEN I WILL TOO. BECAUSE I AM NOT LEAVING HERE WITHOUT HUGGING EVERY ONE.
THIS IS THE CHAMBER OF THE ORACLE.
NEXT UP...
OOOOH.

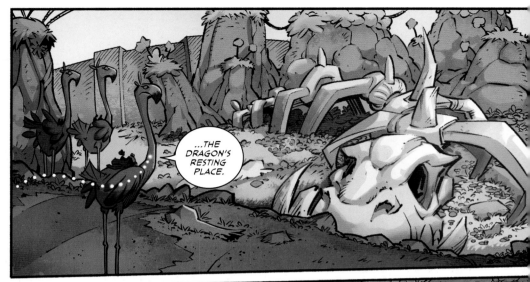

...THE DRAGON'S RESTING PLACE.

THE HAUNTED ISLE. WHERE EVERY NIGHT IS HALLOWEEN.

FOREVER WINTER. HOME OF THE ICE CRABS.

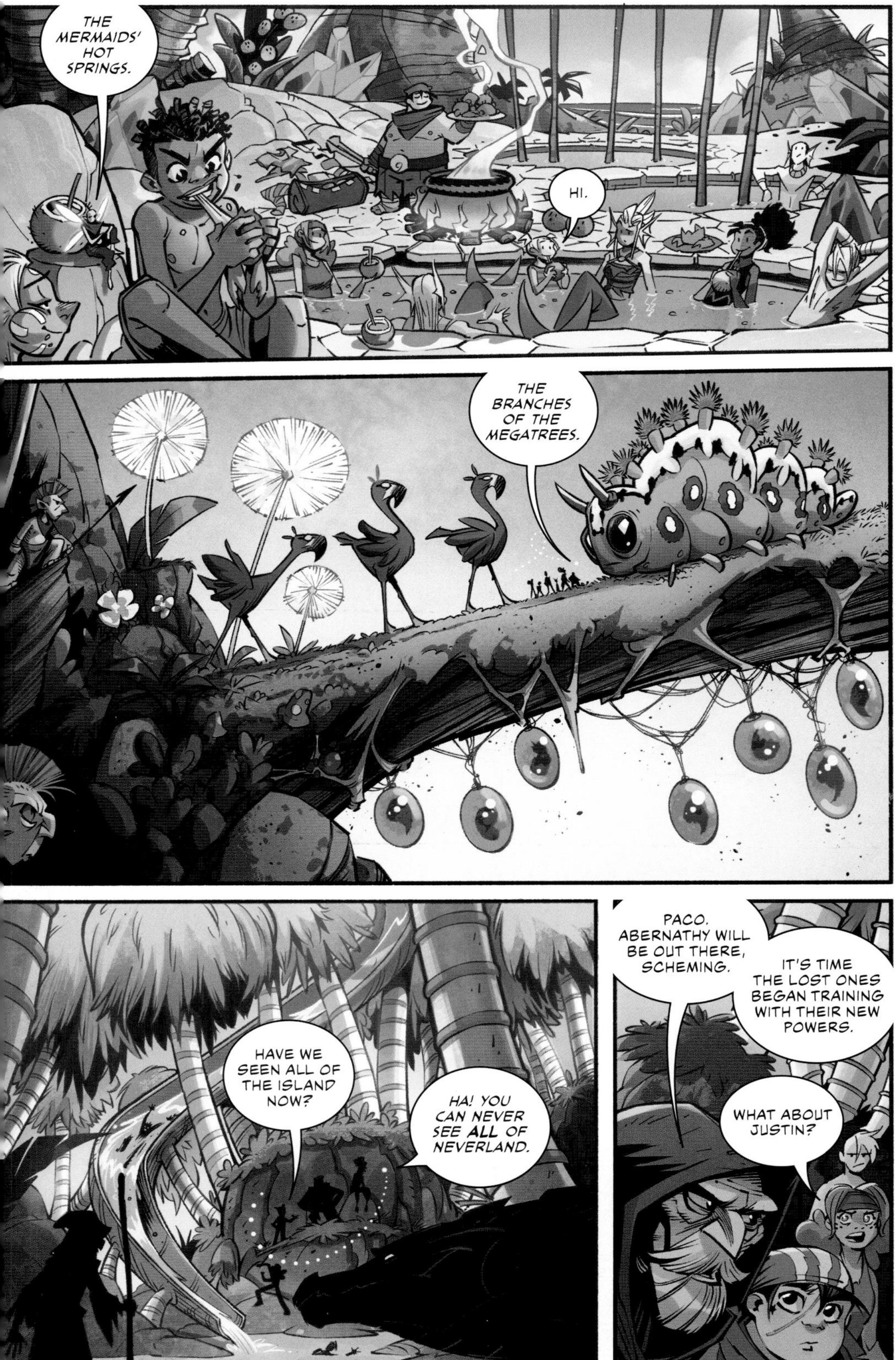
THE MERMAIDS' HOT SPRINGS.
HI.
THE BRANCHES OF THE MEGATREES.
HAVE WE SEEN ALL OF THE ISLAND NOW?
HA! YOU CAN NEVER SEE ALL OF NEVERLAND.
PACO. ABERNATHY WILL BE OUT THERE, SCHEMING.
IT'S TIME THE LOST ONES BEGAN TRAINING WITH THEIR NEW POWERS.
WHAT ABOUT JUSTIN?

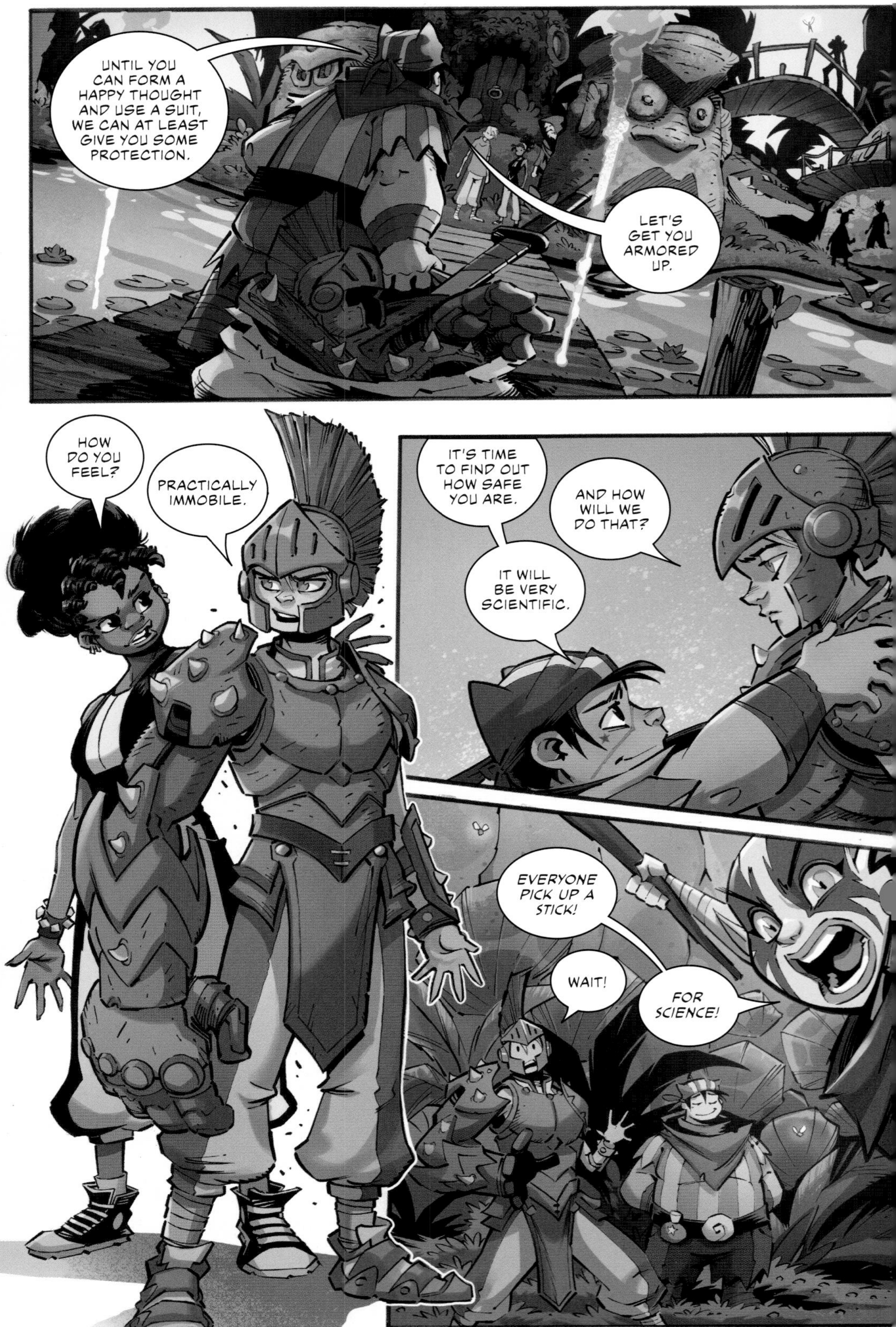
UNTIL YOU CAN FORM A HAPPY THOUGHT AND USE A SUIT, WE CAN AT LEAST GIVE YOU SOME PROTECTION.
LET'S GET YOU ARMORED UP.
HOW DO YOU FEEL?
PRACTICALLY IMMOBILE.
IT'S TIME TO FIND OUT HOW SAFE YOU ARE.
AND HOW WILL WE DO THAT?
IT WILL BE VERY SCIENTIFIC.
EVERYONE PICK UP A STICK!
WAIT!
FOR SCIENCE!

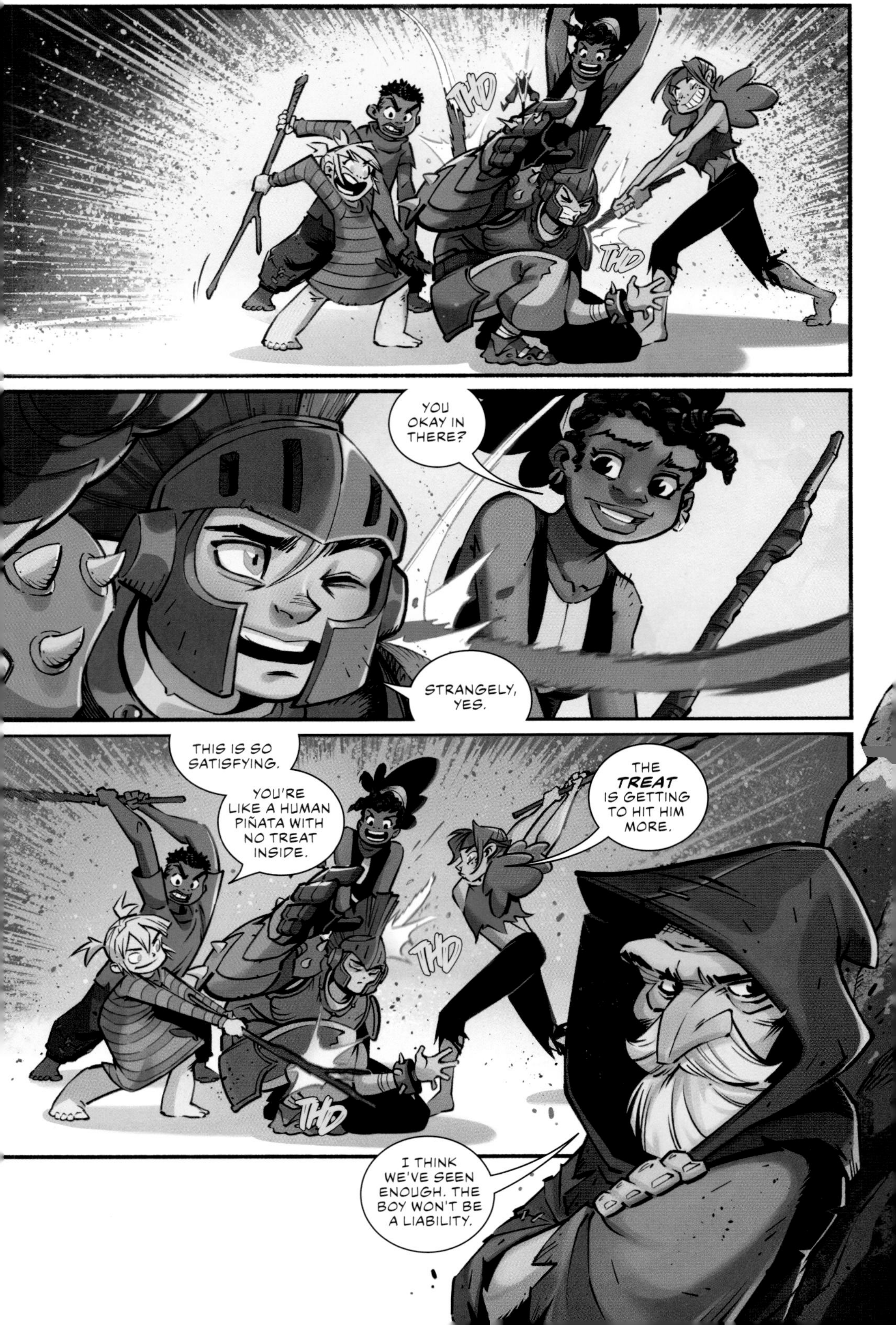

THD
THD
YOU OKAY IN THERE?
STRANGELY, YES.
THIS IS SO SATISFYING.
YOU'RE LIKE A HUMAN PIÑATA WITH NO TREAT INSIDE.
THE TREAT IS GETTING TO HIT HIM MORE.
THD
THD
I THINK WE'VE SEEN ENOUGH. THE BOY WON'T BE A LIABILITY.

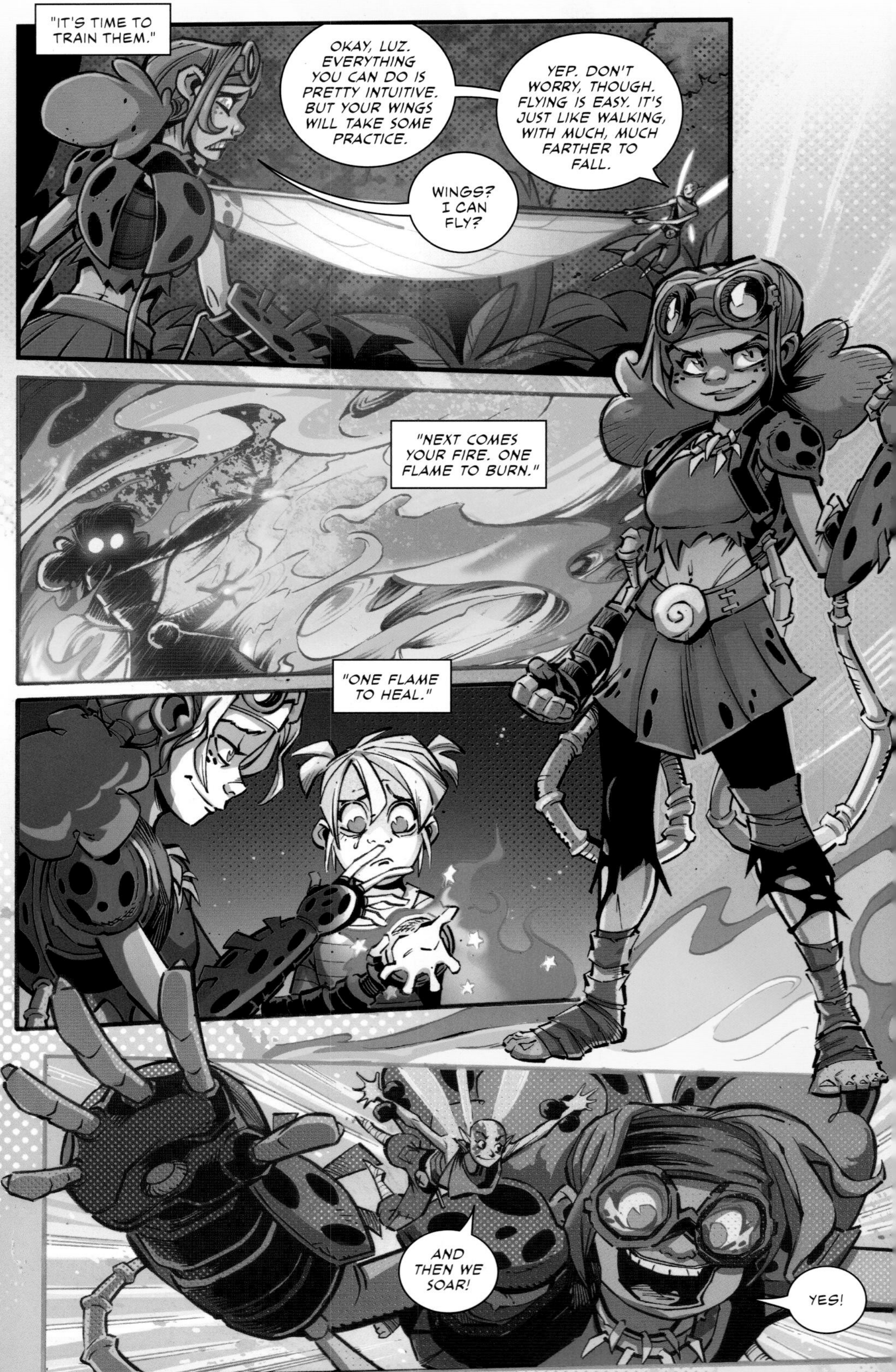
"IT'S TIME TO TRAIN THEM."
OKAY, LUZ. EVERYTHING YOU CAN DO IS PRETTY INTUITIVE. BUT YOUR WINGS WILL TAKE SOME PRACTICE.
YEP. DON'T WORRY, THOUGH. FLYING IS EASY. IT'S JUST LIKE WALKING, WITH MUCH, MUCH FARTHER TO FALL.
WINGS? I CAN FLY?
"NEXT COMES YOUR FIRE. ONE FLAME TO BURN."
"ONE FLAME TO HEAL."
AND THEN WE SOAR!
YES!

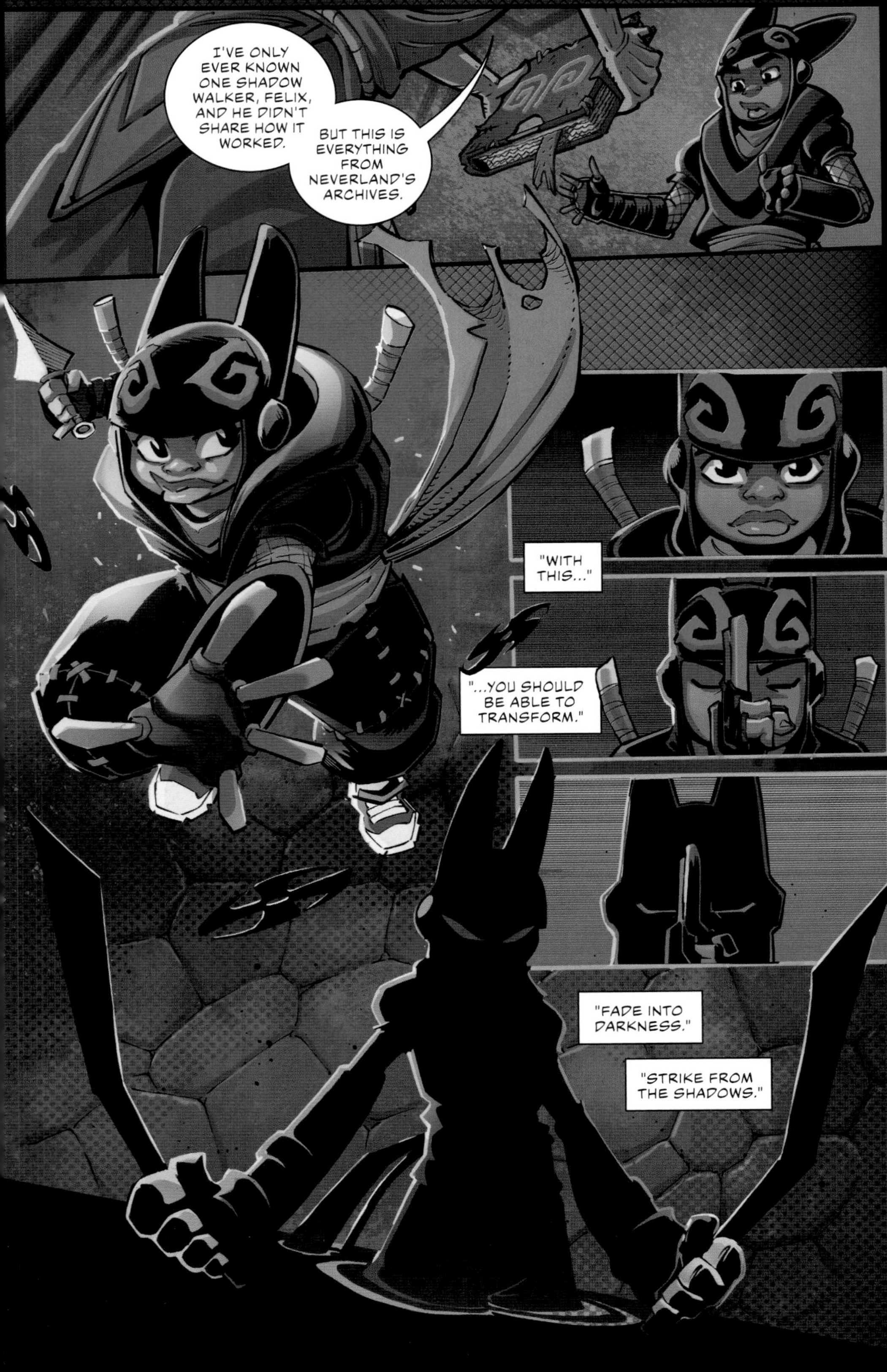
I'VE ONLY EVER KNOWN ONE SHADOW WALKER, FELIX, AND HE DIDN'T SHARE HOW IT WORKED.
BUT THIS IS EVERYTHING FROM NEVERLAND'S ARCHIVES.
"WITH THIS..."
"...YOU SHOULD BE ABLE TO TRANSFORM."
"FADE INTO DARKNESS."
"STRIKE FROM THE SHADOWS."

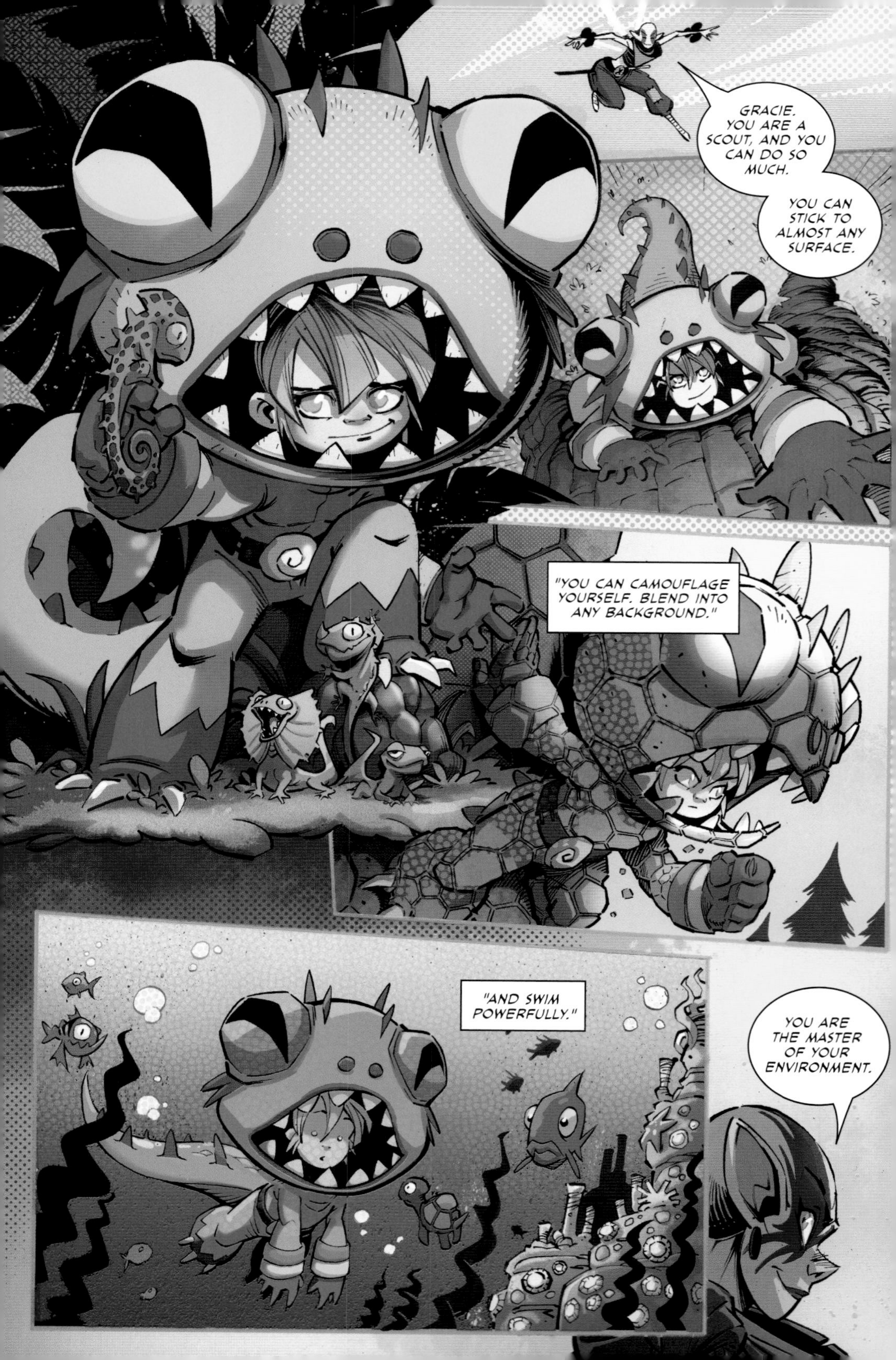
GRACIE. YOU ARE A SCOUT, AND YOU CAN DO SO MUCH.
YOU CAN STICK TO ALMOST ANY SURFACE.
"YOU CAN CAMOUFLAGE YOURSELF. BLEND INTO ANY BACKGROUND."
"AND SWIM POWERFULLY."
YOU ARE THE MASTER OF YOUR ENVIRONMENT.

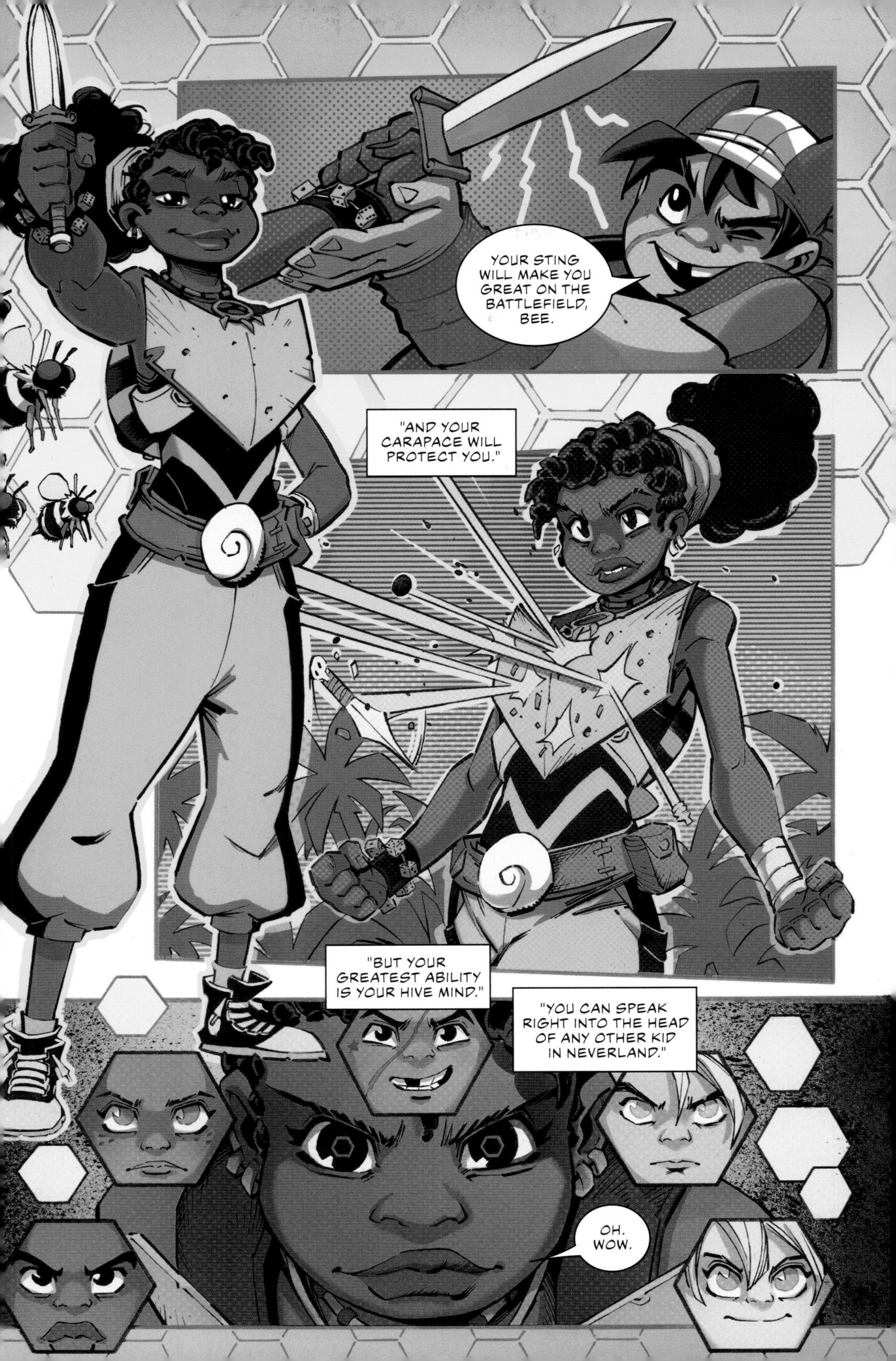
YOUR STING WILL MAKE YOU GREAT ON THE BATTLEFIELD, BEE.
"AND YOUR CARAPACE WILL PROTECT YOU."
"BUT YOUR GREATEST ABILITY IS YOUR HIVE MIND."
"YOU CAN SPEAK RIGHT INTO THE HEAD OF ANY OTHER KID IN NEVERLAND."
OH. WOW.

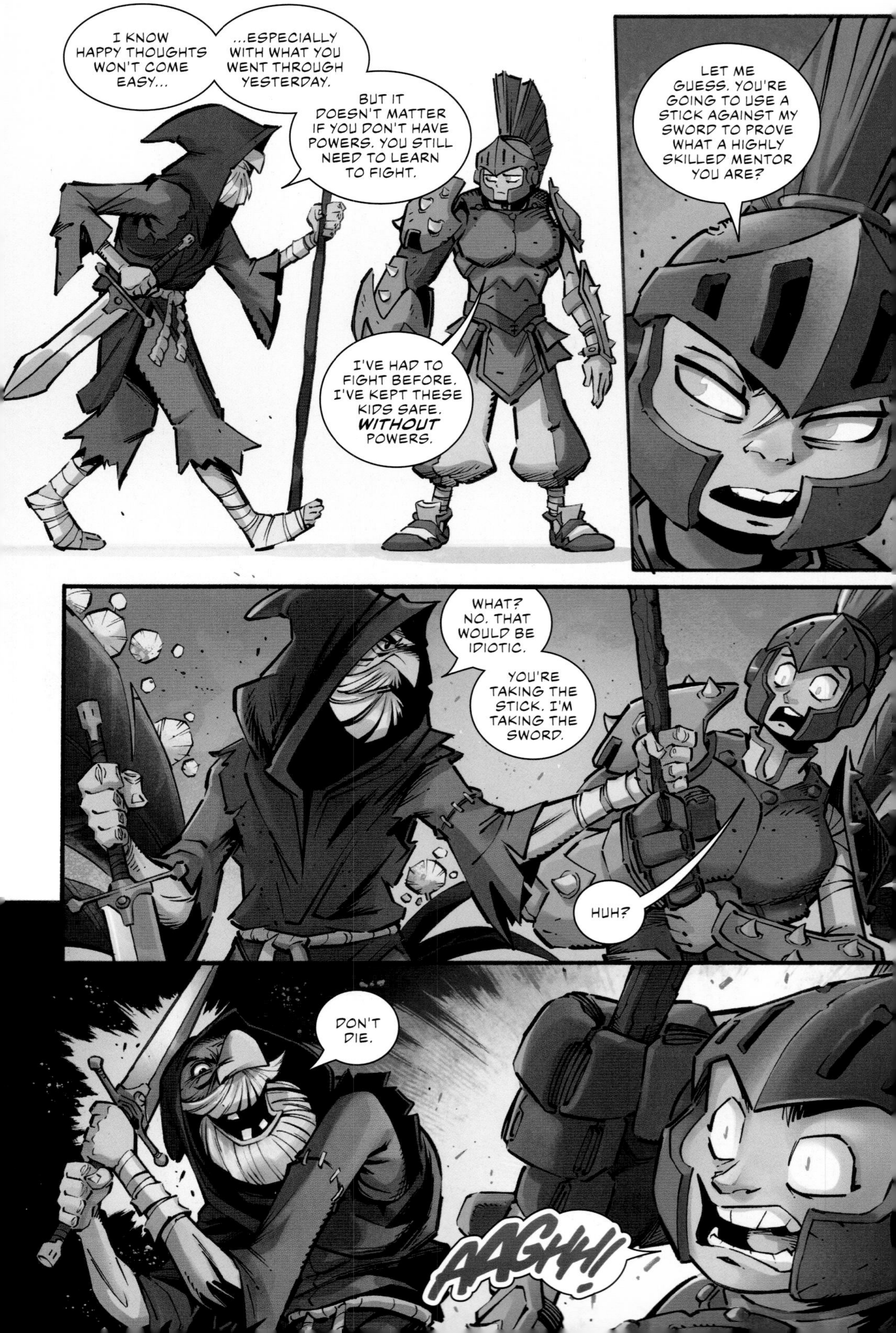

I KNOW HAPPY THOUGHTS WON'T COME EASY...
...ESPECIALLY WITH WHAT YOU WENT THROUGH YESTERDAY.
BUT IT DOESN'T MATTER IF YOU DON'T HAVE POWERS. YOU STILL NEED TO LEARN TO FIGHT.
I'VE HAD TO FIGHT BEFORE. I'VE KEPT THESE KIDS SAFE. *WITHOUT* POWERS.
LET ME GUESS. YOU'RE GOING TO USE A STICK AGAINST MY SWORD TO PROVE WHAT A HIGHLY SKILLED MENTOR YOU ARE?
WHAT? NO. THAT WOULD BE IDIOTIC.
YOU'RE TAKING THE STICK. I'M TAKING THE SWORD.
HUH?
DON'T DIE.
AAGHH!!

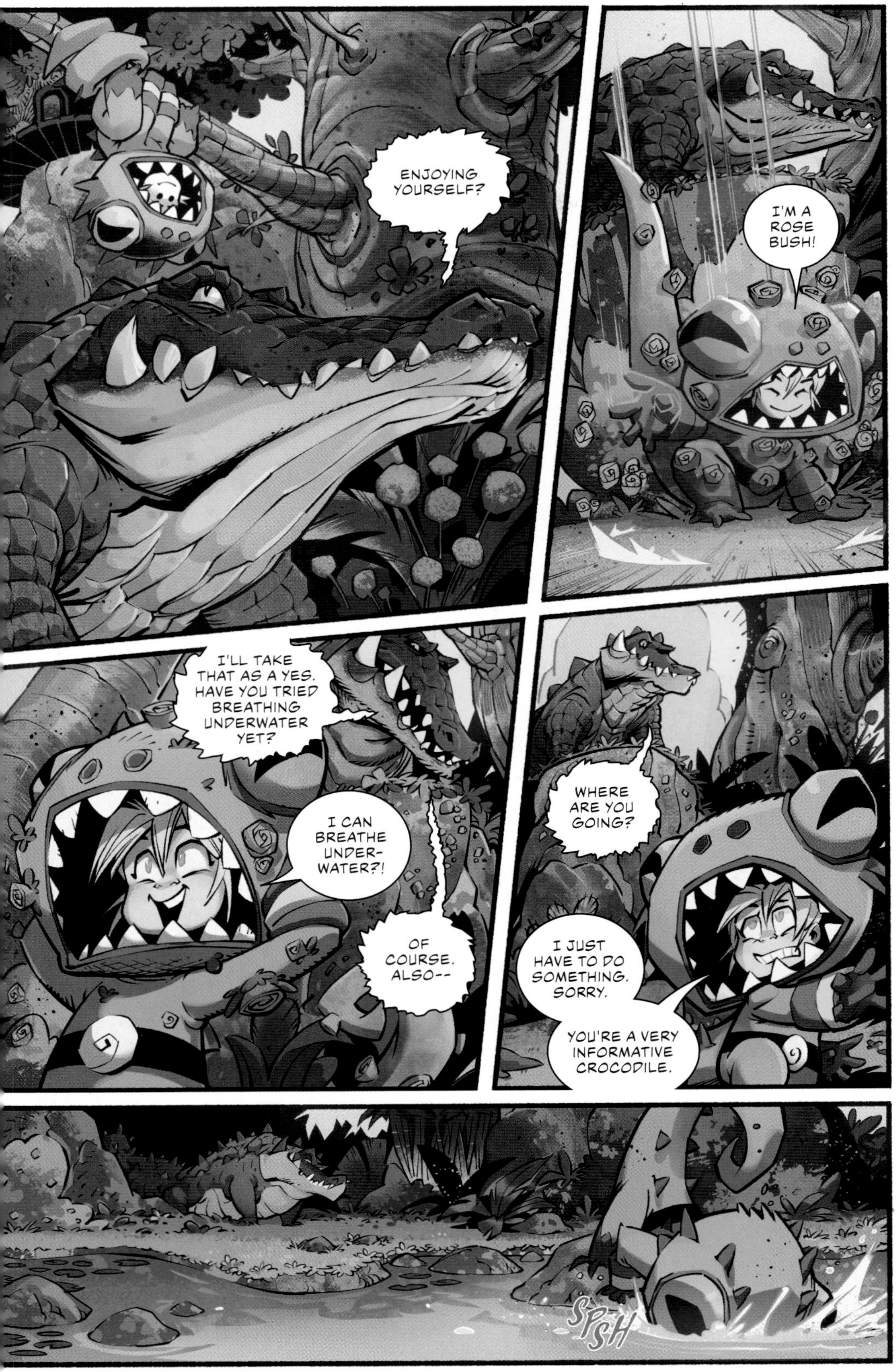

ENJOYING YOURSELF?
I'M A ROSE BUSH!
I'LL TAKE THAT AS A YES. HAVE YOU TRIED BREATHING UNDERWATER YET?
I CAN BREATHE UNDER-WATER?!
OF COURSE. ALSO--
WHERE ARE YOU GOING?
I JUST HAVE TO DO SOMETHING. SORRY.
YOU'RE A VERY INFORMATIVE CROCODILE.
SPSH

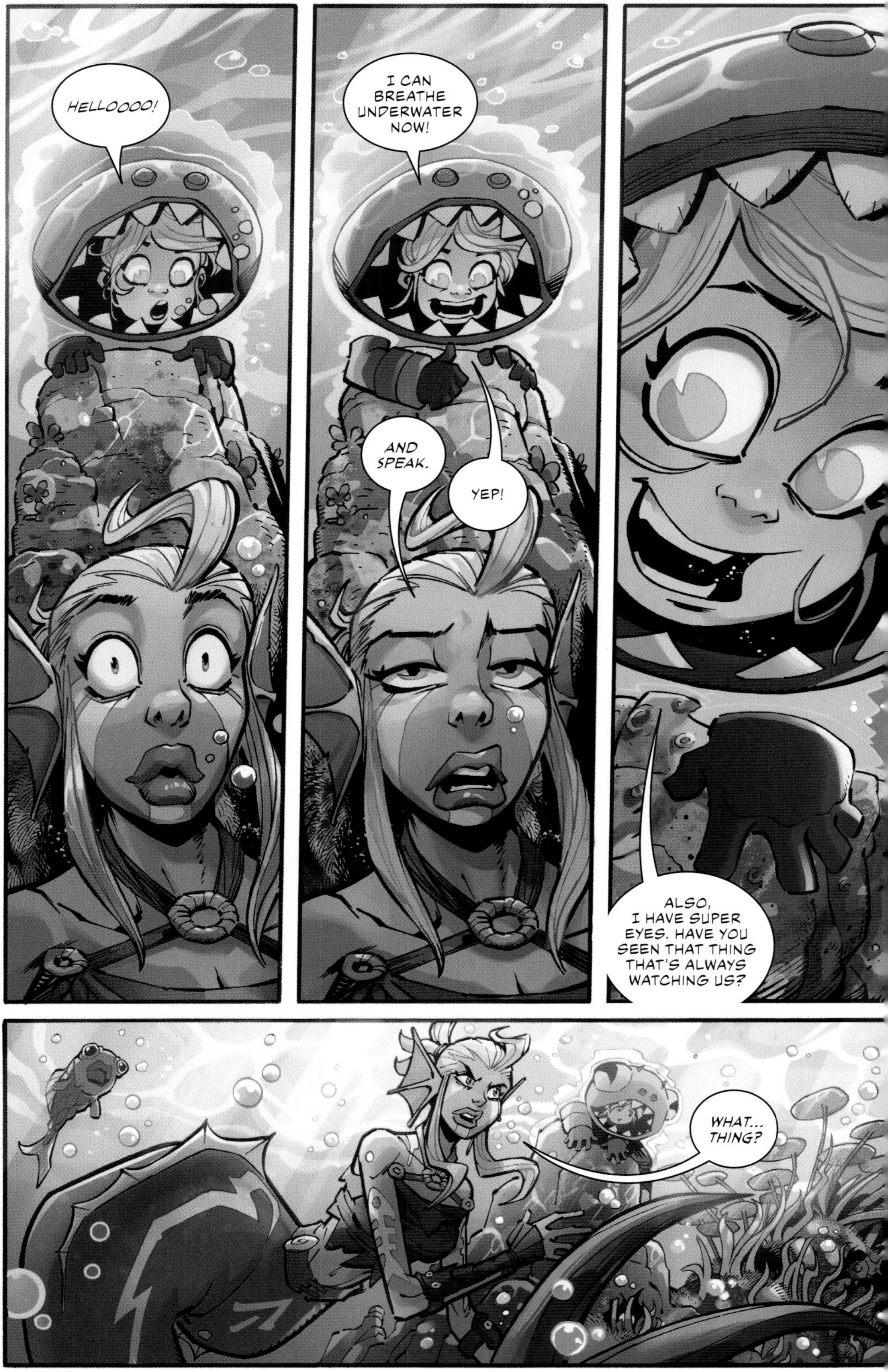
HELLOOOO!
I CAN BREATHE UNDERWATER NOW!
AND SPEAK.
YEP!
ALSO, I HAVE SUPER EYES. HAVE YOU SEEN THAT THING THAT'S ALWAYS WATCHING US?
WHAT... THING?

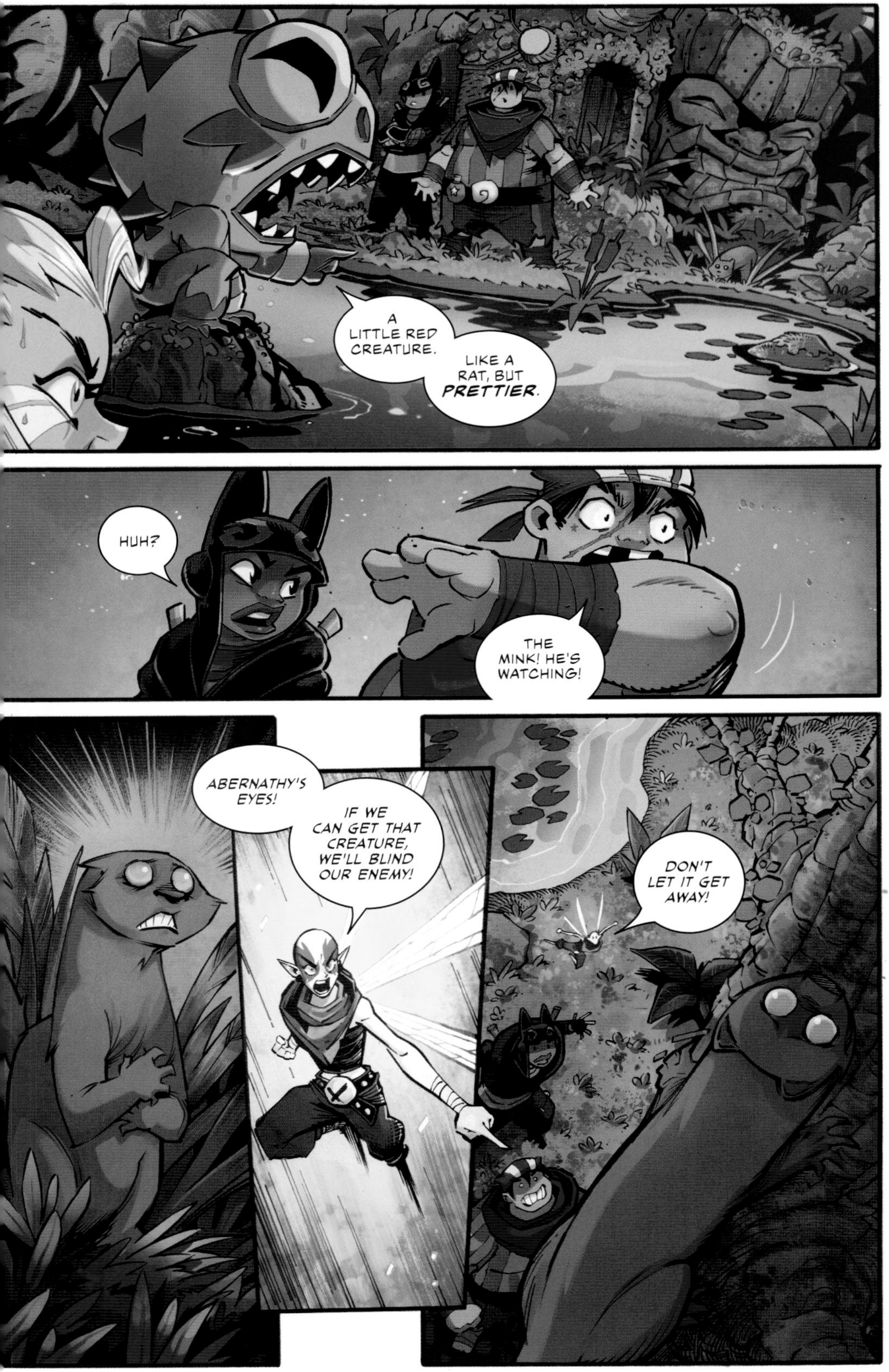
A LITTLE RED CREATURE.
LIKE A RAT, BUT *PRETTIER*.
HUH?
THE MINK! HE'S WATCHING!
ABERNATHY'S EYES!
IF WE CAN GET THAT CREATURE, WE'LL BLIND OUR ENEMY!
DON'T LET IT GET AWAY!

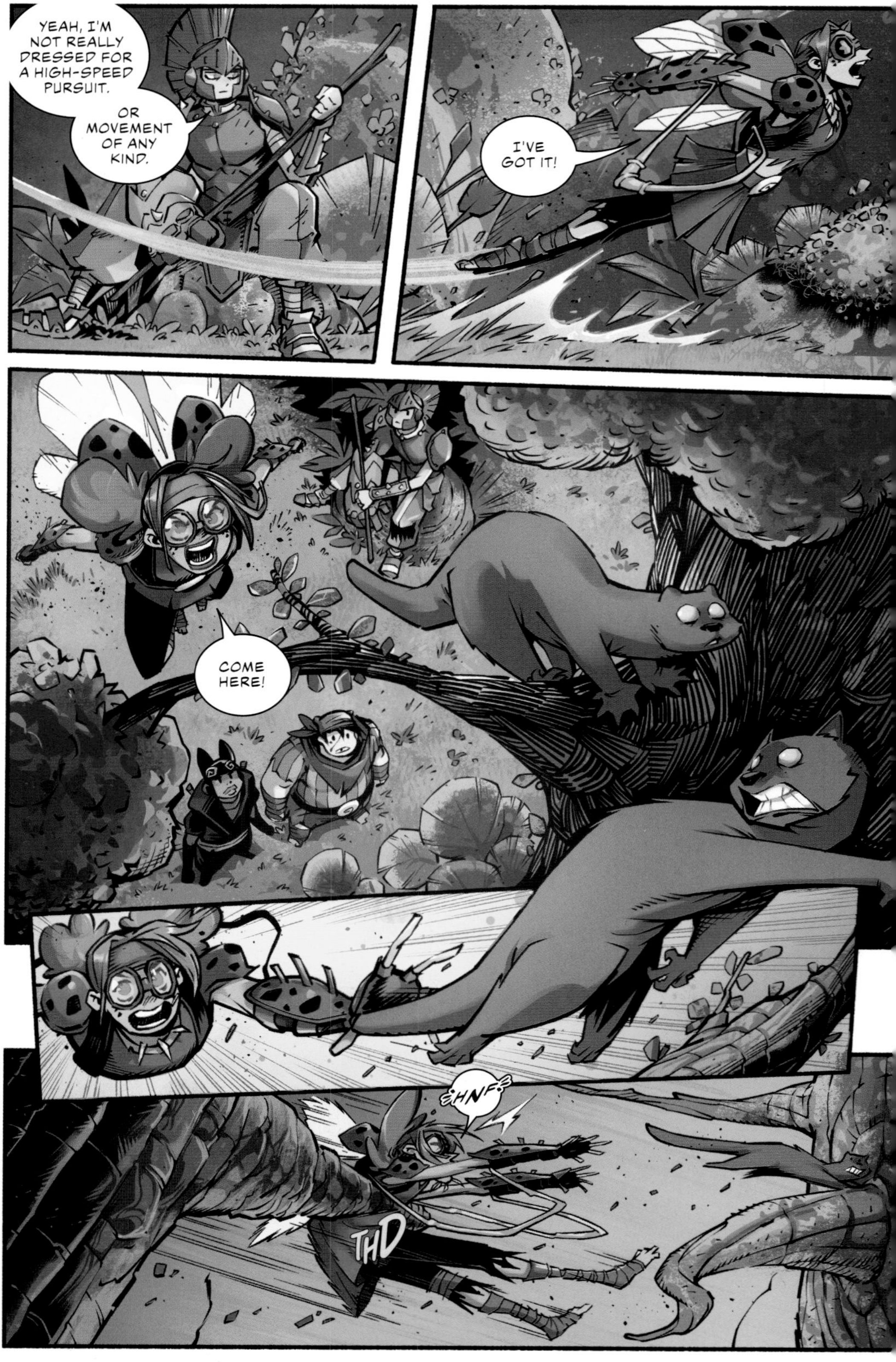
YEAH, I'M NOT REALLY DRESSED FOR A HIGH-SPEED PURSUIT.
OR MOVEMENT OF ANY KIND.
I'VE GOT IT!
COME HERE!
HNF
THD

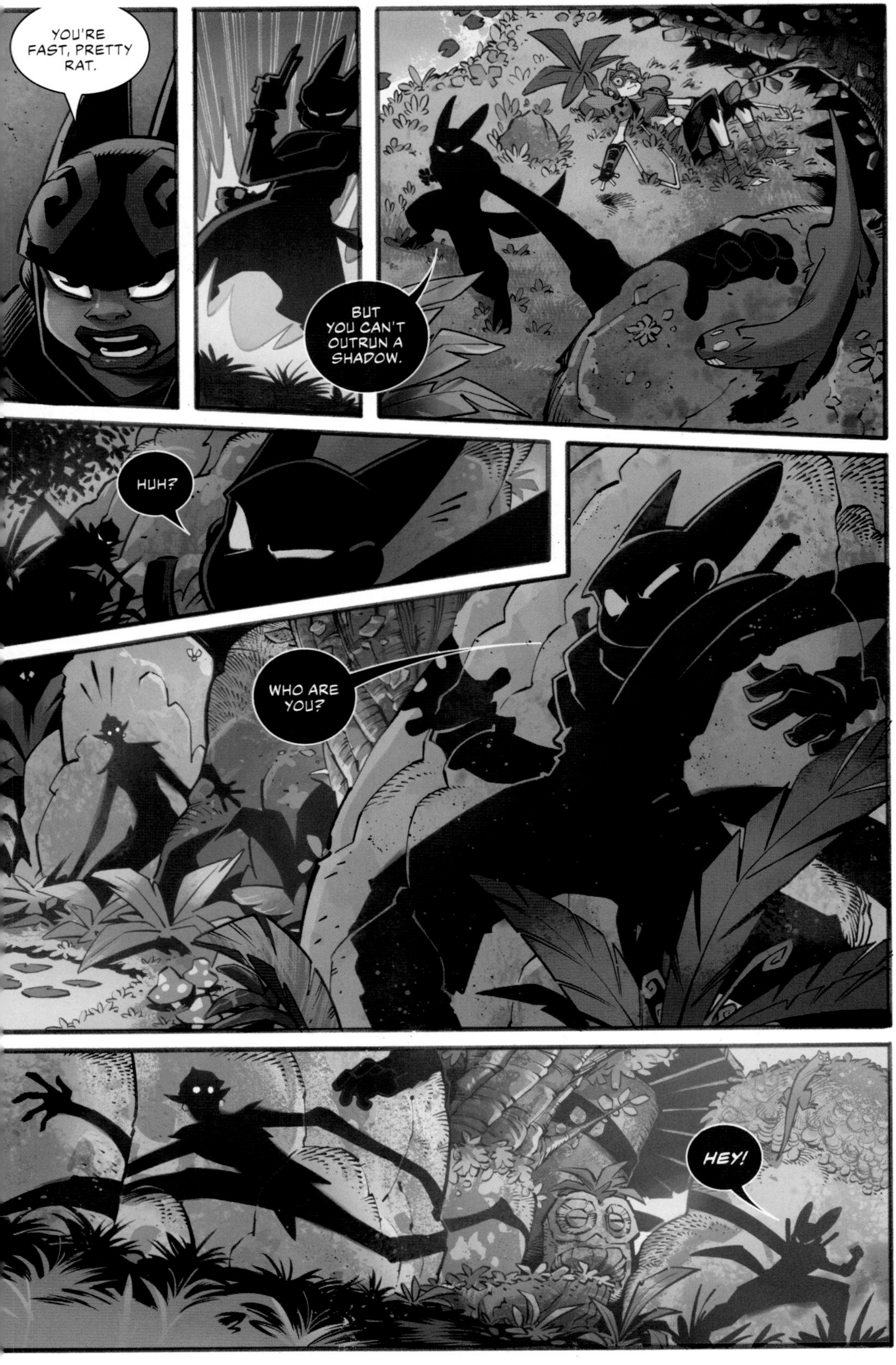
YOU'RE FAST, PRETTY RAT.
BUT YOU CAN'T OUTRUN A SHADOW.
HUH?
WHO ARE YOU?
HEY!

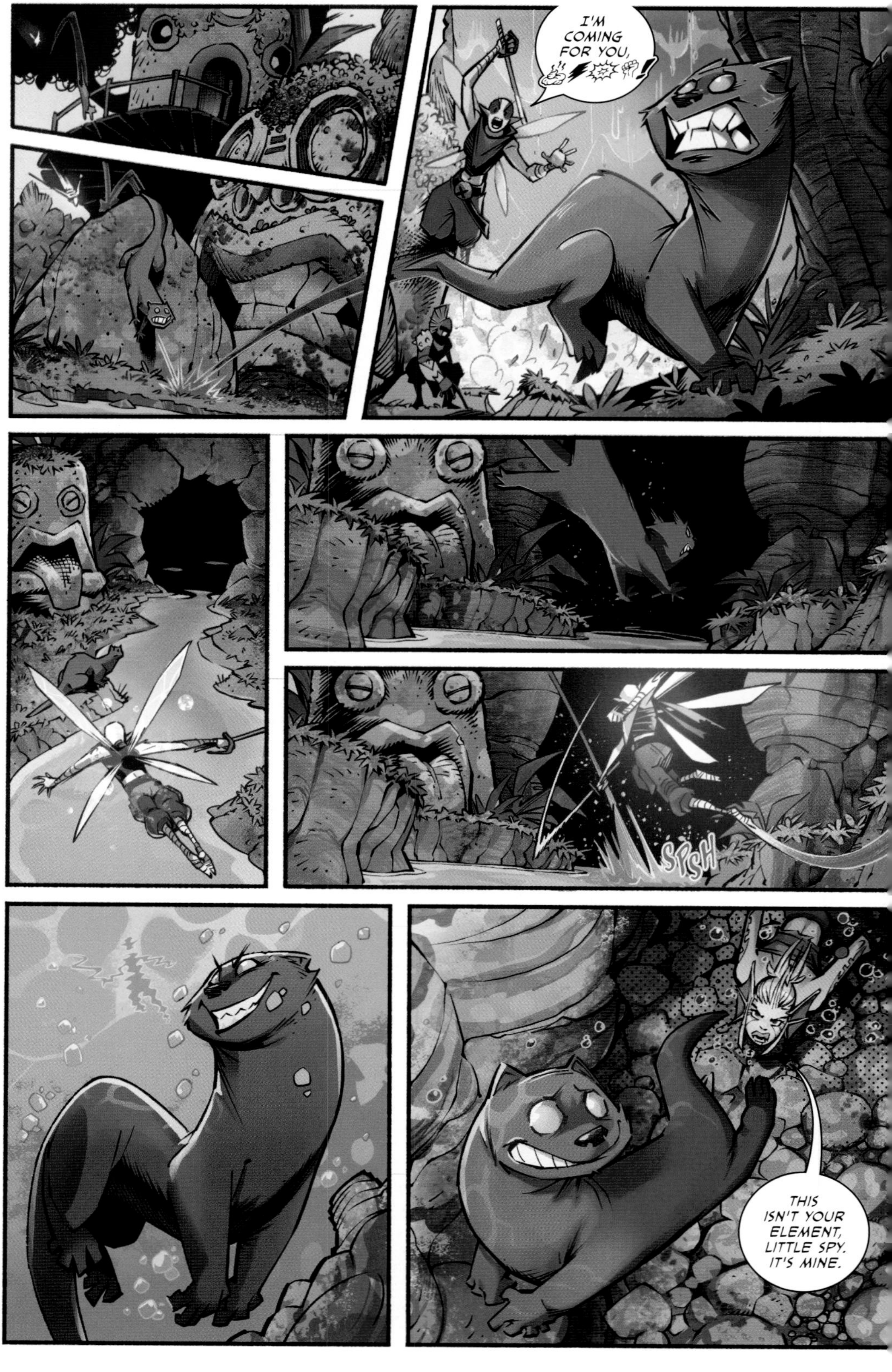
I'M COMING FOR YOU,
SPSH
THIS ISN'T YOUR ELEMENT, LITTLE SPY. IT'S MINE.

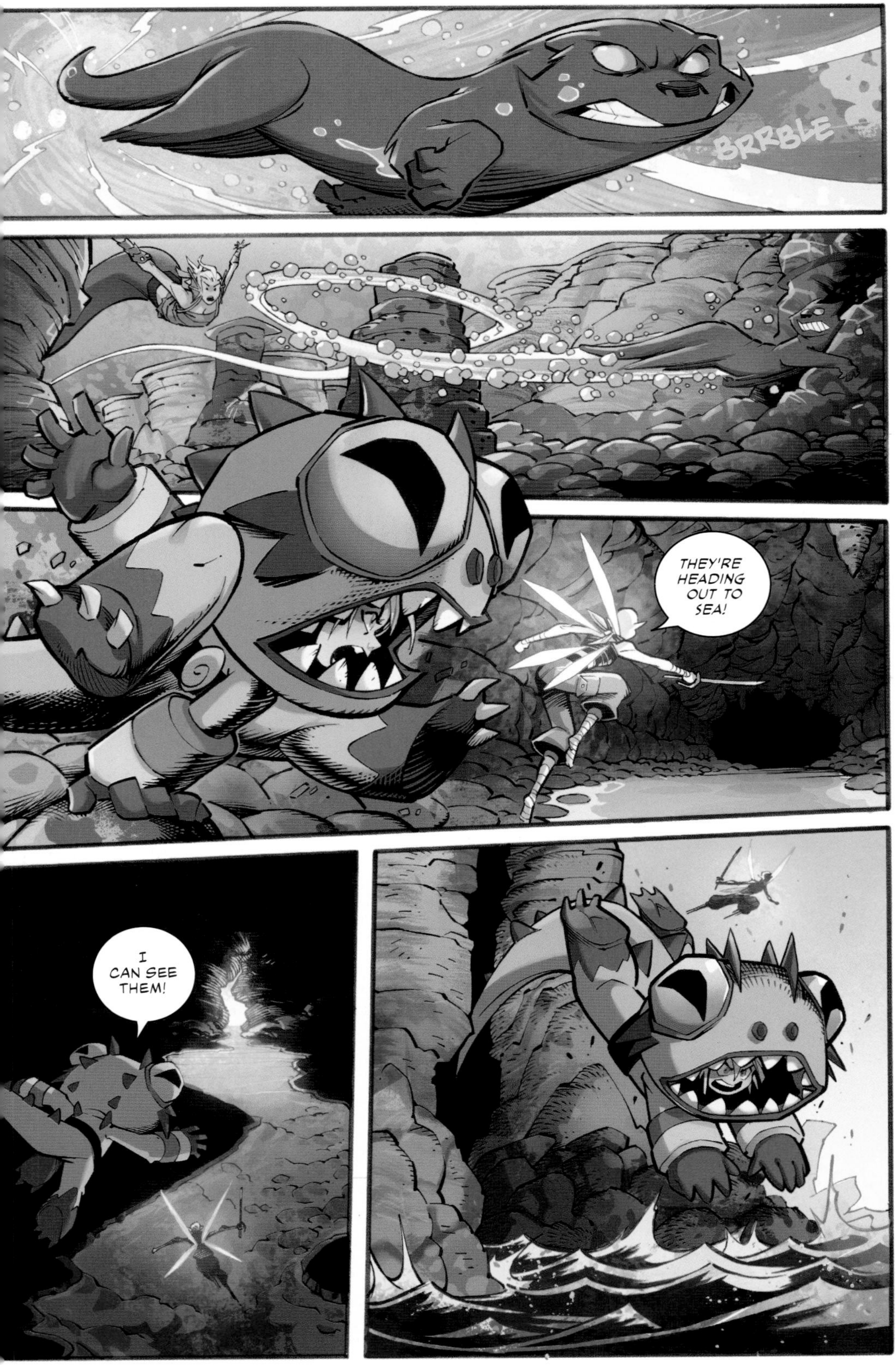
BRRBLE
THEY'RE HEADING OUT TO SEA!
I CAN SEE THEM!

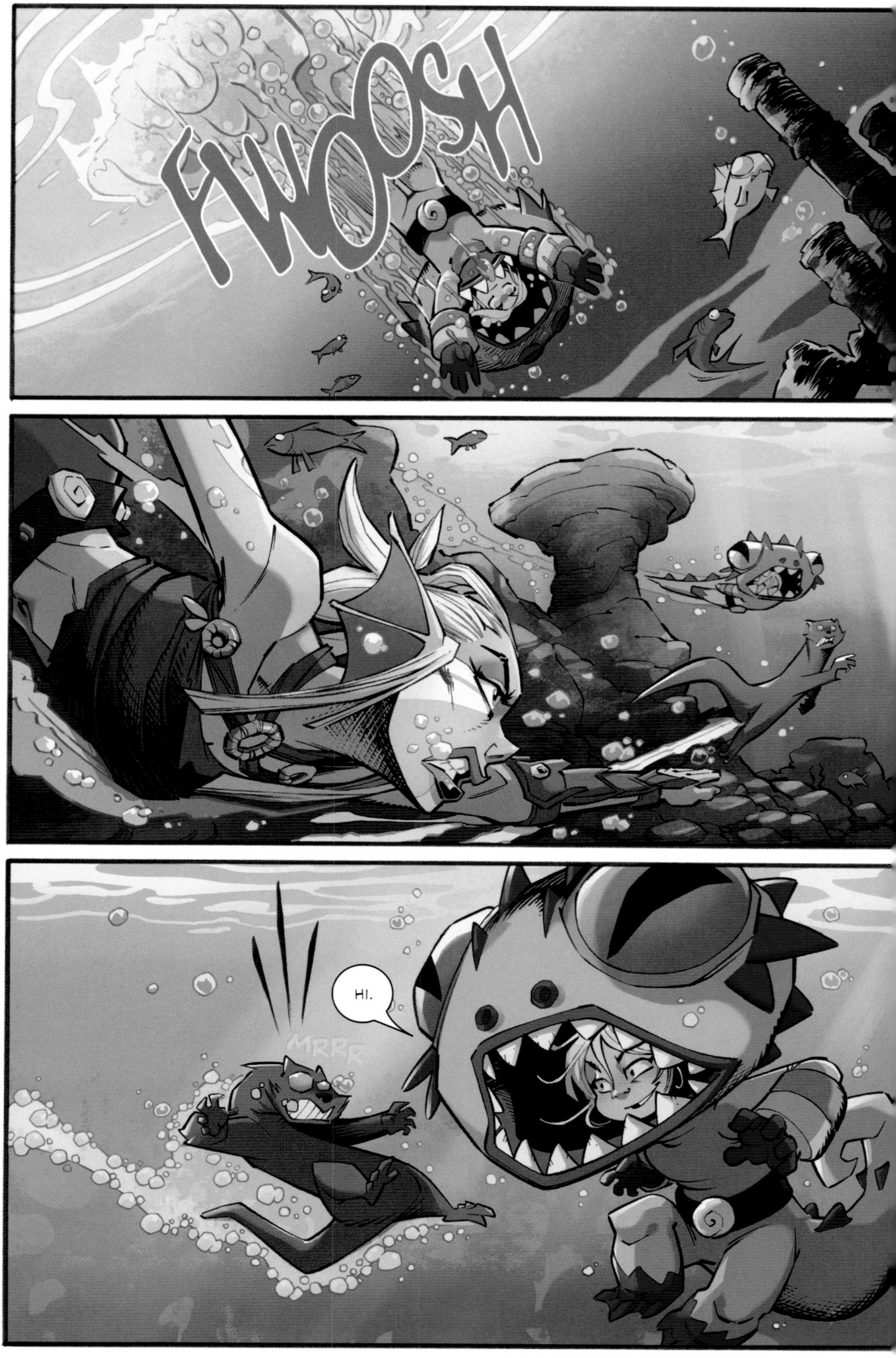
FWOOSH
HI.
MRRR

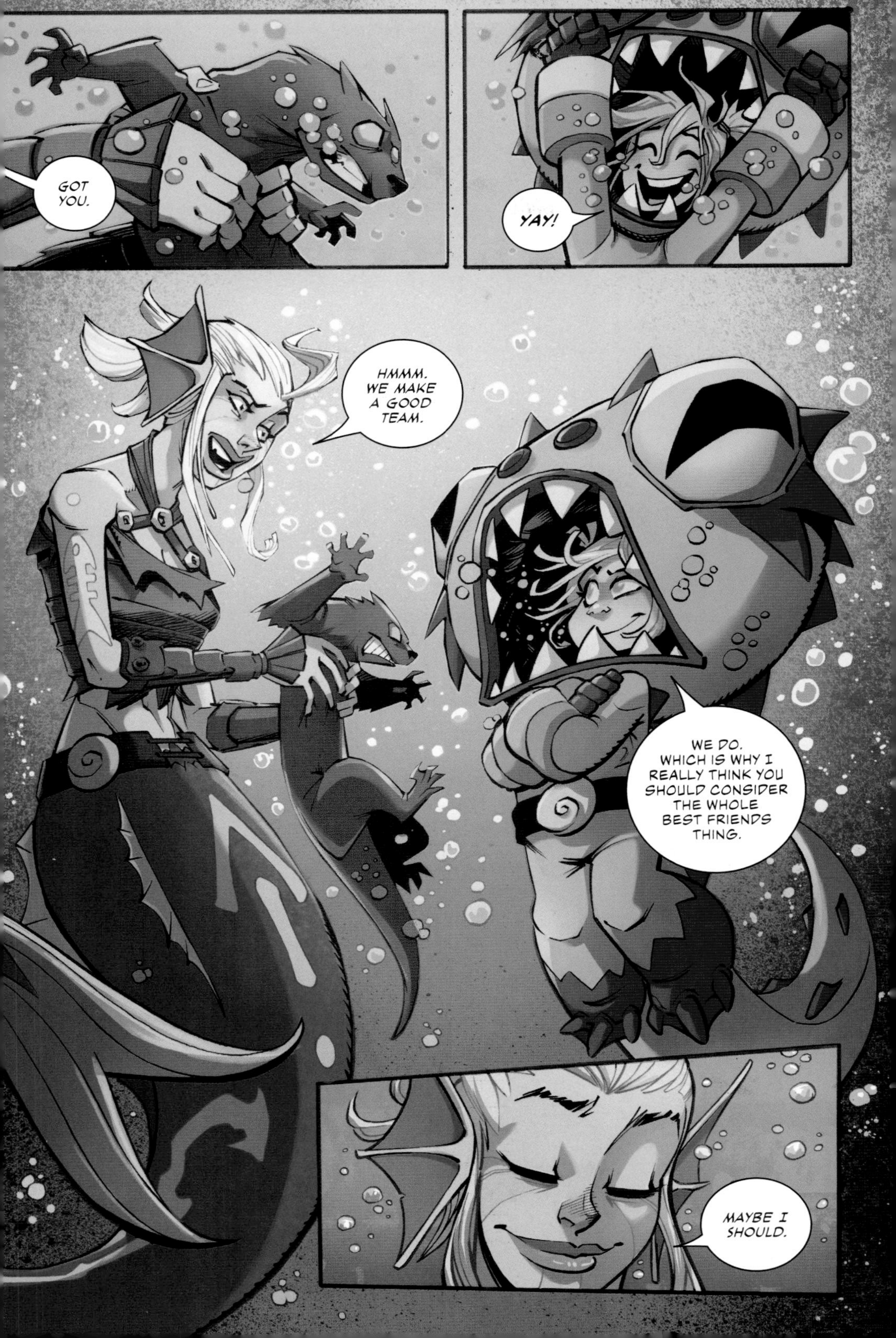
GOT YOU.
YAY!
HMMM. WE MAKE A GOOD TEAM.
WE DO. WHICH IS WHY I REALLY THINK YOU SHOULD CONSIDER THE WHOLE BEST FRIENDS THING.
MAYBE I SHOULD.

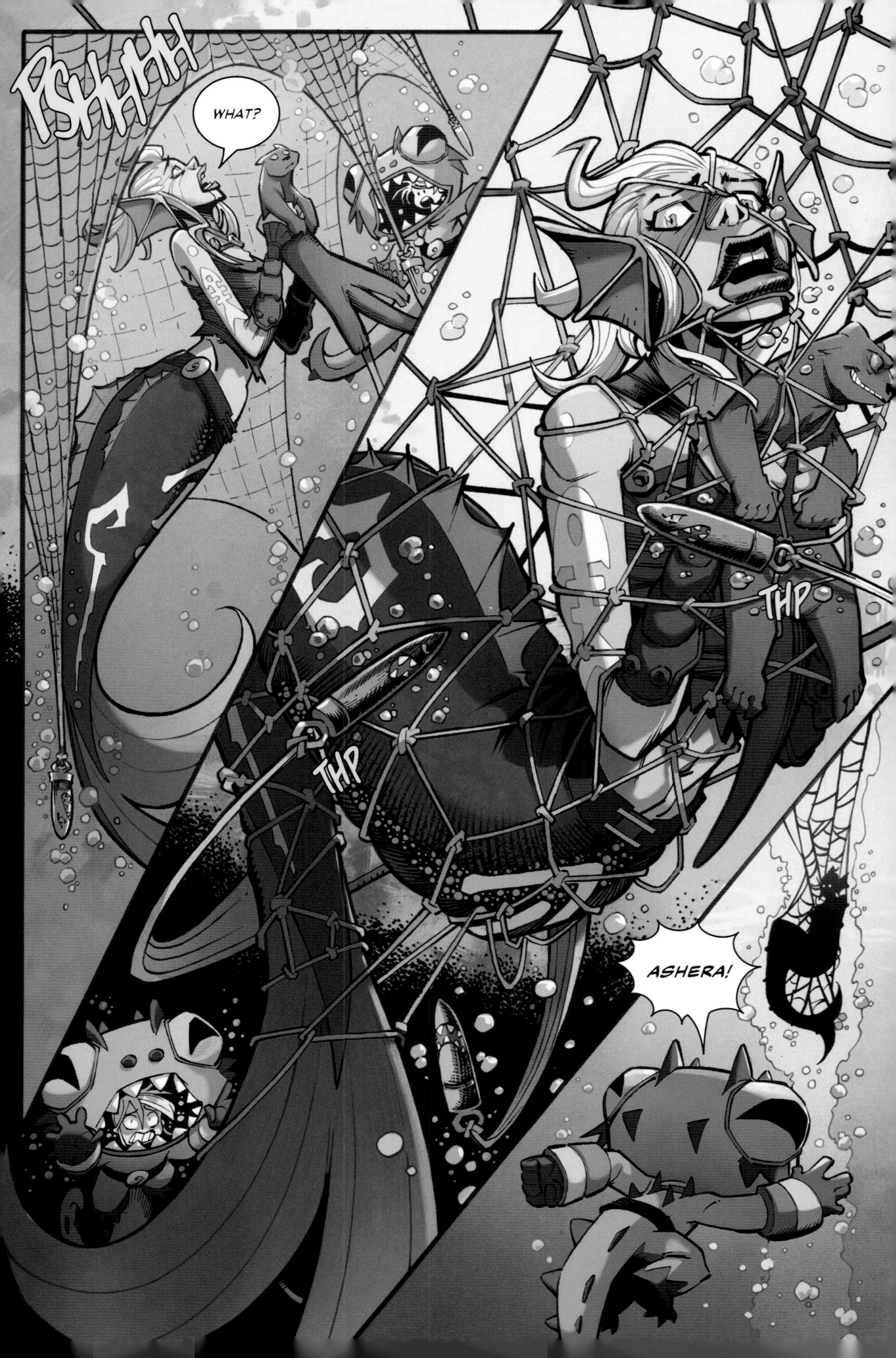
PSHHHH
WHAT?
THP
THP
ASHERA!

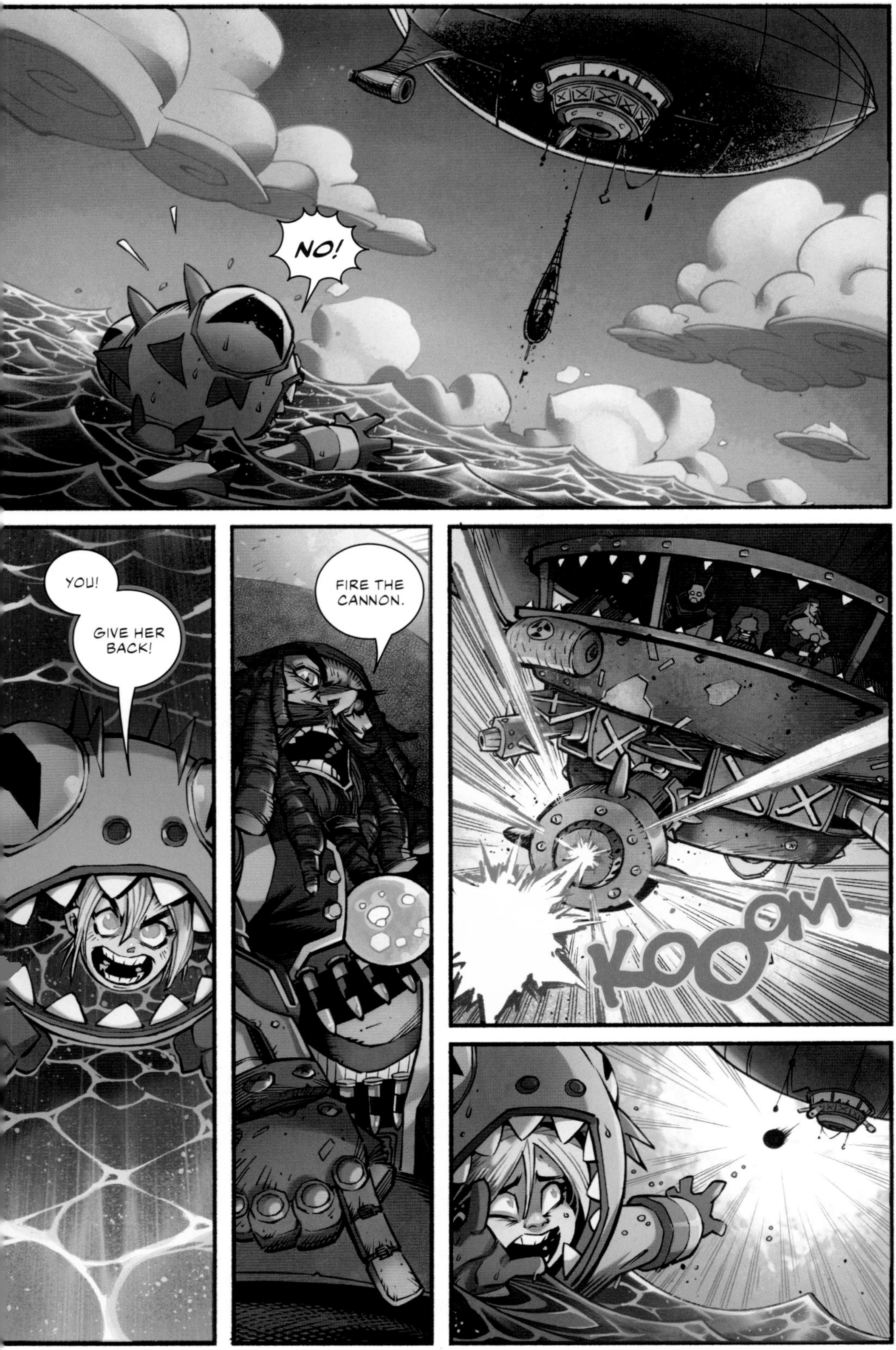
NO!
YOU!
GIVE HER BACK!
FIRE THE CANNON.
KOOOOM

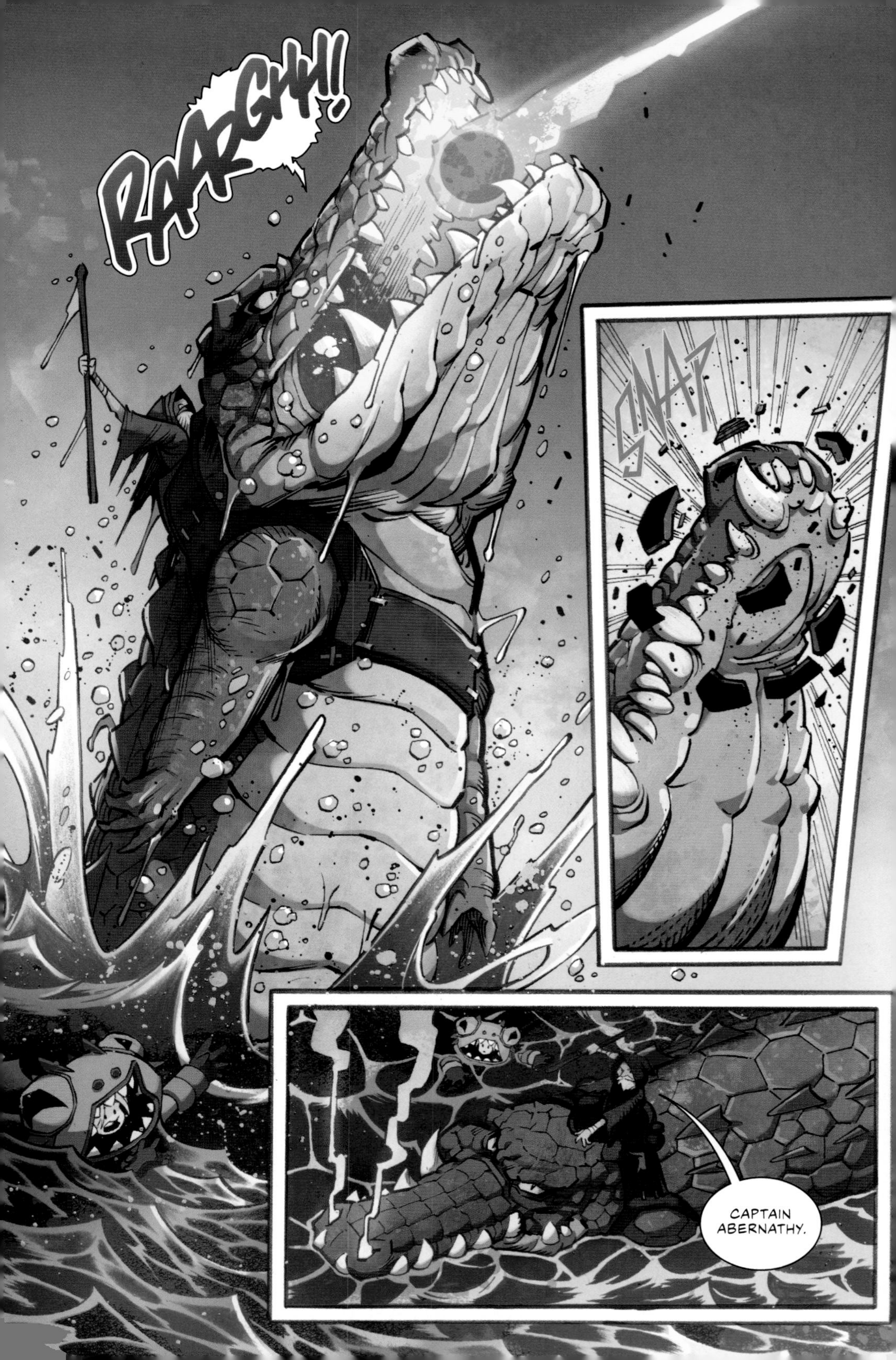
RAARGHH!!
SNAP
CAPTAIN ABERNATHY.

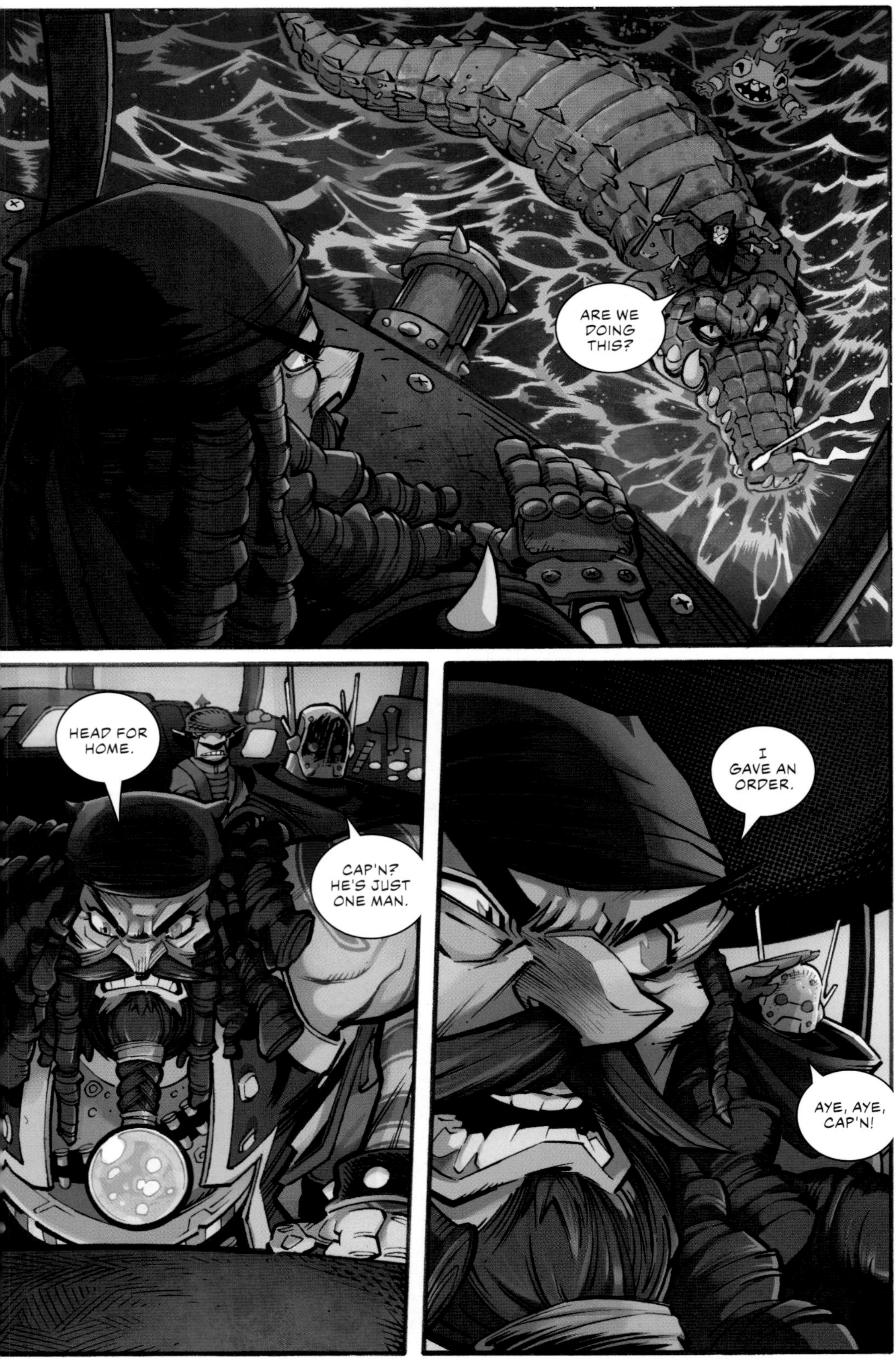
ARE WE DOING THIS?
HEAD FOR HOME.
CAP'N? HE'S JUST ONE MAN.
I GAVE AN ORDER.
AYE, AYE, CAP'N!

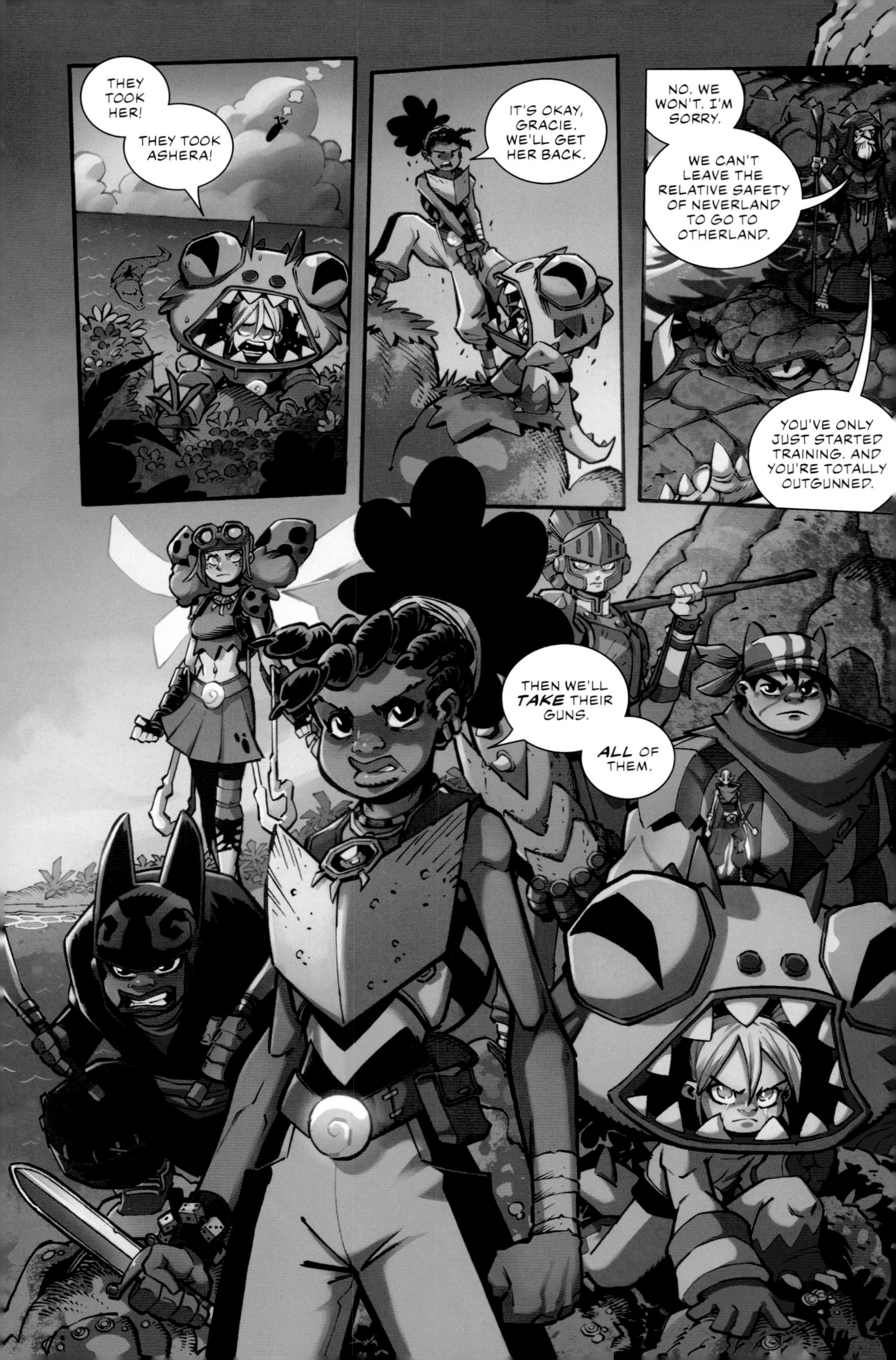
THEY TOOK HER!
THEY TOOK ASHERA!
IT'S OKAY, GRACIE. WE'LL GET HER BACK.
NO. WE WON'T. I'M SORRY.
WE CAN'T LEAVE THE RELATIVE SAFETY OF NEVERLAND TO GO TO OTHERLAND.
YOU'VE ONLY JUST STARTED TRAINING. AND YOU'RE TOTALLY OUTGUNNED.
THEN WE'LL TAKE THEIR GUNS.
ALL OF THEM.

CHAPTER
FIVE

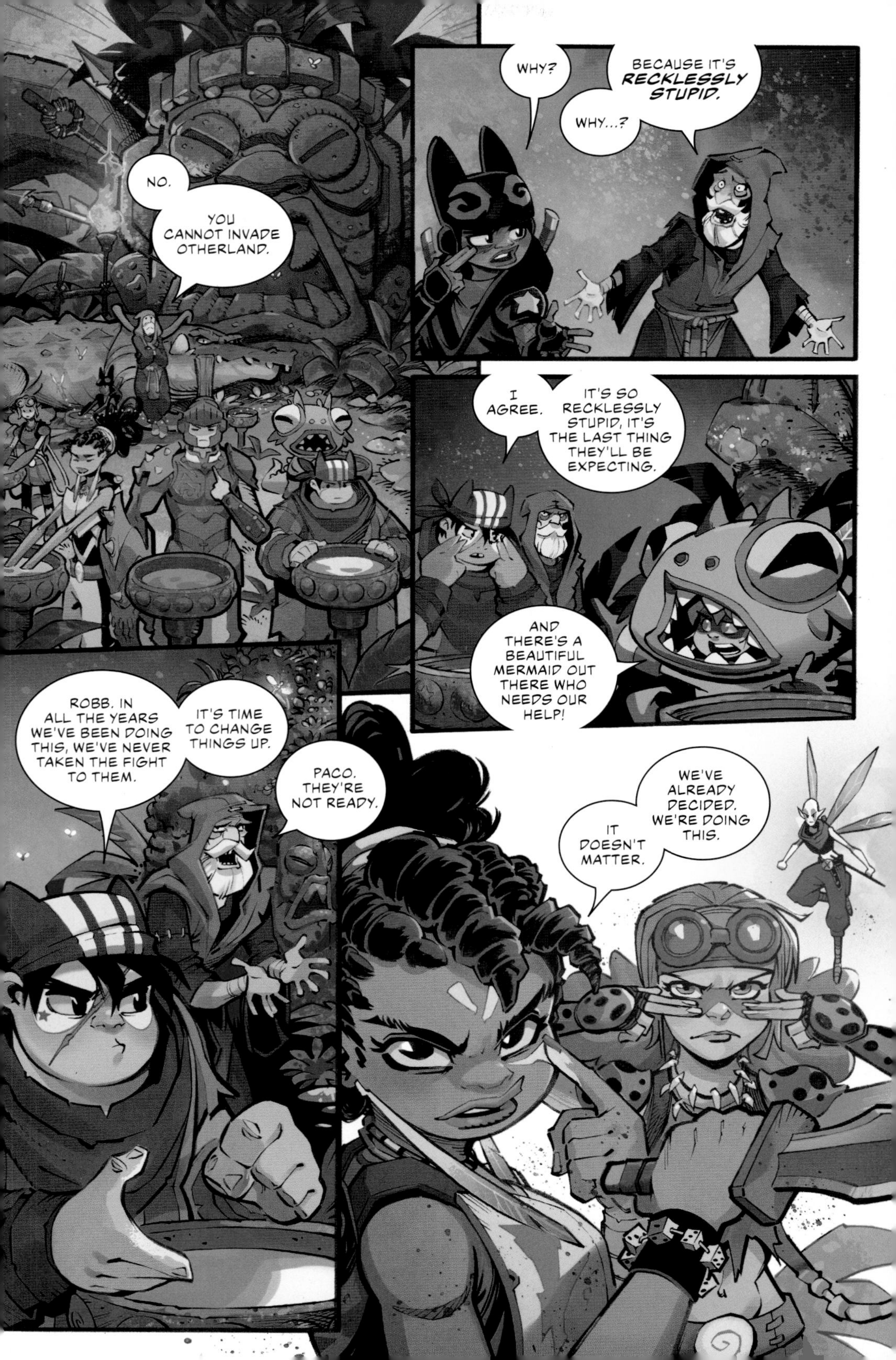
NO.
YOU CANNOT INVADE OTHERLAND.
WHY?
BECAUSE IT'S RECKLESSLY STUPID.
WHY...?
I AGREE.
IT'S SO RECKLESSLY STUPID, IT'S THE LAST THING THEY'LL BE EXPECTING.
AND THERE'S A BEAUTIFUL MERMAID OUT THERE WHO NEEDS OUR HELP!
ROBB. IN ALL THE YEARS WE'VE BEEN DOING THIS, WE'VE NEVER TAKEN THE FIGHT TO THEM.
IT'S TIME TO CHANGE THINGS UP.
PACO. THEY'RE NOT READY.
IT DOESN'T MATTER.
WE'VE ALREADY DECIDED. WE'RE DOING THIS.

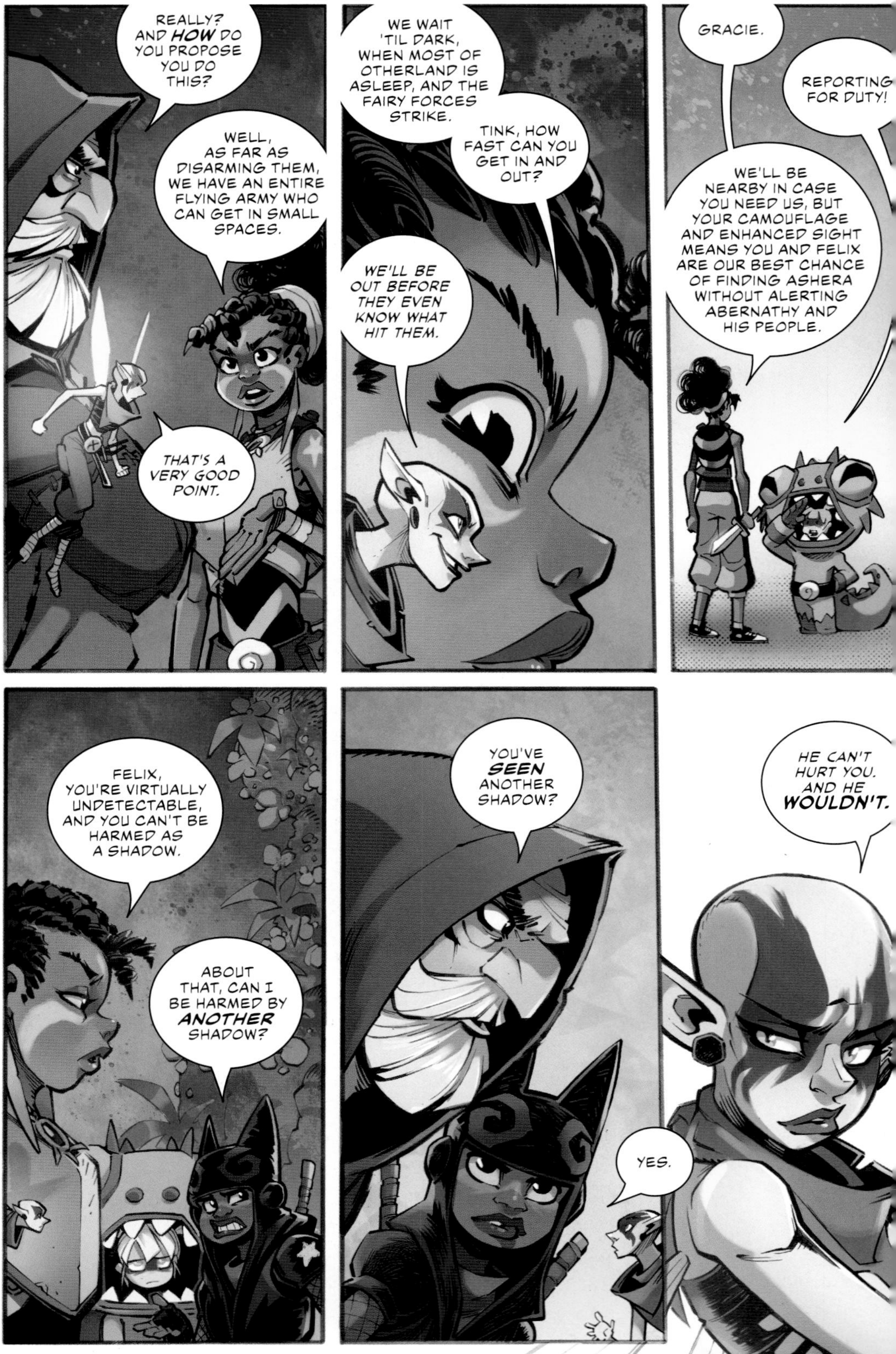
REALLY? AND HOW DO YOU PROPOSE YOU DO THIS?
WELL, AS FAR AS DISARMING THEM, WE HAVE AN ENTIRE FLYING ARMY WHO CAN GET IN SMALL SPACES.
THAT'S A VERY GOOD POINT.
WE WAIT 'TIL DARK, WHEN MOST OF OTHERLAND IS ASLEEP, AND THE FAIRY FORCES STRIKE.
TINK, HOW FAST CAN YOU GET IN AND OUT?
WE'LL BE OUT BEFORE THEY EVEN KNOW WHAT HIT THEM.
GRACIE.
REPORTING FOR DUTY!
WE'LL BE NEARBY IN CASE YOU NEED US, BUT YOUR CAMOUFLAGE AND ENHANCED SIGHT MEANS YOU AND FELIX ARE OUR BEST CHANCE OF FINDING ASHERA WITHOUT ALERTING ABERNATHY AND HIS PEOPLE.
FELIX, YOU'RE VIRTUALLY UNDETECTABLE, AND YOU CAN'T BE HARMED AS A SHADOW.
ABOUT THAT, CAN I BE HARMED BY ANOTHER SHADOW?
YOU'VE SEEN ANOTHER SHADOW?
YES.
HE CAN'T HURT YOU. AND HE WOULDN'T.

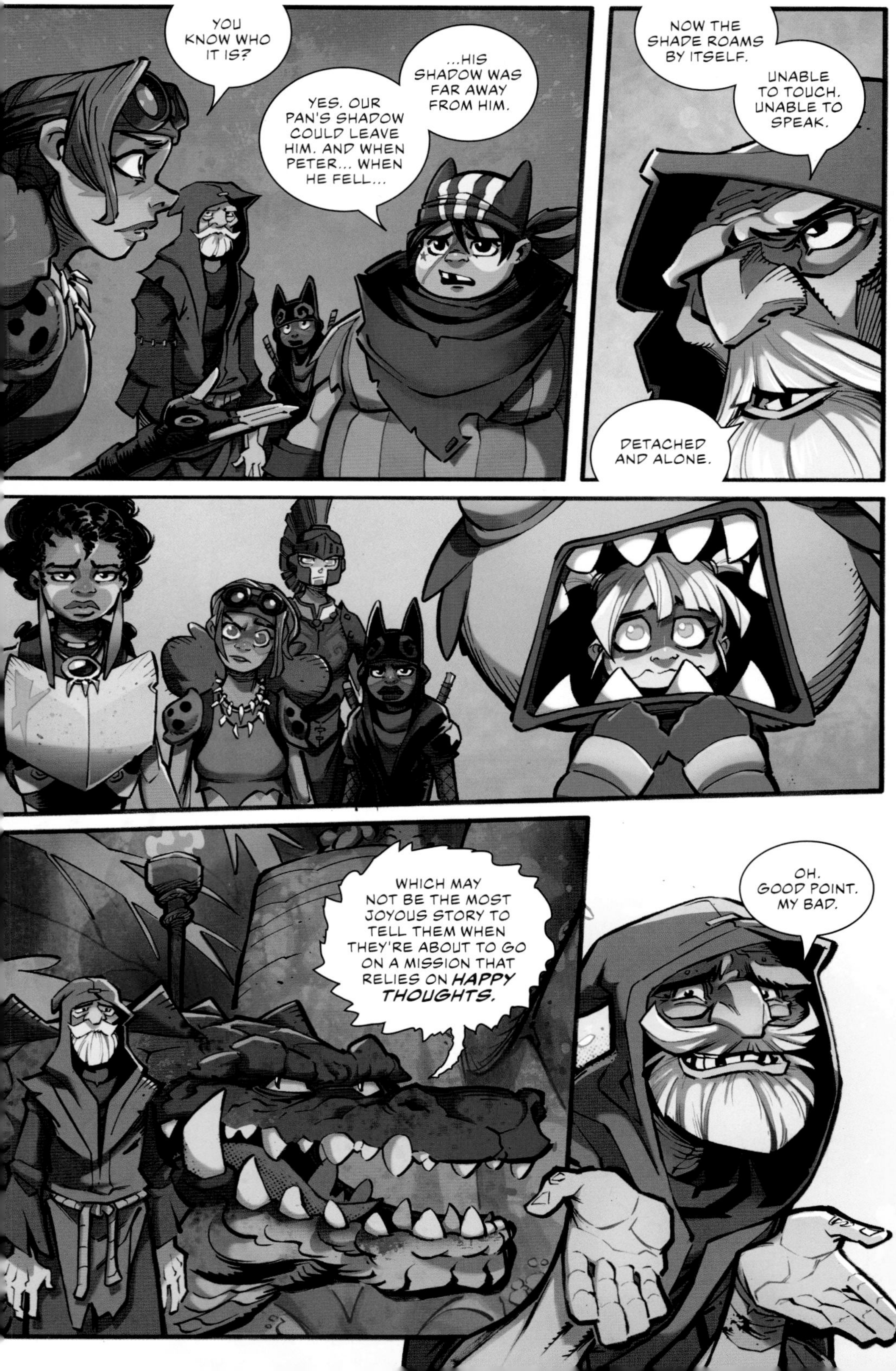
YOU KNOW WHO IT IS?
YES. OUR PAN'S SHADOW COULD LEAVE HIM. AND WHEN PETER... WHEN HE FELL...
...HIS SHADOW WAS FAR AWAY FROM HIM.
NOW THE SHADE ROAMS BY ITSELF.
UNABLE TO TOUCH. UNABLE TO SPEAK.
DETACHED AND ALONE.
WHICH MAY NOT BE THE MOST JOYOUS STORY TO TELL THEM WHEN THEY'RE ABOUT TO GO ON A MISSION THAT RELIES ON *HAPPY THOUGHTS.*
OH. GOOD POINT. MY BAD.

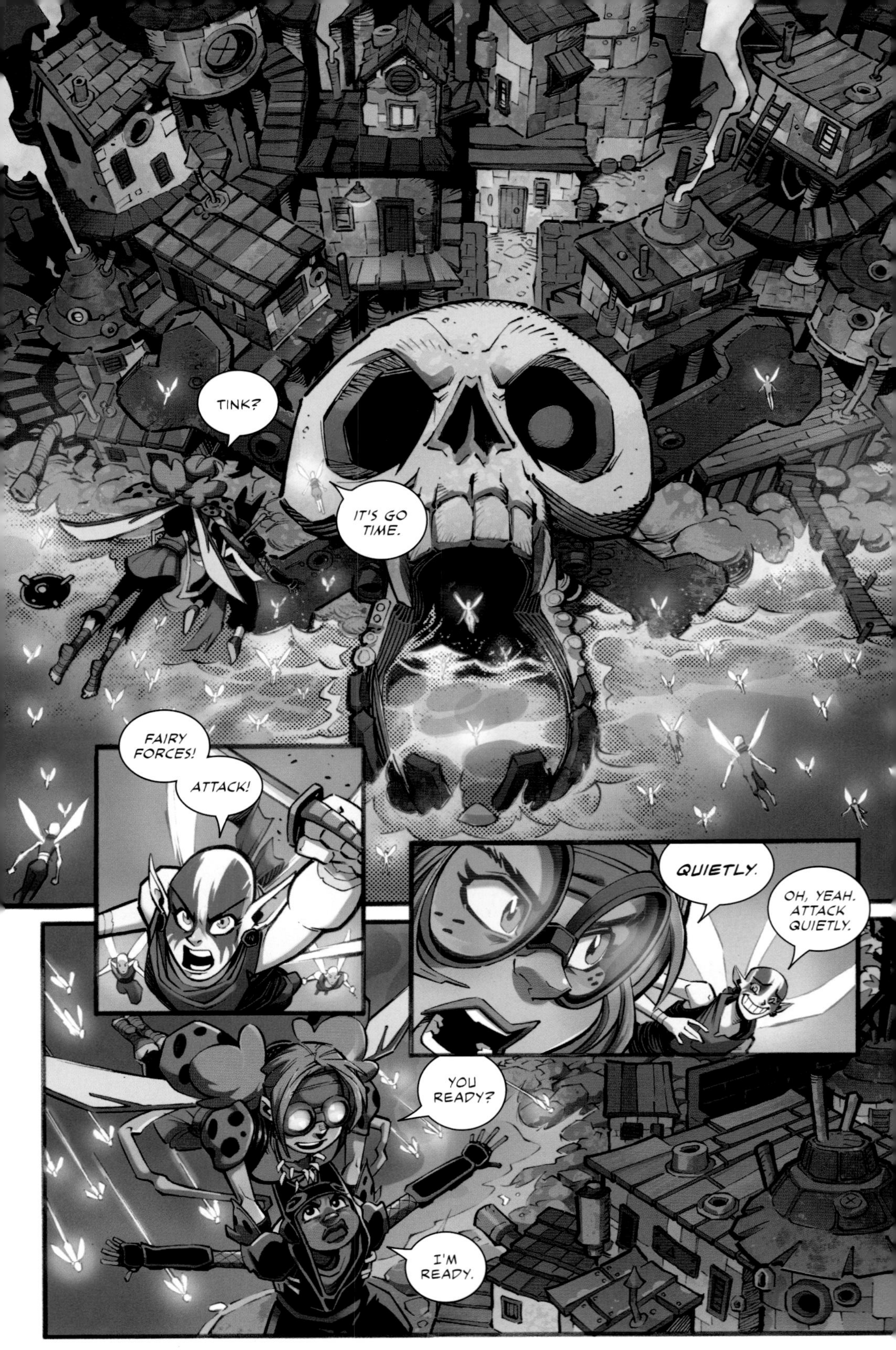
TINK?
IT'S GO TIME.
FAIRY FORCES!
ATTACK!
QUIETLY.
OH, YEAH. ATTACK QUIETLY.
YOU READY?
I'M READY.

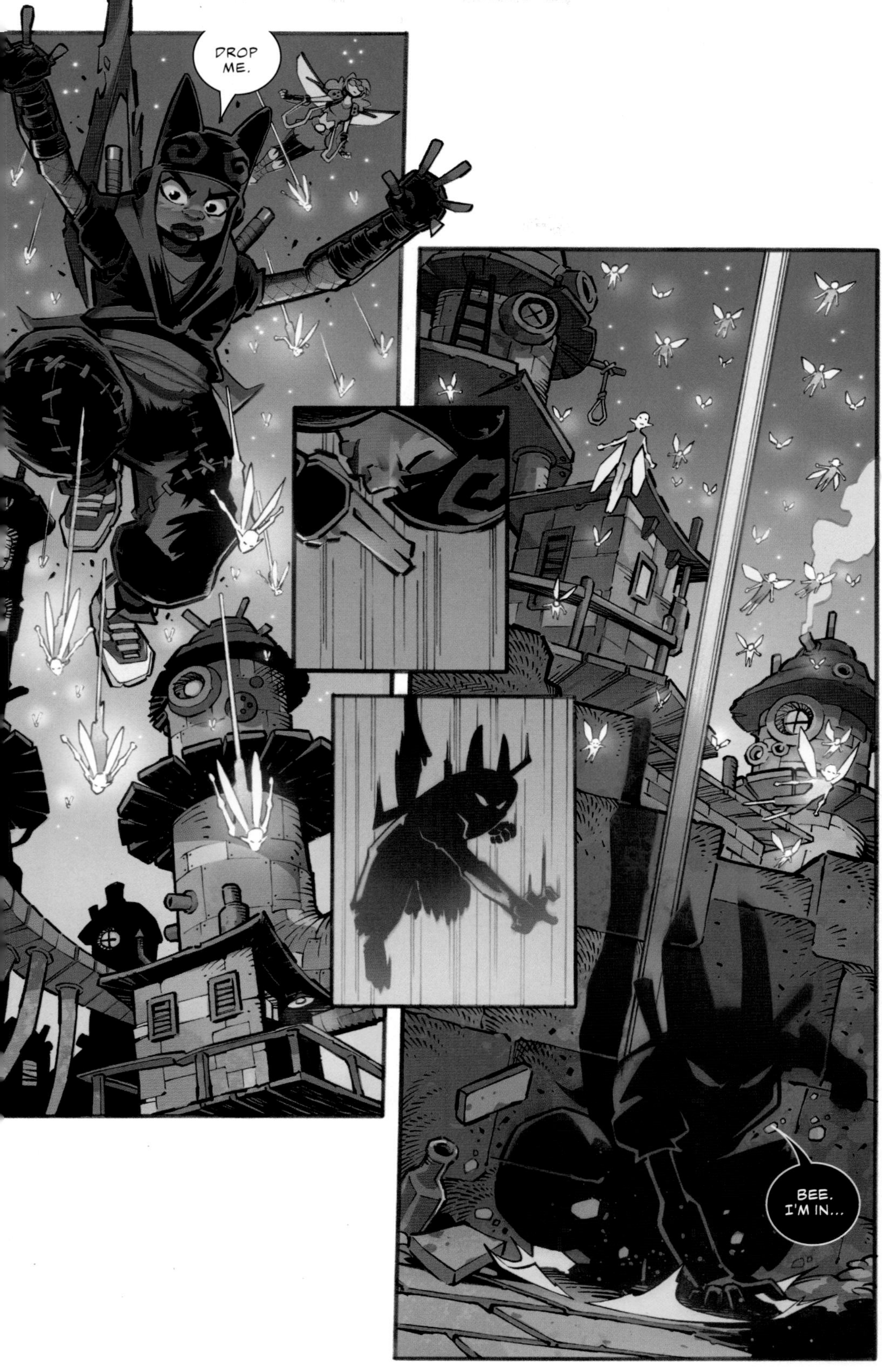
DROP ME.
BEE. I'M IN...

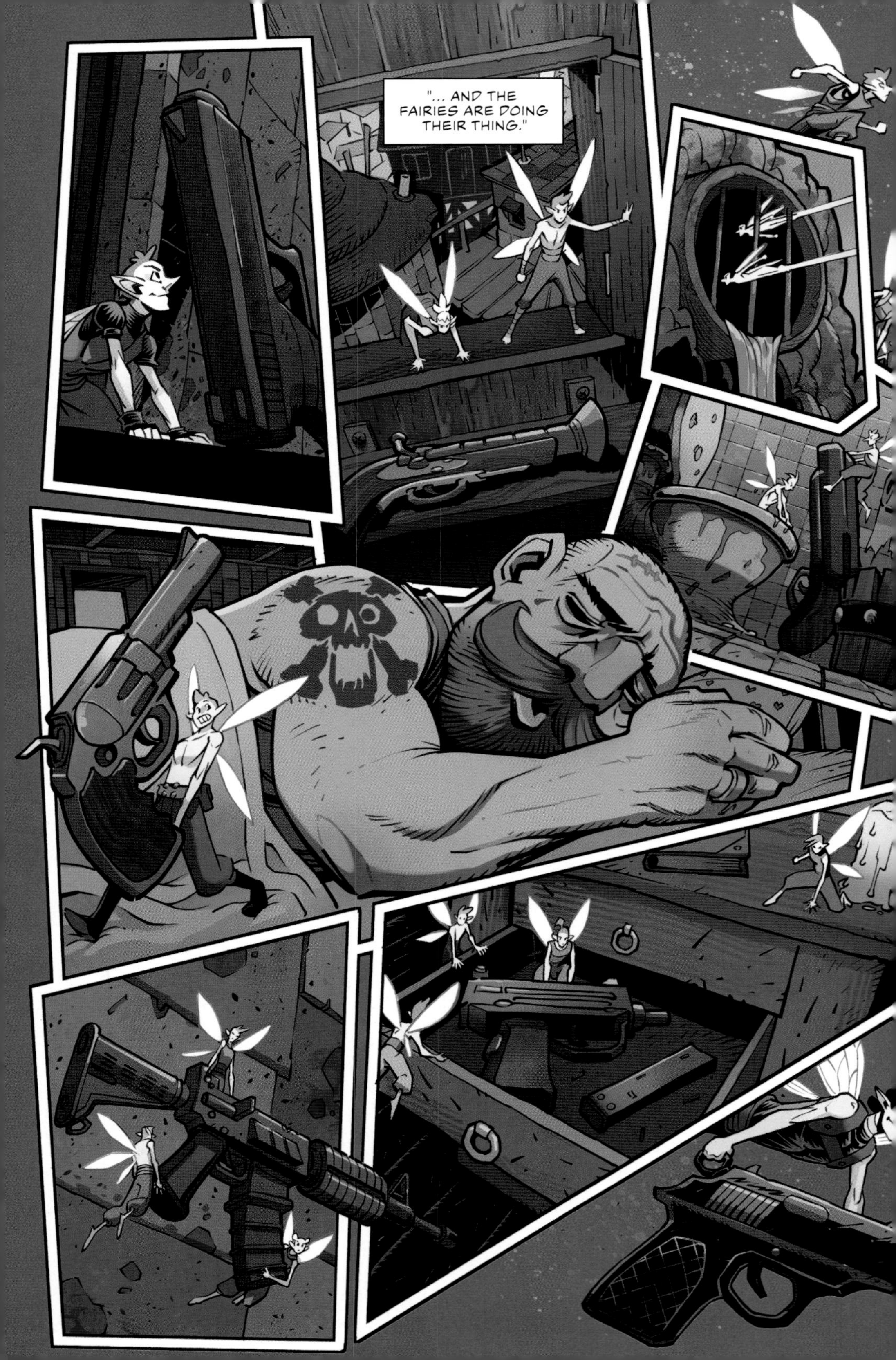
"... AND THE FAIRIES ARE DOING THEIR THING."

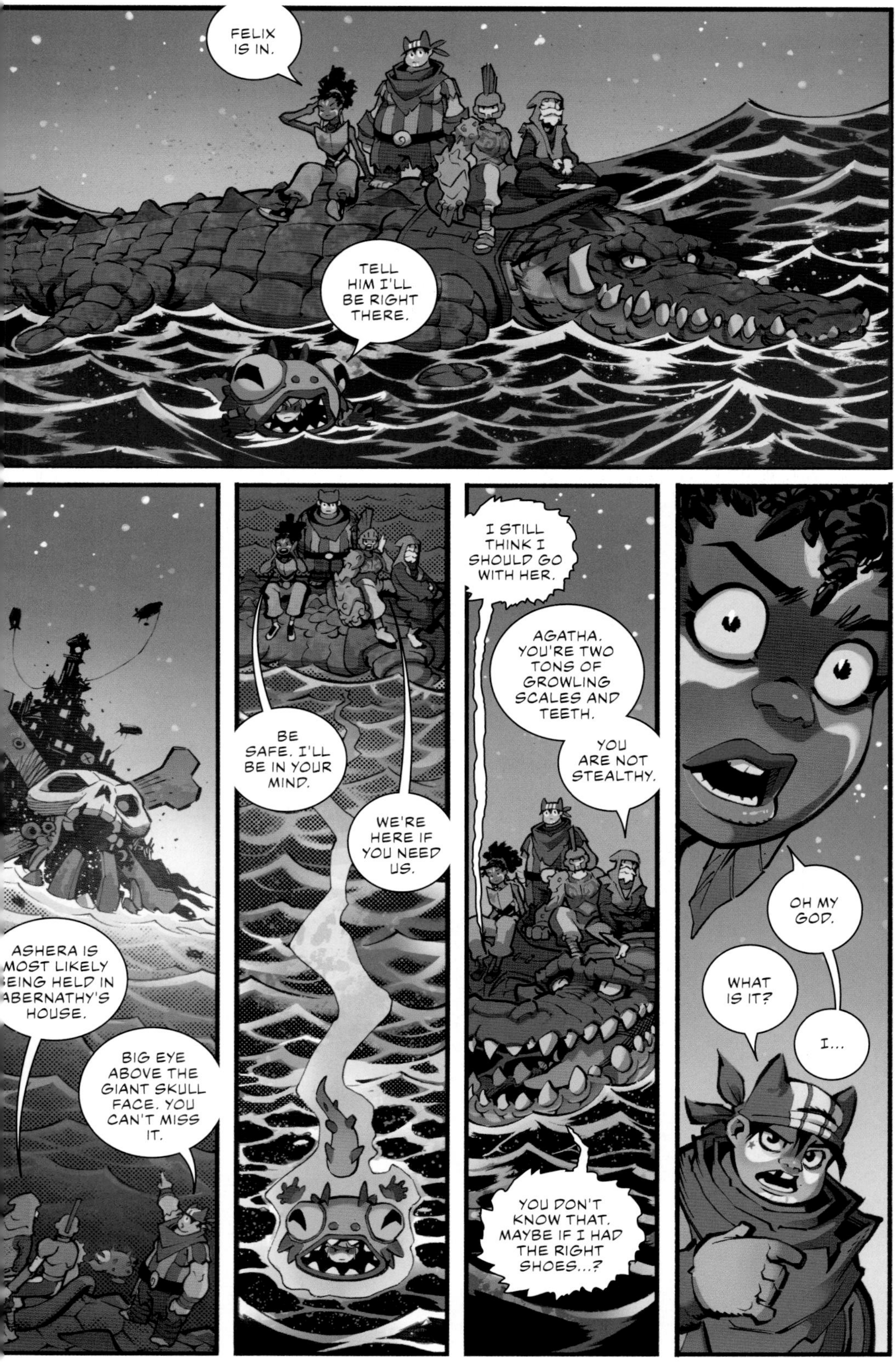
FELIX IS IN.
TELL HIM I'LL BE RIGHT THERE.
ASHERA IS MOST LIKELY BEING HELD IN ABERNATHY'S HOUSE.
BIG EYE ABOVE THE GIANT SKULL FACE. YOU CAN'T MISS IT.
BE SAFE. I'LL BE IN YOUR MIND.
WE'RE HERE IF YOU NEED US.
I STILL THINK I SHOULD GO WITH HER.
AGATHA. YOU'RE TWO TONS OF GROWLING SCALES AND TEETH.
YOU ARE NOT STEALTHY.
YOU DON'T KNOW THAT. MAYBE IF I HAD THE RIGHT SHOES...?
OH MY GOD.
WHAT IS IT?
I...

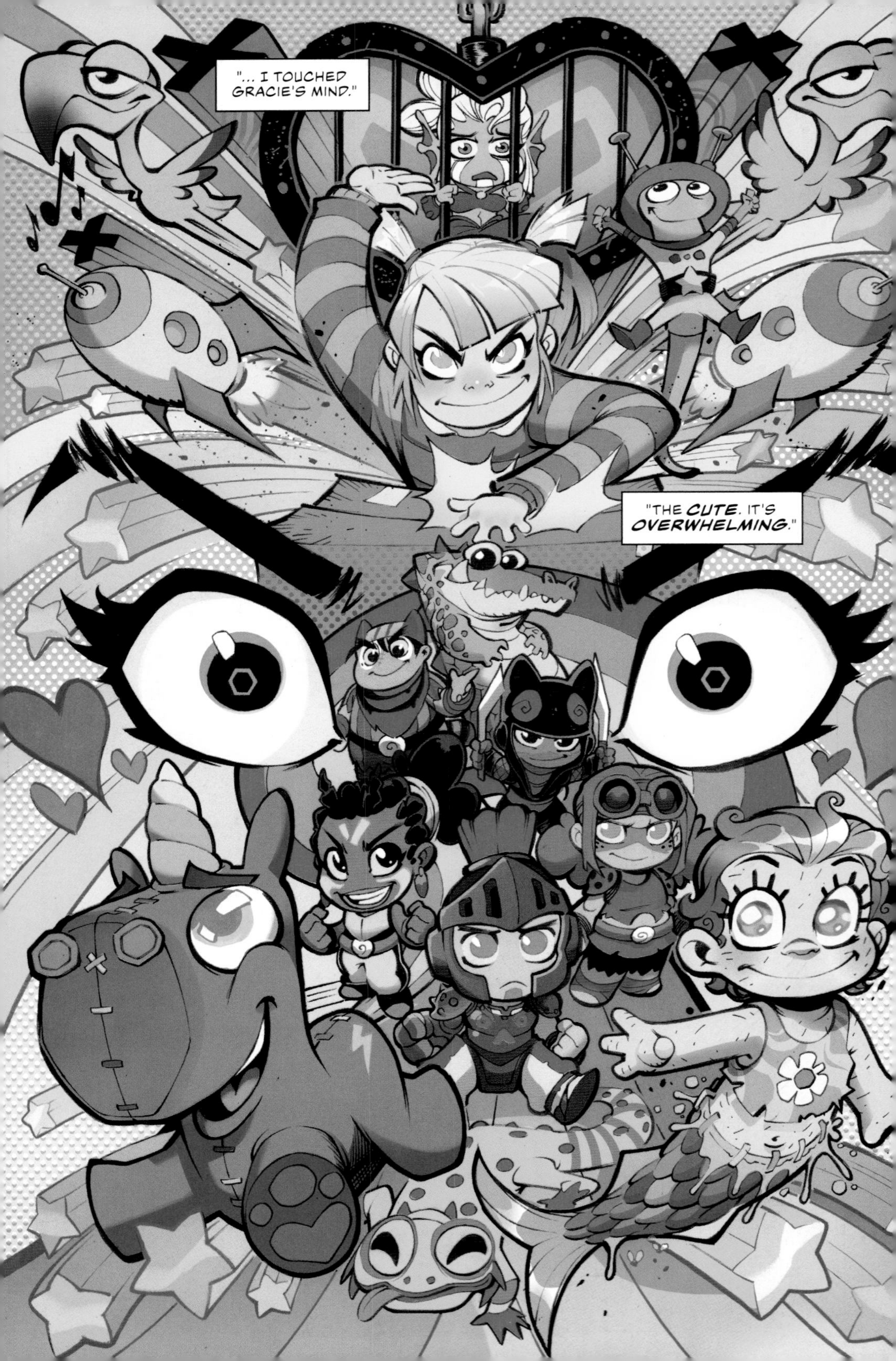
"... I TOUCHED GRACIE'S MIND."
"THE *CUTE*. IT'S *OVERWHELMING*."

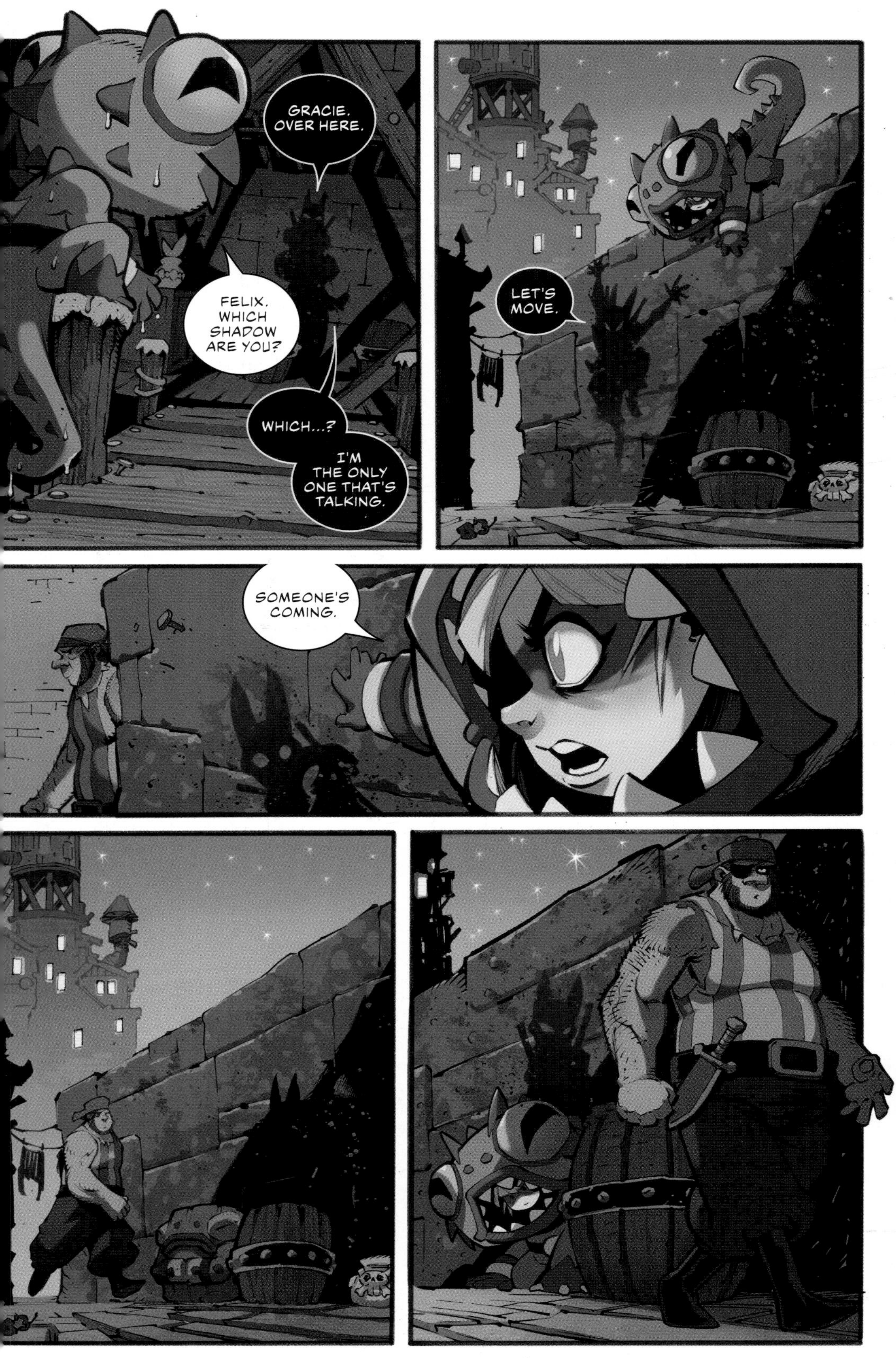
GRACIE. OVER HERE.
FELIX. WHICH SHADOW ARE YOU?
WHICH...?
I'M THE ONLY ONE THAT'S TALKING.
LET'S MOVE.
SOMEONE'S COMING.

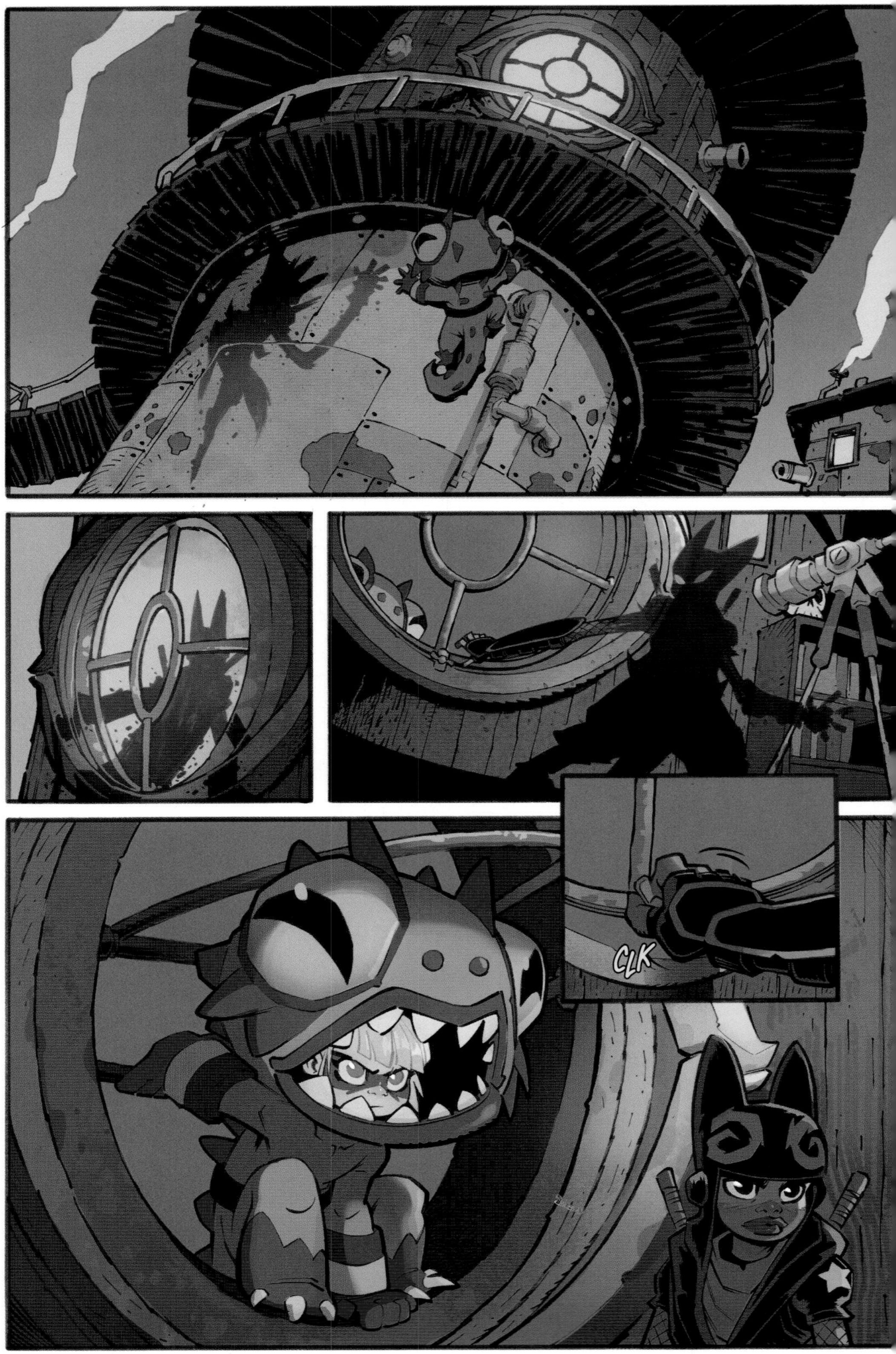
CLK

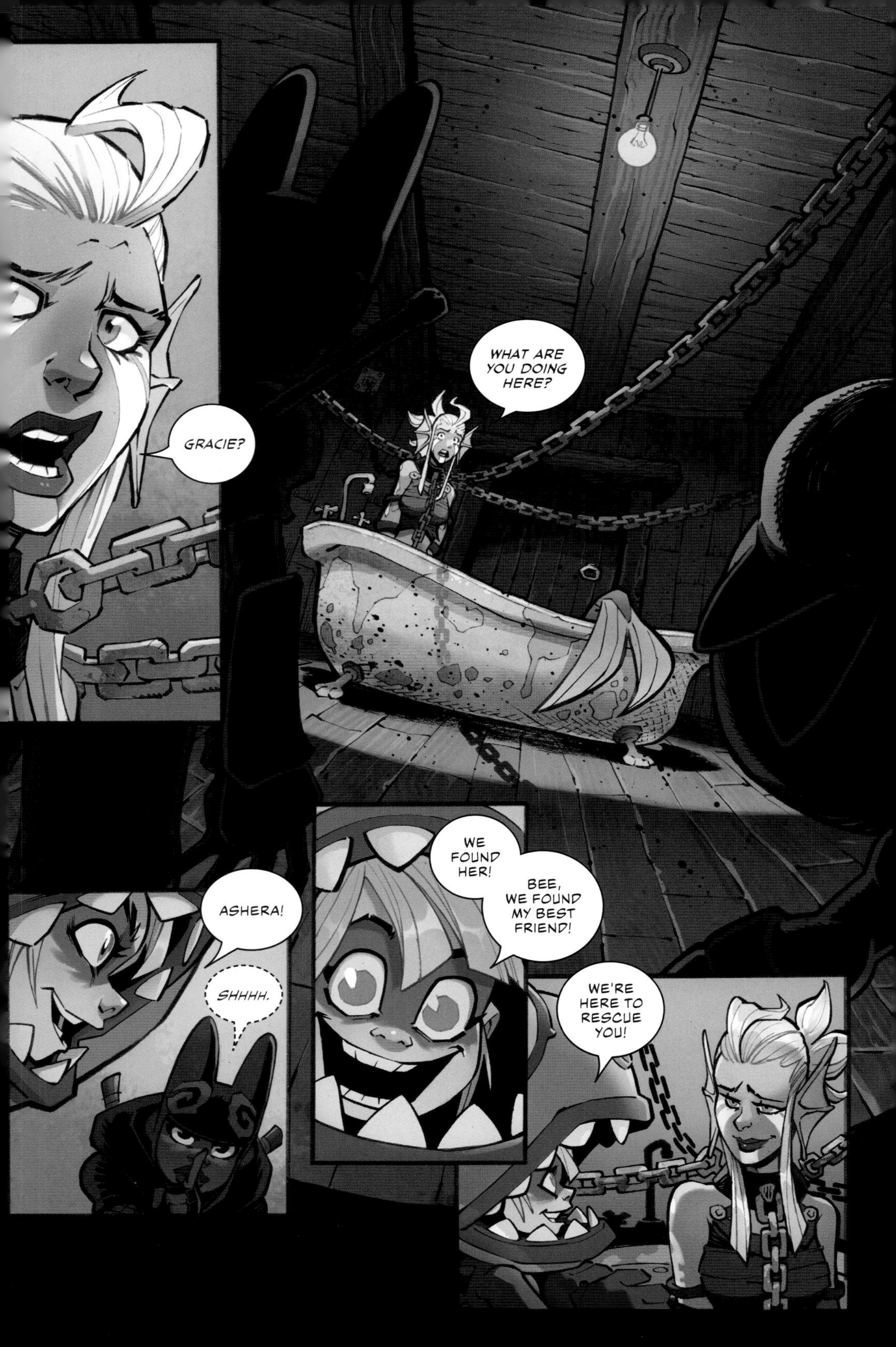
GRACIE?
WHAT ARE YOU DOING HERE?
ASHERA!
SHHHH.
WE FOUND HER!
BEE, WE FOUND MY BEST FRIEND!
WE'RE HERE TO RESCUE YOU!

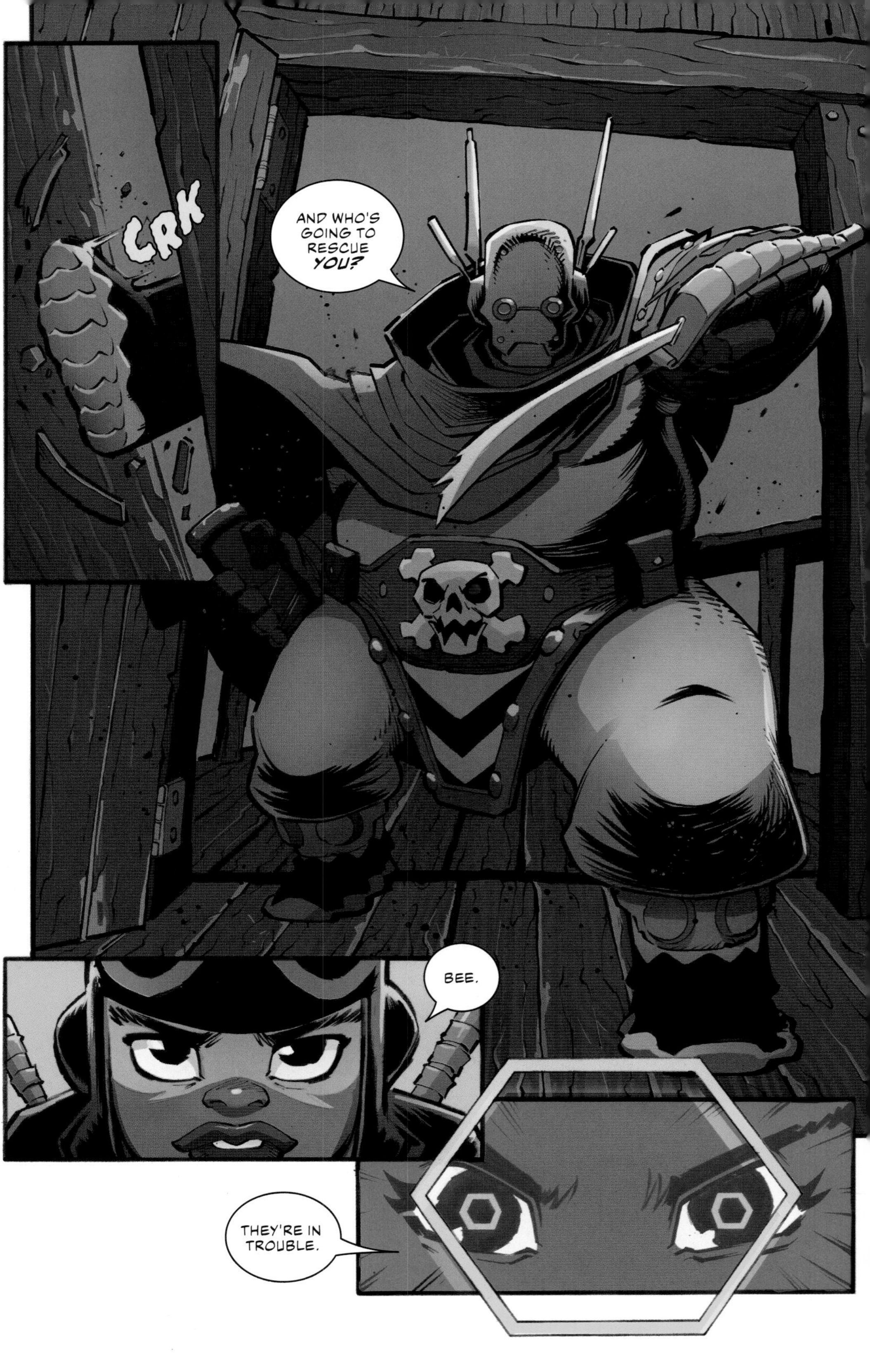
CRK
AND WHO'S GOING TO RESCUE *YOU?*
BEE.
THEY'RE IN TROUBLE.

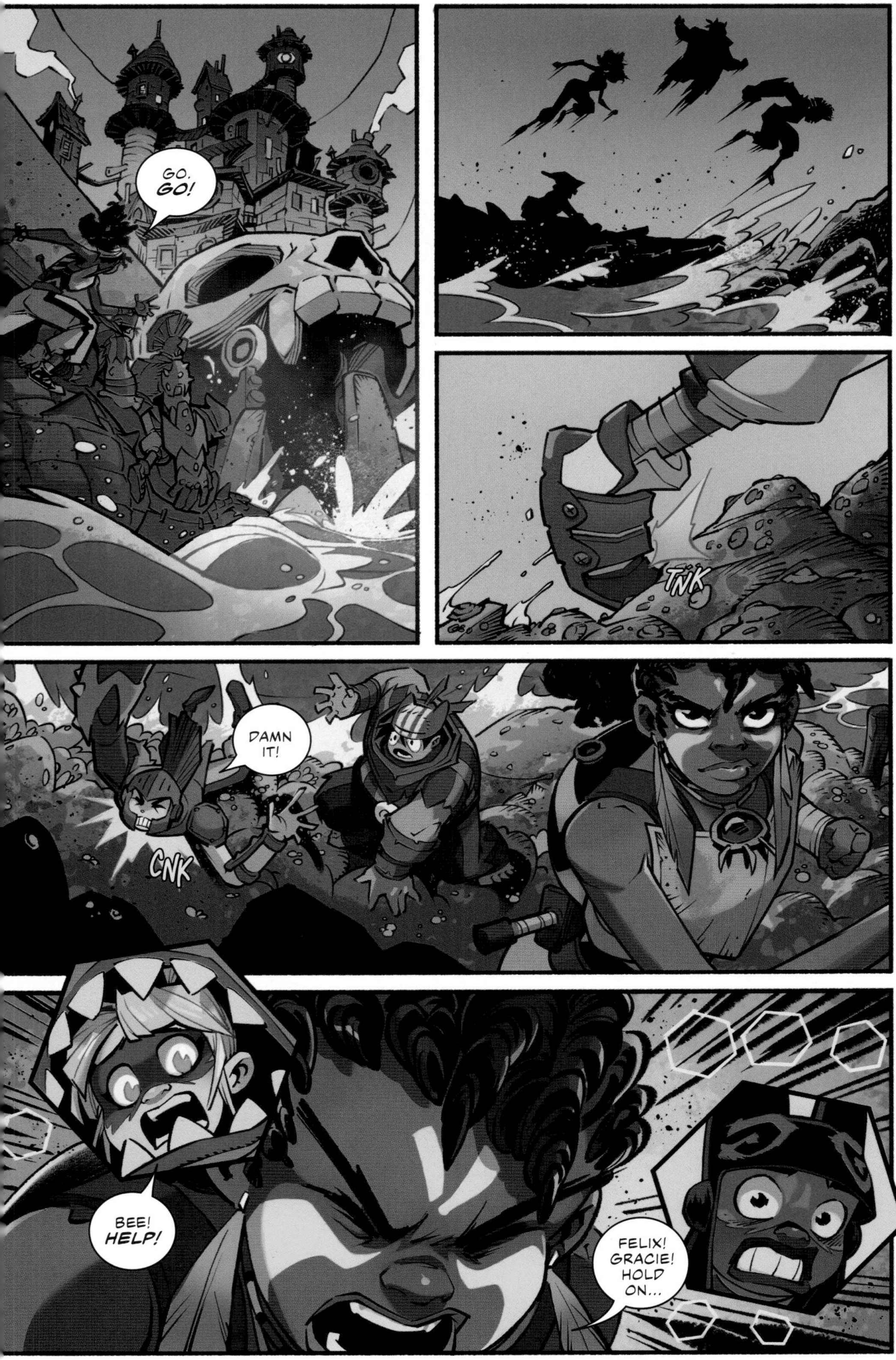
GO. GO!
TNK
DAMN IT!
CNK
BEE! HELP!
FELIX! GRACIE! HOLD ON...

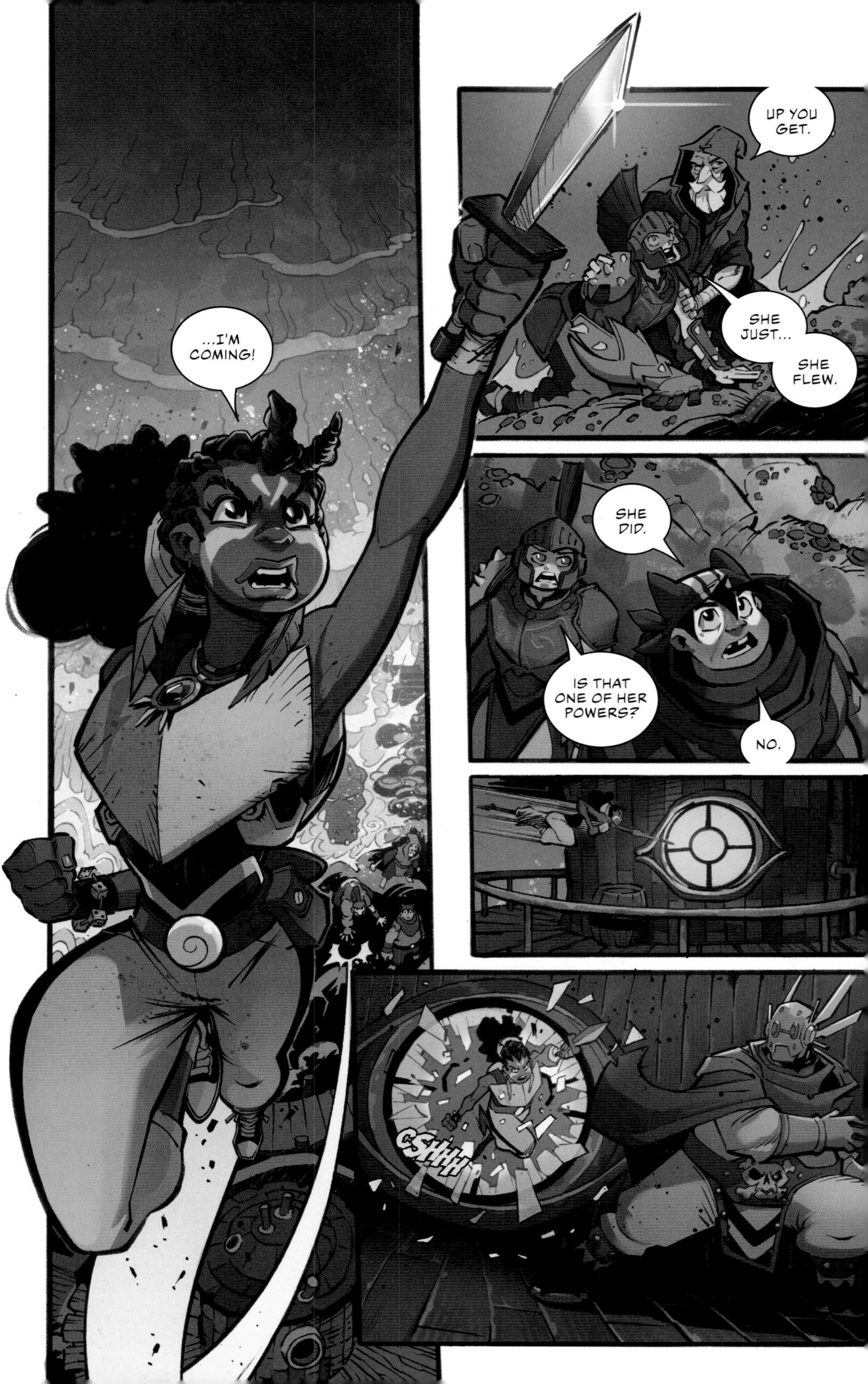
...I'M COMING!
UP YOU GET.
SHE JUST...
SHE FLEW.
SHE DID.
IS THAT ONE OF HER POWERS?
NO.
CSHHH

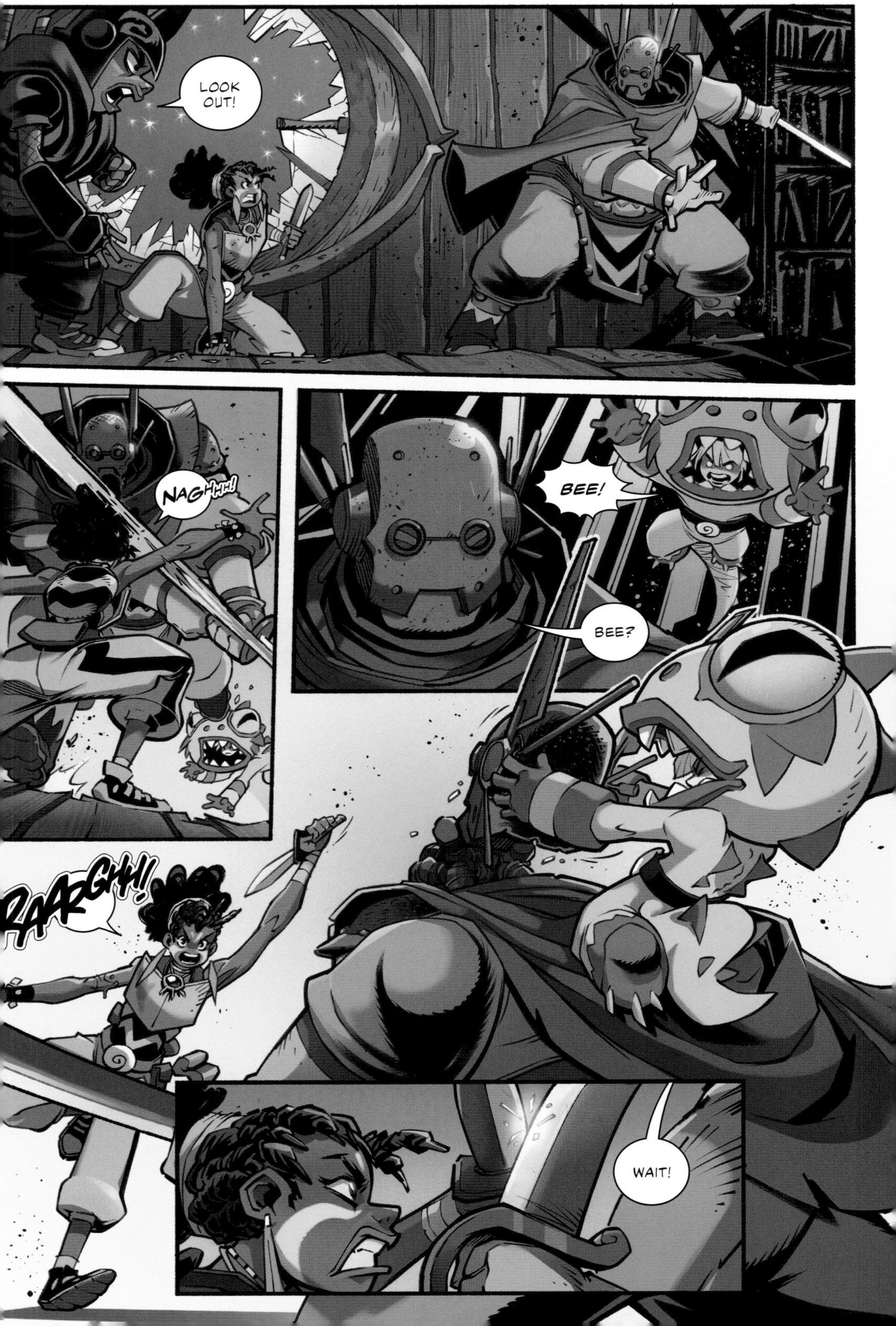
LOOK OUT!
NAGHHH!
BEE!
BEE?
RAARGHH!!
WAIT!

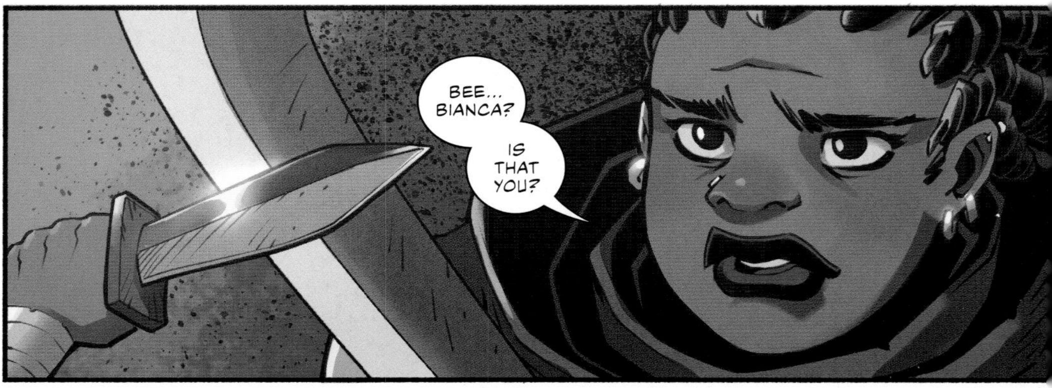
BEE... BIANCA?
IS THAT YOU?
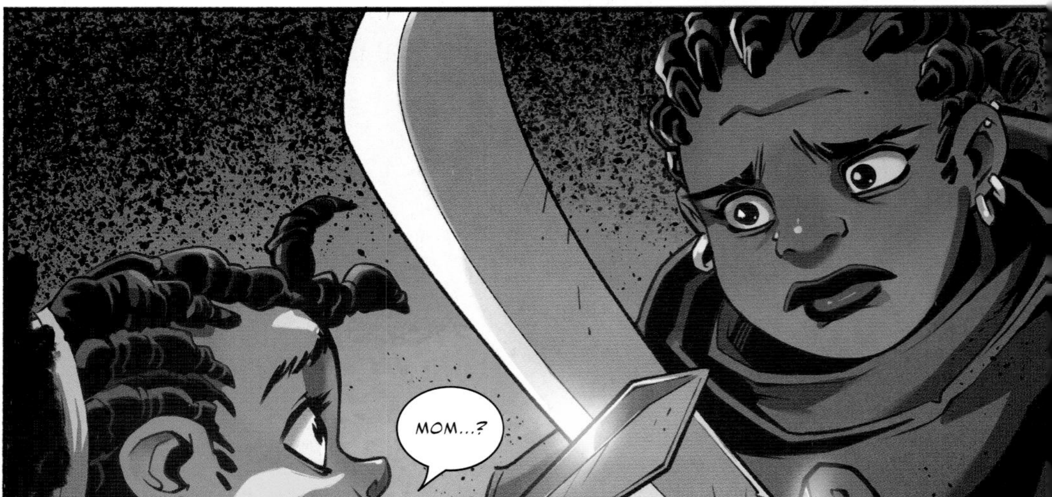
MOM...?
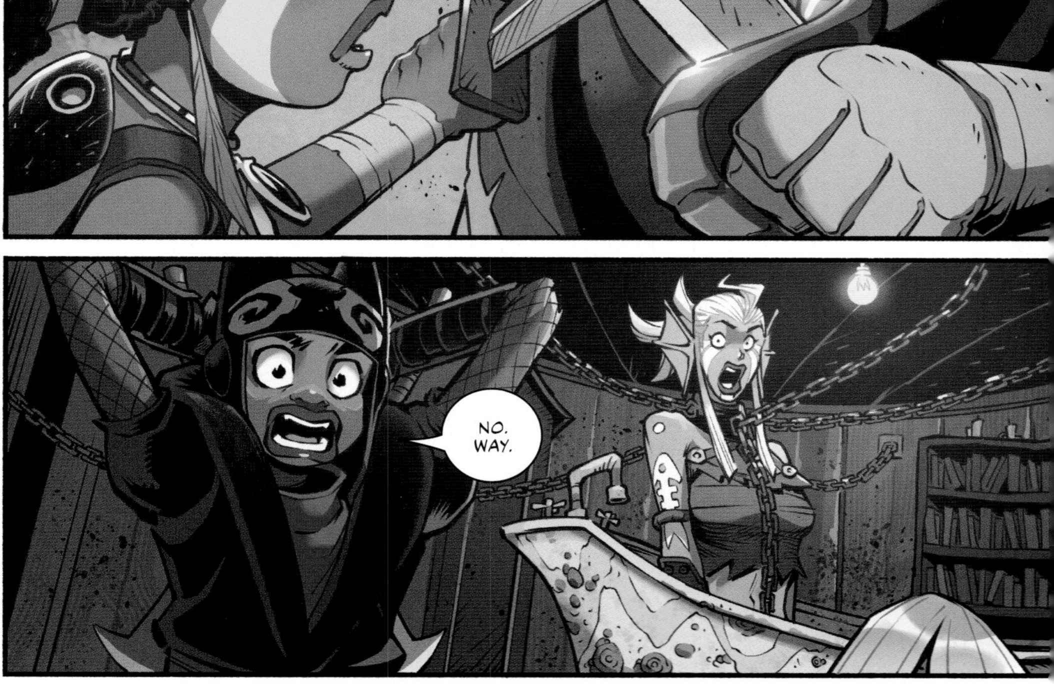
NO. WAY.

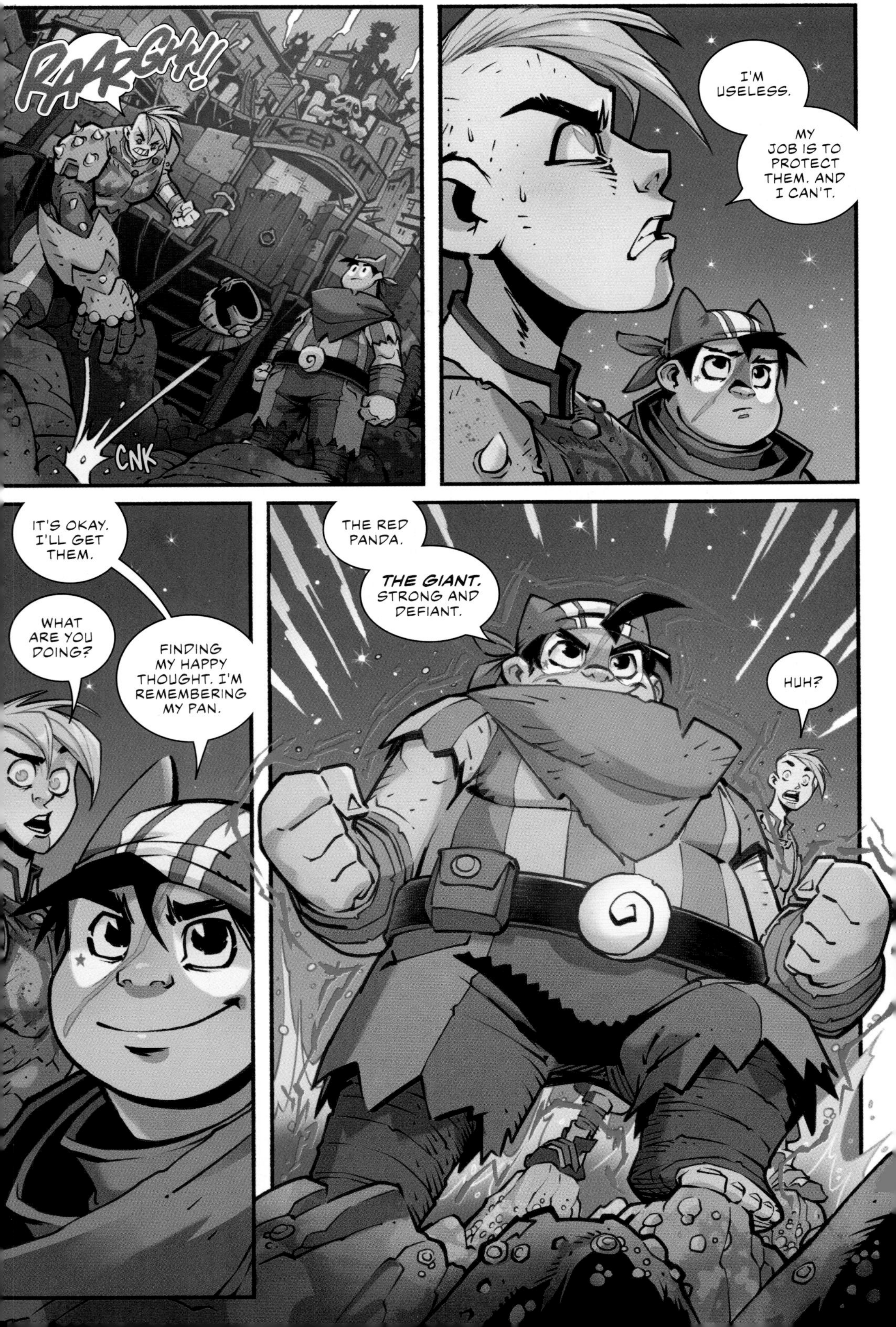
RAAARGHH!!
KEEP OUT
CNK
I'M USELESS.
MY JOB IS TO PROTECT THEM. AND I CAN'T.
IT'S OKAY. I'LL GET THEM.
WHAT ARE YOU DOING?
FINDING MY HAPPY THOUGHT. I'M REMEMBERING MY PAN.
THE RED PANDA.
THE GIANT. STRONG AND DEFIANT.
HUH?

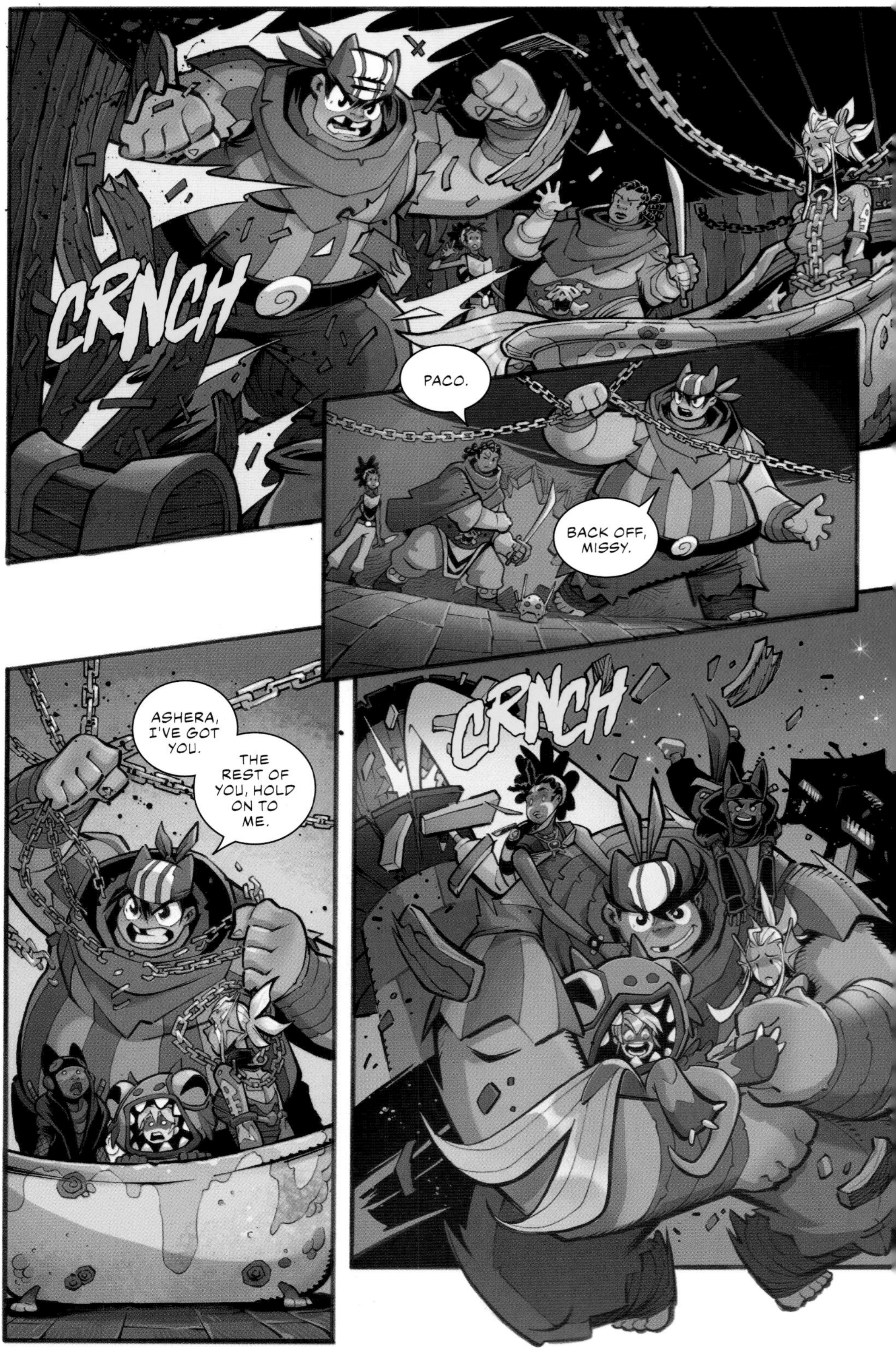
CRNCH
PACO.
BACK OFF, MISSY.
ASHERA, I'VE GOT YOU.
THE REST OF YOU, HOLD ON TO ME.
CRNCH

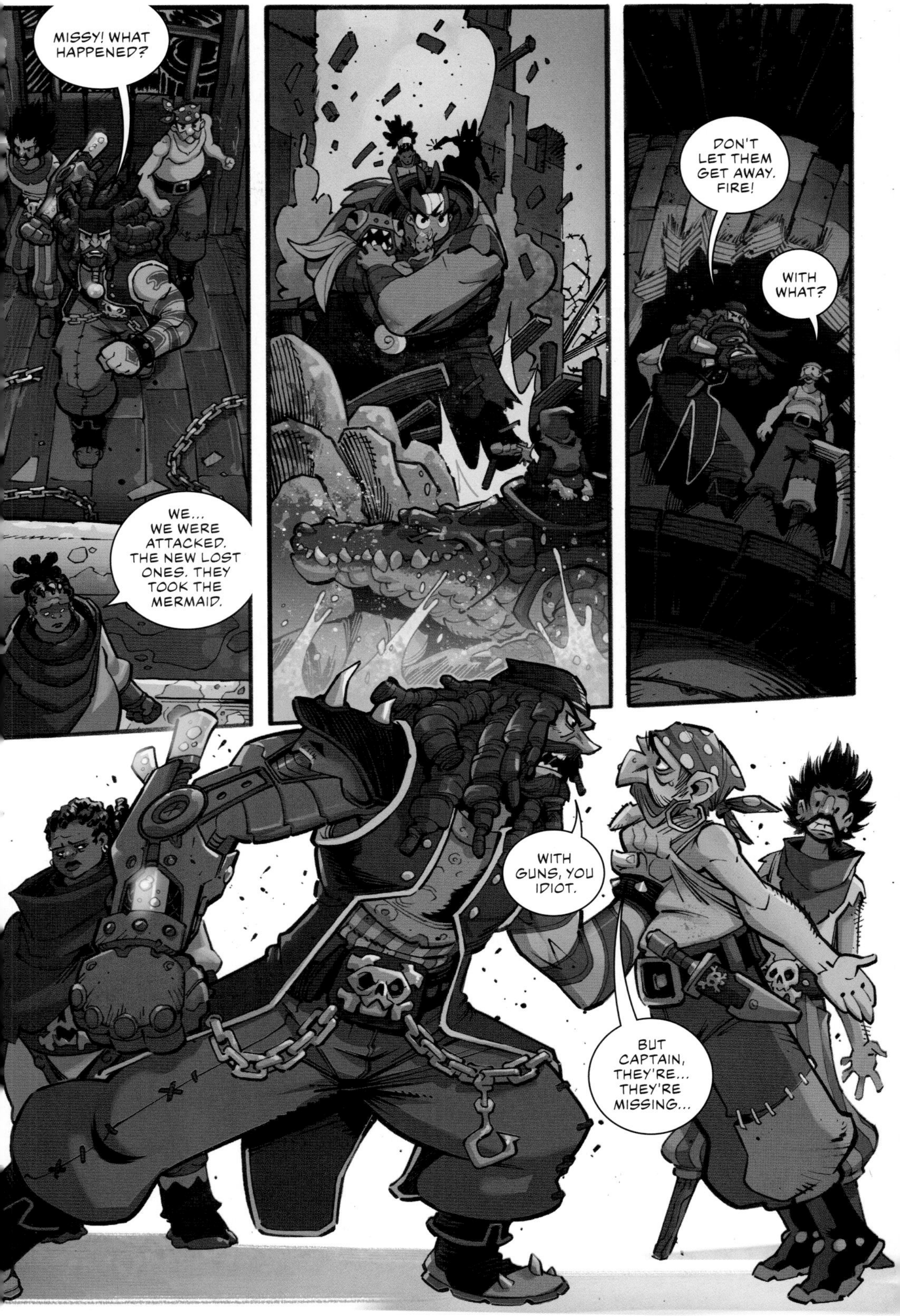
MISSY! WHAT HAPPENED?
WE... WE WERE ATTACKED. THE NEW LOST ONES. THEY TOOK THE MERMAID.
DON'T LET THEM GET AWAY. FIRE!
WITH WHAT?
WITH GUNS, YOU IDIOT.
BUT CAPTAIN, THEY'RE... THEY'RE MISSING...

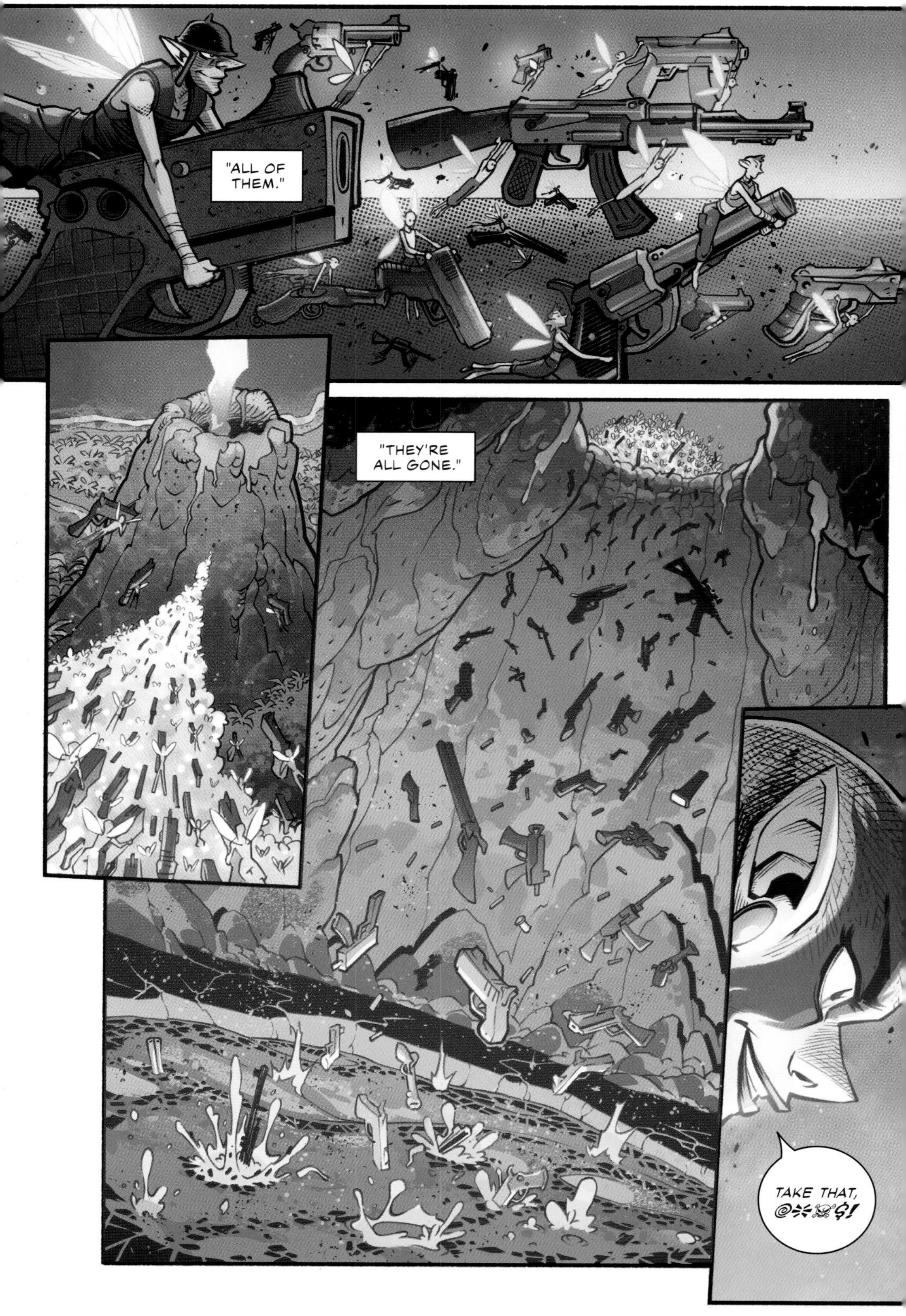
"ALL OF THEM."
"THEY'RE ALL GONE."
TAKE THAT, @*☠$!

CHAPTER
SIX

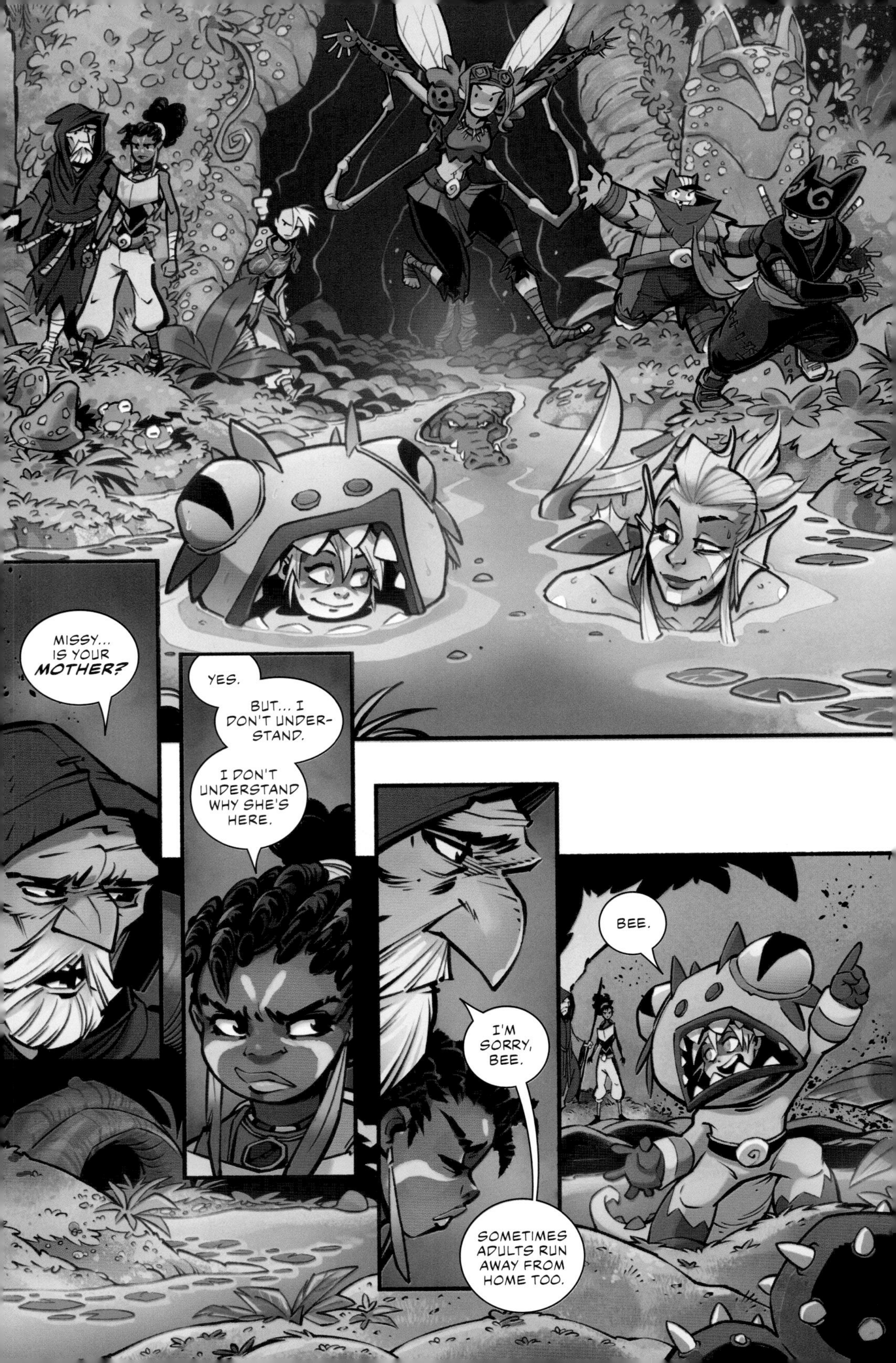
MISSY... IS YOUR MOTHER?
YES.
BUT... I DON'T UNDERSTAND.
I DON'T UNDERSTAND WHY SHE'S HERE.
I'M SORRY, BEE.
SOMETIMES ADULTS RUN AWAY FROM HOME TOO.
BEE.

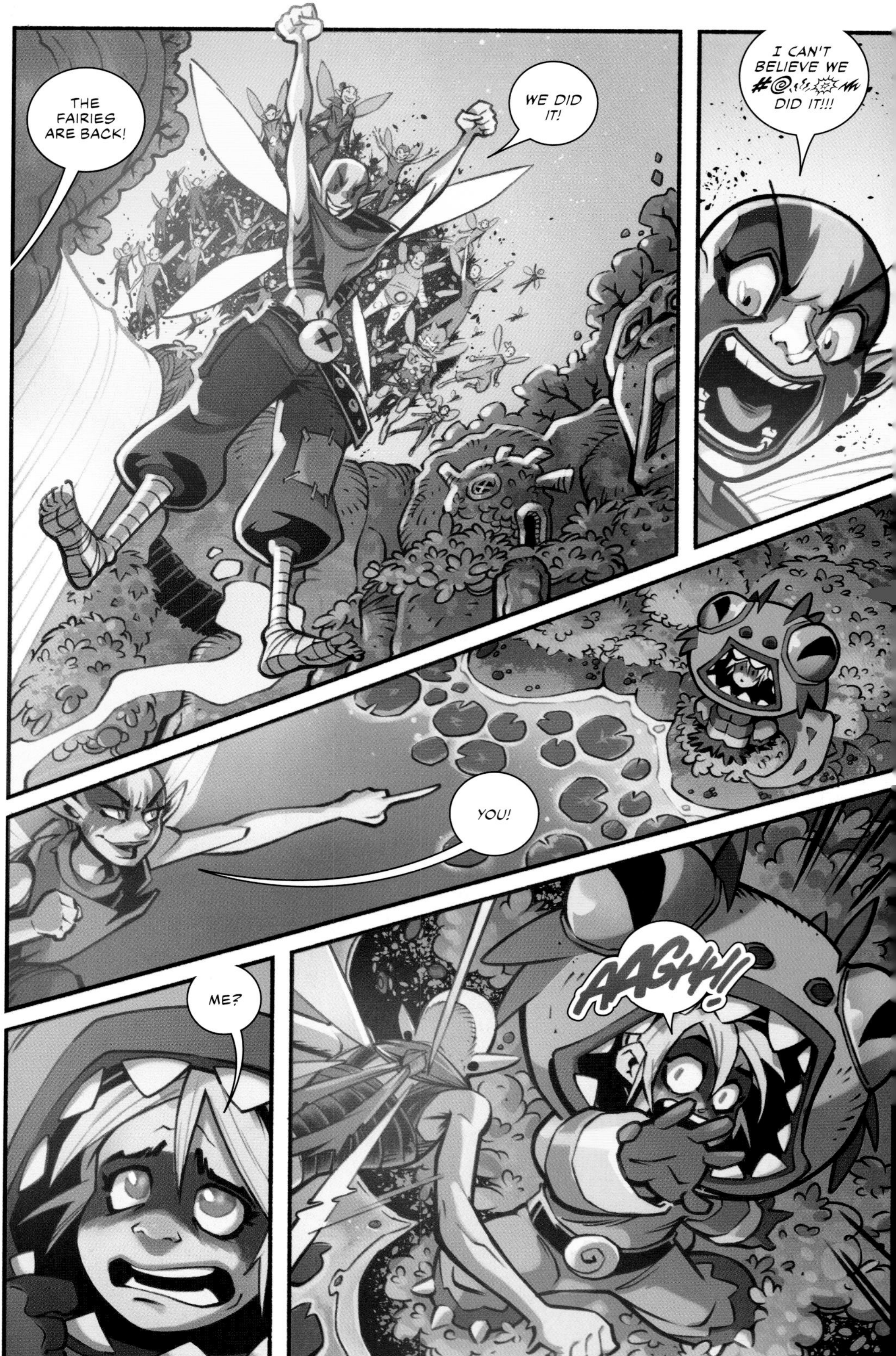
THE FAIRIES ARE BACK!
WE DID IT!
I CAN'T BELIEVE WE #@!*! DID IT!!!
YOU!
ME?
AAGH!!

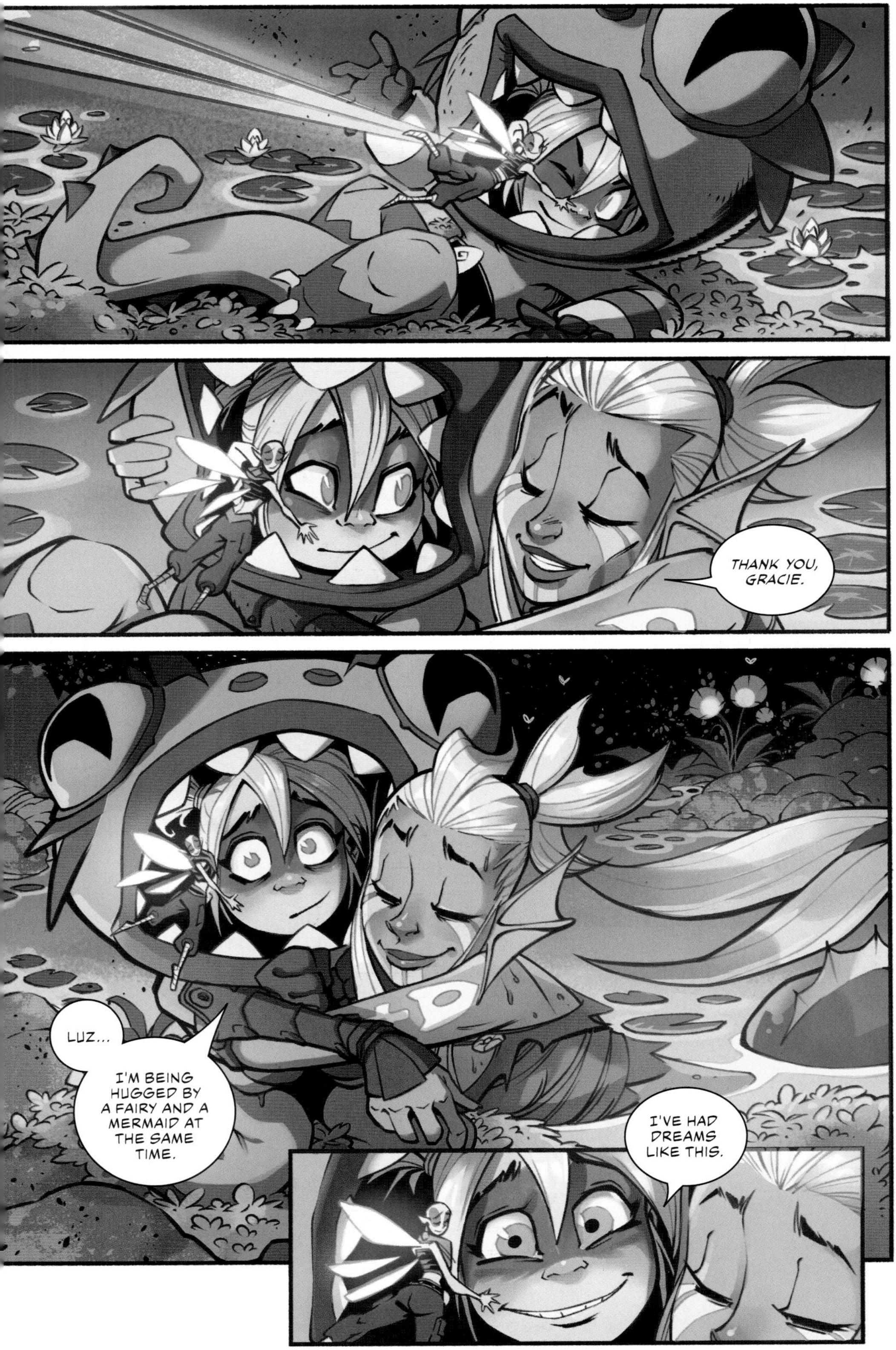
THANK YOU, GRACIE.
LUZ...
I'M BEING HUGGED BY A FAIRY AND A MERMAID AT THE SAME TIME.
I'VE HAD DREAMS LIKE THIS.

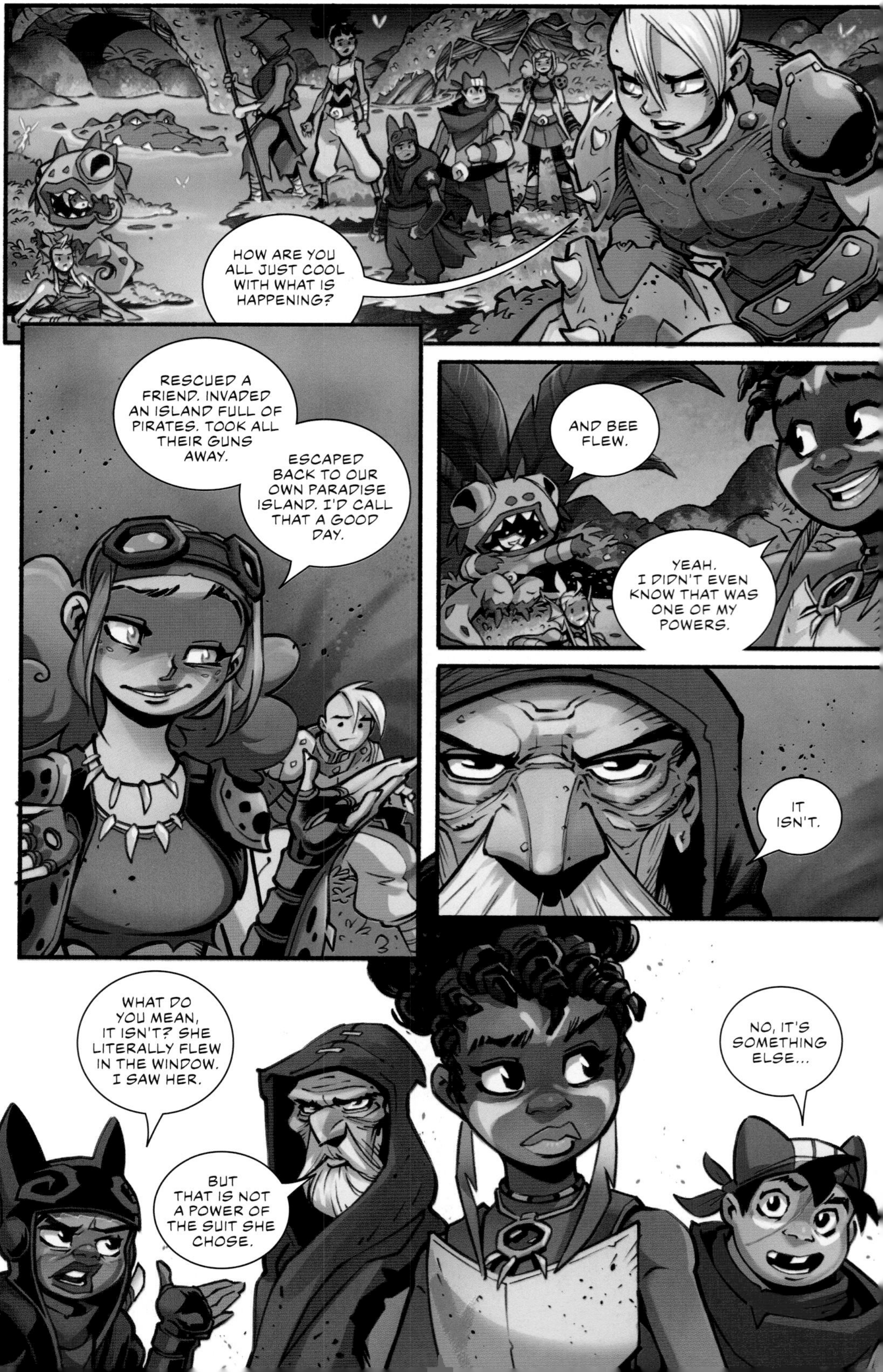
HOW ARE YOU ALL JUST COOL WITH WHAT IS HAPPENING?
RESCUED A FRIEND. INVADED AN ISLAND FULL OF PIRATES. TOOK ALL THEIR GUNS AWAY.
ESCAPED BACK TO OUR OWN PARADISE ISLAND. I'D CALL THAT A GOOD DAY.
AND BEE FLEW.
YEAH. I DIDN'T EVEN KNOW THAT WAS ONE OF MY POWERS.
IT ISN'T.
WHAT DO YOU MEAN, IT ISN'T? SHE LITERALLY FLEW IN THE WINDOW. I SAW HER.
BUT THAT IS NOT A POWER OF THE SUIT SHE CHOSE.
NO, IT'S SOMETHING ELSE...

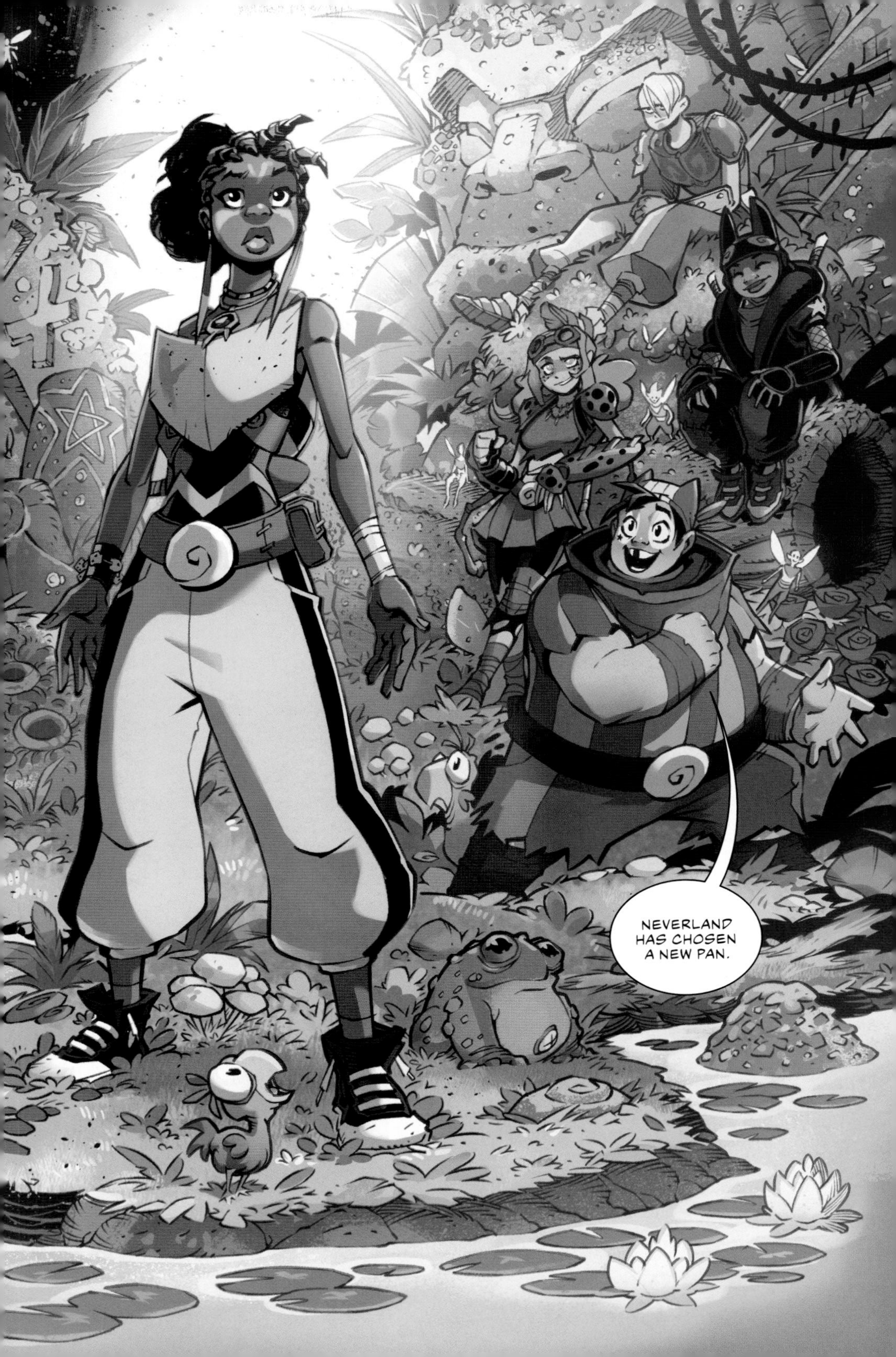
NEVERLAND HAS CHOSEN A NEW PAN.

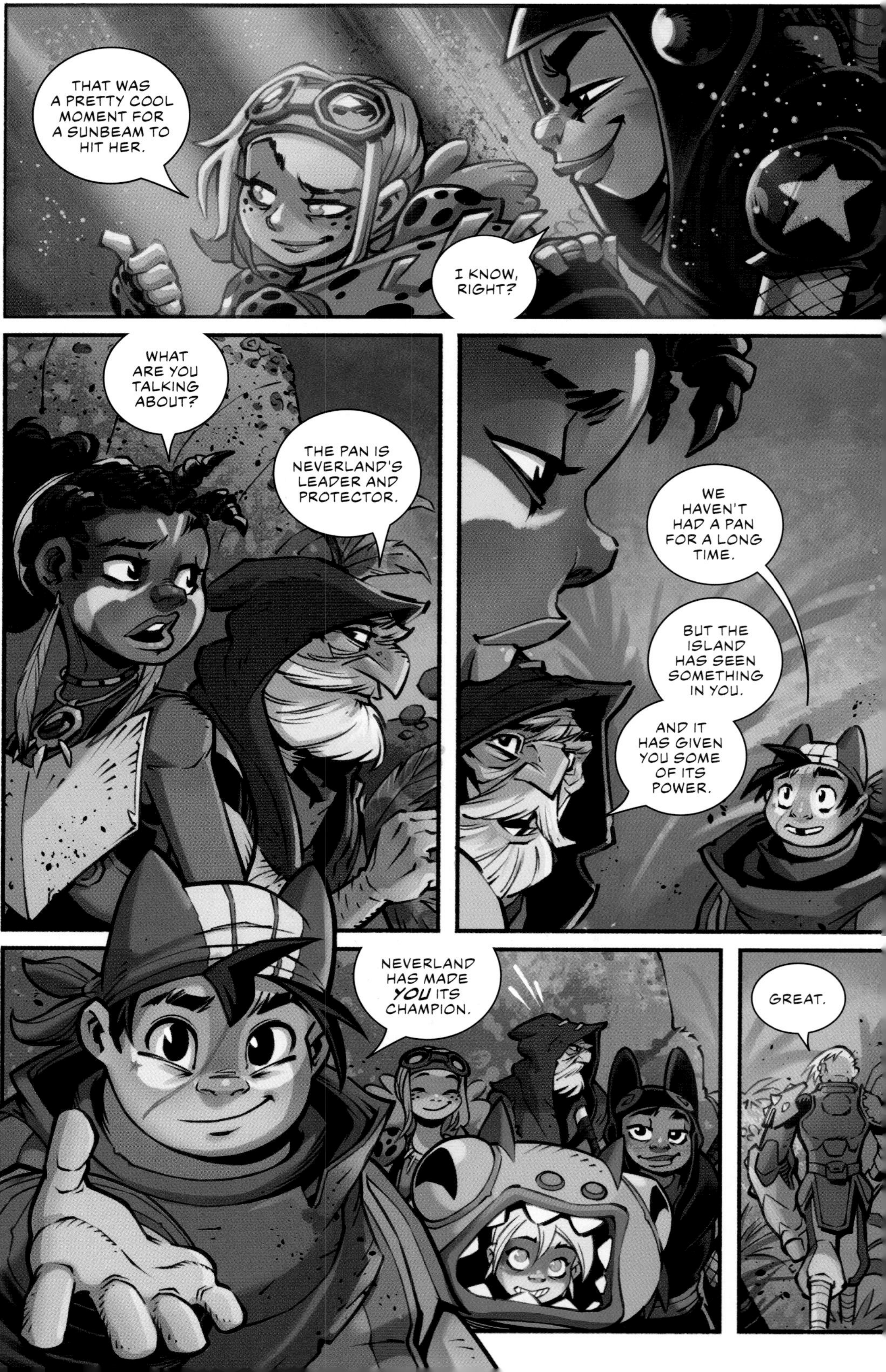
THAT WAS A PRETTY COOL MOMENT FOR A SUNBEAM TO HIT HER.
I KNOW, RIGHT?
WHAT ARE YOU TALKING ABOUT?
THE PAN IS NEVERLAND'S LEADER AND PROTECTOR.
WE HAVEN'T HAD A PAN FOR A LONG TIME.
BUT THE ISLAND HAS SEEN SOMETHING IN YOU.
AND IT HAS GIVEN YOU SOME OF ITS POWER.
NEVERLAND HAS MADE YOU ITS CHAMPION.
GREAT.

JUSTIN?

WHAT?

BEE BEING PAN... IT DOESN'T MAKE YOU LESSER.

SURE.

YOU HAVE A LOT OF ANGER IN YOU.

YOU SENSE THAT OR SOMETHING?

WHAT? NO.

YOU'RE JUST ALWAYS SCOWLING.

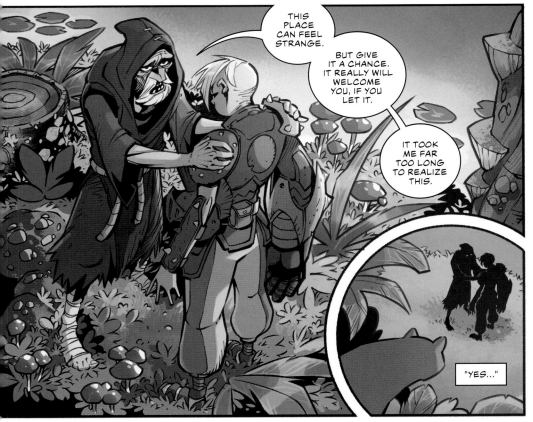

THIS PLACE CAN FEEL STRANGE.

BUT GIVE IT A CHANCE. IT REALLY WILL WELCOME YOU, IF YOU LET IT.

IT TOOK ME FAR TOO LONG TO REALIZE THIS.

"YES..."

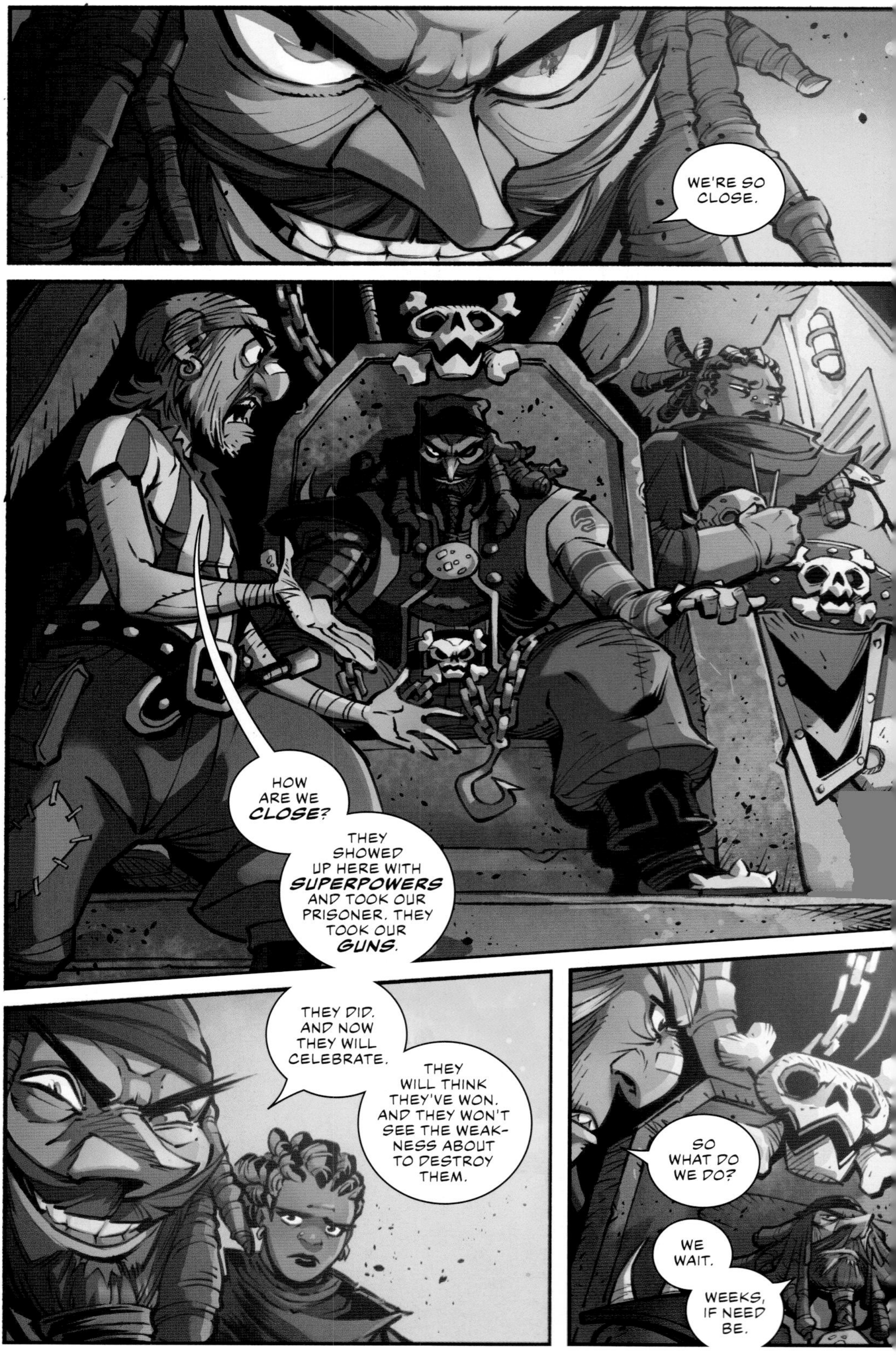
WE'RE SO CLOSE.
HOW ARE WE *CLOSE?*
THEY SHOWED UP HERE WITH ***SUPERPOWERS*** AND TOOK OUR PRISONER. THEY TOOK OUR ***GUNS.***
THEY DID. AND NOW THEY WILL CELEBRATE.
THEY WILL THINK THEY'VE WON. AND THEY WON'T SEE THE WEAK-NESS ABOUT TO DESTROY THEM.
SO WHAT DO WE DO?
WE WAIT.
WEEKS, IF NEED BE.

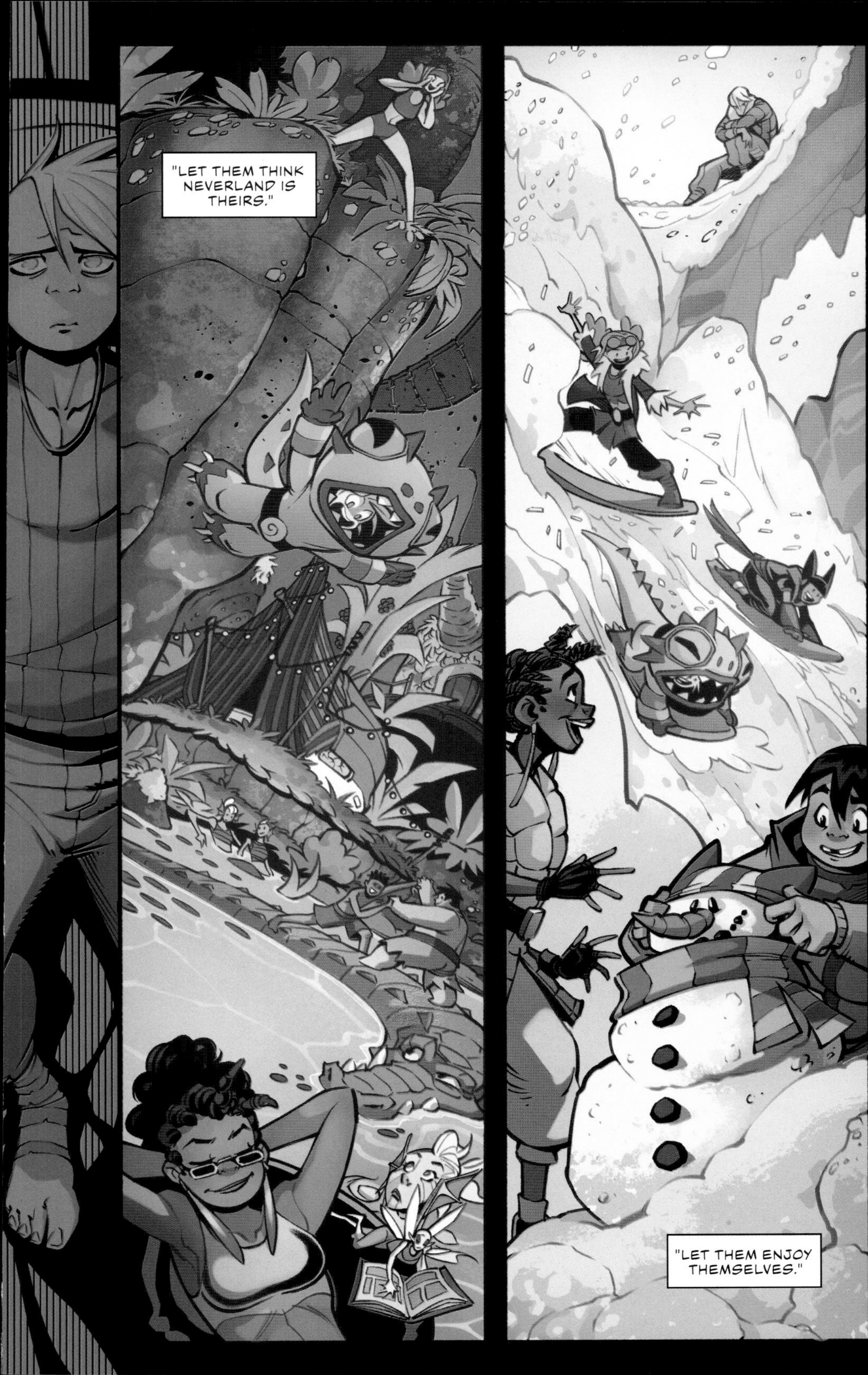
"LET THEM THINK NEVERLAND IS THEIRS."
"LET THEM ENJOY THEMSELVES."

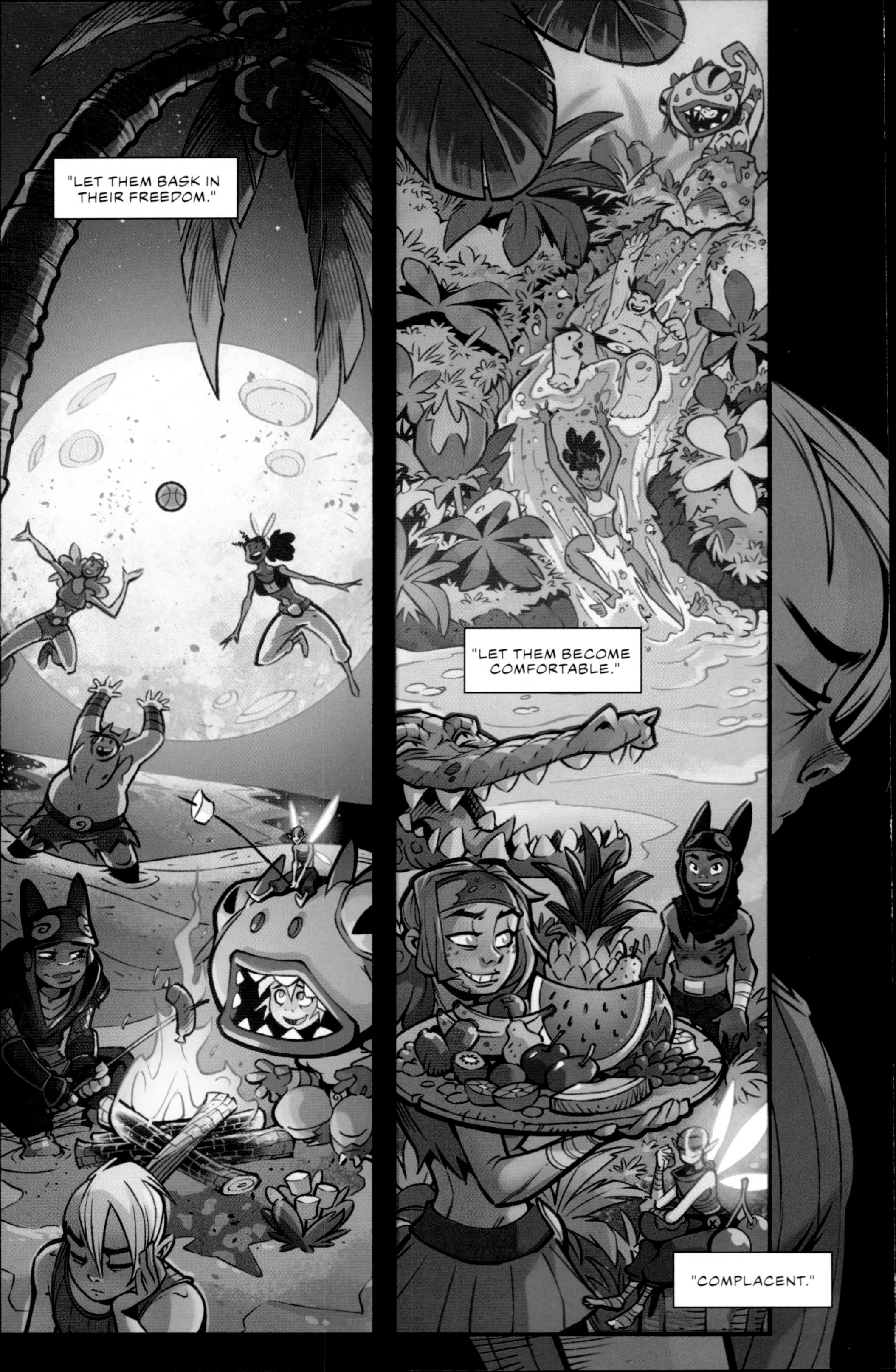
"LET THEM BASK IN THEIR FREEDOM."
"LET THEM BECOME COMFORTABLE."
"COMPLACENT."

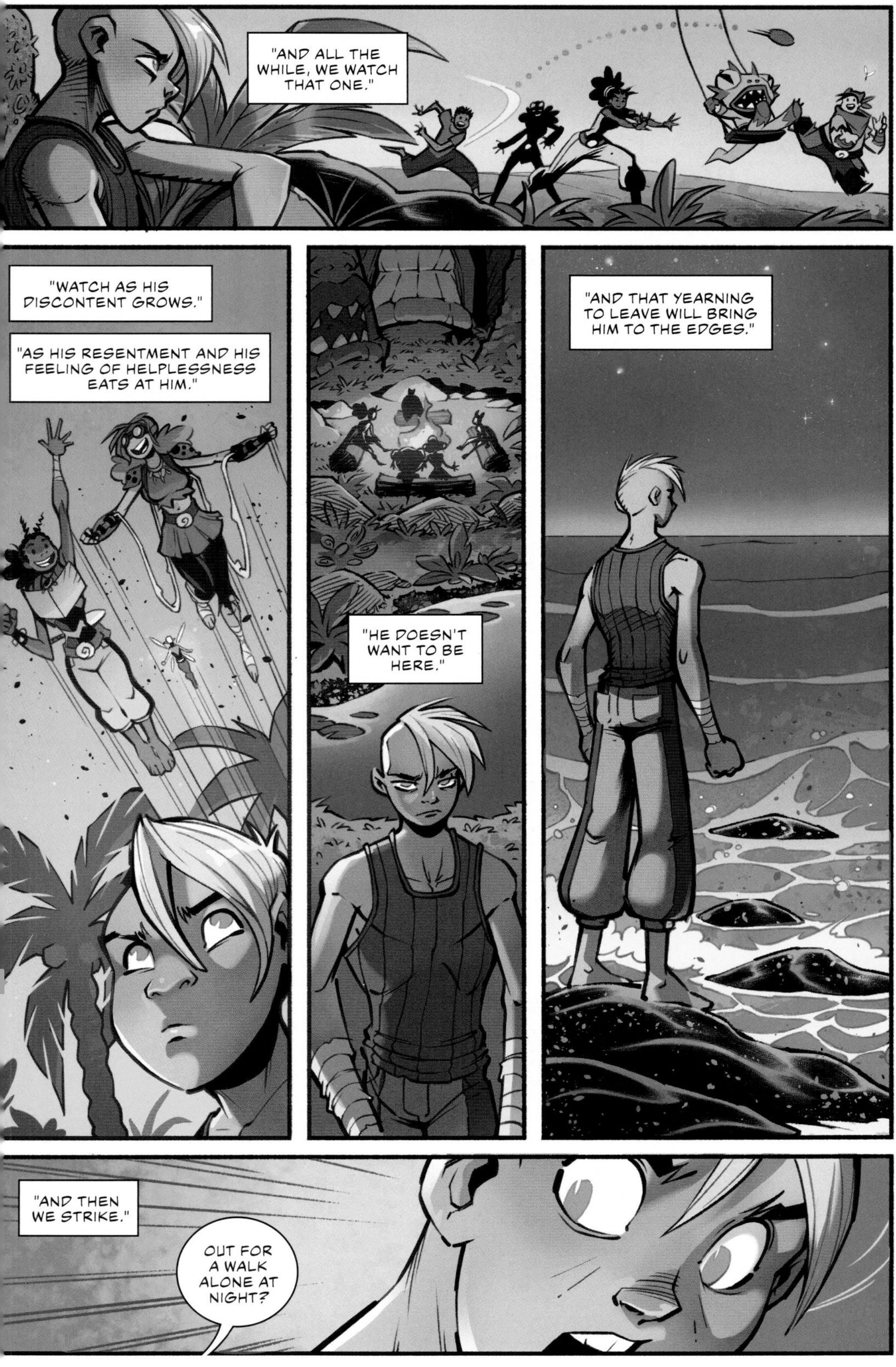
"AND ALL THE WHILE, WE WATCH THAT ONE."
"WATCH AS HIS DISCONTENT GROWS."
"AS HIS RESENTMENT AND HIS FEELING OF HELPLESSNESS EATS AT HIM."
"HE DOESN'T WANT TO BE HERE."
"AND THAT YEARNING TO LEAVE WILL BRING HIM TO THE EDGES."
"AND THEN WE STRIKE."
OUT FOR A WALK ALONE AT NIGHT?

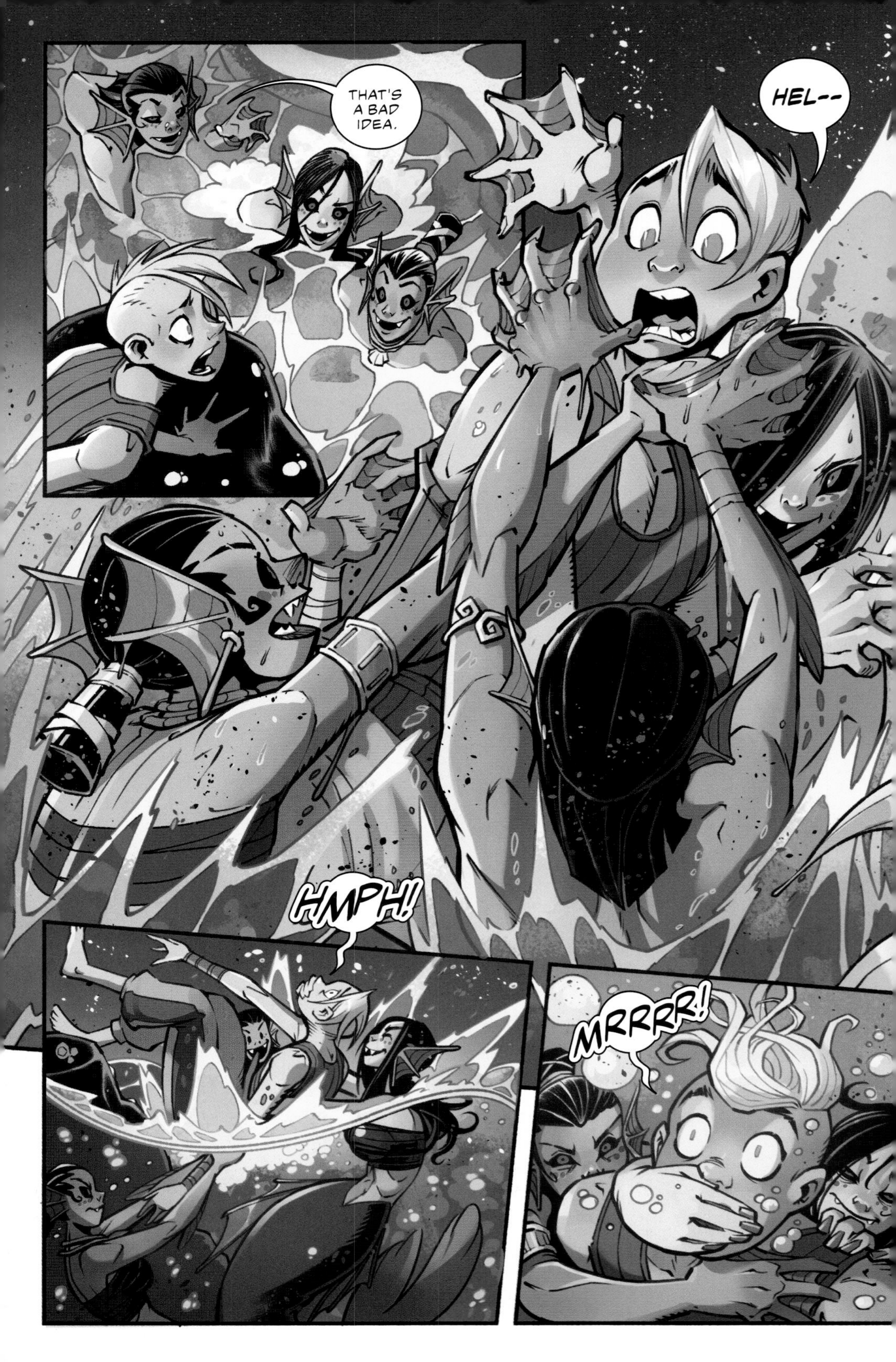
THAT'S A BAD IDEA.
HEL--
HMPH!
MRRRR!

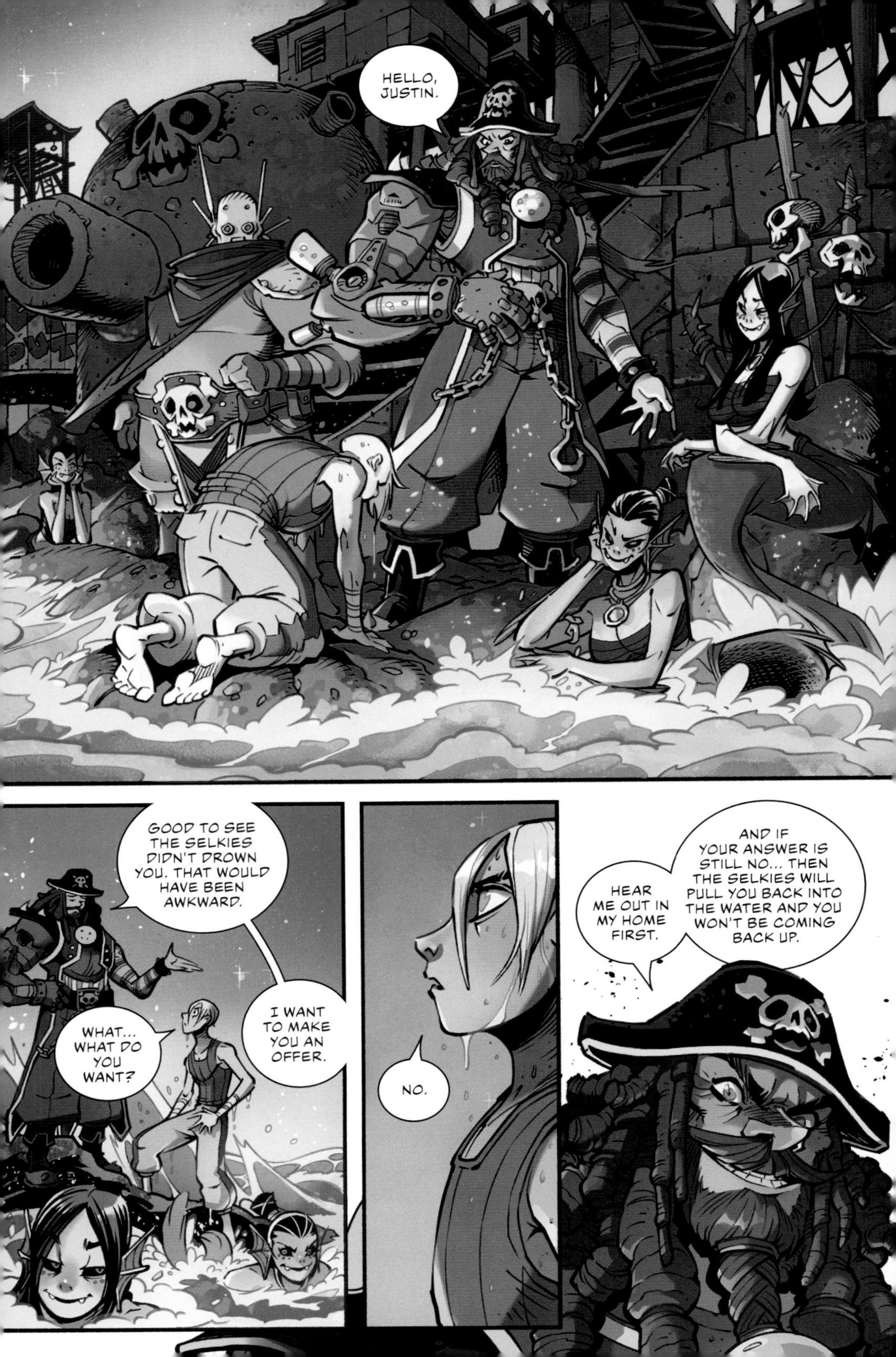
HELLO, JUSTIN.
GOOD TO SEE THE SELKIES DIDN'T DROWN YOU. THAT WOULD HAVE BEEN AWKWARD.
WHAT... WHAT DO YOU WANT?
I WANT TO MAKE YOU AN OFFER.
NO.
HEAR ME OUT IN MY HOME FIRST.
AND IF YOUR ANSWER IS STILL NO... THEN THE SELKIES WILL PULL YOU BACK INTO THE WATER AND YOU WON'T BE COMING BACK UP.

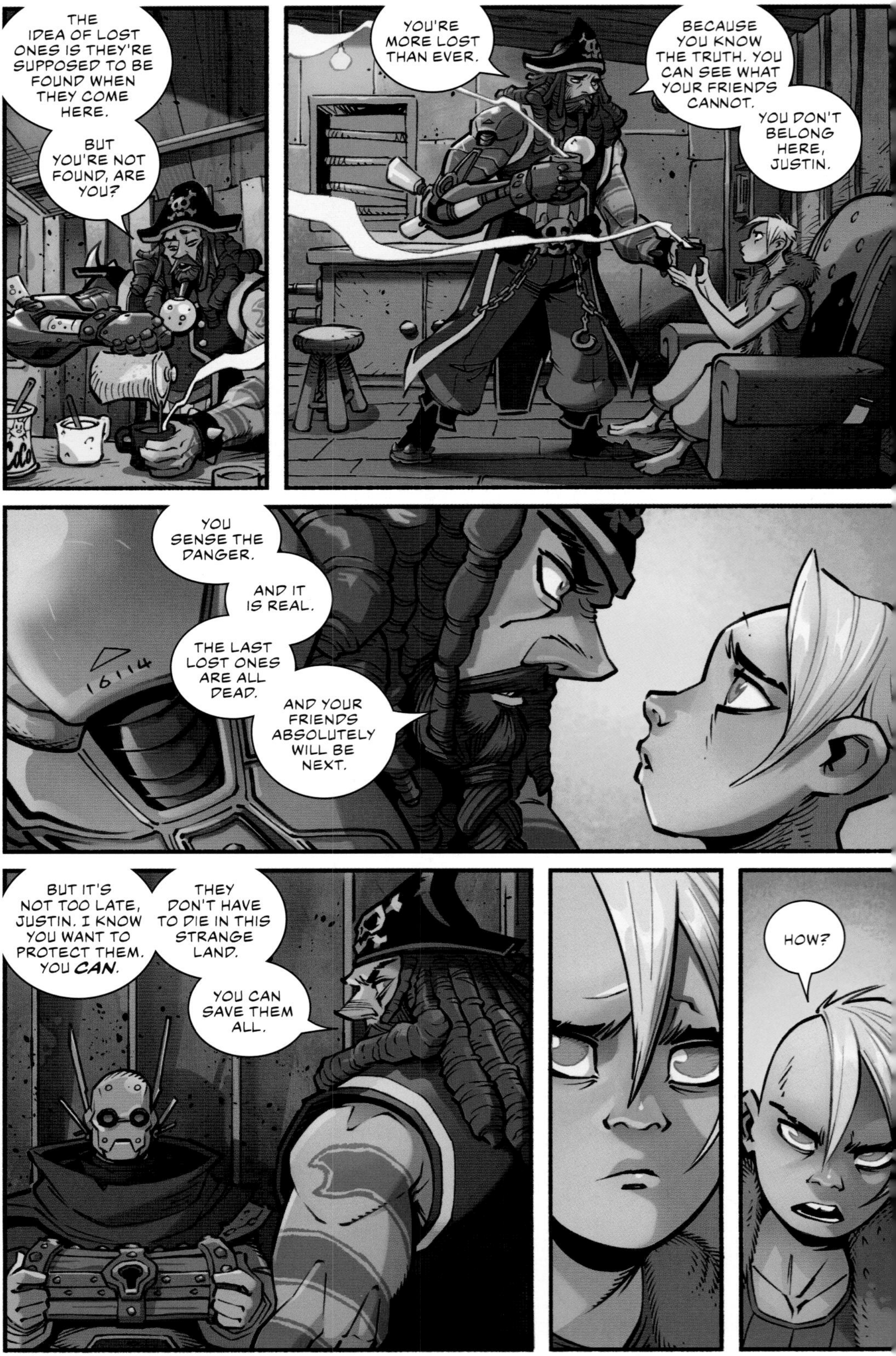
THE IDEA OF LOST ONES IS THEY'RE SUPPOSED TO BE FOUND WHEN THEY COME HERE.
BUT YOU'RE NOT FOUND, ARE YOU?
YOU'RE MORE LOST THAN EVER.
BECAUSE YOU KNOW THE TRUTH. YOU CAN SEE WHAT YOUR FRIENDS CANNOT.
YOU DON'T BELONG HERE, JUSTIN.
YOU SENSE THE DANGER.
AND IT IS REAL.
THE LAST LOST ONES ARE ALL DEAD.
AND YOUR FRIENDS ABSOLUTELY WILL BE NEXT.
16114
BUT IT'S NOT TOO LATE, JUSTIN. I KNOW YOU WANT TO PROTECT THEM. YOU ***CAN***.
THEY DON'T HAVE TO DIE IN THIS STRANGE LAND.
YOU CAN SAVE THEM ALL.
HOW?

WITH THIS.

A SWORD?

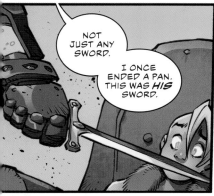

NOT JUST ANY SWORD.

I ONCE ENDED A PAN. THIS WAS *HIS* SWORD.

IT CONTAINS A PART OF NEVERLAND'S POWER. IT CAN BRING THE ISLAND'S MAGICAL WALLS DOWN.

TAKE IT.

AND YOU CAN ALSO TAKE THIS.

ENOUGH FOR YOU AND YOUR FRIENDS TO LIVE HAPPILY EVER AFTER.

DO WHAT NEEDS TO BE DONE AND YOUR FRIENDS GET TO LIVE.

YOU WILL HAVE SAVED THEM, AND I WILL TAKE YOU ALL HOME.

WITH ENOUGH TREASURE TO MAKE YOUR OWN WORLD A PARADISE.

WHY CAN'T YOU OR ONE OF YOUR MONSTERS DO THIS?

ONLY A CHILD CAN STRIKE AT THE HEART OF NEVERLAND.

WHAT DO I HAVE TO DO?

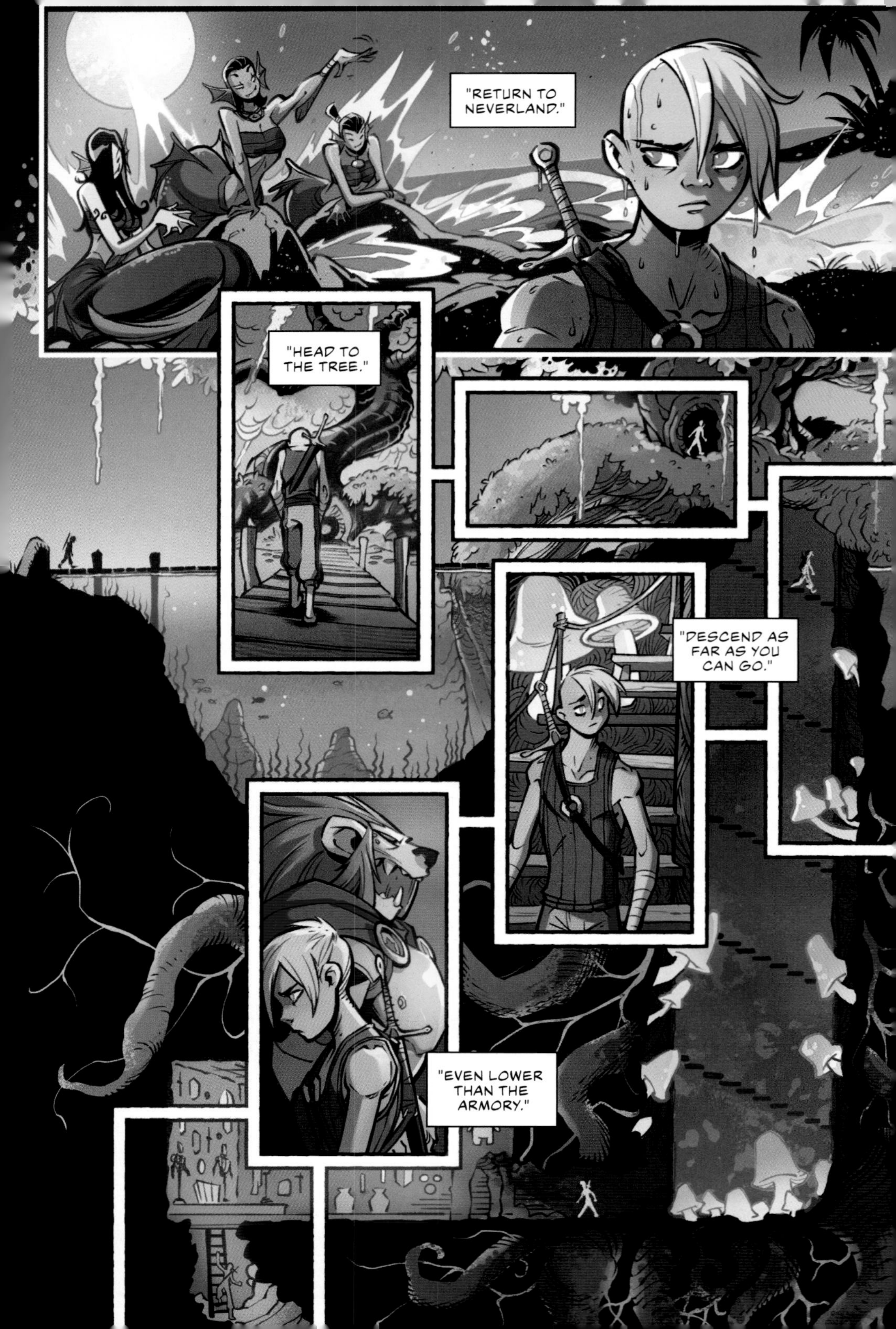
"RETURN TO NEVERLAND."
"HEAD TO THE TREE."
"DESCEND AS FAR AS YOU CAN GO."
"EVEN LOWER THAN THE ARMORY."

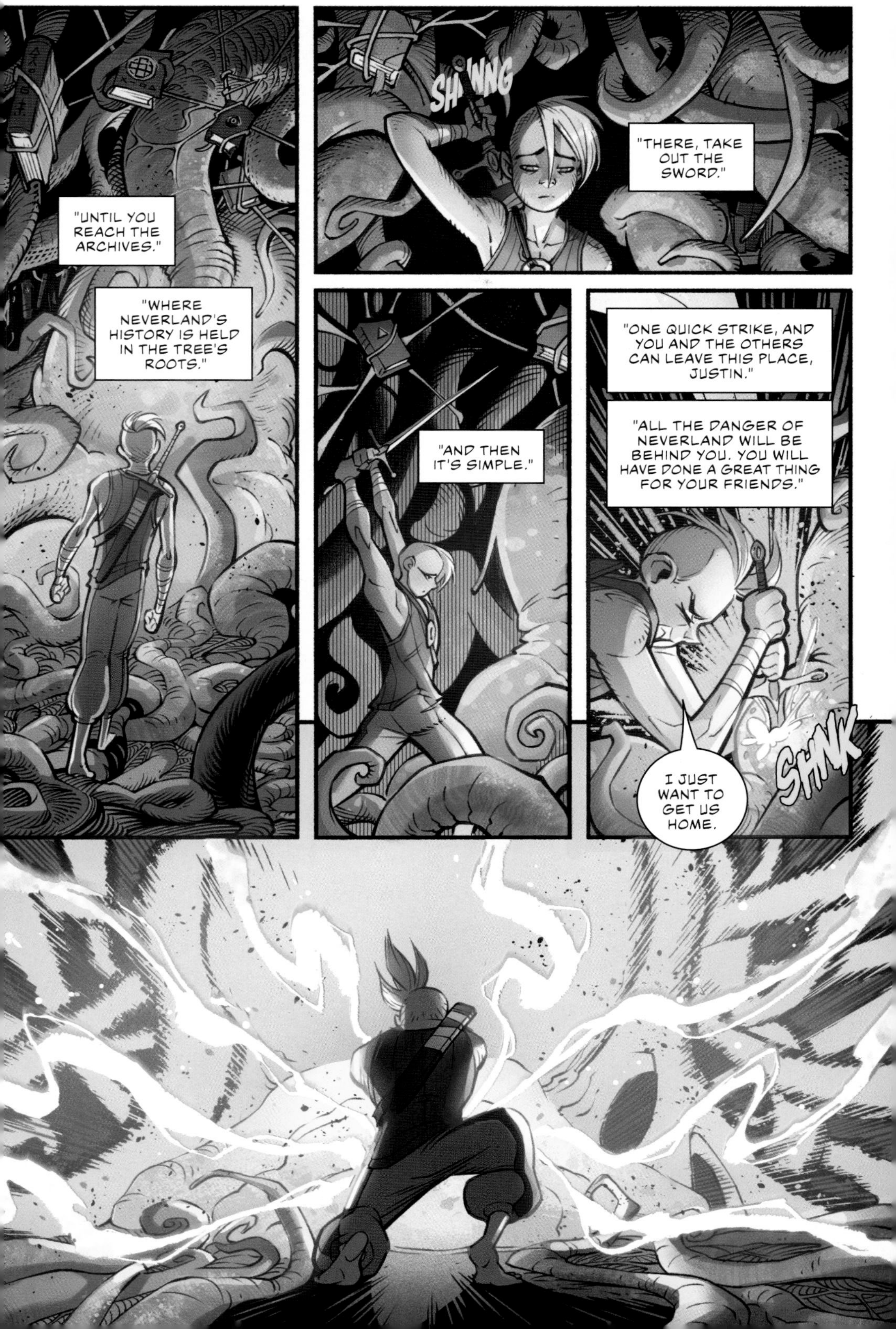
"UNTIL YOU REACH THE ARCHIVES."
"WHERE NEVERLAND'S HISTORY IS HELD IN THE TREE'S ROOTS."
SHINNG
"THERE, TAKE OUT THE SWORD."
"AND THEN IT'S SIMPLE."
"ONE QUICK STRIKE, AND YOU AND THE OTHERS CAN LEAVE THIS PLACE, JUSTIN."
"ALL THE DANGER OF NEVERLAND WILL BE BEHIND YOU. YOU WILL HAVE DONE A GREAT THING FOR YOUR FRIENDS."
I JUST WANT TO GET US HOME.
SHINK

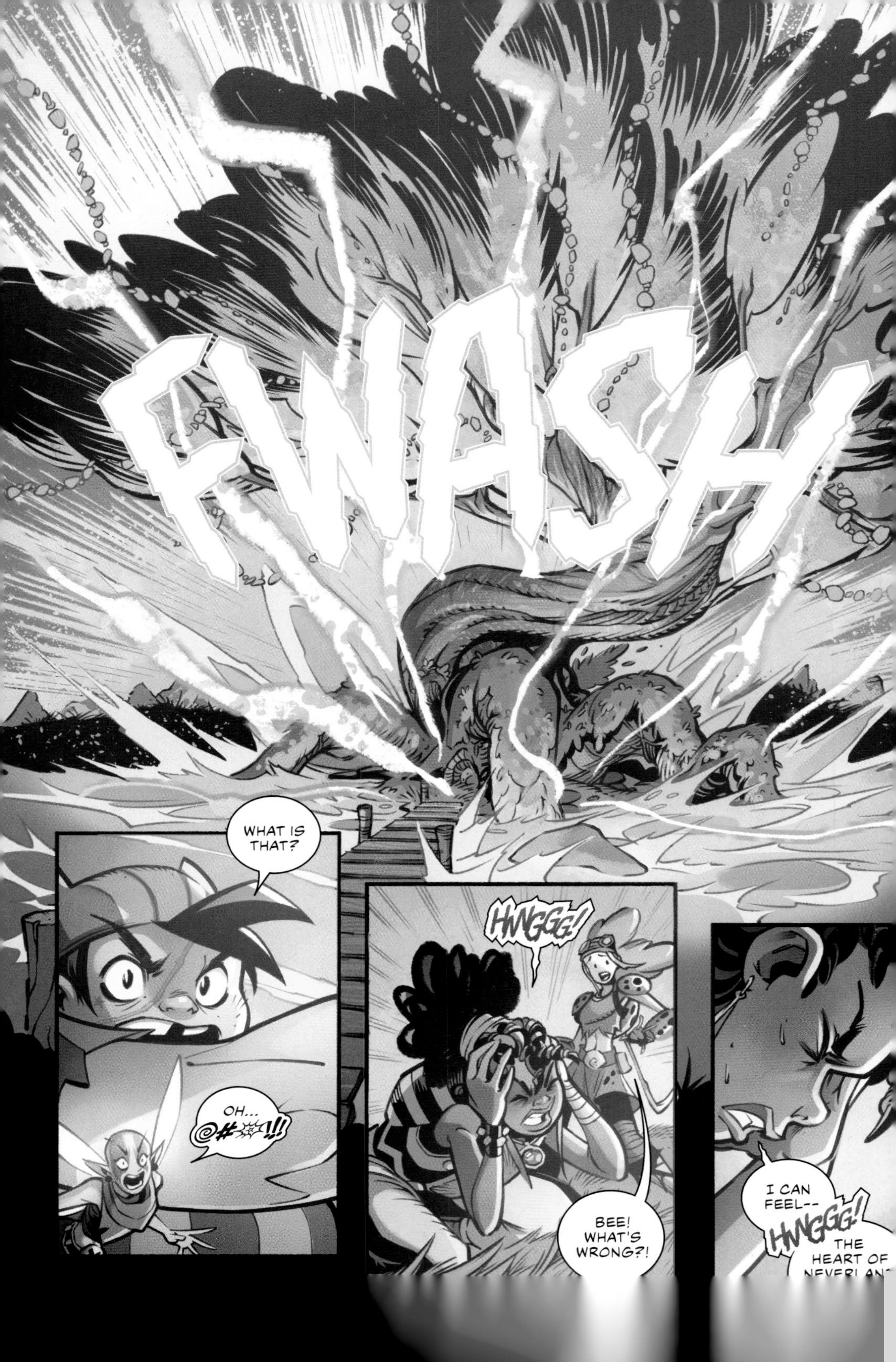
FWASH
WHAT IS THAT?
OH... @#☼!!!
HNGGG!
BEE! WHAT'S WRONG?!
I CAN FEEL--
HNGGG!
THE HEART OF

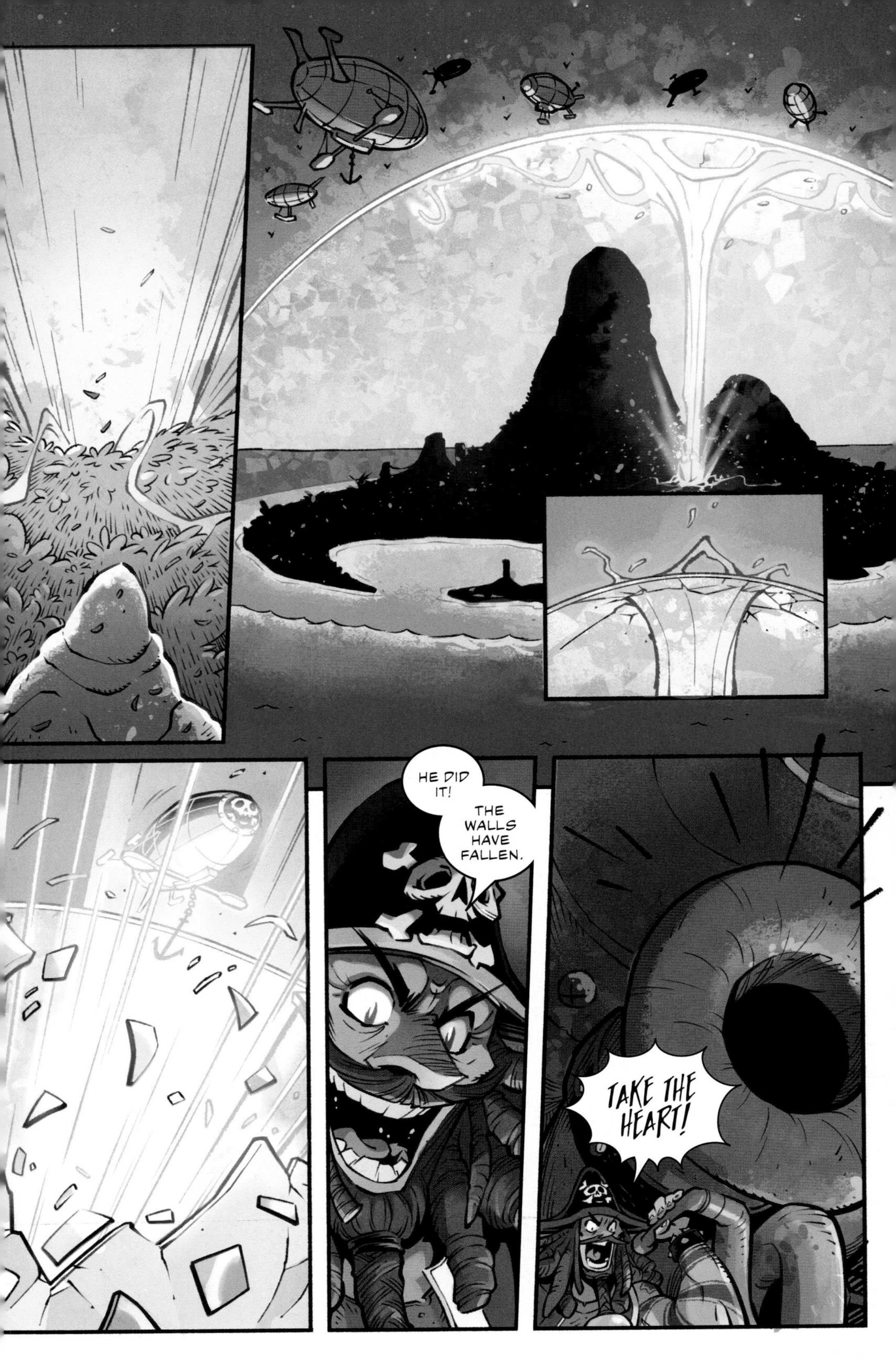
HE DID IT!
THE WALLS HAVE FALLEN.
TAKE THE HEART!

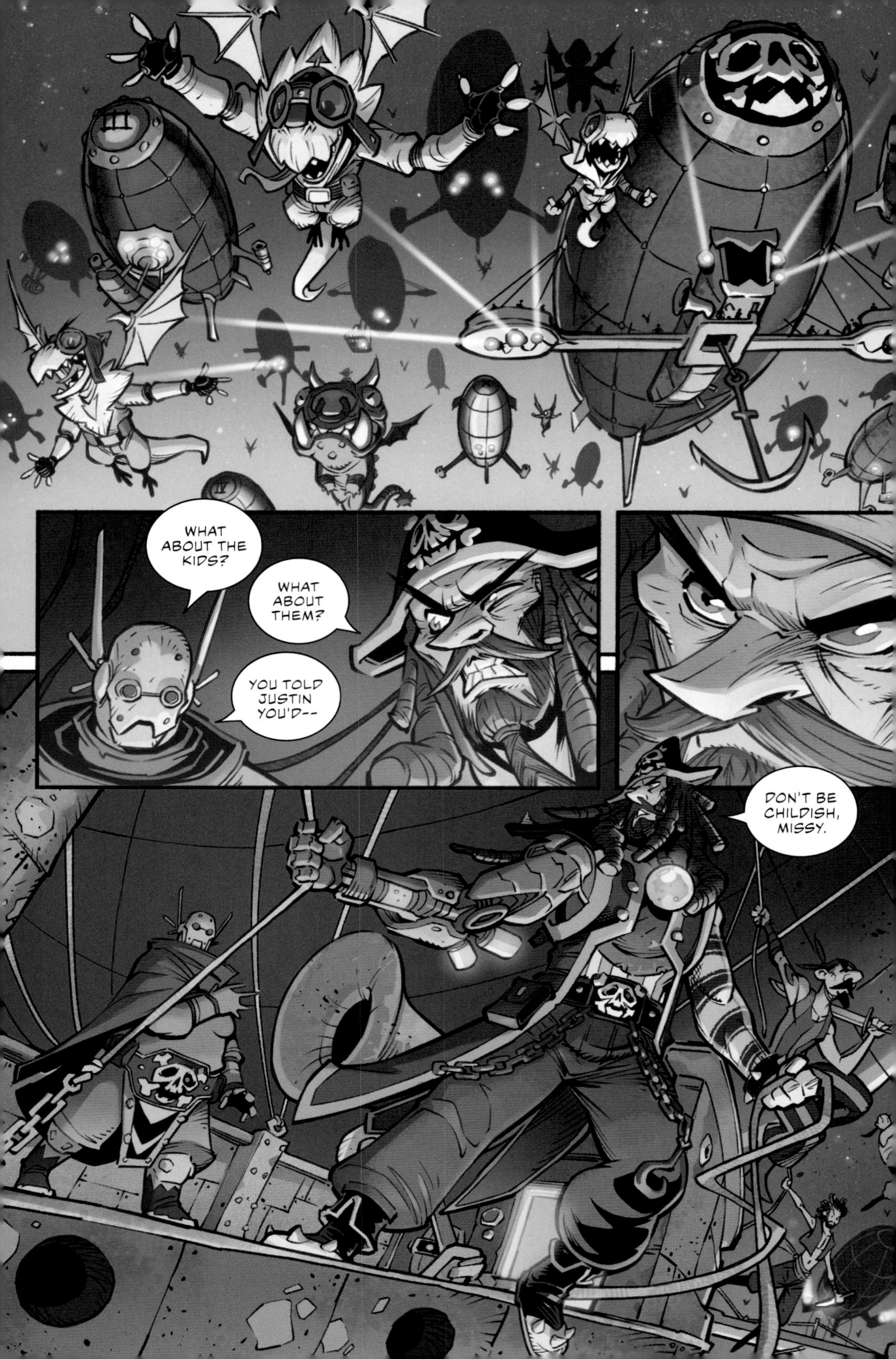
WHAT ABOUT THE KIDS?
WHAT ABOUT THEM?
YOU TOLD JUSTIN YOU'D--
DON'T BE CHILDISH, MISSY.

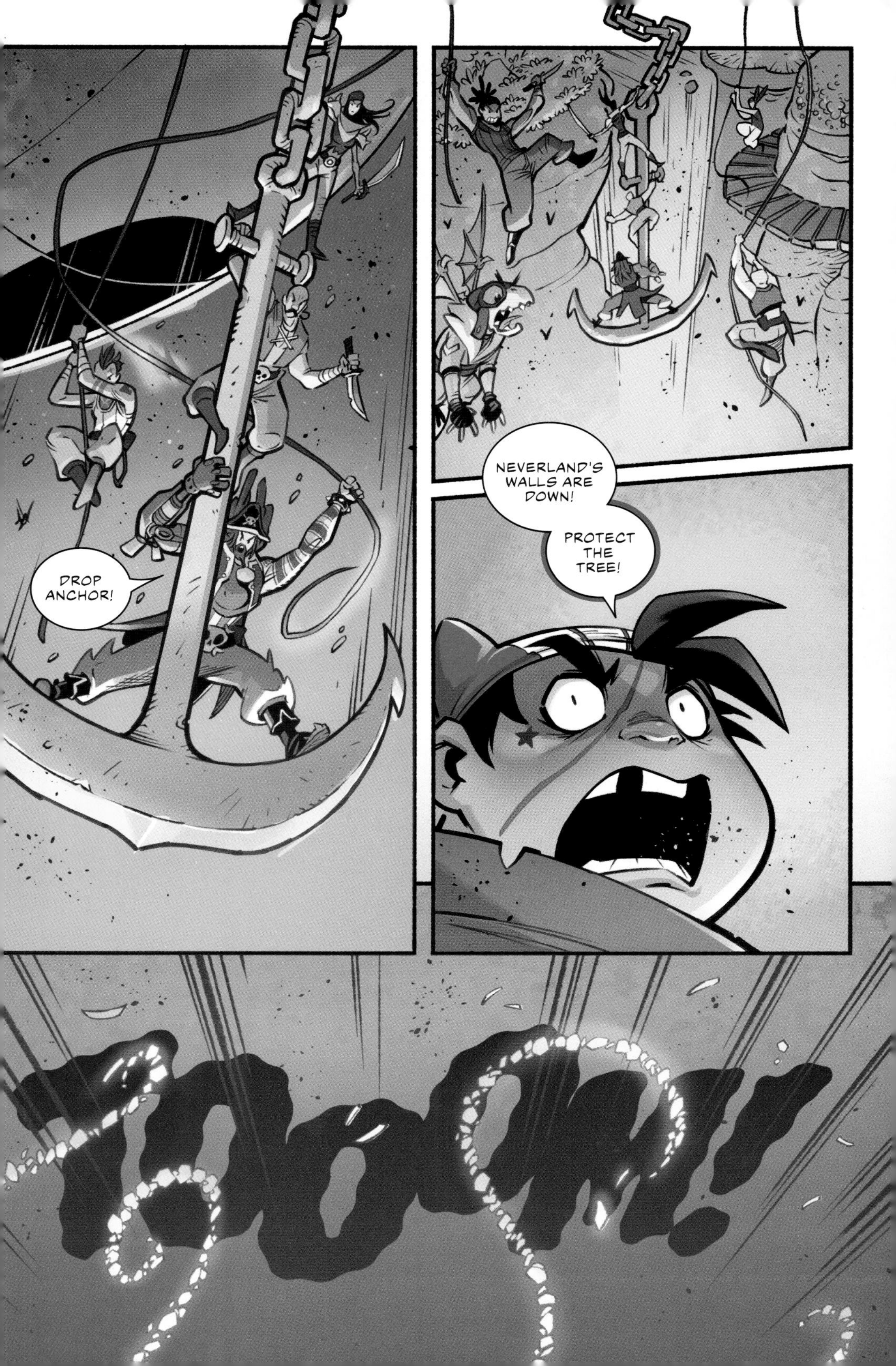
DROP ANCHOR!
NEVERLAND'S WALLS ARE DOWN!
PROTECT THE TREE!
THOOOM!!

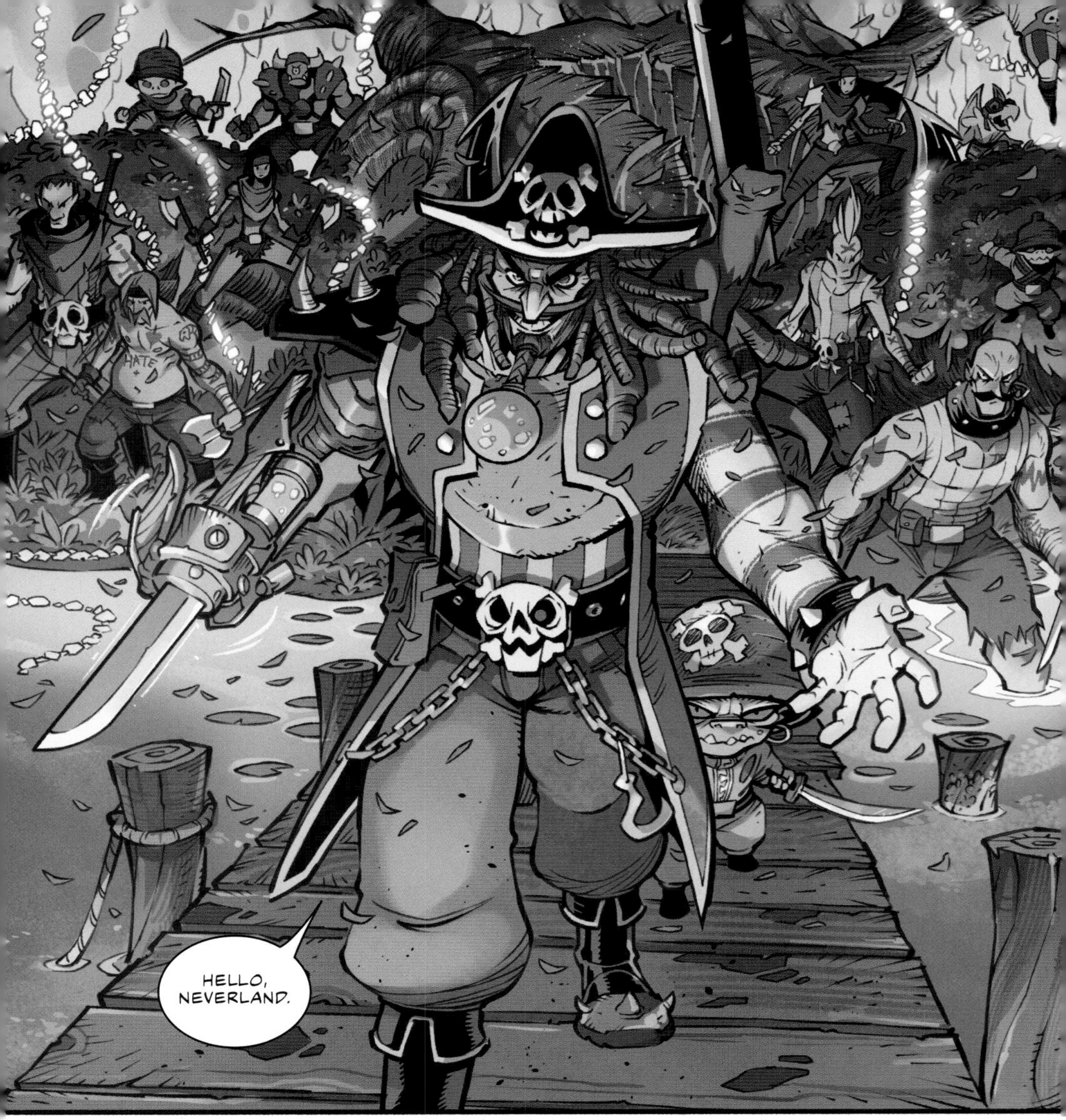
HELLO, NEVERLAND.

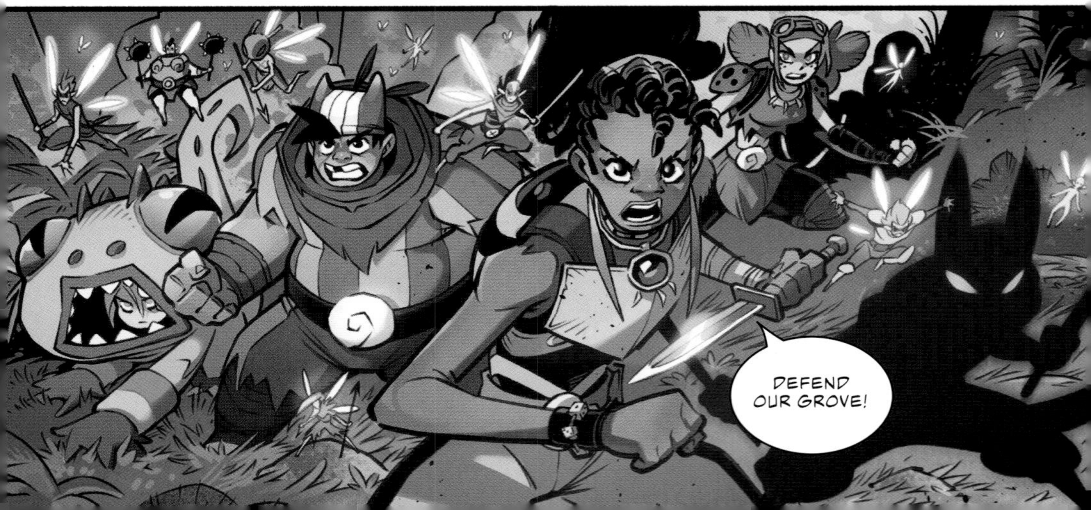
DEFEND OUR GROVE!

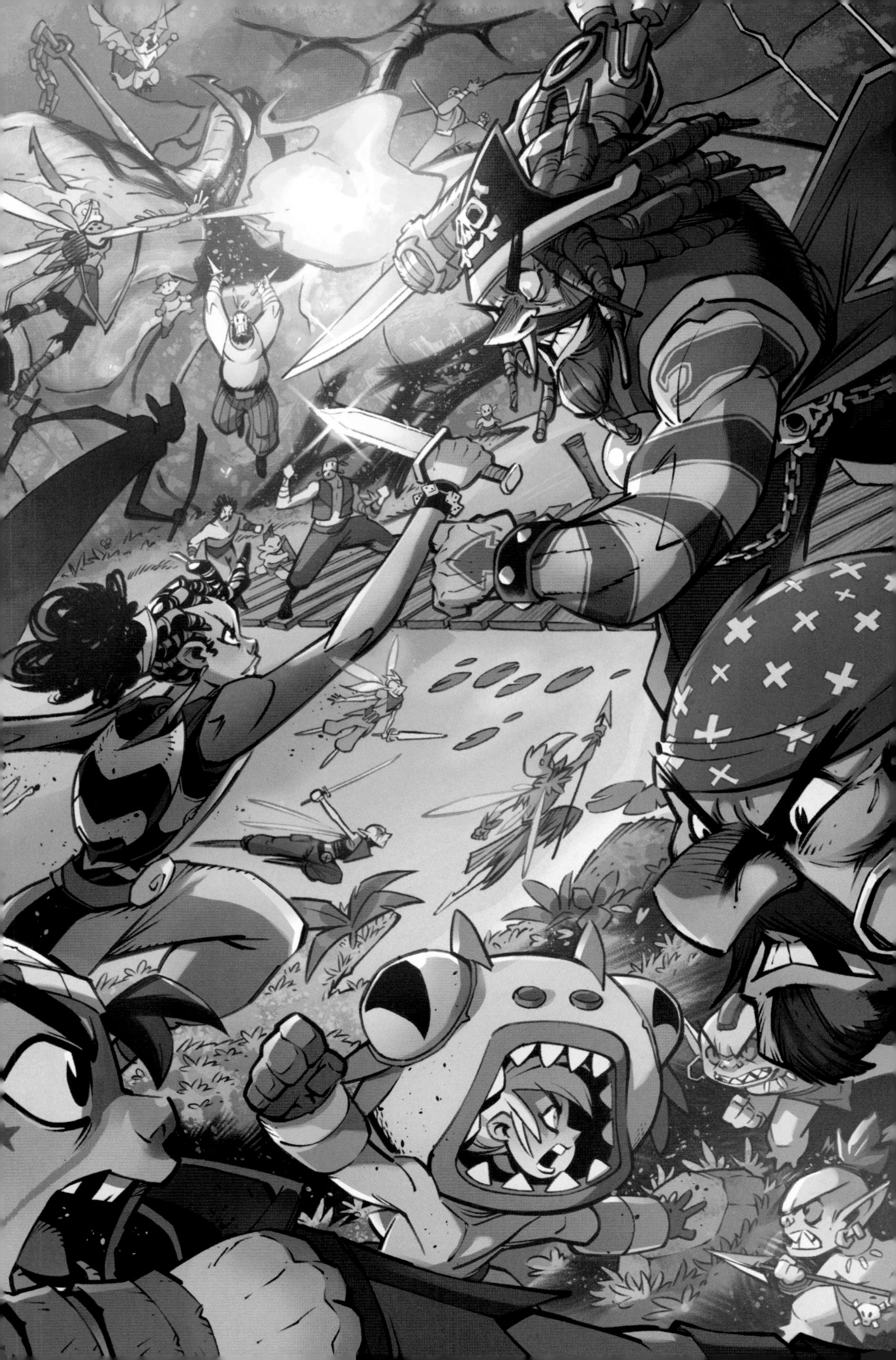

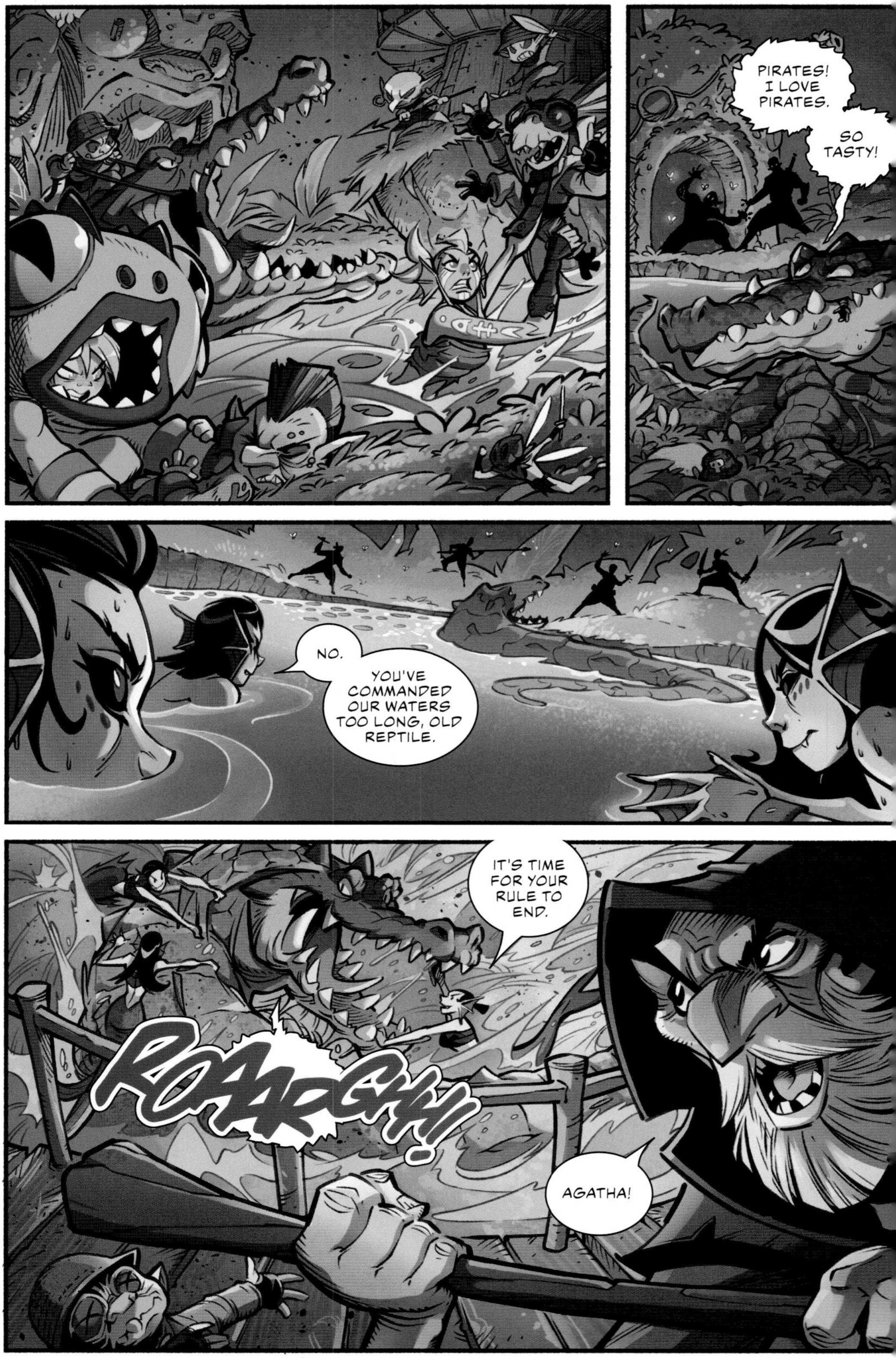
PIRATES! I LOVE PIRATES.
SO TASTY!
NO.
YOU'VE COMMANDED OUR WATERS TOO LONG, OLD REPTILE.
IT'S TIME FOR YOUR RULE TO END.
ROARGH!!
AGATHA!

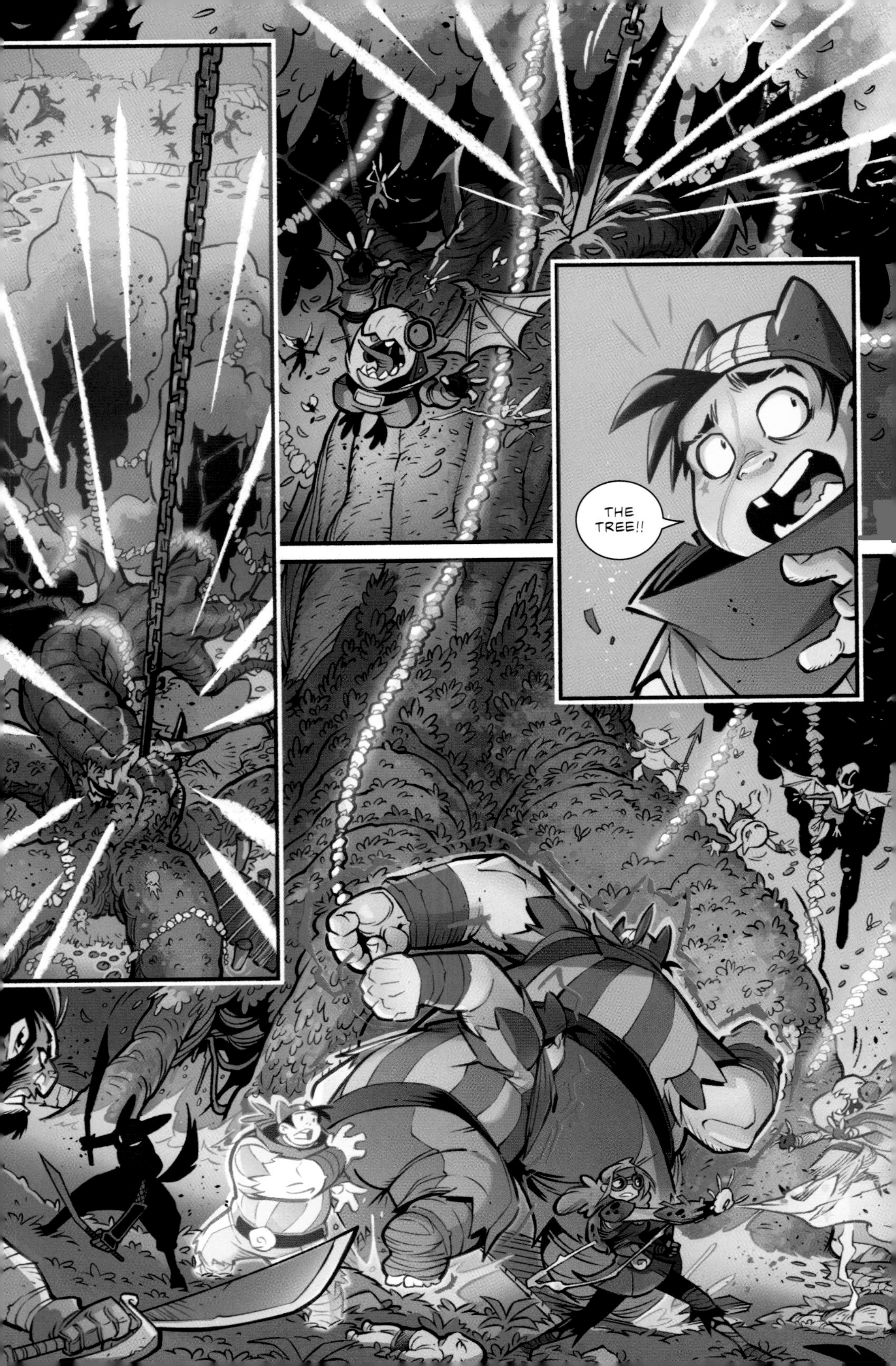
THE TREE!!

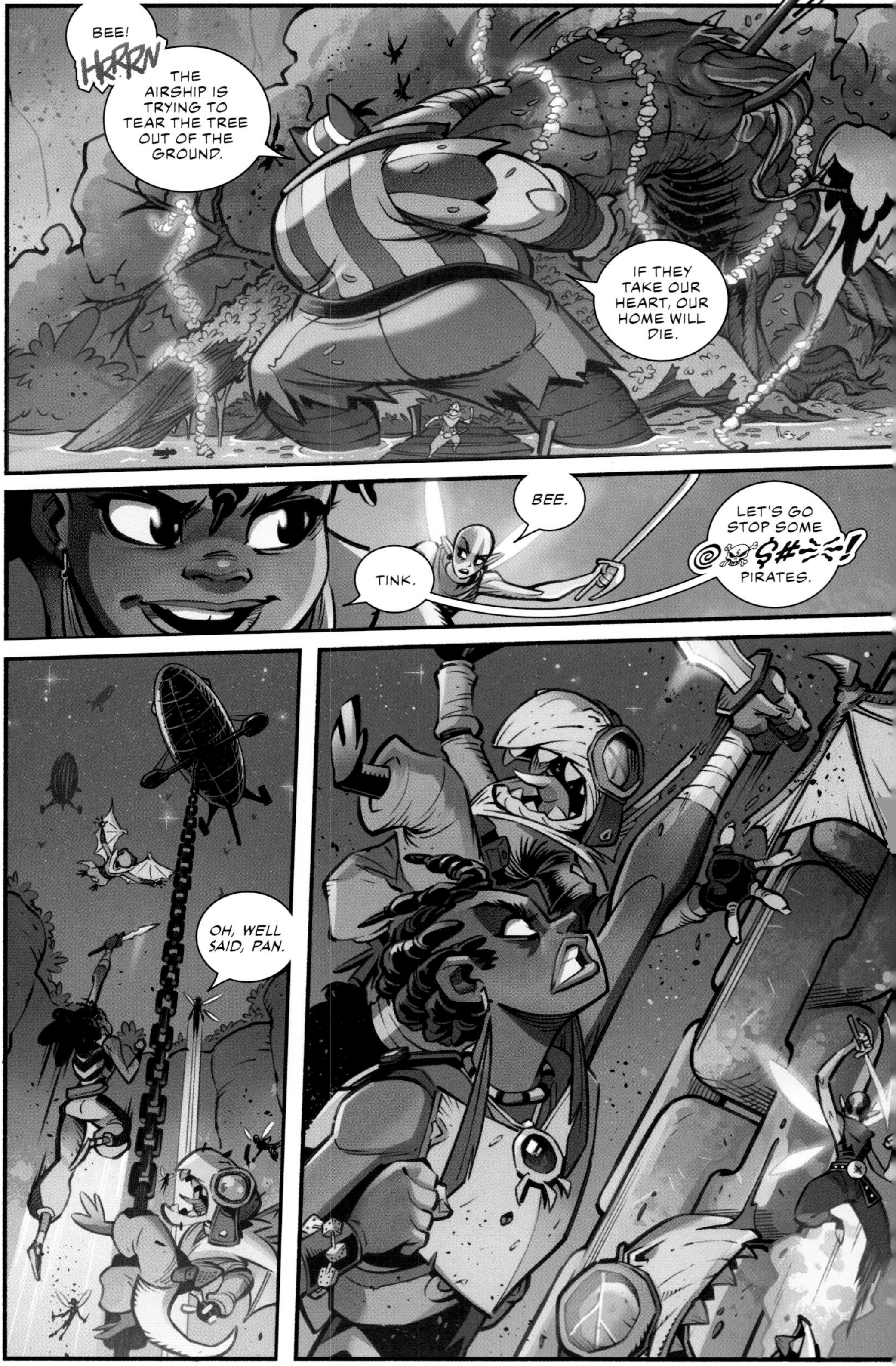
BEE!
HRRRN
THE AIRSHIP IS TRYING TO TEAR THE TREE OUT OF THE GROUND.
IF THEY TAKE OUR HEART, OUR HOME WILL DIE.
BEE.
TINK.
LET'S GO STOP SOME @☠$#~~! PIRATES.
OH, WELL SAID, PAN.

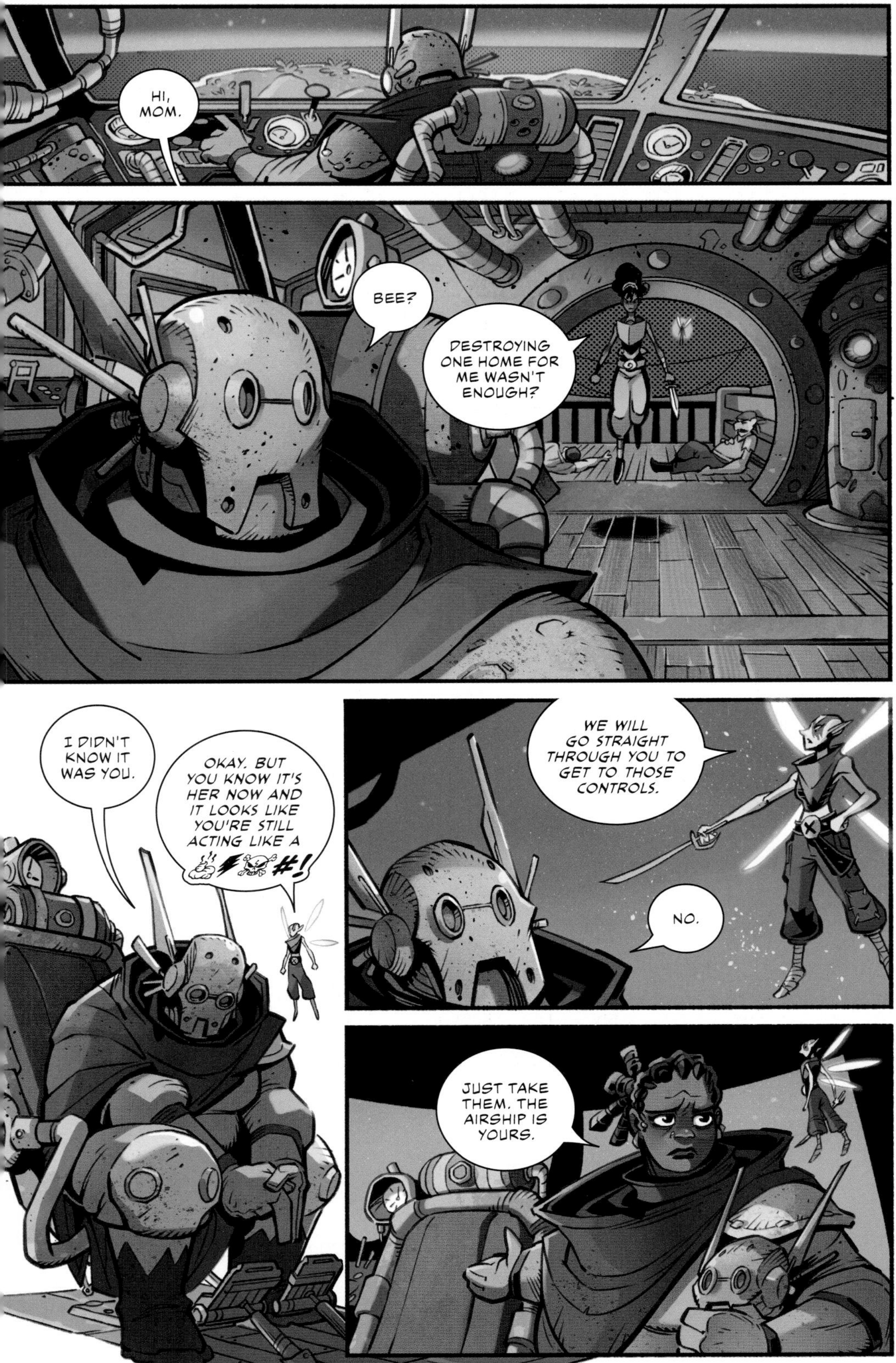
HI, MOM.
BEE?
DESTROYING ONE HOME FOR ME WASN'T ENOUGH?
I DIDN'T KNOW IT WAS YOU.
OKAY. BUT YOU KNOW IT'S HER NOW AND IT LOOKS LIKE YOU'RE STILL ACTING LIKE A #!
WE WILL GO STRAIGHT THROUGH YOU TO GET TO THOSE CONTROLS.
NO.
JUST TAKE THEM. THE AIRSHIP IS YOURS.

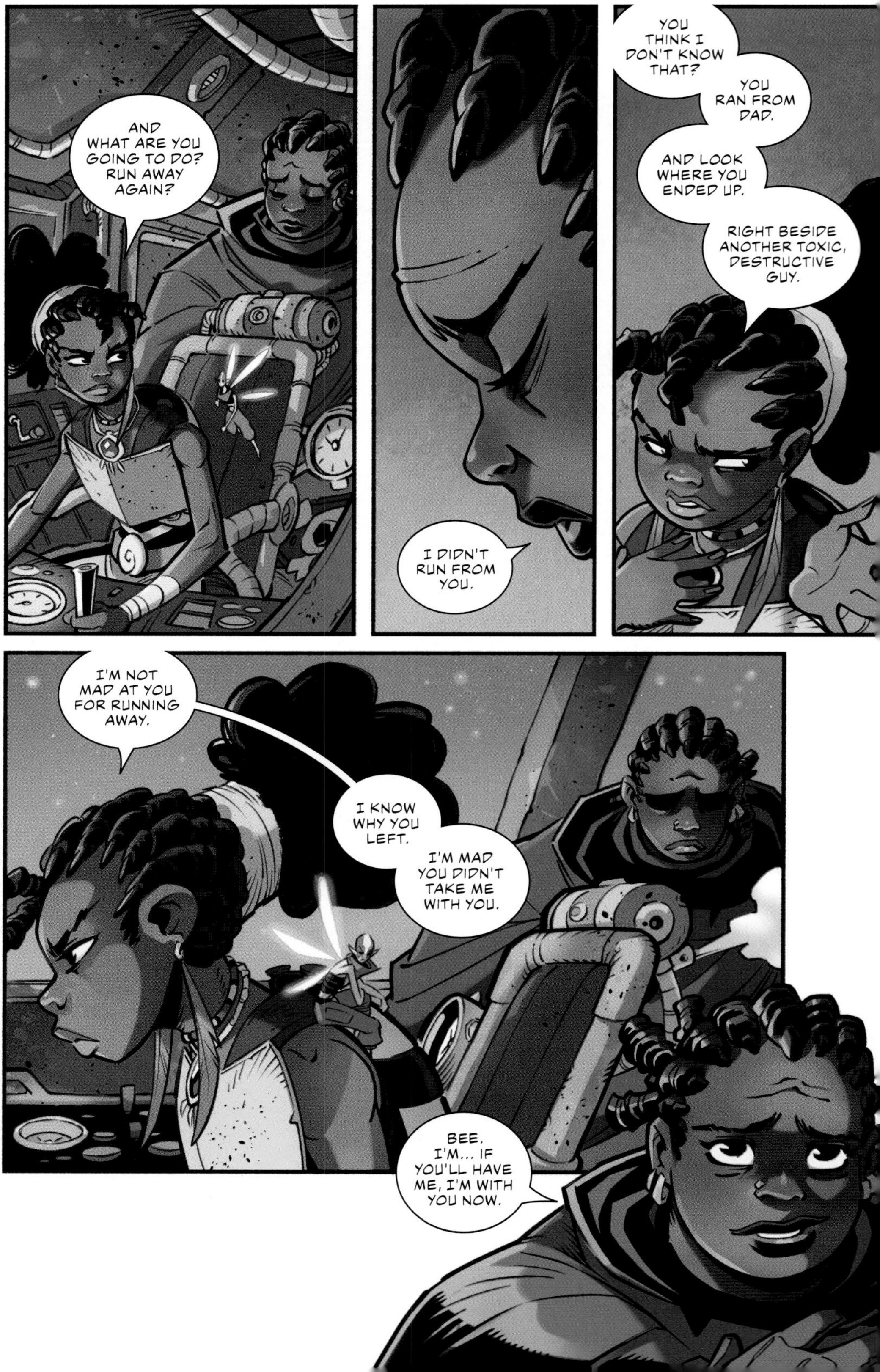

AND WHAT ARE YOU GOING TO DO? RUN AWAY AGAIN?
I DIDN'T RUN FROM YOU.
YOU THINK I DON'T KNOW THAT?
YOU RAN FROM DAD.
AND LOOK WHERE YOU ENDED UP.
RIGHT BESIDE ANOTHER TOXIC, DESTRUCTIVE GUY.
I'M NOT MAD AT YOU FOR RUNNING AWAY.
I KNOW WHY YOU LEFT.
I'M MAD YOU DIDN'T TAKE ME WITH YOU.
BEE. I'M... IF YOU'LL HAVE ME, I'M WITH YOU NOW.

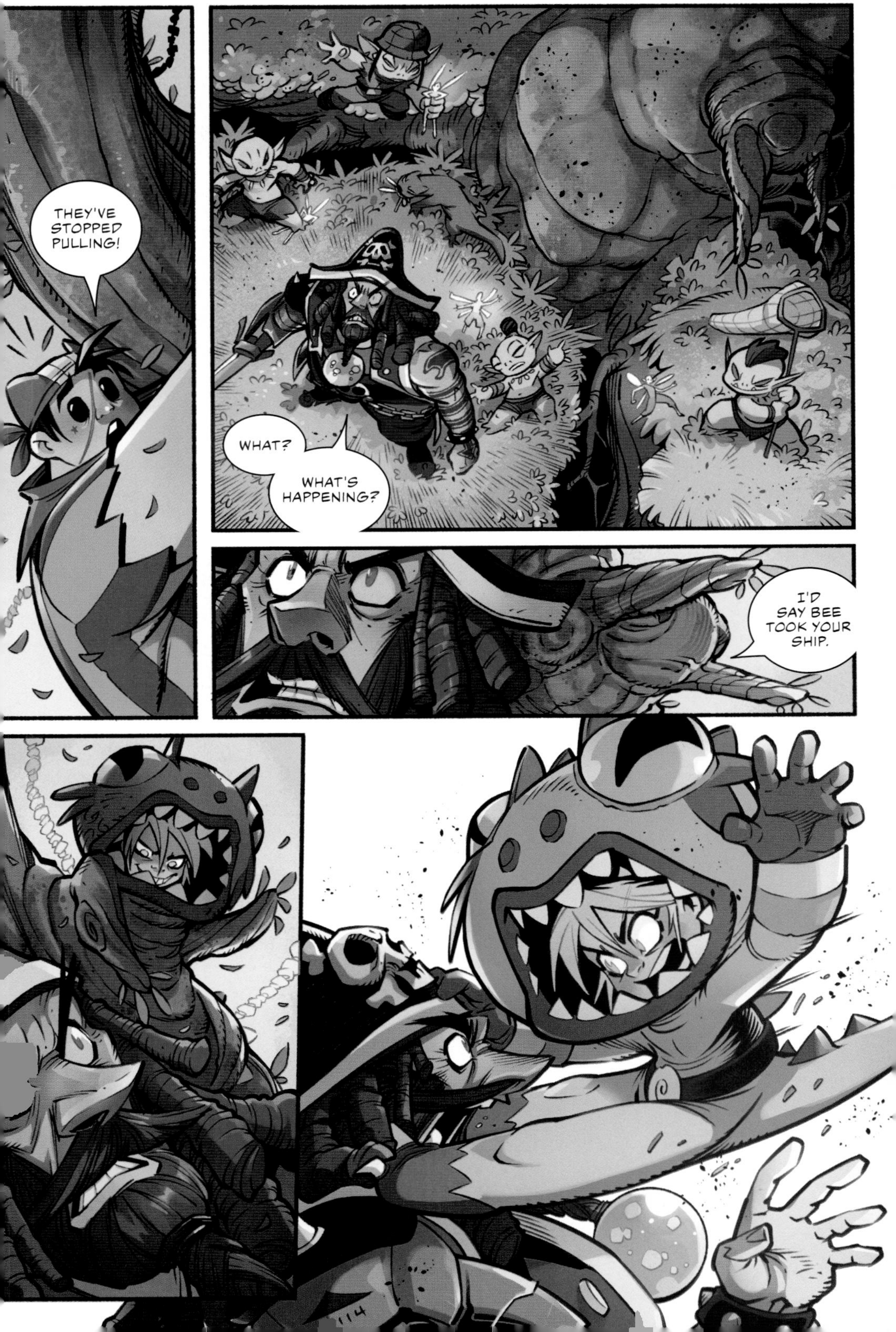
THEY'VE STOPPED PULLING!
WHAT?
WHAT'S HAPPENING?
I'D SAY BEE TOOK YOUR SHIP.

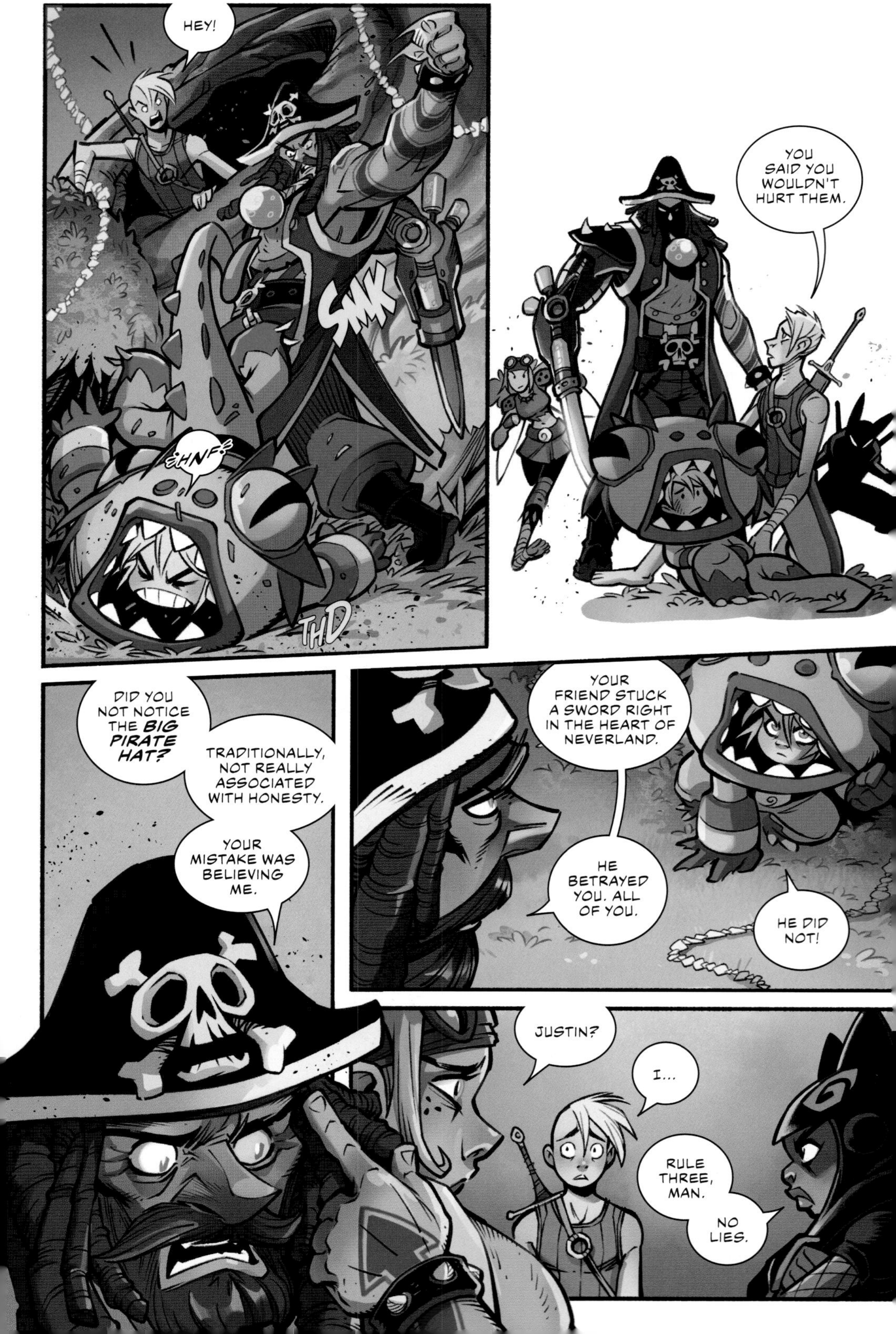
HEY!
SMK
HNF
THD
YOU SAID YOU WOULDN'T HURT THEM.
DID YOU NOT NOTICE THE BIG PIRATE HAT?
TRADITIONALLY, NOT REALLY ASSOCIATED WITH HONESTY.
YOUR MISTAKE WAS BELIEVING ME.
YOUR FRIEND STUCK A SWORD RIGHT IN THE HEART OF NEVERLAND.
HE BETRAYED YOU. ALL OF YOU.
HE DID NOT!
JUSTIN?
I...
RULE THREE, MAN.
NO LIES.

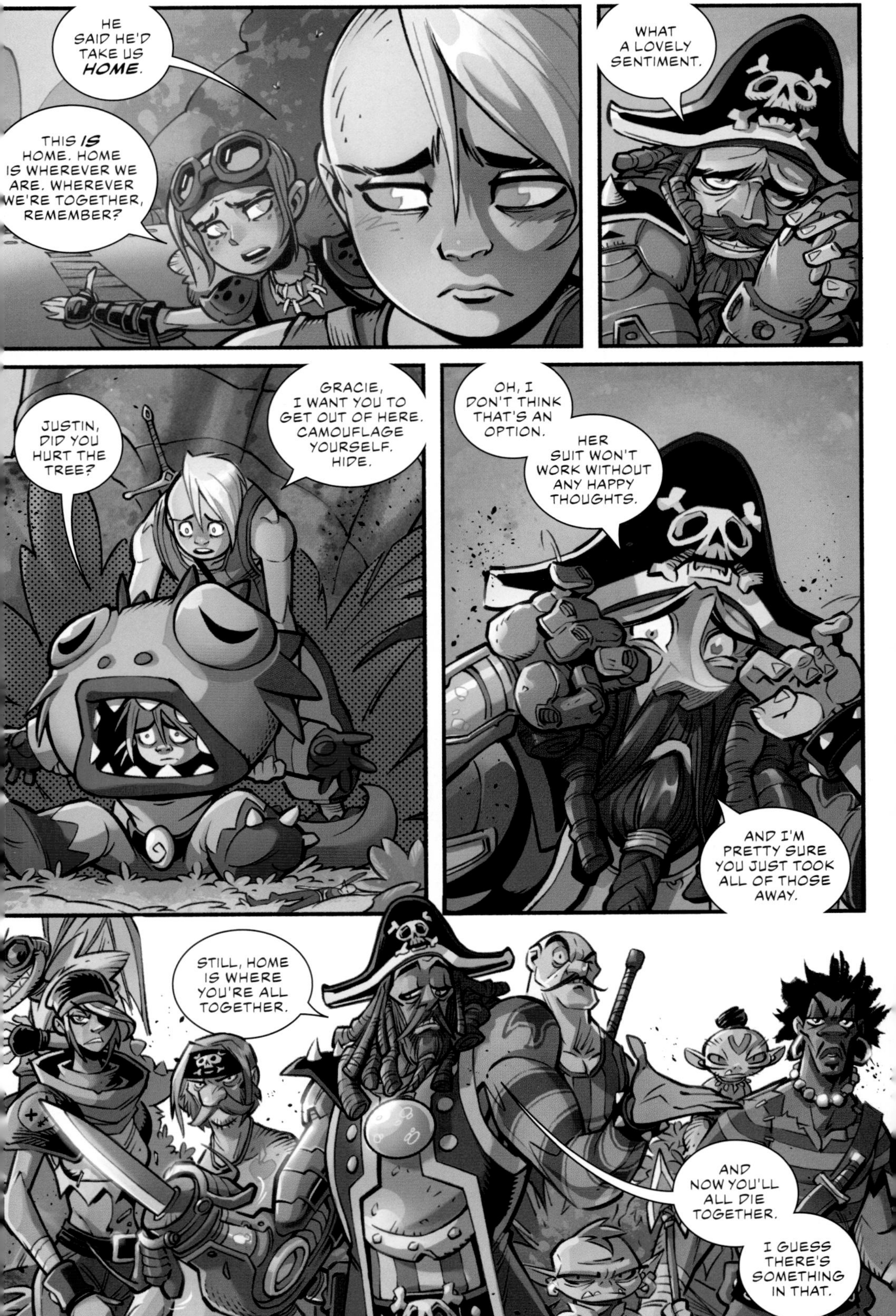
HE SAID HE'D TAKE US *HOME*.
THIS *IS* HOME. HOME IS WHEREVER WE ARE. WHEREVER WE'RE TOGETHER, REMEMBER?
WHAT A LOVELY SENTIMENT.
JUSTIN, DID YOU HURT THE TREE?
GRACIE, I WANT YOU TO GET OUT OF HERE. CAMOUFLAGE YOURSELF. HIDE.
OH, I DON'T THINK THAT'S AN OPTION.
HER SUIT WON'T WORK WITHOUT ANY HAPPY THOUGHTS.
AND I'M PRETTY SURE YOU JUST TOOK ALL OF THOSE AWAY.
STILL, HOME IS WHERE YOU'RE ALL TOGETHER.
AND NOW YOU'LL ALL DIE TOGETHER.
I GUESS THERE'S SOMETHING IN THAT.

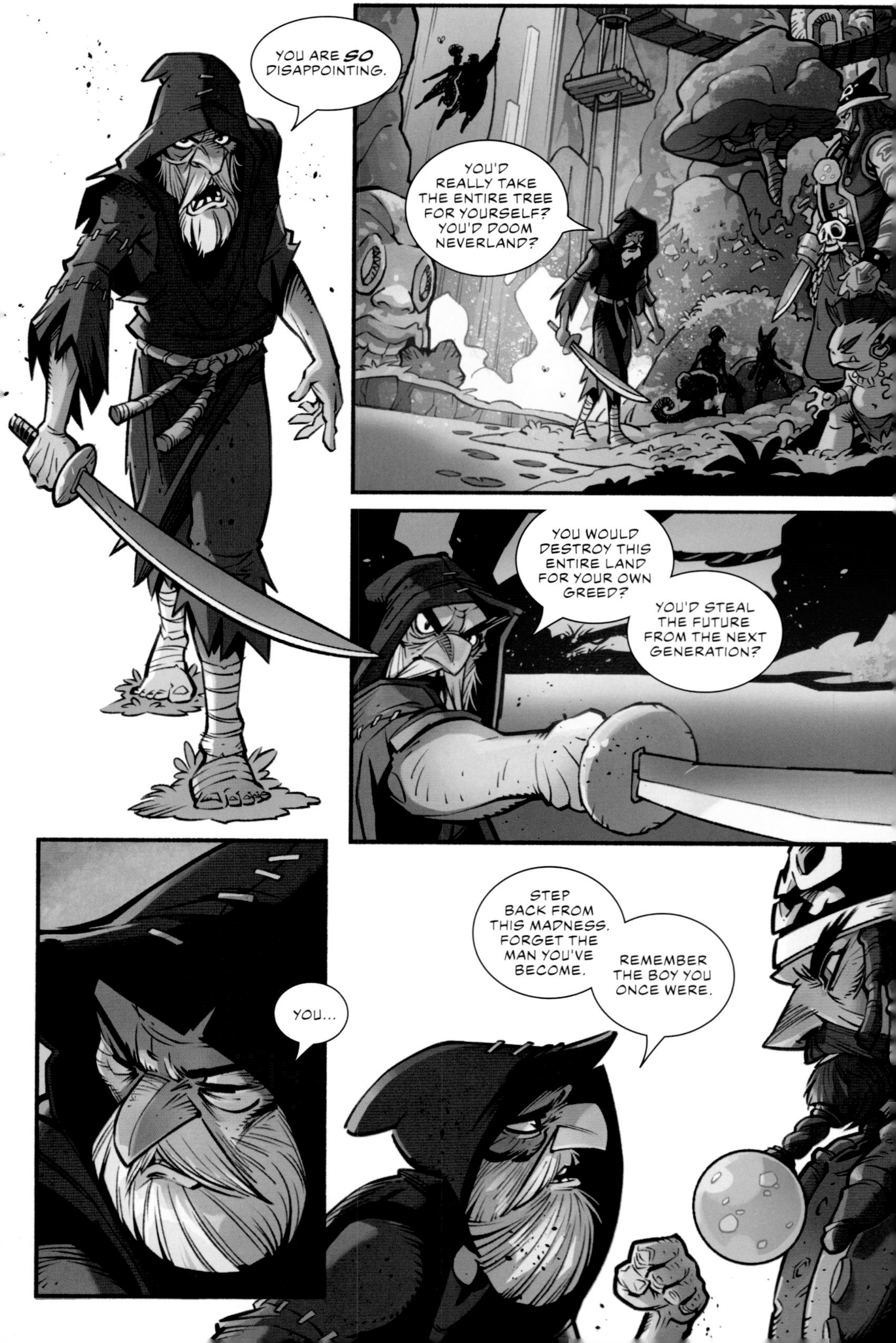
YOU ARE SO DISAPPOINTING.
YOU'D REALLY TAKE THE ENTIRE TREE FOR YOURSELF? YOU'D DOOM NEVERLAND?
YOU WOULD DESTROY THIS ENTIRE LAND FOR YOUR OWN GREED?
YOU'D STEAL THE FUTURE FROM THE NEXT GENERATION?
YOU...
STEP BACK FROM THIS MADNESS. FORGET THE MAN YOU'VE BECOME.
REMEMBER THE BOY YOU ONCE WERE.

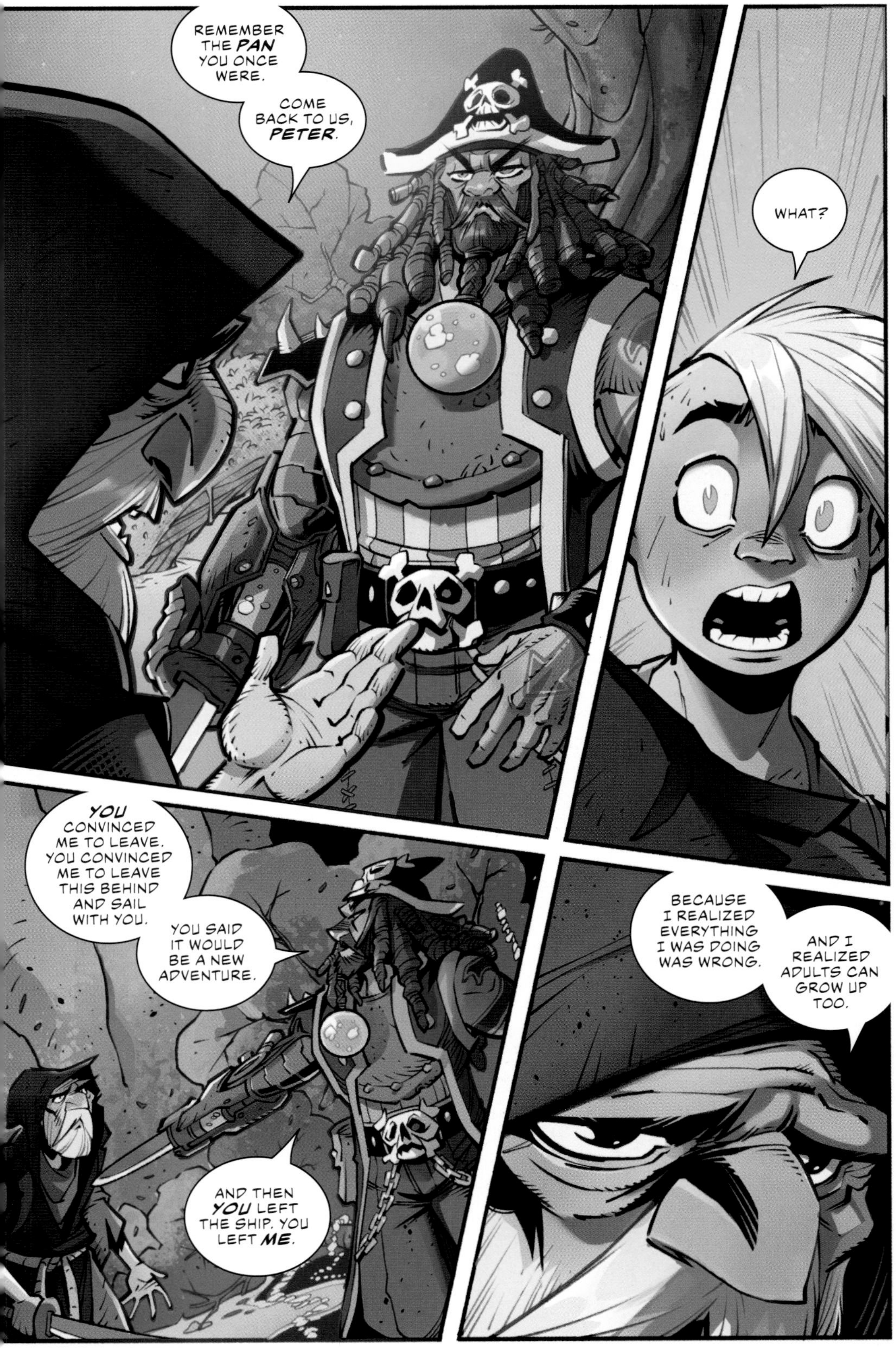
REMEMBER THE PAN YOU ONCE WERE.
COME BACK TO US, PETER.
WHAT?
YOU CONVINCED ME TO LEAVE. YOU CONVINCED ME TO LEAVE THIS BEHIND AND SAIL WITH YOU.
YOU SAID IT WOULD BE A NEW ADVENTURE.
AND THEN YOU LEFT THE SHIP. YOU LEFT ME.
BECAUSE I REALIZED EVERYTHING I WAS DOING WAS WRONG.
AND I REALIZED ADULTS CAN GROW UP TOO.

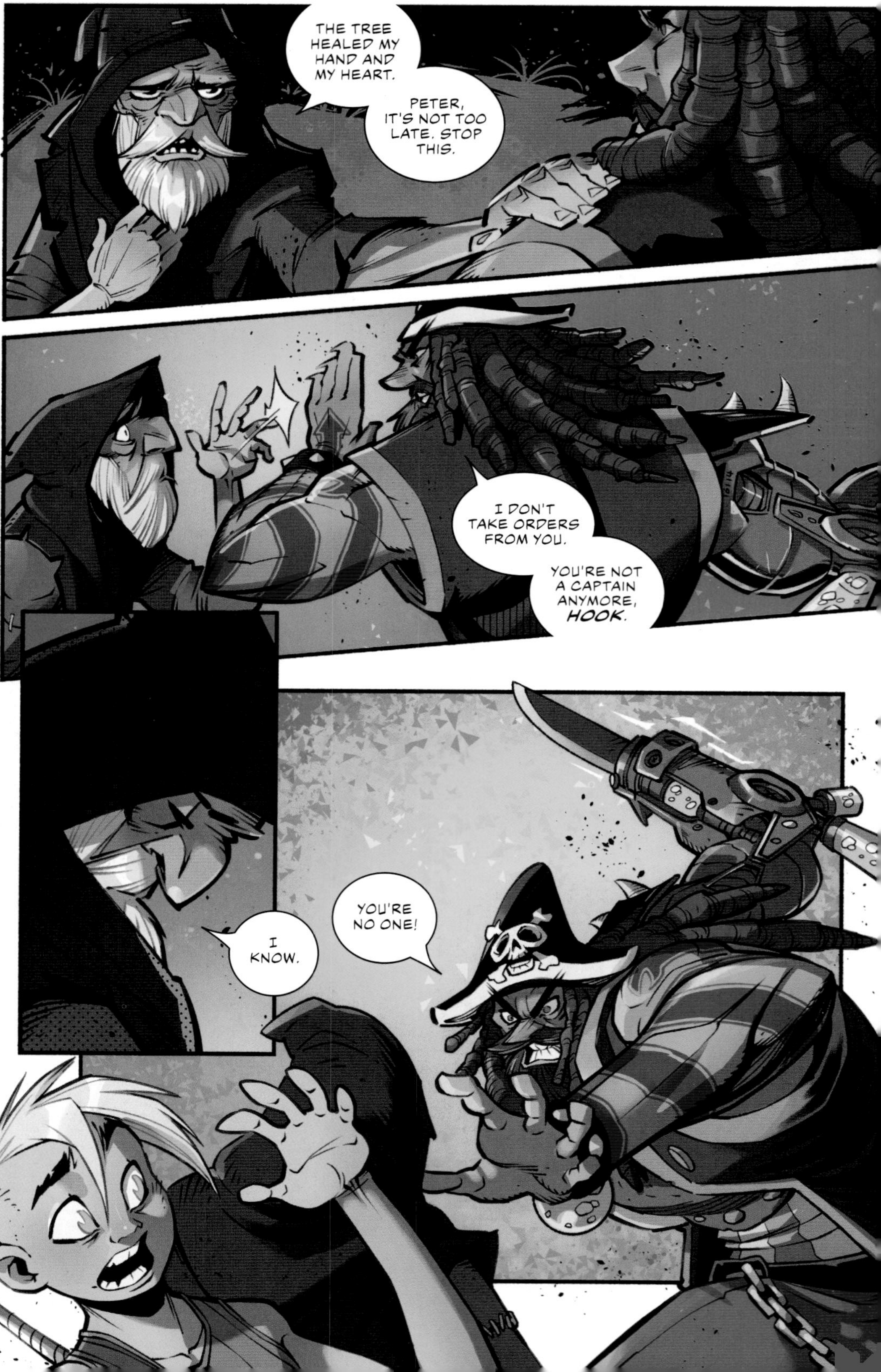
THE TREE HEALED MY HAND AND MY HEART.
PETER, IT'S NOT TOO LATE. STOP THIS.
I DON'T TAKE ORDERS FROM YOU.
YOU'RE NOT A CAPTAIN ANYMORE, ***HOOK***.
I KNOW.
YOU'RE NO ONE!

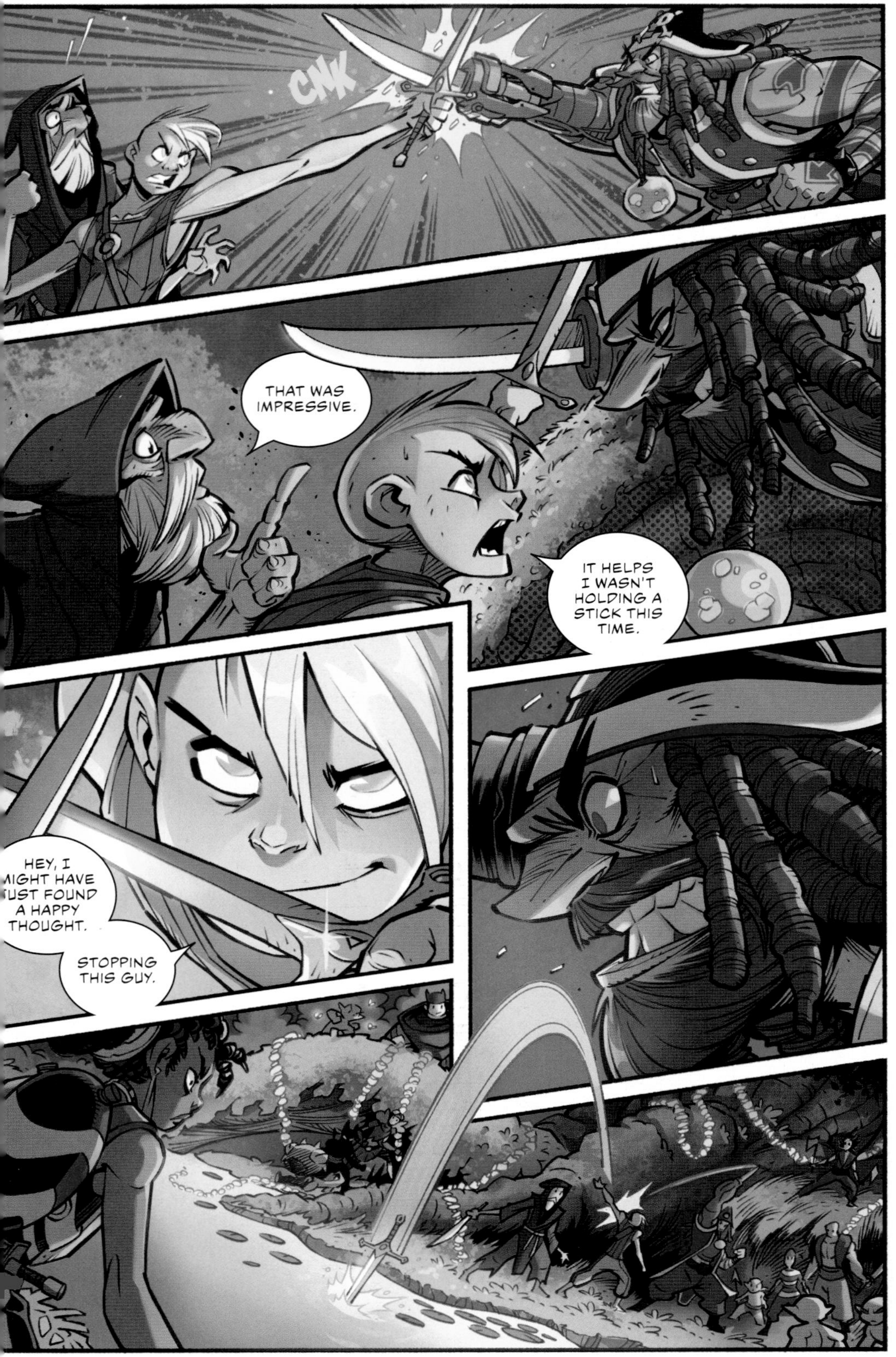
CNK
THAT WAS IMPRESSIVE.
IT HELPS I WASN'T HOLDING A STICK THIS TIME.
HEY, I MIGHT HAVE JUST FOUND A HAPPY THOUGHT.
STOPPING THIS GUY.

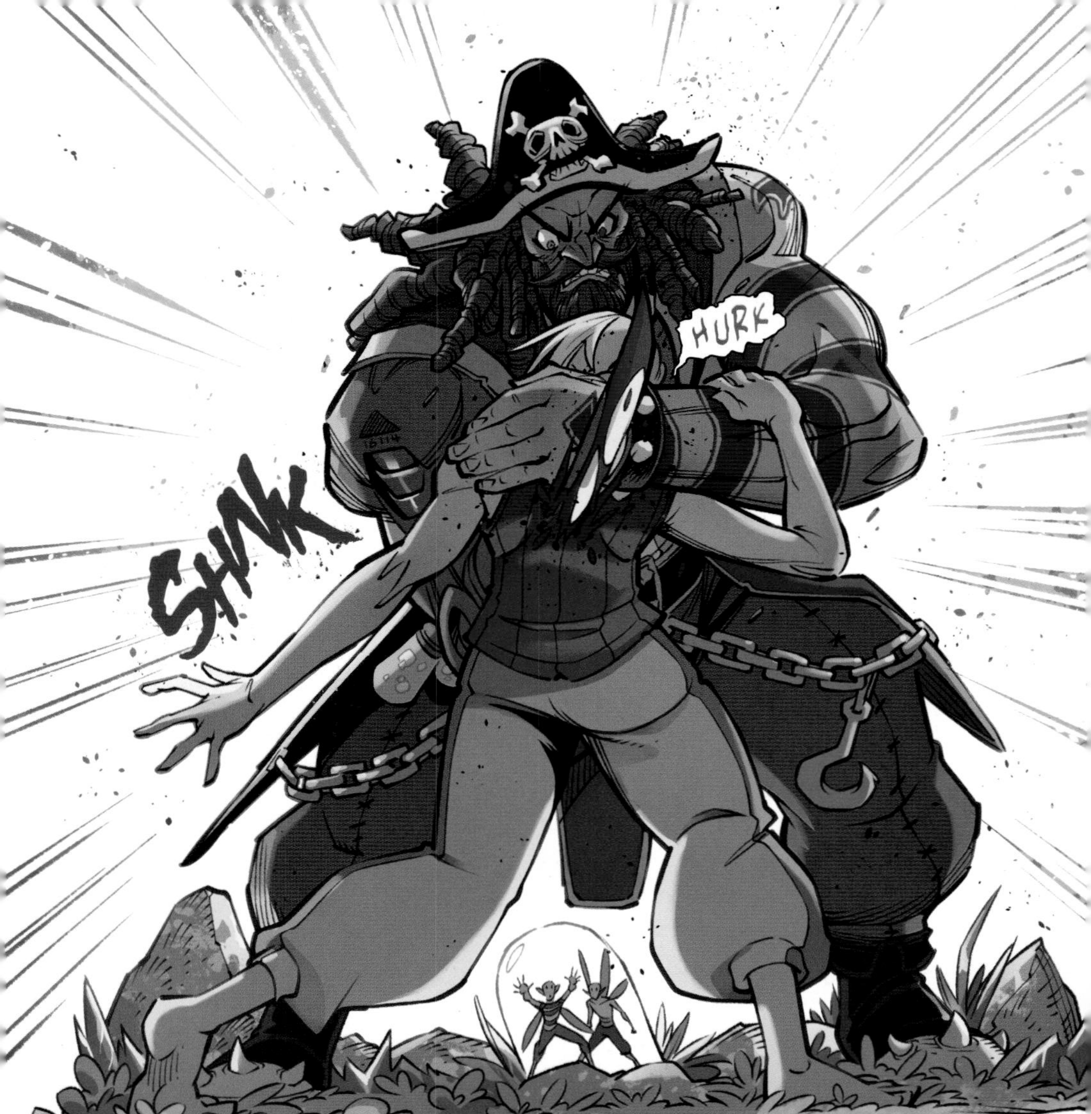
SHNK
HURK

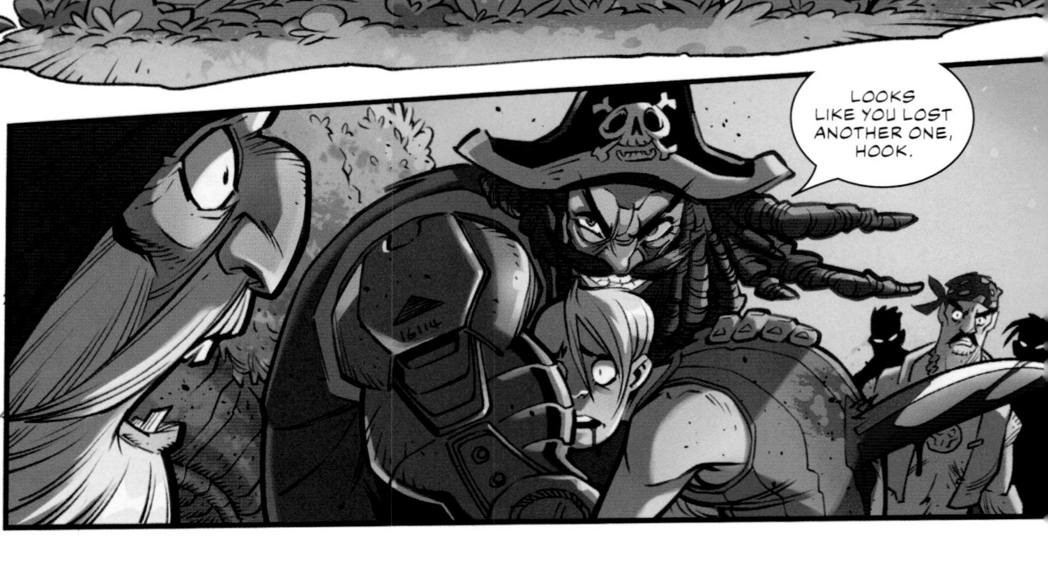
LOOKS LIKE YOU LOST ANOTHER ONE, HOOK.

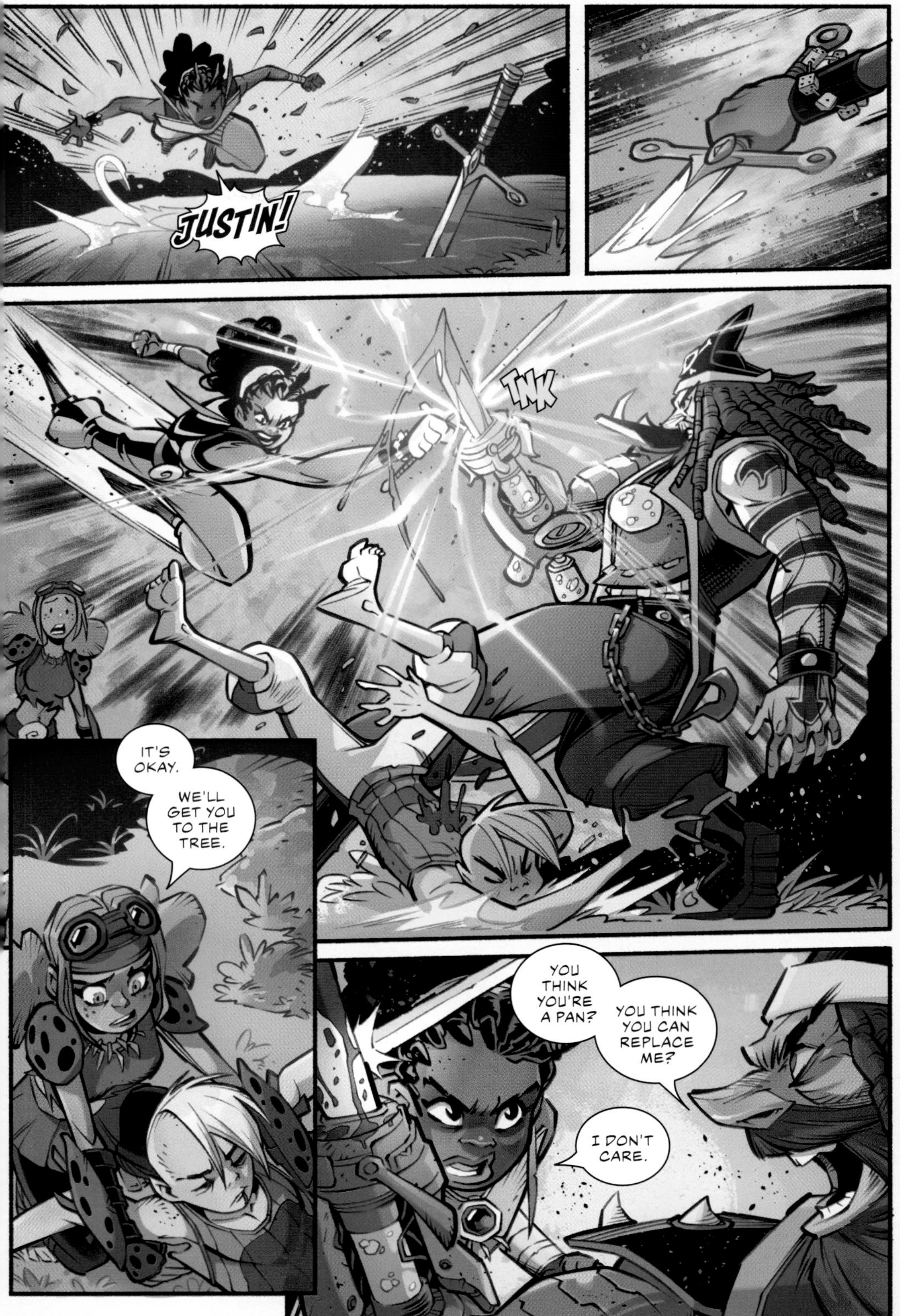
JUSTIN!
TNK
IT'S OKAY.
WE'LL GET YOU TO THE TREE.
YOU THINK YOU'RE A PAN?
YOU THINK YOU CAN REPLACE ME?
I DON'T CARE.

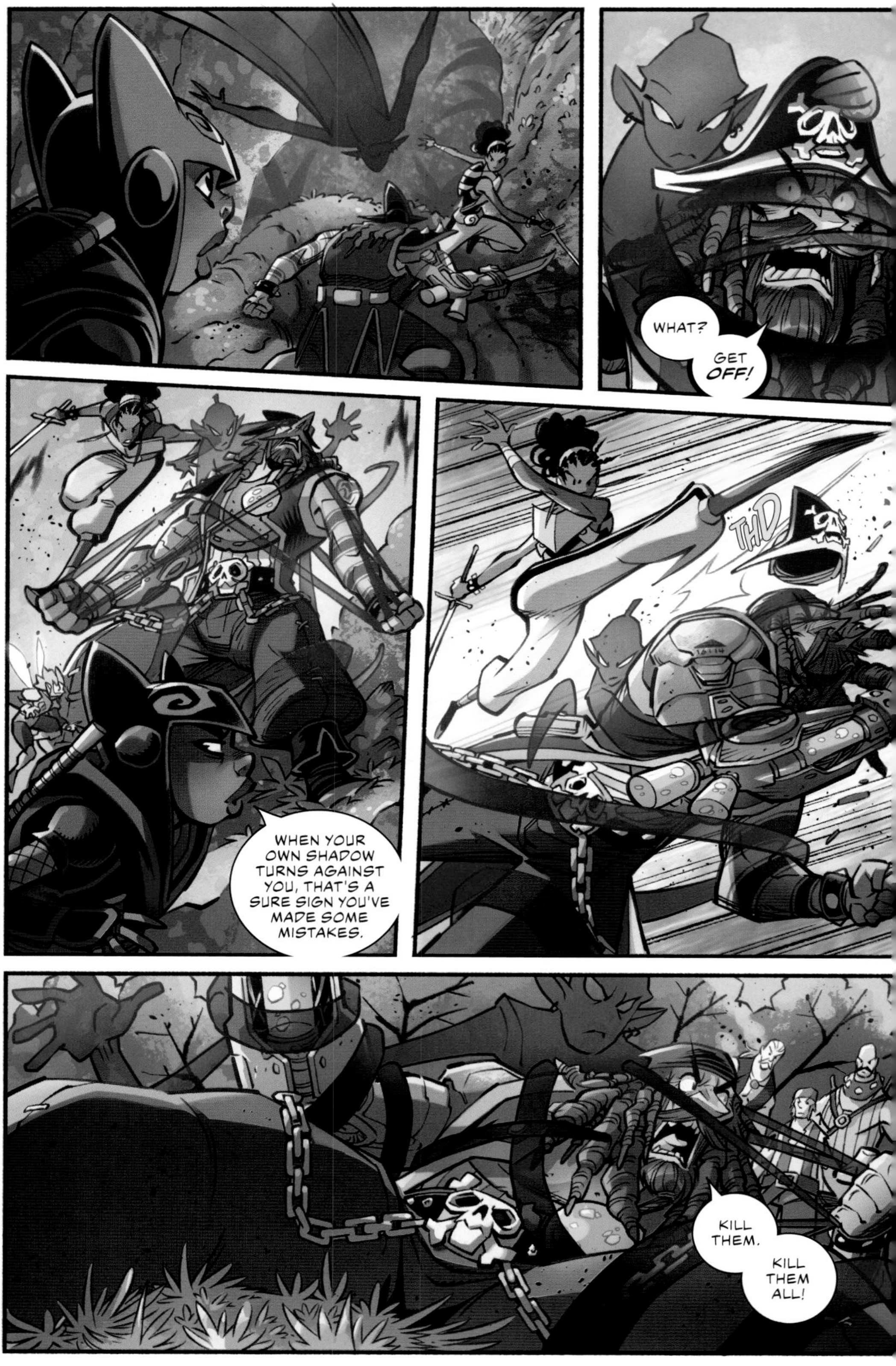
WHAT?
GET OFF!
WHEN YOUR OWN SHADOW TURNS AGAINST YOU, THAT'S A SURE SIGN YOU'VE MADE SOME MISTAKES.
THD
KILL THEM.
KILL THEM ALL!

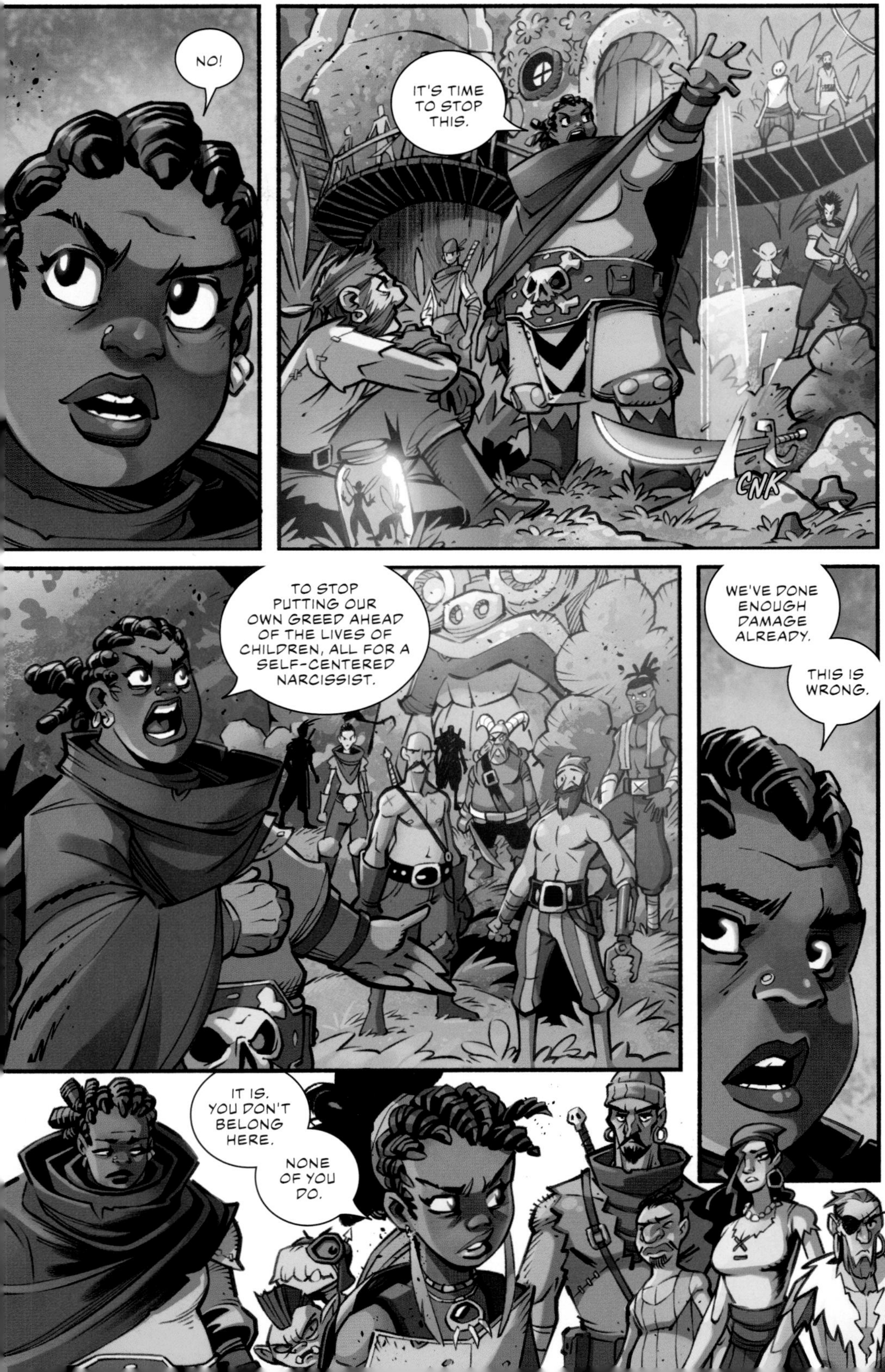

NO!
IT'S TIME TO STOP THIS.
CNK
TO STOP PUTTING OUR OWN GREED AHEAD OF THE LIVES OF CHILDREN, ALL FOR A SELF-CENTERED NARCISSIST.
WE'VE DONE ENOUGH DAMAGE ALREADY.
THIS IS WRONG.
IT IS. YOU DON'T BELONG HERE.
NONE OF YOU DO.

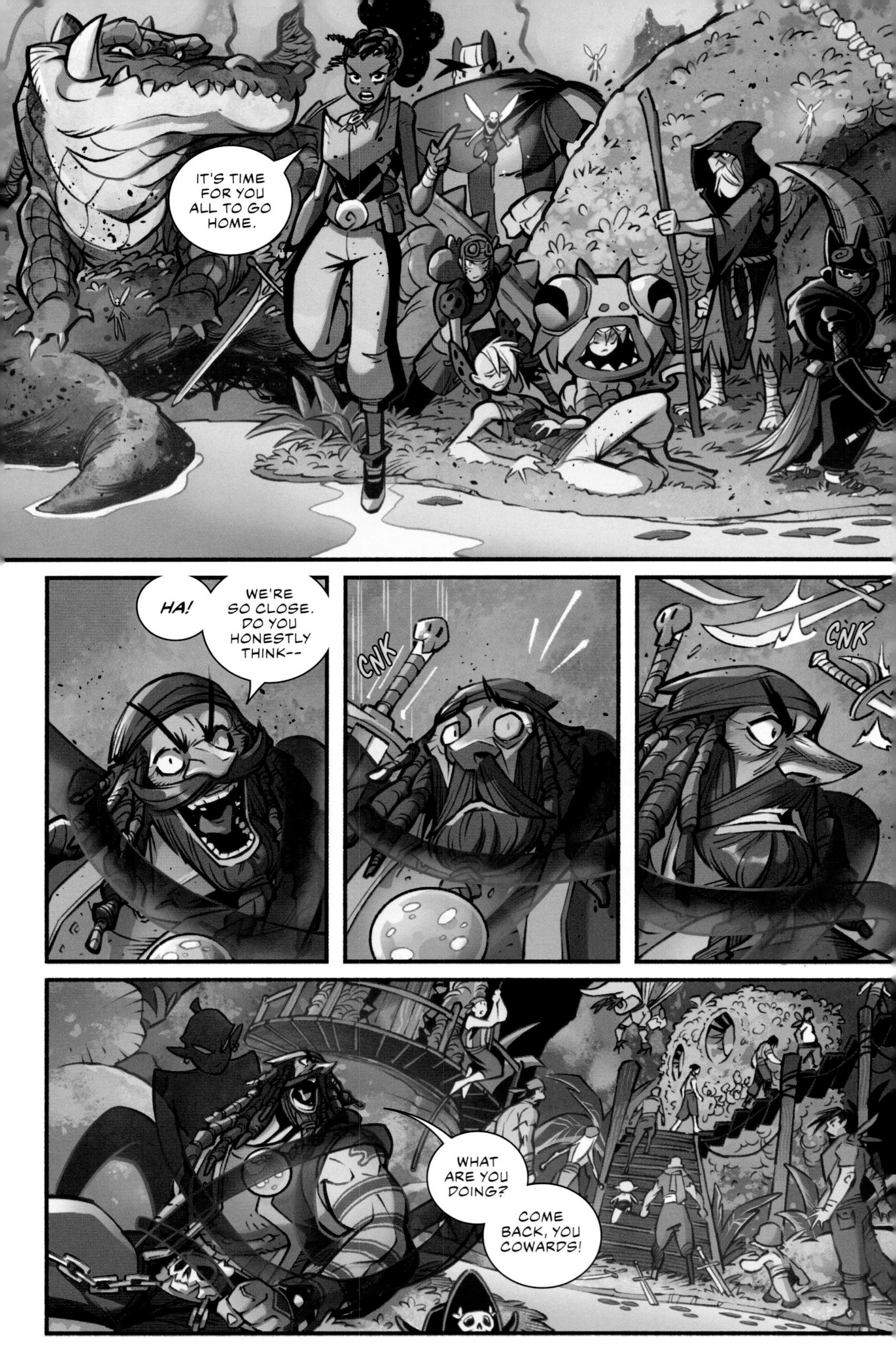
IT'S TIME FOR YOU ALL TO GO HOME.
HA!
WE'RE SO CLOSE. DO YOU HONESTLY THINK--
CNK
CNK
WHAT ARE YOU DOING?
COME BACK, YOU COWARDS!

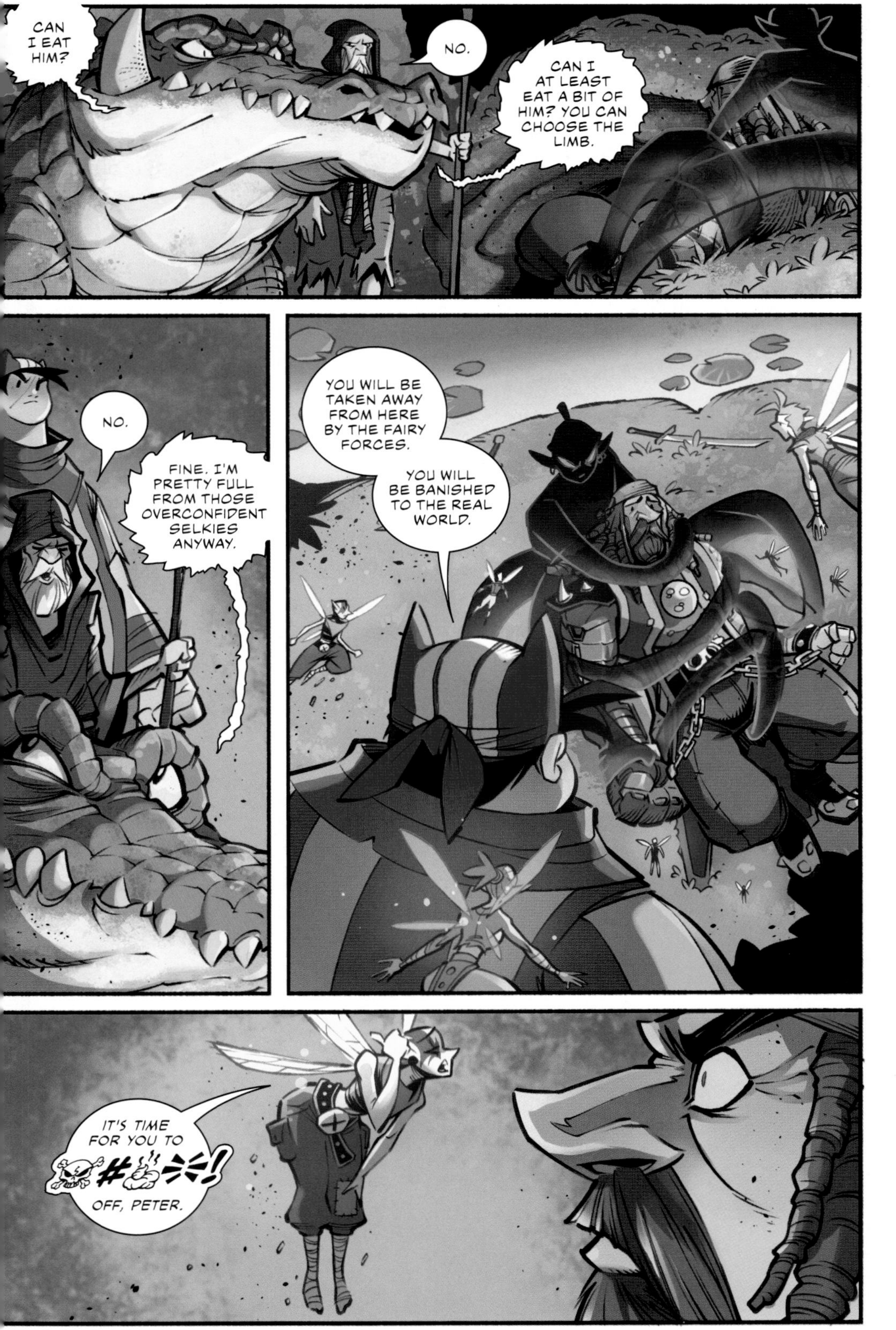
CAN I EAT HIM?
NO.
CAN I AT LEAST EAT A BIT OF HIM? YOU CAN CHOOSE THE LIMB.
NO.
FINE. I'M PRETTY FULL FROM THOSE OVERCONFIDENT SELKIES ANYWAY.
YOU WILL BE TAKEN AWAY FROM HERE BY THE FAIRY FORCES.
YOU WILL BE BANISHED TO THE REAL WORLD.
IT'S TIME FOR YOU TO #!
OFF, PETER.

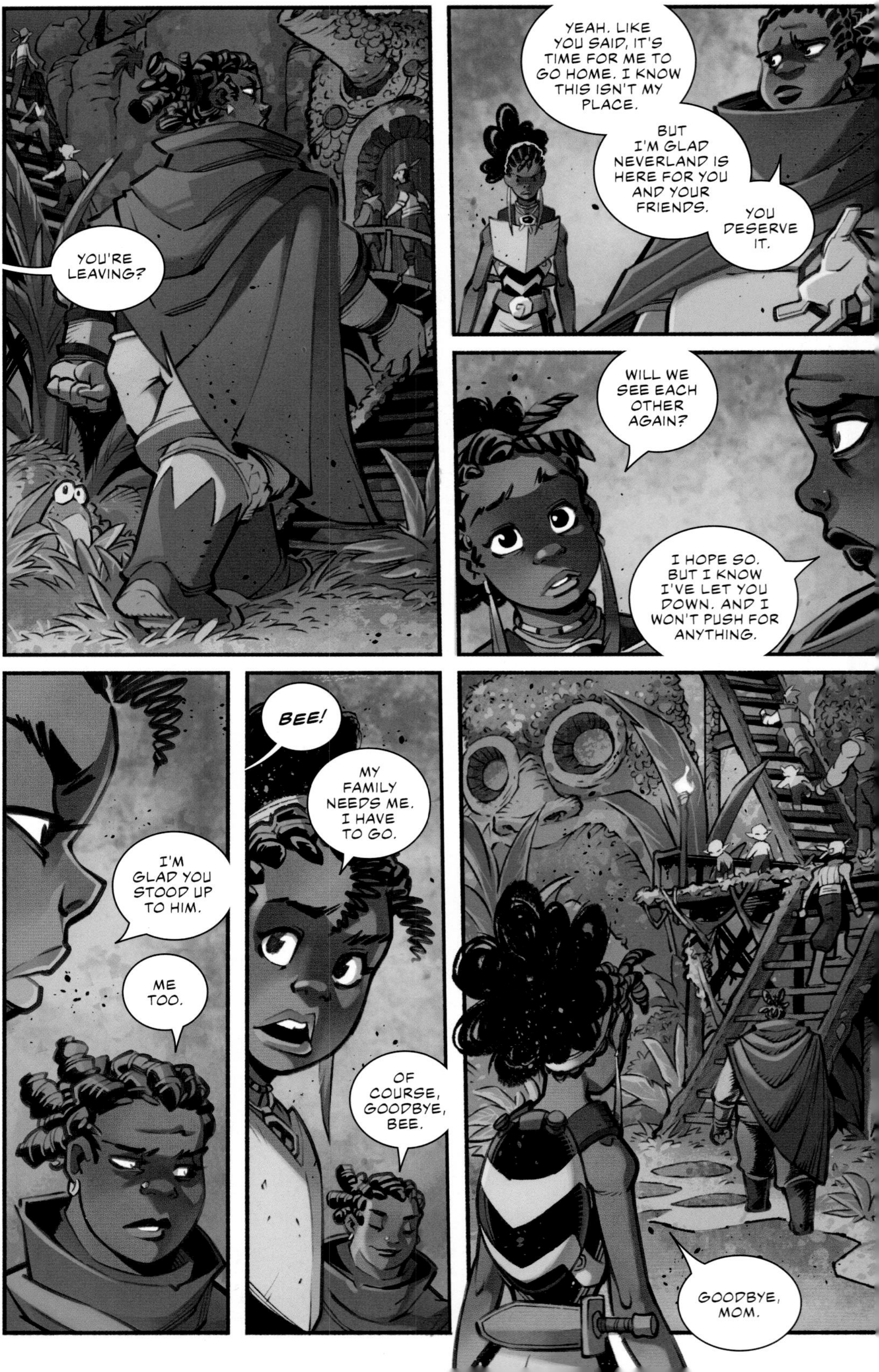
YOU'RE LEAVING?
YEAH. LIKE YOU SAID, IT'S TIME FOR ME TO GO HOME. I KNOW THIS ISN'T MY PLACE.
BUT I'M GLAD NEVERLAND IS HERE FOR YOU AND YOUR FRIENDS.
YOU DESERVE IT.
WILL WE SEE EACH OTHER AGAIN?
I HOPE SO. BUT I KNOW I'VE LET YOU DOWN. AND I WON'T PUSH FOR ANYTHING.
I'M GLAD YOU STOOD UP TO HIM.
ME TOO.
BEE!
MY FAMILY NEEDS ME. I HAVE TO GO.
OF COURSE, GOODBYE, BEE.
GOODBYE, MOM.

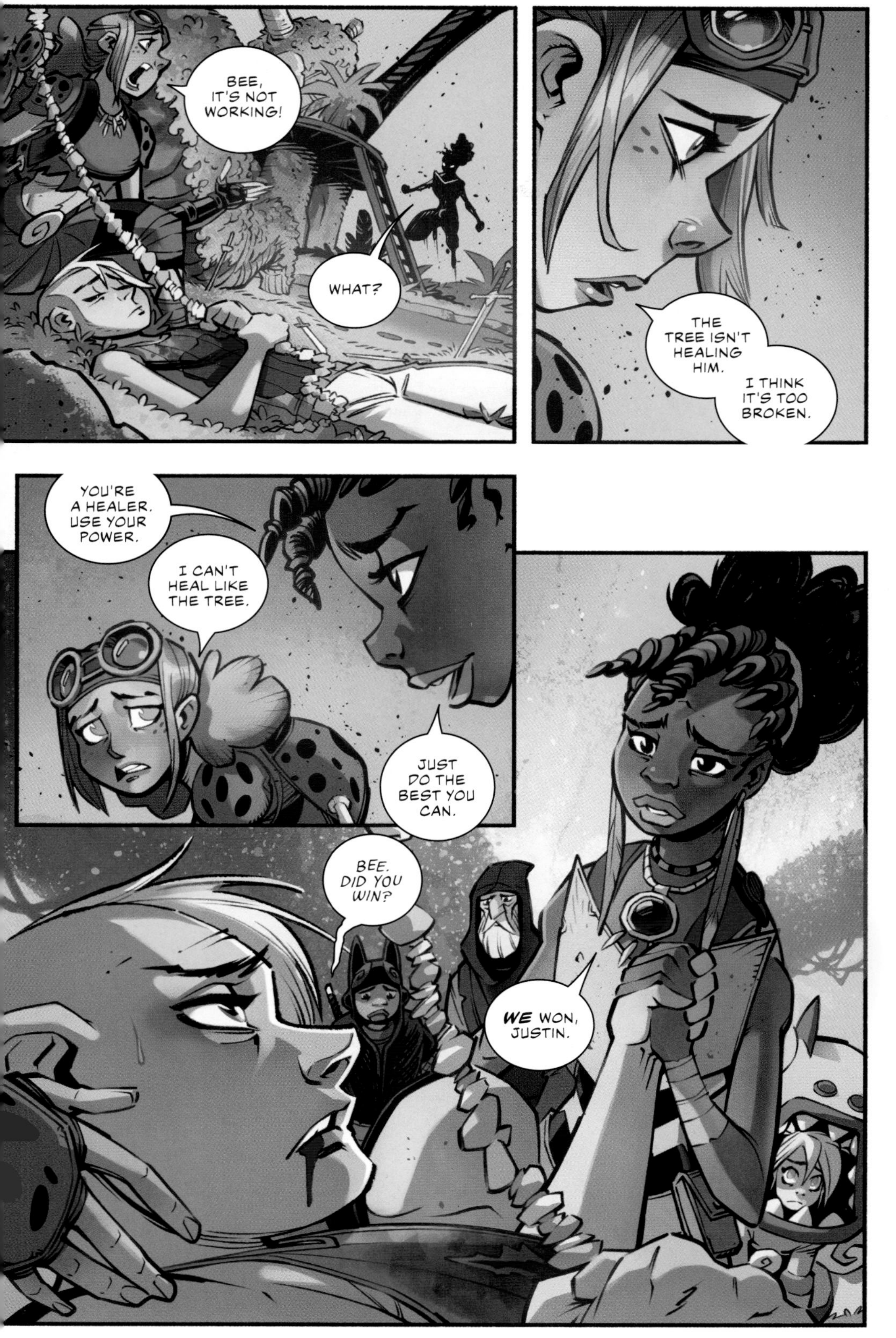
BEE, IT'S NOT WORKING!
WHAT?
THE TREE ISN'T HEALING HIM.
I THINK IT'S TOO BROKEN.
YOU'RE A HEALER. USE YOUR POWER.
I CAN'T HEAL LIKE THE TREE.
JUST DO THE BEST YOU CAN.
BEE. DID YOU WIN?
WE WON, JUSTIN.

I'M... **HNGGG!** ...SO SORRY.

YOU WERE JUST TRYING TO PROTECT US.

LIKE YOU'VE ALWAYS DONE.

WE ALL MAKE MISTAKES, SON. YOU WORKED TO FIX YOURS IMMEDIATELY.

HEY, DON'T YOU GO ANYWHERE.

NOT SURE I HAVE A CHOICE... GRACIE.

LOOK AT THE EYES. DO YOU WANT TO DISAPPOINT THE EYES?

HEH.

I'LL... TRY NOT TO...

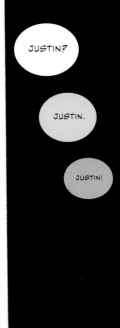

JUSTIN?

JUSTIN.

JUSTIN!

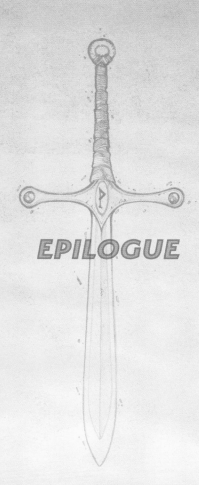

EPILOGUE

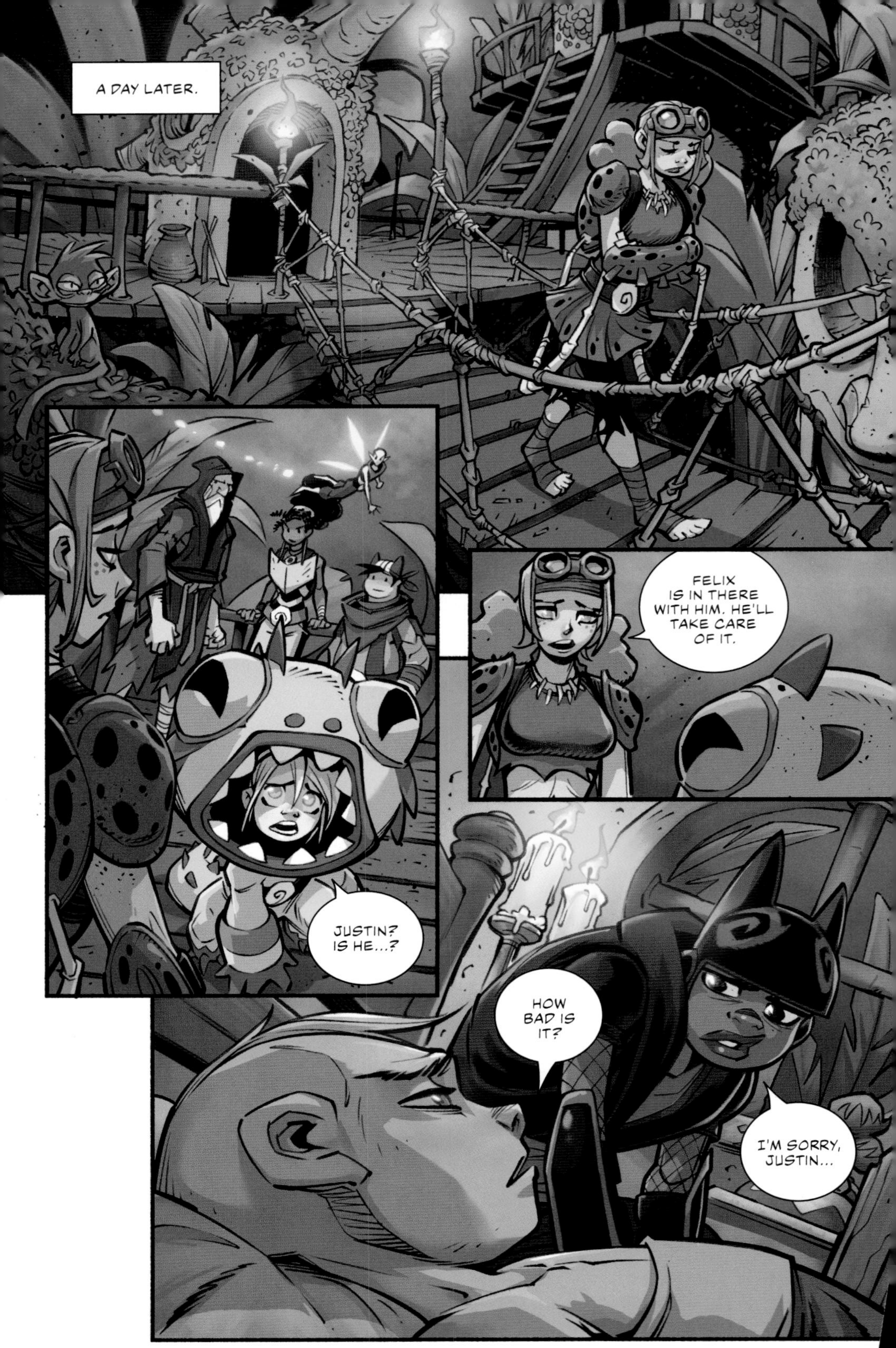
A DAY LATER.
JUSTIN? IS HE...?
FELIX IS IN THERE WITH HIM. HE'LL TAKE CARE OF IT.
HOW BAD IS IT?
I'M SORRY, JUSTIN...

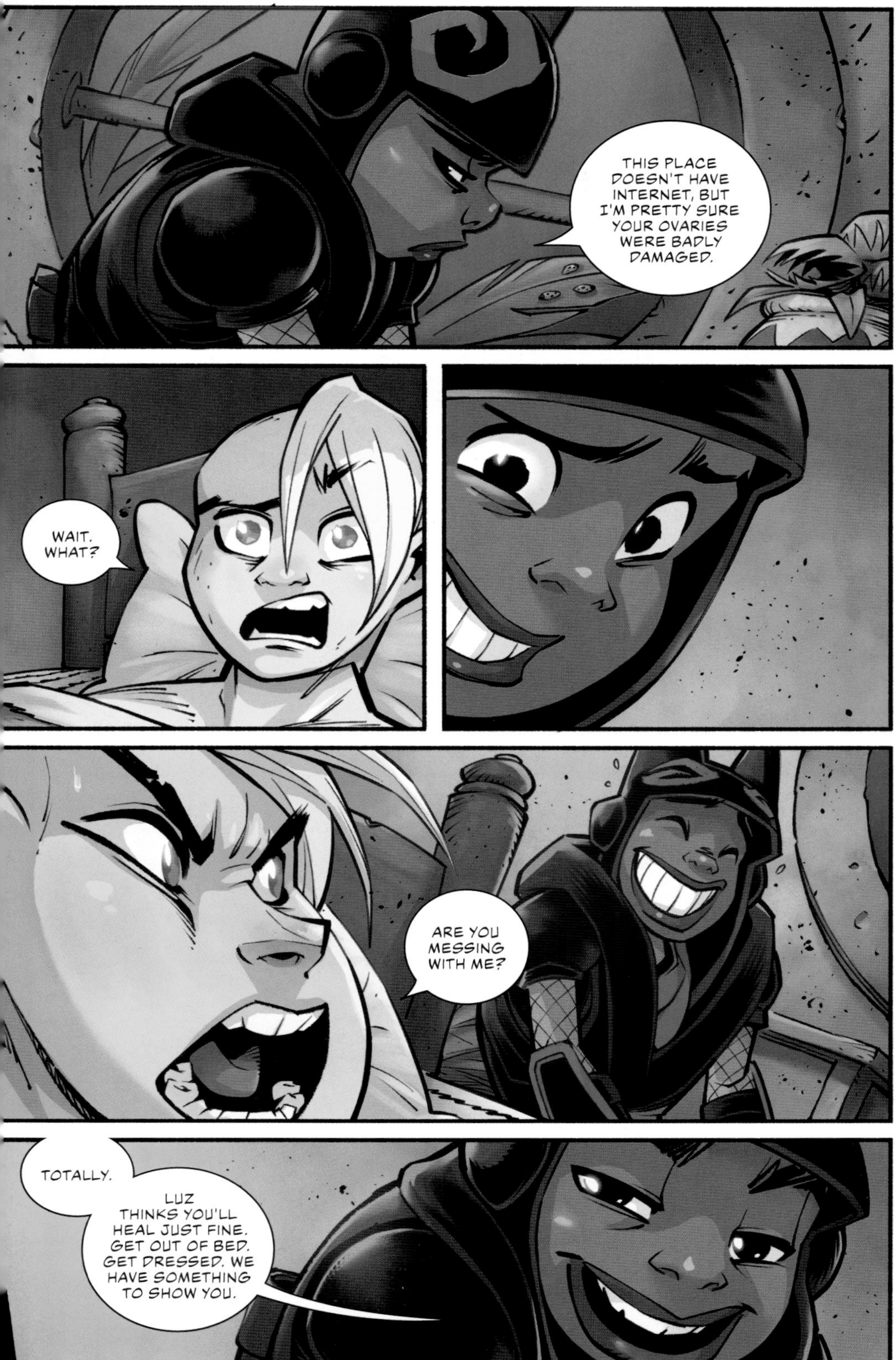
THIS PLACE DOESN'T HAVE INTERNET, BUT I'M PRETTY SURE YOUR OVARIES WERE BADLY DAMAGED.
WAIT. WHAT?
ARE YOU MESSING WITH ME?
TOTALLY.
LUZ THINKS YOU'LL HEAL JUST FINE. GET OUT OF BED. GET DRESSED. WE HAVE SOMETHING TO SHOW YOU.

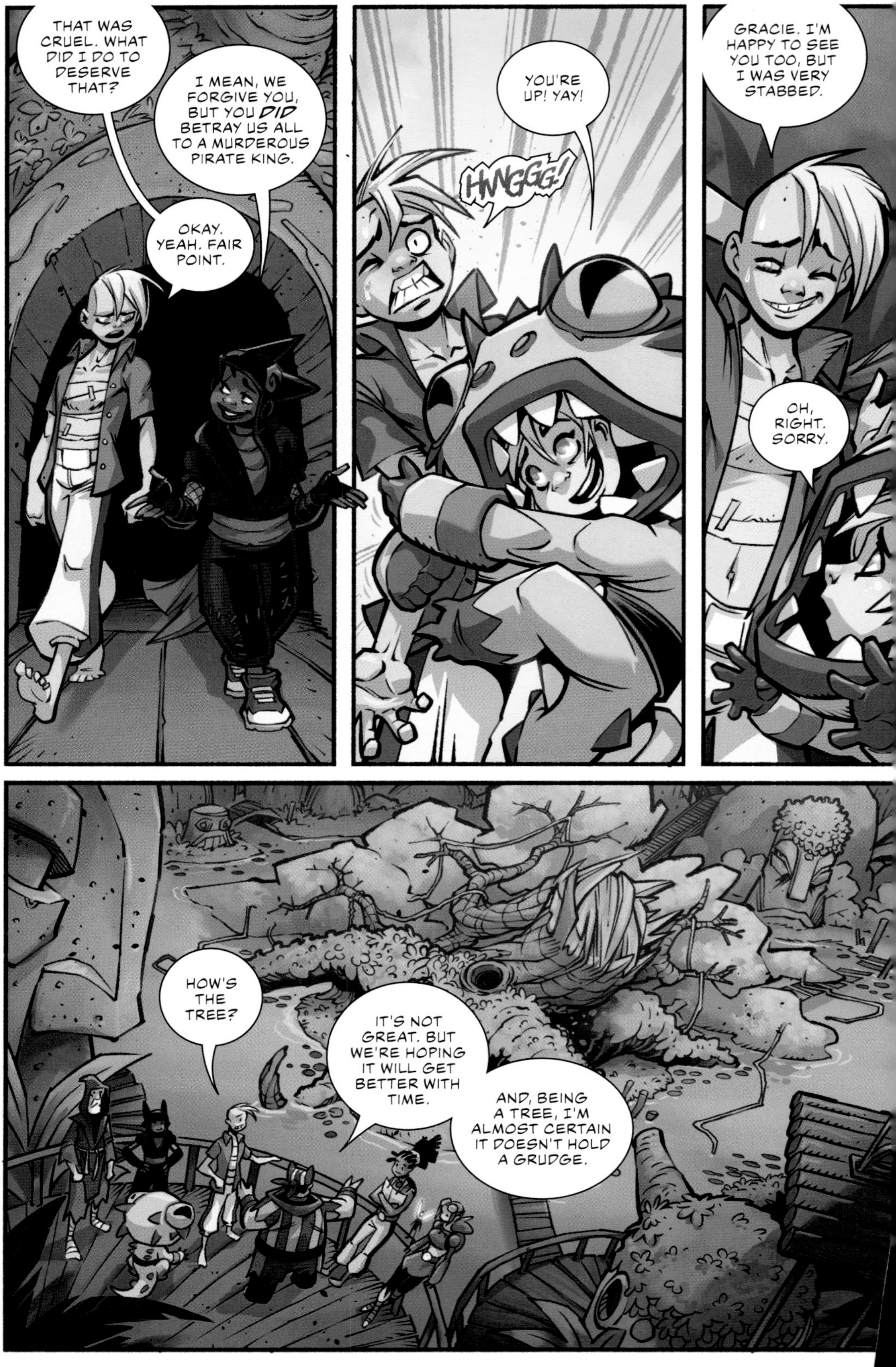
THAT WAS CRUEL. WHAT DID I DO TO DESERVE THAT?
I MEAN, WE FORGIVE YOU, BUT YOU DID BETRAY US ALL TO A MURDEROUS PIRATE KING.
OKAY. YEAH. FAIR POINT.
YOU'RE UP! YAY!
HNGGG!
GRACIE. I'M HAPPY TO SEE YOU TOO, BUT I WAS VERY STABBED.
OH, RIGHT. SORRY.
HOW'S THE TREE?
IT'S NOT GREAT. BUT WE'RE HOPING IT WILL GET BETTER WITH TIME.
AND, BEING A TREE, I'M ALMOST CERTAIN IT DOESN'T HOLD A GRUDGE.

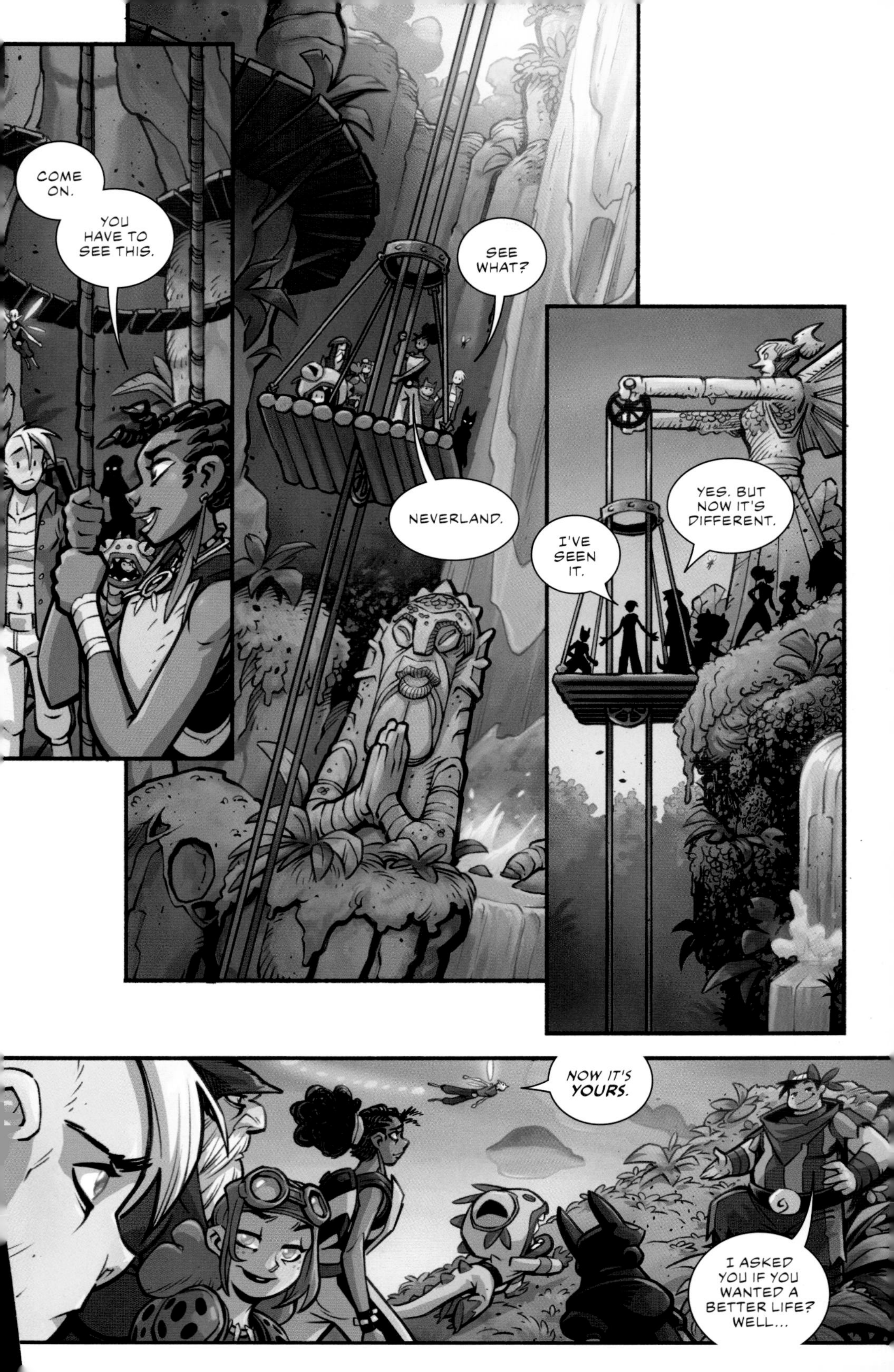
COME ON.
YOU HAVE TO SEE THIS.
SEE WHAT?
NEVERLAND.
I'VE SEEN IT.
YES. BUT NOW IT'S DIFFERENT.
NOW IT'S *YOURS.*
I ASKED YOU IF YOU WANTED A BETTER LIFE? WELL...

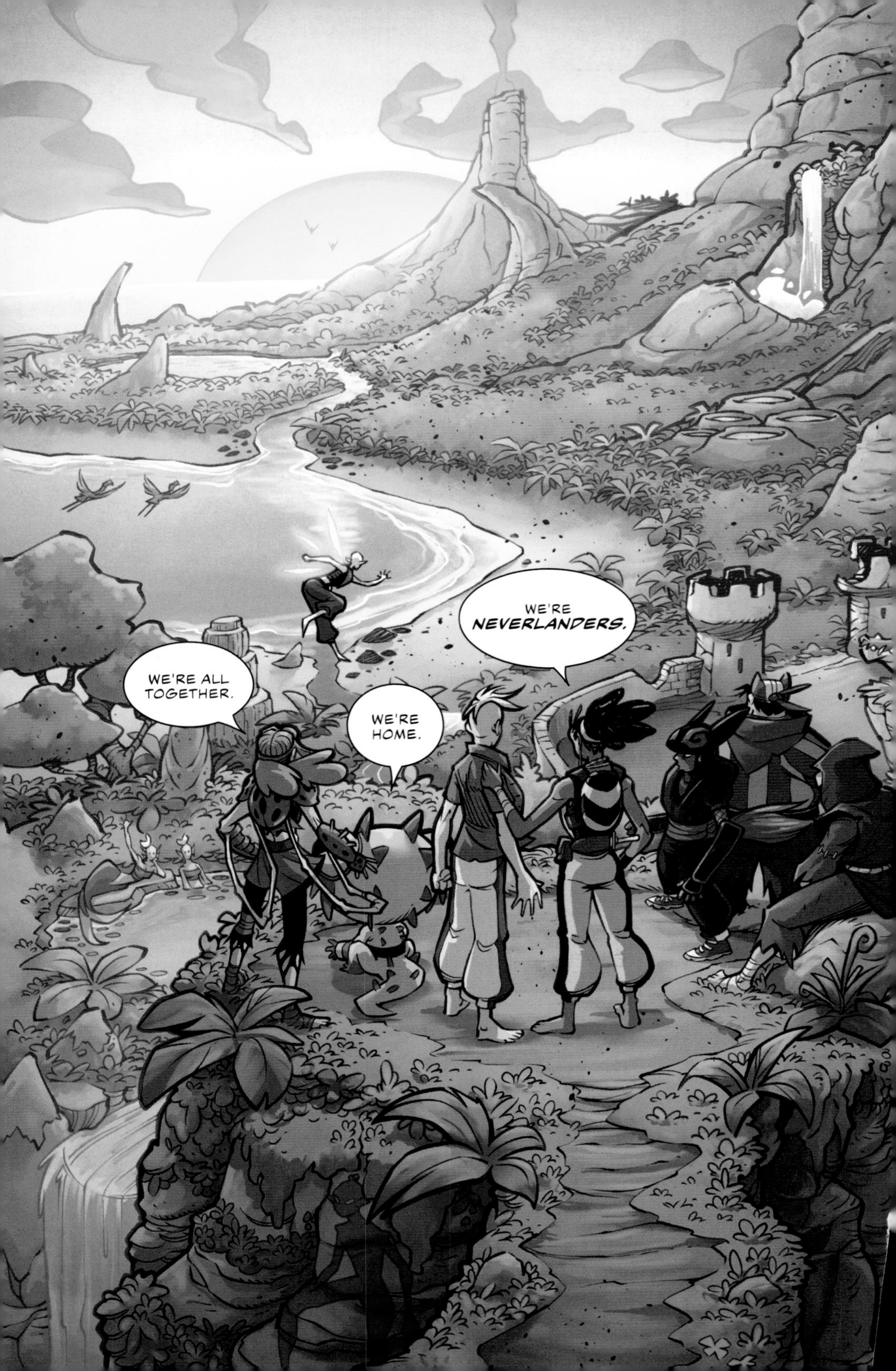
WE'RE ALL TOGETHER.
WE'RE HOME.
WE'RE NEVERLANDERS.